Coastal Whispers

Maya Dawn

Published by Maya Dawn, 2024.

COASTAL WHISPERS

First edition. October 21, 2024.

ISBN: 979-8227489821

Written by Maya Dawn.

I approached a small café, its sign swinging gently in the breeze, "The Foggy Bean." The scent of freshly brewed coffee wafted through the air, beckoning me inside like a siren's song. As I entered, the warmth enveloped me, a stark contrast to the chill outside. The interior was cozy, with wooden beams overhead and mismatched furniture that spoke of comfort and stories shared. A few patrons sat huddled at tables, their hushed conversations punctuated by the clinking of mugs and the froth of milk being steamed. I spotted a corner table and made my way over, my fingers itching to jot down my observations.

As I settled in, I caught the barista's eye—a young woman with vibrant red hair and an apron that seemed to have a life of its own, covered in splashes of cream and espresso. "What can I get you?" she asked, a warm smile lighting up her freckled face.

"Black coffee, please. Strong enough to wake the dead," I replied, returning her smile with one of my own. She laughed, a bright sound that filled the space with warmth.

"Good choice! I think we have just the brew for that," she said, moving to the espresso machine with an easy grace. As she worked, I observed the café patrons—a mix of local fishermen, elderly couples, and a few solitary figures who looked like they were waiting for something or someone.

"First time in Misty Shores?" the barista asked, her voice teasing as she placed my coffee on the table with a flourish.

"Is it that obvious?" I replied, taking a tentative sip. The rich flavor danced on my tongue, instantly invigorating me. "Just here for a little investigation into some... unusual happenings."

Her eyebrows shot up, and her expression turned serious. "Oh, you mean the lights? And the disappearances? People don't like to talk about it much. It's been a little... strange lately."

"Strange is my specialty," I said, a playful smirk tugging at my lips. "What can you tell me?"

Chapter 1: Into the Mist

The salty air clung to my skin as I drove into the quaint, fog-laden town of Misty Shores. The towering cliffs loomed over me like silent sentinels, hiding secrets within their rocky embrace. I had come here as an investigative journalist, sent to unravel the threads of bizarre occurrences that had shaken this seemingly peaceful coastal community. The locals were guarded, their lips sealed tighter than the fog that enveloped the streets. As I parked my car near the dilapidated lighthouse, an eerie sense of anticipation washed over me, igniting my journalistic instincts.

The lighthouse stood like a crooked finger pointing toward the sky, its paint peeling and windows shattered. It was a relic of a forgotten era, each crack in the stone whispering tales of shipwrecks and lost souls. I stepped out of my car, the crunch of gravel beneath my boots mingling with the rhythmic crashing of waves against the rocks. The scent of brine filled my lungs, mixing with something earthy and sweet—perhaps the distant smell of blooming wildflowers that dared to grow in the cracks of the cobblestone streets. I pulled my jacket tighter around me, feeling both exhilarated and apprehensive as I wandered toward the town's heart.

Misty Shores was a tapestry of narrow streets lined with quaint cottages, their faded paint and weathered shingles telling stories of years gone by. Colorful flowers spilled from window boxes, and the occasional seagull cried overhead, its sharp call piercing the heavy silence. A foghorn sounded mournfully in the distance, a reminder of the dangers that lurked beneath the surface of the tranquil facade. I could see the villagers peering through lace-curtained windows, their expressions a blend of curiosity and caution. It was as if they sensed my purpose, and I couldn't help but feel like an intruder in their closely-knit community.

She leaned in, her voice dropping to a conspiratorial whisper. "There are rumors of ghostly figures appearing on the cliffs at night, and strange lights flickering in the lighthouse. Some folks swear they've seen ships that aren't supposed to be there." Her eyes sparkled with a mix of intrigue and fear, and I felt the pulse of the town's mystery thrumming through me.

I could feel the threads of my story weaving together, the tapestry of this coastal town becoming more vibrant and complex with each whispered word. "And the disappearances?" I pressed, unable to mask my curiosity.

She hesitated, glancing toward the window as if expecting someone to be watching. "Well, there have been a few people who've gone missing over the last couple of months. No one really knows why. Some think they wandered off during a storm, but others... others think it's something else entirely."

The café door swung open, bringing with it a gust of wind and a figure wrapped in a long, dark coat. The newcomer stepped inside, shaking off the mist that clung to him like a second skin. He had sharp features and eyes that seemed to hold the weight of the ocean within them, a deep blue that sparkled like the sea under a full moon. I felt an electric charge in the air as he scanned the room, finally settling his gaze on me.

"Are you the one stirring up trouble in Misty Shores?" he asked, his voice smooth yet laced with an edge of amusement.

"Trouble? Me?" I shot back, unable to suppress a grin. "I prefer to think of it as uncovering the truth."

The barista exchanged glances with the newcomer, her expression shifting from playful to wary. "You might want to be careful with that, especially if you're asking about the disappearances," she murmured, her voice barely above a whisper.

"Careful is my middle name," I replied, feeling the weight of my own bravado, but also the undeniable thrill of the chase. As I locked eyes with the stranger, the feeling that Misty Shores held secrets—dark and alluring—grew stronger, pulling me deeper into its foggy embrace.

"Trouble? Me?" I shot back, unable to suppress a grin. "I prefer to think of it as uncovering the truth." The stranger, who had strolled in with the air of someone used to commanding attention, leaned against the café counter, the corners of his mouth curving into a smirk that was both inviting and infuriating.

"Uncovering the truth in Misty Shores is like trying to catch smoke with your bare hands," he replied, his tone light but edged with a seriousness that made my heart race. "People here don't take kindly to nosy outsiders. You might want to watch your back."

I raised an eyebrow, intrigued. "And what exactly makes you the authority on that? Do you have a 'Welcome to Misty Shores' badge tucked under that coat?"

He chuckled, the sound deep and rich, as if it had been smoothed by years of experience. "Maybe not a badge, but I've lived here long enough to know what happens to those who poke their noses where they don't belong."

"Consider me curious, not poky," I quipped, taking another sip of my coffee. It had grown cold, but the bitter taste matched the thrill I felt at the prospect of diving into the unknown. "I suppose you're going to tell me the locals are just being friendly by not inviting me to their bonfires?"

"Bonfires?" he echoed, feigning shock. "More like a warning to stay clear of the cliffs at night. You really don't want to be out there after dark."

I leaned closer, the thrill of the chase igniting my senses. "And why's that? Ghosts? Creatures of the deep?"

"More like locals who might think you're a ghost," he said, his eyes glinting with mischief. "Or maybe something worse. You're not the first reporter to come sniffing around. Last one—well, he didn't leave with a very pleasant story."

The air in the café shifted, thickening with the weight of unspoken tales. I could feel the eyes of the other patrons on me, their interest piqued by our exchange. "I take it he's one of the missing?" I asked, my voice lowered, trying to match the gravity of the moment.

"Not quite," he replied, his expression growing serious. "He ended up leaving town, but let's just say it wasn't entirely voluntary. The town has a way of... persuading people to keep quiet."

"Interesting technique," I said, the corners of my mouth twitching up. "But I'm not easily intimidated."

"Good," he said, straightening up, his expression morphing from playful to something deeper. "You'll need that spirit if you're going to dig into these mysteries."

Just then, the door swung open again, and in strode a middle-aged man with a face like a weathered map—lines etched deep with the stories of the sea. He approached the counter with a purposeful stride, nodding at the barista. "One black coffee, please. And a slice of that pecan pie. I need the calories to keep my strength up."

As he turned, his gaze fell on me, and he squinted, as if trying to place me. "You're new around here, aren't you?"

"Guilty as charged," I replied, my curiosity piqued by the air of authority he exuded. "Just here to explore a few of the town's mysteries."

He chuckled darkly, his laugh like the rumble of thunder. "Mysteries are all we have left, girl. This town used to be full of life, but now? It's just ghosts and whispers."

"Sounds poetic," I said, leaning forward. "What do you mean by 'ghosts and whispers'?"

"Don't mind him," the stranger interjected, his smile returning but tinged with caution. "The locals have their own ways of keeping the stories alive. But trust me, they're best left unspoken."

The man waved a dismissive hand. "You can't silence the truth. Not forever." He took his coffee and pie, casting a wary glance at the stranger before retreating to a table at the back.

"Is it always like this?" I asked the stranger, my intrigue growing. "What's the deal with the disappearances? Are people really vanishing into thin air?"

He sighed, leaning closer as if sharing a secret. "Let's just say the cliffs have a way of keeping secrets. People go there, especially at night, looking for something—maybe answers, maybe closure. But some never return."

"Do you?" I challenged, looking straight into his eyes. "Do you believe in ghosts?"

He chuckled again, this time more subdued. "Ghosts? Not so much. But the past? That haunts us all. Here, the line between the living and the dead is thin."

My heart raced. I was in the presence of something bigger than myself, something shrouded in mystery and charged with emotion. "So what are you saying? That I should just pack my bags and go home?"

"Not at all," he replied, his voice smooth like the coffee sliding down my throat. "I just think you should know what you're getting into."

"And what if I like a little danger?" I challenged, my blood thrumming with excitement.

"Then you're going to love Misty Shores," he said, a teasing glint in his eye. "But remember, curiosity killed the cat, and it might do worse to an investigative journalist."

I took a deep breath, savoring the blend of caffeine and adrenaline coursing through me. The sense of foreboding that had initially washed over me morphed into an intoxicating thrill. "Bring it on, I say. What's the worst that could happen?"

As I finished my coffee, I glanced out the window at the thick mist gathering on the cliffs. It seemed to pulse with life, whispering secrets that begged to be uncovered. I felt a magnetic pull toward it, a need to delve deeper into the shadows that draped Misty Shores.

The barista returned, a knowing smile playing on her lips. "You've got that look, you know. The one that says you're about to dive headfirst into trouble."

I laughed lightly, a tinge of excitement warming my cheeks. "And what if I am?"

"Then just remember to bring a flashlight and some good shoes," she said, handing me my bill. "You're going to need them."

As I stood up to leave, I couldn't shake the feeling that the town had wrapped itself around me, its mysteries inviting me in like an old friend. I turned back to the stranger, who was now watching me with an intensity that sent a shiver down my spine. "So, what's your name, anyway?"

"Jake," he replied, that same smirk returning. "And you? Just 'Curiosity'?"

"No, I'm afraid I'm a bit more complicated than that," I replied, a smile tugging at my lips. "But you can call me Violet. And you, Jake, are going to regret ever getting involved with me."

With that, I stepped out into the fog, the air cool and charged with the promise of untold stories. I could feel the weight of the town's history pressing down on me, its pulse quickening as I embarked on my journey into the unknown.

I stepped out into the embrace of the chill, my breath mingling with the mist that swirled around me like ghostly fingers. The salty air, so crisp and alive, beckoned me deeper into the heart of Misty Shores. I wandered down the main street, glancing into shops that seemed to hold secrets in every corner, their windows fogged over like memories obscured by time. Each step echoed the thrill of discovery, the weight of the stories waiting to be unearthed.

As I passed a small bookstore, a bell chimed softly above the door, and I paused, drawn to the quaint charm of its interior. The scent of old paper and polished wood wafted out, inviting and warm. Inside, shelves creaked under the weight of dusty tomes and novels, their spines faded yet proud. An elderly man stood behind the counter, his spectacles perched precariously on the edge of his nose as he peered at me over the latest bestseller.

"Ah, a newcomer," he said, his voice rich and gravelly, like the sound of rolling waves. "Looking for a good read or perhaps something to unravel the mysteries of this town?"

"Both, actually," I replied, stepping closer. "I'm a journalist, and I hear there are stories here worth telling."

"Stories?" He chuckled, a twinkle in his eye. "Oh, there are plenty of those. But beware, my dear. Some tales are best left untold."

"Where's the fun in that?" I shot back playfully. "What's a good mystery without a bit of danger?"

He leaned back, arms crossed over his plaid shirt, as if assessing my resolve. "You remind me of my daughter, bless her heart. She had the same spark, running around town chasing ghosts."

"Did she catch any?" I asked, intrigued.

"Not the kind you'd want to encounter," he replied, his gaze turning somber. "Some things are better left in the shadows. But if you're set on exploring, I'd recommend 'The Secrets of Misty Shores.' It's been sitting on the shelf for ages, and you might find it enlightening—or chilling."

I nodded, accepting the book he handed me, its cover embossed with gold lettering that seemed to shimmer in the dim light. "Thanks, I'll give it a look."

As I left the bookstore, I felt the weight of the town's history pressing in on me, each whispered story curling around my thoughts.

I tucked the book under my arm and continued my stroll, my mind alive with the possibilities of what lay ahead. The streets twisted and turned like a maze, leading me down toward the rocky shore, where the ocean churned beneath the gray sky.

The beach was almost deserted, save for a few gulls dancing along the shoreline. I stepped onto the damp sand, feeling it squish between my toes as I approached the water's edge. The waves crashed against the rocks, each one sending up a spray that glistened like diamonds in the light. I closed my eyes, letting the sound wash over me, a rhythmic lullaby that both soothed and excited my restless spirit.

My phone buzzed, breaking the moment. I pulled it out to find a text from Jake. Meet me at the lighthouse. There's something I think you should see. My heart raced at his abrupt invitation, a mixture of curiosity and concern swirling within me. What could possibly await me at the lighthouse?

I started back up the path, my pulse quickening with each step. The fog thickened around me, shrouding the town in an ethereal blanket that obscured everything but the looming silhouette of the lighthouse. The air was electric, as if the very atmosphere was charged with secrets waiting to be revealed.

When I reached the base of the lighthouse, I found Jake standing there, hands tucked into his pockets, his expression serious. "You came," he said, his voice low and gravelly, cutting through the stillness of the mist.

"Of course. You didn't exactly leave me with a choice," I replied, my tone teasing to mask the flutter of nerves in my stomach. "What's so urgent?"

He gestured toward the entrance, a wooden door creaking on its hinges as if inviting me into its depths. "I found something. Something strange."

I stepped closer, peering inside. The dim light cast long shadows across the stone walls, revealing a spiral staircase that wound upward into darkness. "And you thought I'd be interested because...?" I prompted, trying to sound more nonchalant than I felt.

"Because it might help explain the disappearances," he said, his gaze locked onto mine, earnest and intense. "And because I think it might be linked to you."

"Me?" I echoed, taken aback. "Why would I have anything to do with it?"

"Just trust me, Violet," he urged, his voice steady. "You need to see this for yourself."

Reluctantly, I nodded, a mixture of apprehension and intrigue propelling me forward. As we ascended the staircase, the air grew thick with the smell of salt and decay. Each step creaked underfoot, a reminder of the many who had passed this way before. We reached the top, where the lantern room opened up before us, encased in glass that was fogged and worn from years of exposure.

Jake gestured toward a dark corner of the room, where shadows danced ominously. "Look over there."

I squinted, straining to see through the dim light. My heart raced as I caught sight of what appeared to be a large, weathered trunk nestled against the wall, half-hidden in shadows. "What is that?" I asked, stepping closer, drawn by an unseen force.

"That's what I need you to see," Jake said, his voice barely above a whisper, as if the very walls were listening.

I knelt beside the trunk, feeling a chill creep up my spine. The surface was covered in barnacles and age, a testament to its long and weary journey. I brushed away some debris, revealing an intricately carved lock, though no key was in sight. "What do you think it holds?" I asked, my voice trembling slightly.

"Whatever it is, I don't think it's good," he said, taking a step back, his expression tense. "And I don't think we should open it."

"Then why did you bring me here?" I challenged, a sense of urgency bubbling up inside me.

"Because it's part of the mystery," he replied, frustration lacing his voice. "And it's too late to turn back now."

A sudden gust of wind slammed against the lighthouse, rattling the glass panes and sending a shiver through the room. I glanced at Jake, the tension between us palpable. The light flickered, casting long, eerie shadows that danced on the walls like specters come to life.

"Violet..." he began, but before he could finish, the sound of splintering wood echoed through the air, drawing my attention back to the trunk.

The lock shattered as if a powerful force had shattered it, and the lid creaked open, revealing a darkness that seemed to pulse with a life of its own. My heart raced as an icy chill swept through the room, and I felt as if the very air around me was thickening, coiling like a serpent ready to strike.

"Get back!" Jake shouted, but it was too late. As I leaned closer, something surged from the trunk, a dark mist swirling upward, enveloping us in a suffocating embrace. The shadows writhed and twisted, coalescing into a figure that hovered just beyond the threshold of comprehension.

Panic ignited in my chest as the figure took shape, and I stumbled back, my mind racing with disbelief. "What... what is that?" I gasped, but my voice was swallowed by the storm brewing around us.

Jake's eyes widened, a mix of fear and determination lighting his features. "I don't know, but we need to leave. Now!"

As the mist lunged toward us, tendrils reaching out like grasping hands, I realized that whatever lay ahead was no longer just a story to uncover. It was a dangerous game we were playing, and the stakes had just risen higher than I could have ever anticipated. In that moment,

I knew one thing for certain: Misty Shores was not just a town filled with secrets—it was alive with them, and I was caught in the very heart of the storm.

Chapter 2: Whispers of the Past

The air was thick with the scent of roasted beans and the salty tang of the nearby ocean, a curious combination that wrapped around me like a well-worn blanket. Mabel's café was a sanctuary, adorned with mismatched chairs that looked as though they had been plucked from various eras, each one holding its own secrets. The walls, painted a muted seafoam green, were adorned with faded photographs of ships in full sail, their proud masts reaching skyward, forever captured in the amber glow of the past. A tattered flag hung from a corner, its colors bleached by years of sun and storms, whispering tales of a bygone era to anyone willing to listen.

Mabel, a small woman with silver hair piled haphazardly atop her head like a seagull's nest, bustled behind the counter. Her apron was smudged with flour and coffee stains, a testament to the countless pastries she baked daily. I could see her eyes flicker with the wisdom of someone who had witnessed both joy and sorrow in equal measure. As she handed me my coffee, her fingers brushed against mine, and I felt a shiver run through me, a fleeting connection that made me momentarily forget the weight of the world outside.

"Careful with that one," she warned, a sly smile tugging at the corners of her lips. "Might bite you if you're not paying attention."

I chuckled, raising the cup to my lips, the rich bitterness awakening something deep inside me. "I've always had a thing for the bold and dangerous," I replied, my voice light but tinged with sincerity. "Maybe that's why I ended up here."

Mabel leaned closer, her voice dropping to a conspiratorial whisper. "Ah, Misty Shores has a way of drawing in the lost souls, doesn't it? It's like the ocean itself calls to you." Her gaze drifted past me, as if she were recalling someone long gone. "But be wary, dear. The sea gives and it takes. Many have tried to unearth its secrets, only to find themselves consumed."

Her words settled around me like the fog that rolled in each evening, thickening the air and blurring the edges of reality. I glanced out the window, where the waves crashed against the rocky shore, frothy tendrils reaching for the land as though they were grasping for something—or someone. It felt as though the sea were holding its breath, waiting for a moment to exhale a truth that had been buried for far too long.

As I sipped my coffee, my thoughts drifted to the reason I had come to Misty Shores in the first place. The postcard from my late grandmother had arrived unexpectedly, its faded colors a stark contrast to the vibrancy of my life in the city. "Come find me," it read in her spidery handwriting, alongside an address I had never known. It felt like a summons, a final wish that had drawn me away from my comfortable but empty existence. The decision had been made in a moment of impulsive clarity, the kind that leaves you wondering whether you were truly brave or just a fool dancing on the edge of chaos.

A sudden gust of wind rattled the window, drawing my attention back to Mabel. She was now gazing out at the sea with an intensity that made me shiver. "There's a storm coming," she murmured, almost to herself. "One that stirs up memories better left alone."

I felt a knot tighten in my stomach. "What do you mean?" I asked, intrigued and unnerved all at once.

Mabel turned her gaze to me, her eyes darkening with a weight of stories yet untold. "The cliffs hold many secrets, dear. My mother spoke of them—glimmers of light that flicker like lost souls searching for something. She said they could lead you to what you desire, but also to what you fear."

"Is that why you keep the lights burning here?" I teased lightly, attempting to lift the tension. "To ward off the ghosts?"

She chuckled, a sound like the tinkling of wind chimes. "Perhaps. Or maybe I keep them burning for the living." There was a gravity in her voice that made me pause. "The past has a way of reaching out to us, my dear. It's like a tide that pulls you under before you even realize you're swimming."

I set my cup down, the bitter taste lingering on my tongue, and leaned forward. "Have you ever felt the pull? Have you ever seen the lights?"

Her expression turned serious, a shadow passing over her features. "Once, long ago. I was a fool then, much like you. I chased after those lights, thinking they would reveal the answers to all my questions. But sometimes, the answers we seek are better left buried in the depths of the ocean."

A silence enveloped us, thick with unspoken words. The café faded away, the world outside becoming a blur of gray and mist. I could feel a storm brewing not just in the skies but within me, a tempest of curiosity and dread. I had always been the kind of person to face the unknown head-on, to seek out the wild and unexpected. Yet here, with Mabel's cautionary tale echoing in my mind, I found myself hesitating.

"What if I want to uncover those secrets?" I asked, my voice barely above a whisper. "What if I want to know the truth about my family, about my grandmother?"

Mabel met my gaze, her expression softening. "Then you must be prepared, dear. The truth can be a double-edged sword. It can free you or shackle you in ways you never imagined."

The door swung open, the chime above ringing like a warning bell, and a figure stepped inside, shaking off droplets of rain. I turned, curious, but my heart raced as I caught sight of the newcomer—a tall man with dark hair, his eyes a piercing blue that seemed to see right through me. An inexplicable connection sparked between us, a recognition that sent a jolt through my entire being.

He approached the counter, and as our eyes met, the air crackled with unspoken possibilities. I felt Mabel's gaze shift between us, her knowing smile returning as though she sensed the storm brewing between us—one that had the potential to change everything.

His entrance shifted the atmosphere like a sudden gust of wind that rattles the leaves. The moment he stepped into Mabel's café, I felt the air thicken, charged with a strange energy. He shook his dark hair away from his forehead, droplets of rain cascading like a waterfall, leaving trails on his leather jacket. There was a ruggedness to him that suggested he was no stranger to the elements, yet his features held a softness that made my heart skip in unexpected ways.

He approached the counter with a casual confidence that sent a flutter through me, as if I had just realized I was standing on the edge of something thrilling yet terrifying. Mabel eyed him with a mix of amusement and caution, like she had seen this play out before, perhaps with other lost souls drawn to the town's magnetic pull.

"Coffee?" she asked, her voice gruff yet warm, her hand already hovering over the steaming pot.

"Please," he replied, his voice low and inviting, rich like the coffee he was about to receive. "Black." He glanced at me, and our eyes locked for a brief moment. I felt a jolt, a connection that seemed to transcend the chaos swirling outside. It was a flicker of understanding, as if he could sense the whirlwind of questions rattling in my mind.

I cleared my throat, finding my voice again. "Are you new here?" I asked, intrigued despite myself.

"Just passing through," he said, taking a seat at a nearby table. "But it seems like I stumbled into something far more interesting than I expected."

Mabel served him his coffee, a knowing smile playing on her lips as she shuffled back to me. "You've got a way with words, young man. A bit of mystery is just what this sleepy town needs."

I leaned back, a smirk creeping onto my face. "And you, Mabel, are the keeper of all the mysteries, I presume?"

Her eyes twinkled, and she replied, "Only the ones worth telling. And this young man? He's got a story to share if he's willing."

"Do tell," I prompted, turning my attention back to the stranger, eager to peel back the layers of his enigmatic persona.

He looked at me, amusement dancing in his blue eyes. "Well, it's not much of a tale, really. Just a traveler searching for some peace and quiet."

I raised an eyebrow, unconvinced. "That's a classic line. Peace and quiet is a tall order in a place that's home to secrets and stories waiting to be uncovered."

"Touché," he said, leaning forward, his tone playful. "What about you? You look like you're in search of something, too. A lost treasure, perhaps? Or just a good cup of coffee?"

"Ah, the elusive treasure," I said, feeling the tension ease a bit, as if we were trading verbal blows in a lighthearted duel. "I'm here to find a piece of my family's history, something that was left behind like driftwood on the shore. Just trying to connect the dots, you know?"

His expression shifted, a flicker of interest igniting in those deep-set eyes. "Family history can be a labyrinth. You never know what you might uncover—or who you might meet along the way."

I tilted my head, intrigued. "What makes you say that? Are you an expert in family mysteries?"

He chuckled, a sound that resonated in the small space, making the shadows retreat just a little. "Let's just say I've had my share of adventures—some of which involve a great deal of digging into the past. A family secret or two can change everything."

"Is that so?" I replied, leaning closer, captivated. "And what about your own secrets? What are you burying beneath that charming smile?"

He grinned, a flash of something untamed in his gaze. "If I told you, they wouldn't be secrets anymore. But I'll share this: there's a lighthouse on the cliffs. They say it's haunted by the lightkeeper's ghost, a tale as old as the stones that make up this town. I've heard stories about those who sought the lighthouse only to find their fate entwined with the past."

Mabel interrupted, setting down a fresh slice of pie that steamed enticingly. "Now that's a story worth telling," she said, her voice laced with excitement. "That lighthouse has seen more than its fair share of tragedies and triumphs."

"Tragedies?" I echoed, feeling a shiver creep up my spine.

"Oh, yes," Mabel continued, her eyes narrowing as she leaned in. "Many have ventured to the cliffs, drawn by the lights, only to vanish into the fog. Some say it's the lighthouse calling to them, a siren's song that lures them to their doom."

I couldn't help but feel a mix of thrill and dread. "And what happened to those who vanished?"

"Some were found, but many were not," she said, her voice lowering. "Their stories remain forever intertwined with the whispers of the past. It's a cautionary tale, dear. Always respect the pull of the sea."

The stranger nodded, his expression thoughtful. "That sounds like the kind of place that holds secrets beneath its waves, just waiting for someone daring enough to uncover them."

"I might just be that someone," I said, half-teasing, half-serious. The allure of the lighthouse seemed to shimmer in the air between us, pulling me in like a moth to a flame.

"Just be careful," he cautioned, a hint of seriousness in his tone that intrigued me even more. "The sea may be calling, but it can also be unforgiving. Not everyone who answers returns to tell the tale."

The café was growing busier, the murmur of conversations blending with the clinking of cups, but in that moment, it felt as if we were the only two souls in existence, suspended in a bubble of curiosity and unspoken connection. I felt the weight of his gaze, heavy yet comforting, and suddenly, my mission felt less like a solitary journey and more like a shared adventure.

"Who knows? Maybe we could unravel a few secrets together," I suggested, the idea sparking with excitement. "After all, you're already here in Misty Shores, flirting with danger."

His lips quirked in a smirk. "Flirting with danger, huh? Sounds like my kind of day. But I should warn you, I have a knack for finding trouble."

"Then you're in good company," I replied, laughing lightly. "Trouble and I have been friends for as long as I can remember."

Mabel chuckled, joining in on our playful banter. "Well, if you two are off to chase ghosts and secrets, don't forget to come back for a slice of my famous pie. It might just give you the strength to face whatever lurks in the dark."

I nodded, a sense of exhilaration swelling within me. Here I was, caught in a web of intrigue, surrounded by whispers of the past and the promise of adventure. With the stranger's intense gaze steady upon me, I felt a spark of possibility igniting, as if the very fabric of the town had woven itself around us, threading our fates together. The storm brewing outside echoed the tempest in my heart, and I couldn't shake the feeling that Misty Shores had become a place where the past and present collided, where every choice I made could lead me deeper into the unknown.

The atmosphere in the café shifted subtly, charged with an energy that made every shared glance between the stranger and me feel electrifying. The aroma of coffee mingled with the sweet scent of Mabel's baking, but beneath that delightful veneer was something heavier, a lingering weight of unspoken truths that clung to the air like the mist rolling in from the ocean.

"So, what brings you to this quaint little corner of the world?" he asked, leaning back in his chair, his gaze unwavering. "You don't strike me as the type who'd be content sitting in a café, sipping coffee and listening to old wives' tales."

I felt the heat of his scrutiny but managed to keep my cool. "You're right. I'm not one to shy away from a good adventure. I came here to find a piece of my family's history, something my grandmother left behind."

He regarded me with a mix of intrigue and caution. "And what exactly did your grandmother leave behind? A treasure map? A diary filled with secrets?"

"More like a postcard," I said, pulling it from my pocket and handing it to him. "It was cryptic—just an address in Misty Shores and a line that read, 'Come find me.'"

He studied the card, tracing his finger over the faded ink. "Mysterious indeed. Sounds like a call to adventure, if you ask me. But sometimes, what you find can change everything."

Mabel returned, placing a slice of her legendary pie in front of me, steam rising like an offering. "Here you go, dear. Fuel for your journey into the unknown."

I took a bite, the sweetness exploding on my tongue, grounding me momentarily. "This is incredible," I exclaimed, savoring the warmth that spread through me. "You should charge extra for this."

"Extra?" Mabel scoffed playfully. "I'm practically giving it away to keep you two from chasing ghosts on an empty stomach."

As laughter faded, the weight of the conversation returned, and I felt the stranger's gaze intensify. "So, have you uncovered anything yet?" he asked, his voice low, the playful spark still present.

"Not much," I admitted, the truth lingering like the last bite of pie. "Just whispers of the past and a heavy sense that there's something more waiting for me."

His eyes glimmered with understanding. "That feeling can be disconcerting. It's like walking through fog; you can't see where you're headed but know there's something just beyond your reach."

"Exactly," I said, intrigued. "It's maddening, but exhilarating too. It's like a puzzle begging to be solved."

He leaned closer, a conspiratorial glint in his eyes. "Then let's start solving it together. I might have some local insights that could shed light on your grandmother's connection to this town."

My heart quickened at the prospect. "Really? You'd do that?"

"Why not?" he replied, a devil-may-care smile spreading across his face. "What's life without a little risk? Besides, there's something captivating about a mystery—especially when it involves a family's history."

I felt a rush of gratitude, a swell of hope mingled with trepidation. "Thank you. I'd appreciate any help I can get. It's a little daunting to dive into this alone."

The way he looked at me—like I was a puzzle he was eager to unravel—made me forget about the darkness creeping in from the outside world. "Then it's settled. Let's meet at the lighthouse tomorrow at dusk," he proposed, a mischievous spark lighting his eyes. "We'll see if we can stir up some ghosts together."

I grinned, feeling a mixture of excitement and anxiety. "Sounds like a plan. But I should warn you, I have a bit of a talent for attracting trouble."

"Then we're bound to have a good time," he quipped, raising his coffee cup in a mock toast. "To ghosts and secrets!"

"To ghosts and secrets!" I echoed, the words hanging in the air like a promise.

As the conversation flowed, I felt a bond forming, woven together by shared laughter and the thrill of what was to come. Mabel busied herself behind the counter, casting occasional glances our way, her eyes sparkling with a knowing glint. It felt like she was watching a story unfold, one she had seen before but was no less excited to witness again.

But as the sun began to dip low in the sky, casting long shadows across the cobblestones outside, I sensed a shift in the energy. The wind howled against the windows, and for a moment, the café felt like the last bastion of warmth in a growing storm. Mabel's jovial demeanor shifted slightly, her hands faltering for just a second as she prepared a fresh pot of coffee.

"Ah, but don't let that wind fool you," she said, casting a wary glance outside. "It can change in an instant. Be careful near the cliffs, especially when the fog rolls in. It has a way of hiding what's right in front of you."

I nodded, but her warning only heightened my curiosity. "What exactly should I be watching out for?"

"Just... trust your instincts," Mabel replied cryptically, a shadow flickering across her features before she masked it with a smile. "The sea doesn't always show its cards."

After a few more exchanges filled with light banter, I excused myself to head back to the inn. The air outside was thick with salt and mystery, the waves crashing against the rocks a constant reminder of the forces lurking just beneath the surface. I couldn't shake the feeling that every step I took away from the café was pulling me closer to something monumental.

As I strolled along the shoreline, my mind raced with possibilities—what secrets lay hidden in the lighthouse? What had my grandmother uncovered that had compelled her to reach out to me from beyond? Each question swirled around in my head like the wind that whipped through my hair, tugging me toward the cliffs, a siren's call that echoed louder with every footfall.

Reaching the base of the cliffs, I paused, staring up at the silhouette of the lighthouse against the darkening sky. It stood like a sentinel, a lonely figure marked by time and stories etched into its stones. As the sun dipped below the horizon, the sky burst into a riot of colors, casting an ethereal glow over the landscape.

I inhaled deeply, filling my lungs with the salty air, then stepped closer to the edge. The wind whipped around me, howling like a restless spirit, and a strange chill raced down my spine. It felt like the very essence of Misty Shores was alive, urging me to take a leap into the unknown.

Then, a flicker of light caught my eye at the top of the lighthouse. It wasn't the steady beam of the lantern but a quick, dancing glow that seemed to beckon me forward. My heart raced, excitement mingled with a growing sense of unease.

"Maybe tomorrow," I whispered to myself, yet my feet moved closer to the cliff's edge. The sound of crashing waves grew louder, drowning out all rational thought, pulling me into its depths. Just as I turned to leave, a figure emerged from the shadows behind the lighthouse, silhouetted against the fading light.

I squinted, my breath hitching in my throat. "Hello?"

But as the figure stepped into the glow, I felt the world tilt beneath me, and with it, the very ground I stood upon shifted in a way that sent my heart plummeting. The storm I had sensed brewing was no longer just a metaphor. It was here, and it was real.

Chapter 3: The Fisherman

The air hung thick with the brine of the sea as I stepped onto the worn wooden planks of the docks, my boots creaking softly with every cautious movement. The sun dipped low, casting a golden hue across the water, painting it with strokes of molten amber. I could taste the salt on my lips and feel the pulse of the tide as if it were a living thing, breathing in rhythm with the world. It was here, amidst the calls of gulls and the distant clinking of boats swaying in their moorings, that I first laid eyes on him.

Gavin Thorne stood like a figure carved from stone, his broad shoulders hunched over a tangle of nets. He wore a weathered cap that shadowed his face, but when he looked up, the stormy blue of his eyes pierced through the veil of dusk. They were the kind of eyes that held secrets and sorrows, depths I felt compelled to explore even as I hesitated, acutely aware of the chill that raced down my spine. The world around us faded into a blur, and it felt like we were the only two souls adrift in a sea of muted colors and murmuring waves.

"Need a hand with that?" I asked, my voice surprising me with its lightness against the backdrop of his heavy silence. He glanced up, one brow arching in a silent challenge.

"Unless you've got gills, I reckon you'd be better off staying dry," he replied, a hint of a smirk tugging at the corner of his mouth, revealing a warmth that contradicted his brooding exterior. It was the kind of wit that danced on the edge of sarcasm, inviting yet teasing, and I couldn't help but smile back, a flutter of exhilaration rising within me.

"I've managed to survive in much worse conditions," I countered, stepping closer, drawn to him as if he were a lighthouse in a storm. His hands moved deftly, fingers skillfully untangling knots in the net, each motion deliberate and strong, telling tales of a life lived in harmony with the relentless sea.

"What's a city girl like you doing here?" he asked, his gaze flicking to my worn jeans and oversized sweater, a stark contrast to his ruggedness.

I shrugged, suddenly conscious of how out of place I felt. "Looking for a fresh start, I guess. I've always had a thing for the sea—its unpredictability, its whispers of the unknown."

"Don't we all," he mused, his voice low, a hint of bitterness lacing his words. "The sea promises freedom, but it also demands sacrifices."

His response hung in the air between us, heavy with unspoken history. I took a step back, gauging his demeanor, searching for any hint of vulnerability. "What sacrifices have you made?" I dared to ask, curiosity piqued.

He paused, fingers stilled as he studied me with an intensity that sent shivers skimming across my skin. "Too many to count," he finally replied, his voice gruff, an invisible wall rising between us. I could sense the weight of his past, an anchor that held him in place while the tides of his life roiled around him.

Just then, the wind picked up, tousling my hair and bringing with it the tang of impending rain. The clouds above thickened, casting a shadow over the dock, and I sensed the shift in the atmosphere. "It looks like a storm's coming," I said, glancing at the horizon where dark clouds churned like an angry beast.

"Better get you inside, then," he replied, his tone shifting from wary to protective. "There's a tavern just down the way, good fish stew if you're brave enough to try it."

"Brave enough?" I repeated, a laugh escaping my lips, unplanned and light. "Or foolish enough?"

"Depends on how you look at it," he said, his lips twitching into a half-smile. "Come on, then."

The tavern was nestled against the cliffs, its wooden facade weathered but inviting, the aroma of something simmering wafting through the open door as we stepped inside. The warmth enveloped me like a familiar blanket, contrasting sharply with the crispness of the air outside. Patrons filled the dimly lit space, laughter and conversation blending with the crackling of a fireplace in the corner.

Gavin led me to a table tucked away in a cozy nook, a space where shadows mingled with flickering candlelight. As we settled in, I couldn't help but notice how he seemed to relax, the tension in his shoulders easing as he leaned back, a flicker of amusement dancing in his eyes.

"Not what you expected from a fisherman's haunt?" he asked, studying me as if I were a puzzle he was intent on solving.

"I guess I expected more... bait and tackle," I admitted, grinning as I let my gaze wander around the room. "This is surprisingly charming."

"Charming can be deceiving," he warned, his expression turning serious, eyes narrowing as he took a sip from his mug. "Sometimes it's the pretty places that hide the darkest secrets."

His words sent a ripple of intrigue through me. "Secrets? Like what?"

"Like the legends of the cliffs," he replied, leaning forward, his voice dropping to a conspiratorial whisper. "They say the spirits of the lost wander there, drawn to the sea, waiting for someone to find them."

A thrill raced through me, a mix of trepidation and excitement. "You believe in that?"

"Not sure what I believe," he said, a hint of vulnerability cracking his stoic facade. "But I've seen things. Things that make you question reality."

I could feel the chemistry crackling between us, the air thick with unspoken words and burgeoning connection. As he shared his tales of the cliffs and the mysterious disappearances that had plagued the town for generations, I found myself captivated not just by the stories but by the man behind them. Each word he spoke wove a tapestry of intrigue, painting a vivid picture of a life lived on the precipice of the ordinary and the extraordinary.

"What if I told you I'm not afraid of a little adventure?" I challenged, my pulse quickening as I caught his gaze, daring him to see me beyond the layers of my own cautious facade.

"Adventure, or foolishness?" he countered, a teasing glint in his eyes, and I felt my heart swell with anticipation, ready to plunge into whatever mystery awaited us.

The storm outside raged on, thunder rumbling like a distant warning, yet within this small haven, I felt a flicker of hope igniting—a chance to uncover the hidden corners of not just the town, but of Gavin Thorne himself.

As the storm outside raged with a ferocity that rattled the windows, the tavern transformed into a sanctuary of warmth and chatter, its walls thick with the stories of weary travelers and locals alike. I settled into the comforting embrace of the wooden booth, watching as Gavin's demeanor shifted with the ambiance. The playful glint in his eyes sparked with mischief, and for a moment, the weight of his past seemed to lift.

"Alright, city girl, if you're up for adventure, how about a little wager?" he proposed, leaning forward, his elbows resting on the table, his fingers drumming against the scarred surface. The flickering candlelight danced across his face, illuminating the faint shadows beneath his eyes.

"What kind of wager?" I asked, intrigued.

"If you can drink this stew without grimacing, I'll take you to see the cliffs at dawn. But if you make even a single face, you have to tell me your most embarrassing secret," he challenged, a devilish grin spreading across his lips.

"Really? That's your idea of a wager? That's child's play!" I scoffed, but the thrill of the challenge sparked a playful competitiveness within me.

"Child's play? Just wait until you taste it," he said, a twinkle of mischief in his eyes.

Moments later, the stew arrived, a bubbling cauldron of unidentifiable seafood and spices that sent my senses reeling. The rich aroma enveloped me, hinting at depths of flavor I couldn't quite place. I lifted the spoon, feeling the weight of it in my hand as I took a cautious sip. The moment the stew touched my tongue, an explosion of flavors flooded my mouth—smoky, spicy, and oddly comforting. I fought the instinct to wince, focusing instead on the warmth spreading through me.

Gavin watched with rapt attention, his amusement palpable. "Well?" he prompted, leaning back as he sipped his own drink, clearly savoring the tension.

"Not bad," I replied, masking my surprise. "But I'm not giving you the satisfaction of knowing it's good."

"Feisty. I like it," he said, and I felt a rush of warmth at his compliment, even as I remained resolute.

"Your turn," I challenged, pushing the bowl away as I wiped my mouth with a napkin, feeling the pulse of the night settle in around us. "What's your embarrassing secret?"

He chuckled, the sound deep and rich, sending a thrill through me. "Alright, I'll bite. But it's not pretty," he warned, his expression turning serious as he leaned closer. "When I was a kid, I thought I could impress the girl I liked by fishing without a pole. So, I dove into the lake, caught a fish with my bare hands, and came up gasping for air, covered in mud and algae."

My laughter burst forth, uncontained. "That's hilarious! How did you think that would work out?"

"Clearly, I was a bright child," he replied dryly, but the smile never left his face. "Needless to say, she didn't find it charming."

Our laughter mingled, forming a thread that pulled us closer, and for the first time, I felt a palpable connection—a shared lightness that softened the edges of our earlier conversation. Gavin was more than just the brooding fisherman; he was a man shaped by his experiences, a mosaic of charm and mischief layered over deeper currents of pain.

"So, where do we go tomorrow?" I asked, the thought of the cliffs igniting a flicker of excitement in my chest.

He tilted his head, a look of contemplation passing over his features. "There's a spot known as the Whispering Rocks. They say if you listen closely, you can hear the voices of those who've been lost to the sea."

"Sounds eerie," I replied, the thrill of the supernatural sending shivers down my spine. "Do you really believe in all that?"

He shrugged, an enigmatic expression crossing his face. "I don't know what to believe anymore. Some say they hear their loved ones calling to them. Others claim it's just the wind."

"And you?" I pressed, leaning forward. "What do you hear?"

For a moment, his expression darkened, and I regretted pushing him. "I've heard a lot of things," he said quietly, his voice barely above a whisper.

The atmosphere shifted, the playful banter dissipating as an unspoken tension loomed over us. I could see the ghosts flitting behind his eyes, stories he wasn't ready to share. Sensing my misstep, I changed the subject, desperate to lighten the mood.

"Alright, then! I'm willing to take your tour of the cliffs, but if I do this, you have to show me how to fish without a pole," I declared, a playful challenge dancing on my lips.

Gavin's eyes sparkled with delight, and I was struck again by the warmth that bubbled beneath his surface. "Deal. But prepare yourself; it's an art form."

Our conversation flowed back into lighthearted teasing, each laugh drawing us closer together, weaving a connection that felt both thrilling and terrifying. As the night deepened, the tavern filled with a mix of laughter and music, the atmosphere thrumming with life.

Just as I was beginning to feel entirely at ease, a figure slipped into the tavern, a gust of cold air trailing in behind them. My gaze shifted, and I felt my breath hitch at the sight of a woman with sharp features and dark, stormy eyes that scanned the room like a predator searching for its prey. There was something unsettling about her, an aura that clung to her like fog, and I felt Gavin's posture tense beside me.

"Just ignore her," he murmured, his voice low.

"Who is she?" I whispered, unable to tear my gaze away.

"Someone best left alone," he replied tersely, his expression hardening.

But curiosity was a beast that refused to be silenced, and I watched as she made her way toward us, her movements fluid and purposeful. "Gavin," she said, her voice a silken thread that seemed to draw the entire tavern into her orbit. "I didn't expect to find you here."

"Likewise, Evangeline," he replied, his tone clipped, and I could sense the tension crackling between them.

"Who's your friend?" she asked, her gaze sliding to me, assessing and calculating.

"I'm just passing through," I said, trying to project confidence even as I felt like a rabbit caught in a lion's gaze.

"Passing through? Or running away?" she mused, a knowing smirk curling her lips.

Gavin stiffened beside me, and I caught the flash of something in his eyes—a warning, perhaps, or an unspoken plea for me to hold my ground. The air was charged with a strange energy, and I could feel the precarious balance of the evening teetering on the edge of a precipice.

"Whatever I'm doing, it's none of your business, Evangeline," he said, his voice low and fierce.

"Oh, but it is, Gavin. You have a habit of drawing in the lost, don't you?" she purred, her words dripping with a sweetness that sent chills down my spine.

I could see Gavin's jaw clenching, the tension between them a silent storm. With each heartbeat, I felt the fabric of the evening unravel, a foreboding sense that this encounter was only the beginning of something darker lurking beneath the surface. The whispering cliffs awaited us, but the shadows they cast were beginning to loom larger than the sea itself.

The tavern's lively atmosphere seemed to recede as Evangeline's presence filled the room, her gaze lingering on me like a storm cloud ready to burst. Gavin's body tensed beside me, the warmth of our earlier laughter dissipating into the icy tension that now clung to the air. I had only just begun to peel back the layers of this enigmatic fisherman, and already, shadows were threatening to close in around us.

"Why are you still hanging around this town, Gavin?" Evangeline purred, her tone laced with a teasing familiarity that sent an uncomfortable ripple through me. "You know it's a dangerous place for someone like you."

"Dangerous, or just familiar?" he replied, his voice low, steely.

"Ah, familiarity can be a double-edged sword," she replied, casting a glance my way that felt like an unwelcome intrusion. "Especially for those looking to escape their past."

"Or seeking a new beginning," I shot back, surprising myself with the boldness that surged within me. I wouldn't let her corner me or him.

Evangeline's smile was sharp, revealing a glint of amusement. "You're a brave one, aren't you? Or perhaps just naïve."

Gavin shot me a glance, his eyes holding a warning that urged caution, but I sensed the embers of anger simmering beneath his composed exterior. "What do you want, Evangeline?" he asked, his voice tense as he leaned forward, bracing himself against the table.

"Just checking in on you, darling," she replied, her voice dripping with false sweetness. "I'd hate to see you entangled with someone who doesn't know the danger lurking beneath this charming façade."

My pulse quickened, the air thickening with unspoken threats. "I'm not a child," I retorted, standing my ground. "I can take care of myself."

"Can you?" she challenged, her dark eyes narrowing, and the warmth of the tavern seemed to fade further. "This town has secrets, and you'd do well to stay clear of them."

"Enough," Gavin snapped, his voice sharp, slicing through the tension. "You're not welcome here, Evangeline. Leave."

The atmosphere shifted, and for a fleeting moment, I believed she might back down. Instead, her smile widened, and a sinister light flickered in her eyes. "Very well. But don't say I didn't warn you." With that, she turned, her presence receding as she swept out of the tavern like a dark shadow, leaving behind a heavy silence.

Gavin let out a long breath, tension releasing from his shoulders as he slumped back in his seat. "I'm sorry about that," he murmured, his expression a mix of frustration and concern. "She doesn't know when to stop."

"Is she always like that?" I asked, my curiosity piqued despite the heaviness of the moment.

"Unfortunately, yes. Evangeline has a way of turning up at the worst possible times," he replied, raking a hand through his hair, revealing a vulnerability I hadn't seen before.

"Is she really a danger?" I pressed, sensing that there was more beneath his guarded exterior.

"Let's just say she knows things," he said, his voice low, eyes focused on something far beyond the walls of the tavern. "Things about this town, about me. And she doesn't hesitate to use that knowledge to get what she wants."

The weight of his words hung in the air, and I felt an unsettling chill creep up my spine. "What does she want from you?"

"Power," he replied simply, but the word carried a depth of meaning that resonated between us. "And control. She has a way of getting under people's skin, making them feel small."

"Sounds charming," I remarked, attempting to lighten the mood even as unease gnawed at me.

"It isn't. But I'm not going to let her dictate my life," he said firmly, his blue eyes sparking with resolve. "And I won't let her scare you away."

The warmth of his words wrapped around me like a lifeline, igniting a fierce sense of determination within. "I'm not going anywhere," I declared, a newfound strength surging through me. "I want to know the truth. About the town, about you, about everything."

Gavin studied me, a mixture of admiration and concern flaring in his gaze. "You're not afraid of what you might find?"

"Should I be?" I shot back, my heart racing.

"Maybe," he replied, a shadow of doubt crossing his features. "But that's what makes you interesting. You have a spirit that refuses to be snuffed out."

"Flattery will get you everywhere, fisherman," I quipped, a playful smile breaking through my earlier apprehension. "Just remember, you owe me a tour of the cliffs at dawn."

"Right," he said, the corners of his mouth twitching up as he regained some of his earlier ease. "But only if you promise to keep your wits about you."

"Deal," I agreed, my heart swelling with anticipation.

As the night wore on, laughter returned to our table, the weight of Evangeline's presence fading into the background. We shared stories, dreams, and the thrill of possibilities, the lines of our lives intertwining like the nets he mended earlier. It felt exhilarating to connect, to dance around the edges of our vulnerabilities while the world outside continued its tempestuous rhythm.

Yet, as I glanced out the window, a flicker of movement caught my eye. I squinted, heart skipping a beat as I saw Evangeline standing across the street, shrouded in shadows. Her dark silhouette seemed to pulse with a menacing energy, and though she stood still, I could feel the weight of her gaze, a predatory focus that sent ice through my veins.

"Gavin," I whispered, unable to tear my eyes away. "She's still out there."

He turned, his expression darkening as he caught sight of her. "Damn it," he muttered, pushing himself out of his seat. "We need to go. Now."

"What? Why?" Panic flared within me.

"Trust me," he said, urgency flooding his tone. "We can't stay here."

Before I could ask any more questions, he grabbed my hand, his grip firm and reassuring as he led me toward the door. The tavern, once a warm refuge, now felt like a cage closing in around us. I glanced back, heart pounding, as we stepped out into the cool night, the weight of the storm still looming overhead.

As we rounded the corner of the tavern, I felt a sense of dread settle deep within me. The night was alive with sounds—the wind whispering secrets, the waves crashing against the rocks in a rhythmic dance. Yet something felt off, a prickling awareness that made the hair on the back of my neck stand on end.

"Where are we going?" I asked, my voice barely above a whisper as I followed Gavin into the darkness.

"Somewhere safe," he replied, his eyes scanning the surroundings, alert and tense. "We need to put some distance between us and her."

As we hurried down the deserted street, the shadows stretched around us, and I couldn't shake the feeling that Evangeline was watching us, her eyes boring into my back like a cold blade. My heart raced, not just from fear, but from the exhilaration of the unknown. I was crossing into a world where secrets thrived, where shadows danced along the edges of reality, and where I was now undeniably entwined with a man whose past was as turbulent as the sea.

Just when I thought we had escaped, a cold wind swept through the alley, carrying with it a chilling whisper. "You can't run forever, Gavin," a voice echoed, smooth and serpentine, sending a shiver down my spine.

Gavin's grip tightened around my hand, and we both froze, fear threading through the air like a taut line ready to snap. "We need to move faster," he urged, urgency creeping into his voice.

Before I could respond, the ground trembled beneath us, and I felt an ominous crackling in the air, like the prelude to a storm. Shadows coalesced, and from the darkness, Evangeline emerged, her eyes gleaming with a predatory hunger.

"You think you can escape me?" she taunted, her voice echoing off the walls like a chilling symphony. "This is just the beginning."

My breath caught in my throat, and in that moment, the weight of her words crashed over me, a dark tide threatening to pull us under. The night stretched ahead, a web of uncertainty, and I knew that whatever lay before us was more than I had ever bargained for.

Chapter 4: Secrets Beneath the Surface

The wind whipped around us, tangling my hair in wild knots as Gavin and I navigated the rocky cliffs. Each step was a careful negotiation with the jagged earth, a reminder that beauty often lurked in treacherous places. The cliffs loomed above the crashing waves, their sound a hypnotic rhythm that seemed to echo secrets of the deep. I could taste the salt on my lips, sharp and bracing, like the thrill of the unknown.

"Watch your step," Gavin called out, his voice threaded with amusement. He had that way about him—finding joy even in the most precarious of situations. It was one of the things that drew me to him, the way he embraced life as though it were an uncharted adventure, rather than a series of obstacles. I laughed, my nerves settling into a comfortable flutter as I glanced back at him, his silhouette framed by the vast expanse of the ocean. There was a reckless charm to him, a way of leaning into danger that made my heart race and my mind whirl.

I turned my attention back to the cliff face, where the rock bore strange markings—somewhat like ancient hieroglyphics, worn and weathered by time. My fingertips brushed the grooves, feeling the coolness of the stone beneath the warmth of the sun. Each symbol seemed to pulse with a life of its own, a testament to stories long forgotten. "Gavin, look at this!" I exclaimed, excitement bubbling up inside me like the tide below.

He bounded over, his eyes sparkling with curiosity. "What have you found? An ancient alien landing site? Or maybe a treasure map?" His grin was infectious, and I couldn't help but roll my eyes playfully.

"More like a mysterious code waiting to be cracked," I replied, tracing a particularly elaborate spiral with my fingertip. "These markings...they feel important, like they're trying to tell us something." My imagination ran wild. What if this was the key to unlocking the town's buried history? What if we were standing on the brink of a discovery that could change everything?

Gavin leaned in closer, his breath warm against my ear. "Or maybe it's a warning to get the hell out of here." His tone was teasing, but a flicker of seriousness danced in his eyes. I knew he shared my sense of wonder and apprehension. We both felt it—the unsettling energy that hummed in the air, electrifying the atmosphere around us.

As we stepped back, the sound of the ocean crescendoed, drowning out our laughter. It was as if the cliffs were whispering their secrets, urging us to dig deeper. The lighthouse loomed ahead, its silhouette a stark contrast against the cerulean sky. The structure had long since surrendered to the elements, its paint peeling like forgotten memories, and I felt a pull to explore its depths. "Shall we?" I asked, gesturing toward the building.

"Lead the way, fearless adventurer," Gavin replied, and I couldn't help but bask in the warmth of his encouragement. With a determined nod, I forged ahead, my heart racing with the thrill of discovery and the thrill of having him by my side.

The air inside the lighthouse was thick with dust and the scent of damp wood. The broken windows allowed slivers of light to pierce the shadows, illuminating the remnants of a life once lived here. Each step echoed, the sound reverberating against the walls, creating an eerie symphony. I reached out to touch the railing of the spiral staircase, the wood splintering beneath my fingers, reminding me of the fragility of time.

"Do you think anyone ever comes here?" Gavin mused, his voice a low whisper as if we might wake the ghosts of the past.

"Maybe they're all too scared of what they might find," I said, a shiver racing down my spine. It wasn't just the decrepit state of the lighthouse that unsettled me; it was the stories I imagined hiding within its walls. What had happened here? Who had lived in this lonely place, and why had they left it to rot?

As we climbed the staircase, my heart pounded with anticipation. Each creak of the wood beneath our feet felt like a secret being revealed. When we reached the top, the view stole my breath away. The ocean spread out before us, endless and mesmerizing, while the cliffs rose dramatically at the edges of the horizon. It was both beautiful and haunting—a perfect reflection of the mystery that enveloped this place.

"Wow," Gavin breathed, stepping beside me. "It's incredible up here."

"It is," I agreed, my eyes tracing the horizon, but my thoughts were drawn back to the symbols. "But there's something more down there. I can feel it."

Gavin turned to me, his expression serious. "You really want to find out what it means, don't you?"

"Yes," I said, the resolve settling firmly in my chest. "I need to know."

The wind whipped around us, almost in response, and I could feel the tension building, an invisible thread tugging at me, pulling me toward the answers hidden in the past. Gavin's presence was a grounding force, and I turned to him, ready to share the weight of my determination.

"Let's go back down," I suggested, my voice steady despite the excitement bubbling inside me. "We need to figure out how to decode those symbols."

He nodded, a glimmer of admiration in his eyes that made my heart skip a beat. "Okay, then. But I'll warn you, if we end up unleashing some ancient curse, I'm blaming you."

I laughed, a sound bright and defiant against the looming shadows of the lighthouse. "Fair enough. But if we uncover a treasure, you'll be my partner in crime."

As we descended, my thoughts raced with possibilities. The day was only beginning, and beneath the surface of this sleepy town lay secrets waiting to be unearthed. Together, we would dive headfirst into the unknown, and with each revelation, I felt the thrill of adventure intertwining with something deeper—an unspoken connection that both excited and terrified me.

The afternoon sun hung low in the sky, casting long shadows that danced playfully across the abandoned lighthouse. As Gavin and I emerged from the crumbling structure, the cool breeze off the ocean wrapped around us like a refreshing embrace, teasing away the remnants of dust and uncertainty. I was still reeling from the haunting beauty of the view, my heart thrumming with the thrill of discovery. But now, with each step down the path that wound back toward the cliffs, I was hyper-aware of the pulse of the town around us, as if it were a living entity, holding its breath in anticipation of our next move.

"So, deciphering those symbols? Any thoughts?" Gavin asked, a glint of mischief sparking in his hazel eyes.

"Maybe they're just graffiti from bored sailors," I replied, smirking. "Or a warning about the sea monsters lurking beneath the waves." The sun caught his hair, turning it a soft gold, and for a moment, I forgot the chill creeping up my spine at the thought of what lay beneath the surface of the water.

"Sea monsters, huh?" he laughed, his voice deep and rich. "Should I be concerned about my life choices? Or do you think they prefer their snacks a little more... crunchy?"

I rolled my eyes but couldn't help the laughter that bubbled up. "I'm pretty sure they have a taste for adventure, not just snacks. We'd be safe, right?"

"Unless you plan on becoming their next gourmet meal," he shot back, pretending to contemplate my fate. "Then I'd say it's a whole different story."

The lighthearted banter brought an ease to the air, but beneath it, I sensed a tension brewing, a current of something deeper that neither of us could fully grasp yet. As we navigated the rocky path back to town, I replayed the symbols in my mind, searching for a pattern or meaning. There had to be a story behind them, something that tied them to the lighthouse, the cliffs, and perhaps even the town itself.

Arriving back in the quaint village, the scent of saltwater mingled with freshly baked bread wafting from a nearby bakery, enticing and familiar. It felt like a different world altogether, the hustle and bustle of daily life blending seamlessly with the lingering mysteries of the cliffs. Yet, my heart wasn't in the pastries or the lively chatter. I was drawn back to the enigma that awaited us.

"Let's check in at the library," I suggested, my mind racing. "Maybe we can find something about the history of this place, the lighthouse, those symbols..."

Gavin raised an eyebrow, a playful smirk tugging at the corners of his mouth. "You mean you want to drag me into a dusty, old library? Where the only things that breathe are the books?"

"Ah, but think of all the untold stories! The secrets waiting in those pages." I nudged him playfully. "Besides, we might find some juicy gossip about sea monsters."

He laughed, shaking his head, but the warmth in his eyes told me he was game. "Lead the way, then. Just promise me there won't be any shushing librarians."

With a determined stride, I headed toward the town library, a charming brick building with ivy creeping up its walls and an old oak tree standing sentinel in the yard. Inside, the air was cool and scented with paper and ink, a haven of quiet that felt worlds away from the chaos of the cliffs. Rows of books towered above us, their spines lined like soldiers awaiting orders.

I could practically feel the pulse of knowledge in the air as I moved deeper into the stacks, running my fingers over the spines, searching for anything that might illuminate our discoveries. "If I were a book about local legends and ancient symbols, where would I be?"

"Probably hiding under a pile of dusty encyclopedias," Gavin quipped, his voice a gentle tease.

As I turned a corner, I spotted an elderly woman at the front desk, her hair a soft cloud of white, reading glasses perched precariously on the tip of her nose. She looked up as we approached, her expression shifting from mild curiosity to something like recognition.

"Ah, you two must be the newcomers. The ones causing a stir down at the cliffs."

"We may have stumbled upon some ancient symbols," I admitted, trying to suppress a grin. "Do you know anything about them?"

Her eyes twinkled with mischief. "Oh, there are stories, my dear. Many stories. But they come with a price."

Gavin leaned closer, intrigued. "What's the price?"

"Your patience, of course. And perhaps a bit of your imagination." She smiled, and it was both inviting and daunting. "I have a book that might interest you. Follow me."

We trailed after her as she led us through the maze of shelves, her movements graceful despite the years that seemed to weigh on her. She paused in front of a heavy tome, its cover adorned with intricate designs that mirrored the symbols we had seen.

"This one," she said, pulling it down and handing it to me. "The Secrets of Coastal Lore. It holds the town's history and legends about the cliffs, the lighthouse, and what lies beneath the waves."

Gavin leaned in, examining the cover. "Perfect. Let's dive in."

I opened the book, the pages crinkling softly as I flipped through them, absorbing the words like a sponge. My pulse quickened as I stumbled upon a section dedicated to ancient mariner symbols, their meanings hinting at warnings and guides to the sea. As I read, a story began to unfold—of sailors who had carved their tales into the cliffs, offering sacrifices to the ocean in exchange for safe passage. Each mark told of a shipwreck, a storm survived, or a lost love forever intertwined with the sea.

"This is it," I murmured, feeling a mix of excitement and apprehension. "These symbols—they're not just random markings. They're part of a larger story about this place."

Gavin leaned over, his breath warm against my shoulder. "What does it say? Are we the next chapter in this tale?"

I chuckled nervously, my mind racing. "More like we're uncovering the prologue. There's something ominous here, a warning about the sea—something that hasn't been seen in decades."

"Like a sea monster?" he teased, though the seriousness in his eyes suggested he knew there was more to it than just local lore.

"Yes, but also about the lighthouse and its forgotten keepers," I replied, the weight of the words heavy on my heart. "It mentions a guardian spirit, protecting those who respect the ocean. But it warns against those who seek to exploit its mysteries."

The library fell into a comfortable silence, save for the rustling of pages and the soft patter of footsteps. I could sense Gavin's curiosity mingling with unease as we pieced together fragments of the past.

"What if there's a reason we found those symbols?" he said, a hint of gravity threading his words. "What if we're meant to do something?"

The thought sent a shiver down my spine, a mix of excitement and trepidation. Perhaps we were more than just passive observers in this story; perhaps we were players on a stage set by the ocean itself.

"Then let's find out," I replied, determination flaring within me. The mystery had already begun to entwine itself around us, and as I glanced at Gavin, his unwavering support sparked a new fire. We were diving into something far more profound than I had anticipated, and I was ready for whatever lay ahead.

The book lay open between us like a portal to another world, its pages a mosaic of faded ink and yellowing paper. Gavin leaned in closer, our shoulders almost brushing, the warmth between us an electric contrast to the chill of the library. I could feel the thrum of his curiosity, matched only by my own, and the intensity of the moment sent a thrill down my spine.

"Look at this," I said, tapping a finger on a page adorned with an intricate illustration of the lighthouse surrounded by swirling waves and ghostly figures. "It mentions an artifact—the Keeper's Amulet. According to the legend, it was said to grant its bearer the power to commune with the sea and protect the coast from disaster."

"Commune with the sea? That sounds like something out of a pirate movie," he quipped, but I caught the flicker of intrigue in his eyes. "What happened to it?"

"Here's the kicker." I flipped the page, revealing a hastily scrawled note in the margin. "It states that the amulet was hidden somewhere near the cliffs, the location known only to those who respect the ocean." My heart raced as the implications sank in. "It could still be out there."

Gavin's brows knitted together, his expression shifting from amusement to seriousness. "And if it is, what does that mean for us? For the town?"

I had thought the adventure would be exhilarating, but now a weight settled in my stomach. "It could be dangerous. The stories warn that whoever seeks the amulet without true intent risks unleashing something far worse than mere legends."

"Like a sea monster?" he said, half-joking but half-serious, the corners of his mouth twitching with the strain of holding back a grin.

"Perhaps," I replied, biting my lip, trying to hold back a laugh, but the gravity of the situation clung to us like the musty air of the library. "The guardians of the sea don't take kindly to treasure hunters."

Gavin leaned back, his thoughtful gaze fixed on the ceiling. "So, we're essentially talking about a curse on top of a treasure hunt. Great combo."

"Exactly," I said, my excitement battling with caution. "But if we could find the amulet... just imagine what we could learn about the town's history, about the symbols."

"And if we don't find it?" he countered, his tone suddenly serious, as if the weight of his words was enough to crush the lightness that had settled between us.

"Then we've stirred up something ancient and possibly dangerous for nothing," I admitted, my heart pounding. "But I need to know, Gavin. We need to know."

He studied me for a long moment, his expression shifting as if weighing the risks against the allure of the unknown. "Okay, then. Let's find this amulet, but let's tread carefully. No reckless moves, no sea monster snacks."

A smile broke across my face, the tension easing just a fraction. "Deal. But if we do find it, you owe me a grand adventure."

"Are you really going to insist on dragging me along to face ancient curses for an adventure?" he asked, incredulous.

"Of course! You're my partner in crime now," I replied, lightheartedly, but the truth of it settled in my chest. The thrill of the chase was infectious, and I could feel the magnetic pull of the mystery guiding me.

As we dove back into the pages of the book, I was struck by a sudden chill that swept through the library, causing the hairs on my arms to stand at attention. The air thickened, and for a brief moment, it felt as if the very walls were listening, holding their breath, waiting for the next chapter to unfold.

"What was that?" Gavin's voice was low, the levity gone.

"I'm not sure," I murmured, casting a glance around the room, the silence amplifying the thrum of my heartbeat. "Maybe we stirred something up."

"Great, just what we need—a haunted library," he said, but I could see the edge of concern etched in his features.

Before I could respond, the front door creaked open, and a tall figure stepped inside, the shadows of the evening falling behind them. My breath caught as I recognized the newcomer—a local historian named Eleanor, known for her fervent obsession with the town's legends. She had a reputation for her eccentricity, but there was something unsettling about her presence now.

"Ah, the curious duo," she said, her voice a blend of intrigue and foreboding. "I hear you've taken an interest in the lighthouse."

"We're just looking into the symbols," I replied, trying to gauge her reaction.

"Symbols can tell you stories, but they can also bring you trouble," she warned, her dark eyes locking onto mine with an intensity that sent shivers down my spine. "You don't understand what you're dealing with."

"Or maybe we do," Gavin countered, a spark of defiance igniting in his tone. "We're not afraid of a little trouble."

Eleanor's lips curled into a cryptic smile. "Bravery can lead to folly. The Keeper's Amulet is not to be trifled with. Its power is a double-edged sword, and those who seek it often find themselves lost."

"What do you mean by lost?" I asked, my voice barely above a whisper.

"The ocean has its own desires. It protects what is sacred, and it punishes those who seek to exploit it," she said, stepping closer. "You must heed the warnings if you wish to emerge unscathed."

I felt the weight of her words settle over us like a fog. "But we have to try. We need to know what the symbols mean, what happened at the lighthouse," I replied, my resolve hardening despite the apprehension creeping in.

Eleanor regarded us both with an inscrutable expression, then nodded slowly. "Just remember, curiosity can lead you down paths you never intended to tread. And sometimes, the past doesn't want to be uncovered."

With that, she turned on her heel and strode out of the library, leaving a thick silence in her wake. I exchanged a glance with Gavin, uncertainty sparking between us.

"What was that about?" he asked, his brow furrowing.

"I don't know," I admitted, unease settling in my stomach. "But I think we might be in over our heads."

"Maybe we should take a step back," he suggested, the gravity of our quest sinking in.

But as I looked down at the book open before me, the images of the lighthouse and the symbols beckoned me forward. The thrill of the unknown was stronger than the fear that tugged at my mind, and I couldn't turn back now.

"Just one more look at the symbols before we go," I insisted, my voice steady despite the chaos within.

Gavin hesitated but eventually nodded, the adventurous spark returning to his eyes.

As I flipped the pages, searching for the illustrations, I felt a sudden shift in the air—an ominous rush that swept through the library like a whispered warning. The temperature dropped, and the shadows around us thickened, curling like tendrils reaching for the light.

"What's happening?" Gavin asked, his voice rising with tension.

I opened my mouth to respond, but before I could form the words, the lights flickered and went out, plunging us into darkness. The faint sound of rushing waves outside faded, replaced by an unsettling silence, thick and heavy, wrapping around us like a shroud.

Then, in the inky blackness, a faint glow began to emerge from the pages of the book, illuminating the symbols we had been studying. They pulsed with an otherworldly light, each mark shimmering like a beacon.

"What is that?" Gavin whispered, awe mingled with fear.

I stared, transfixed, as the glow intensified, the symbols dancing before our eyes, forming an intricate pattern that seemed to beckon us closer. But as I reached out, the ground beneath us trembled, and a deep rumble echoed through the library, shaking the very foundations of the building.

"Get back!" Gavin shouted, but it was too late.

The book exploded in a shower of brilliant light, and in that moment, I realized we had awakened something we weren't prepared for—something far more powerful and dangerous than we could have ever imagined. The last thing I saw was the glow consuming everything around us, pulling me into a whirlwind of light and shadow, before everything went dark.

Chapter 5: The Mayor's Game

The air in Misty Shores was damp with the kind of fog that clung to you like a persistent memory, whispering secrets to those who dared to listen. I stood at the edge of the town square, the cobblestones slick beneath my feet, each step echoing the weight of unanswered questions. Mayor Callahan's office was a short stroll away, a stately brick building that loomed over the square, its windows darkened as if holding their breath. It was a fortress of sorts, one that promised protection but was likely hiding much more behind its austere façade.

As I made my way toward the entrance, the remnants of a recent storm still clung to the trees, their branches heavy and bowed, casting long shadows that flickered like specters in the dim light. The townspeople bustled about, their voices mingling with the rustle of leaves. I caught snippets of conversation—words like "funding," "construction," and "improvements." It all felt like a thin veil draped over something more sinister, and my instincts urged me to dig deeper.

I pushed open the heavy oak door to the mayor's office, the creak echoing in the silent hall. The air inside was thick with the smell of polished wood and something metallic, perhaps leftover from the last town hall meeting. A receptionist sat behind a glass partition, her fingers dancing over a keyboard, completely engrossed in her screen. She barely glanced up, her indifference a wall I'd have to scale.

"Hi, I'd like to speak with Mayor Callahan," I said, forcing a smile that felt more like a grimace.

"Do you have an appointment?" she asked without looking up.

"No, but—"

"Then I can't help you," she replied, her tone as final as the closing of a door.

I felt a rush of irritation but chose to swallow it down. The mayor was my only lead, and I needed to keep my cool. "When might he be available?" I pressed, leaning forward slightly, hoping my earnestness would break through her aloofness.

She glanced up at me then, her eyes narrowing. "He's a busy man. If you want, you can leave a message."

I held her gaze for a moment longer, sensing the barriers she had erected. "You know, it would really help the community if I could talk to him about the upcoming festival," I said, testing a different angle.

Her brow arched slightly, a flicker of interest igniting in her expression. "The festival, huh? You think he'd care about that?"

"Given how it brings in tourists and supports local businesses, I think he should," I replied, trying to inject a note of conviction into my voice.

She hesitated, her fingers pausing mid-air as she contemplated my words. Finally, she shrugged, lifting the phone receiver. "Fine. I'll see if he can spare a moment. Just a moment," she added, as if afraid I might try to seize a full hour.

As she dialed, my heart raced with anticipation. The mayor was a master of obfuscation, but the festival was a distraction, and perhaps it could open a door to the truth I sought. I had been in Misty Shores long enough to recognize the discontent simmering beneath the surface. The town was caught in the grip of something oppressive, and Mayor Callahan was at the center of it, his charm and authority cloaking the darker elements of his rule.

The phone clicked, and I caught snippets of her conversation. "Yes, Mr. Callahan. There's a woman here about the festival... Yes, I'll send her in."

With a sigh, she gestured toward the door that led to his office, the wariness returning to her features. I stepped forward, heart thumping with both dread and determination. The heavy door swung open, revealing a room that radiated power. Dark wood paneling lined the walls, adorned with portraits of stern-looking predecessors who seemed to judge my every move.

Mayor Callahan sat behind a large, imposing desk, his fingers steepled in front of him. He had the kind of smile that could disarm even the most cynical of hearts, but I had learned to see past the surface. "Ah, welcome," he said, his voice smooth like velvet. "What can I do for you?"

I took a deep breath, feeling the weight of his gaze. "I wanted to discuss the upcoming festival and how we can better support it this year," I said, keeping my tone light.

"Ah, yes, the festival." He leaned back in his chair, fingers still entwined. "A lovely tradition. But you must understand, my time is limited. What exactly do you propose?"

"More activities, perhaps? Something that might draw more visitors?" I ventured, watching his reaction closely.

He chuckled softly, a sound that held no warmth. "You think that's what we need? More tourists? They come, they gawk, and they leave. What's the benefit of that?"

I hesitated, searching for the right words. "It's about community spirit. The festival can bring people together, showcase local talent. It could mean more for the economy than just a one-day event."

His smile faltered for just a moment, a flicker of irritation crossing his features. "The economy, yes. It's a delicate balance, isn't it? Too many outsiders, and the locals feel overshadowed." He leaned forward slightly, his eyes narrowing as if weighing my words. "But tell me, what do you know of our local businesses? Are they truly struggling, or is it just a myth?"

I felt a chill run down my spine at his shift in tone, sensing he was probing for something deeper. "I've spoken to a few shop owners," I said carefully. "They've mentioned that foot traffic has declined. They're worried."

"Worried?" He leaned back again, a dangerous glint in his eye. "Worry can be a powerful motivator, but sometimes it's simply a matter of perception."

His words hung in the air, heavy with implication. There was something about his demeanor that set my instincts aflame; he was toying with me, testing my resolve. I sensed that beneath his charismatic exterior lay a network of shadows, secrets intertwined with the town's very fabric.

"Mayor Callahan, I want to help," I said, my voice firm, hoping to cut through the tension. "But I need to know what's really happening here. There's more to this than just a festival."

He regarded me with an inscrutable expression, his smile now a mask that concealed the labyrinth of his thoughts. "Ah, but that's the thing, isn't it? Sometimes, the more you know, the less you understand. Are you prepared for that?"

The challenge in his tone ignited a fire within me. "I am. I've faced worse than a few secrets. What I don't understand is why you seem so determined to keep things hidden."

"Hidden?" he echoed, his eyes narrowing slightly. "Or simply...protected? It's all in how you frame the narrative, my dear. Just remember, curiosity can lead to revelations that change everything."

His words resonated like a warning bell, echoing in the cavernous office as I stood my ground. I could feel the weight of his authority pressing down on me, yet I was more resolute than ever. There was a game at play, and I had no intention of backing down. Misty Shores was a tapestry woven with threads of intrigue and tension, and I was determined to unravel its mysteries, even if it meant dancing with shadows.

The conversation with Mayor Callahan left a lingering chill in my bones, a chill that was almost tangible as I stepped out of his office and into the unforgiving cold of Misty Shores. The fog had thickened, swirling around me like a gauzy curtain that separated the known from the unknown, making the quaint town appear ethereal and deceptive all at once. The cobblestones glistened under the dim glow of the streetlamps, casting reflections that danced eerily, as if the very ground was alive with secrets waiting to be uncovered.

As I made my way through the square, I could feel the weight of the mayor's words echoing in my mind. His playful ambiguity was unnerving, as though he reveled in the power of obscurity. Curiosity flared within me, igniting a determination I didn't know I possessed. If he thought he could intimidate me with clever wordplay and evasive answers, he clearly underestimated my resolve.

The warmth of The Whimsical Café beckoned me from across the square, its cheerful yellow façade a stark contrast to the oppressive atmosphere outside. As I stepped inside, the delightful aroma of freshly brewed coffee and baked pastries wrapped around me like a comforting embrace. The café was bustling, filled with townsfolk animatedly chatting over mugs and plates, their laughter punctuating the air, momentarily dispelling the fog's gloom.

I found a small table by the window, the perfect spot to observe and reflect. The barista, a young woman with vibrant pink hair, flashed me a grin as she took my order. "What can I get you? Coffee, tea, or something a little more... daring?" she asked, her eyes twinkling with mischief.

"Surprise me," I replied, feeling a surge of defiance. If I was going to navigate this maze of politics and hidden truths, I might as well fuel my journey with caffeine and a touch of whimsy.

As I waited, I let my gaze wander through the café. It was alive with the kind of energy that felt infectious. I spotted Marjorie, the town's most vocal librarian, gesticulating wildly at a table in the corner, a group of seniors hanging onto her every word. "And then he said, 'That's not how you catch a ghost!'" she exclaimed, eliciting a round of chuckles. Her enthusiasm was contagious, and it reminded me of the warmth this town could exude, despite the encroaching shadows of uncertainty.

Just then, my drink arrived—an extravagant concoction of lavender-infused latte art that felt more like a piece of art than a beverage. I took a sip, and the floral notes danced on my palate, pulling me further into this moment of blissful distraction. It was a sweet escape, but as the steam curled upwards, so did my thoughts of the mayor and his labyrinth of secrets.

I pulled out my notebook, the blank pages awaiting the impressions of the day, the mysteries I was determined to unravel. As I began to jot down notes about the mayor's evasions, my mind drifted to the townsfolk. There was something brewing beneath the surface, and I wondered if they sensed it too. Perhaps they were caught in the same fog, blinded by Callahan's charm and unaware of the storm brewing just out of sight.

My thoughts were interrupted by the ringing of a bell, signaling the entrance of a newcomer. I glanced up to see a figure I hadn't noticed before—an older man with a weathered face and striking silver hair, his presence commanding despite his slight frame. He scanned the café, his eyes settling on me with a piercing intensity. The air shifted, charged with an electric tension.

He approached, and I could see a familiarity in his gaze, as though he had recognized something in me that I hadn't yet realized about myself. "You're the one asking questions about the mayor," he stated, not bothering with pleasantries.

I felt a mix of surprise and intrigue. "And you are?"

"Elliot Dawson," he replied, extending a hand, which I shook cautiously. "Retired fisherman and unofficial town historian. The waves have a way of washing ashore stories, you know?"

His words rolled off his tongue like a melodic chant, and I was captivated. "Stories can be powerful," I said, feeling an invisible thread tethering us. "They can shape perceptions, and sometimes even reality."

He nodded, a spark igniting in his eyes. "Ah, but it's the hidden stories that hold the real weight. The ones the mayor would rather keep buried."

My pulse quickened. "You know something, don't you?"

Elliot leaned closer, lowering his voice. "I've seen things in this town—things that would make your skin crawl. Callahan is a master at spinning tales, but he's not the only player on this board."

His words sent a shiver of excitement through me, a thrill that had nothing to do with the chill in the air. "What do you mean? Who else is involved?"

"Everyone has a secret in Misty Shores, my dear. Even you," he said, leaning back slightly with a knowing grin. "But some secrets are darker than others."

I leaned forward, captivated. "I'm not afraid of the dark."

His laughter was low and rich. "You might be surprised at how well the dark can hide. You see, it's not just the mayor you should watch out for. There are layers here—layers that could swallow you whole if you're not careful."

"What are you suggesting?" I asked, my heart racing as a thousand possibilities unfurled in my mind.

"There's an old saying around here: 'When the tide goes out, you can see who's been swimming naked.' Callahan may be the face of Misty Shores, but there are others who thrive in his shadow, pulling strings and setting traps." His gaze pierced mine, and I could sense the gravity of his warning. "You're not just here to plan a festival. You're seeking answers. But I fear you might be stirring up a hornet's nest."

"I can handle a few hornets," I said, my voice steadier than I felt. "But I need to know what I'm up against."

"Then meet me at the docks tonight. Midnight. I'll share what I know." His expression turned serious, the lightness dissipating like morning fog under the sun. "But be warned: the truth can be a double-edged sword. It cuts both ways."

With that, he stood and walked away, leaving me with a mind racing with possibilities and a heart thumping in my chest. I watched him disappear into the mist outside, the café's warmth feeling almost too stifling in the wake of his revelations. The aroma of lavender now felt distant, overshadowed by the weight of the secrets lurking in the shadows of Misty Shores.

My thoughts circled back to the mayor, the web of influence he had spun, and the threads that Elliot hinted at. I was more determined than ever to untangle them, but a flicker of doubt danced at the edges of my resolve. What if I was in over my head? The stakes were rising, and the fog seemed to thicken once more, wrapping its tendrils around me as if trying to pull me under.

But I couldn't turn back now. The taste of intrigue was too sweet, and I was hungry for the truth, no matter where it led. The docks awaited, and with them, the promise of answers—and perhaps, even danger.

As night draped its velvet cloak over Misty Shores, I felt a thrill of anticipation mixed with trepidation. The town, with its quaint charm and whimsical aura, transformed under the pale moonlight, becoming a world both familiar and hauntingly strange. Shadows danced along the cobblestones, the soft sound of waves lapping at the shore providing an eerie backdrop to my thoughts. I had accepted Elliot's invitation to meet at the docks, a decision that felt both reckless and exhilarating.

The air was cool against my skin, and I hugged my jacket tighter as I approached the water's edge. The dock loomed before me, its wooden planks creaking softly underfoot, the scent of brine and something more potent mingling in the air. I glanced around, the dim glow of the streetlamps illuminating the fog that clung to the night like a forgotten dream. Elliot's warning echoed in my mind, heightening my senses. Was I truly ready to uncover the secrets that lay beneath the surface of this town?

A low sound, like the distant rumble of thunder, caught my attention, but the sky remained clear. I turned to look down the dock, squinting into the darkness. Was that a figure approaching, or merely a trick of the light? I felt my heart race; the thrill of the unknown was intoxicating.

Just as I was about to call out for Elliot, a figure emerged from the shadows. He moved with a deliberate ease, his silver hair catching the moonlight like a beacon. Elliot's weathered face, illuminated in the soft glow, held a serious expression that erased any lightness I had felt earlier.

"You came," he said, a hint of relief mingling with something else—was it concern?

"Of course I did," I replied, trying to inject some bravado into my voice. "You said you had information. I'm all ears."

He motioned for me to follow him further down the dock, away from the dim lights and closer to the water's edge where the moon cast a silver path on the surface. "This isn't the place for idle chatter. We need to be discreet."

I felt a surge of adrenaline as I followed him, the rhythmic sound of the waves matching the quickening beat of my heart. The cool breeze tousled my hair, and the tension in the air was palpable. "What do you know about Callahan? And why do you think he's hiding something?"

Elliot paused, glancing over his shoulder as if ensuring no one was within earshot. "The mayor has a knack for disappearing when the conversation gets too close to the truth. You should know that. It's all part of the game he plays. But there's more—much more. What he's hiding could change everything for Misty Shores."

"Just tell me," I urged, the weight of his words pressing down on me. "What's going on?"

He took a deep breath, the tension in his shoulders easing slightly. "Years ago, before Callahan came into power, the town was teetering on the brink of disaster. There was a scandal involving some property development, land deals that went awry. Callahan swooped in like a knight in shining armor, promising to fix things. But the truth? He's been profiting from the very problems he claimed to solve."

"Profit?" I echoed, piecing together the fragments of the puzzle. "You mean he's lining his pockets?"

Elliot nodded gravely. "And not just his. He's built a network of influence that keeps the townspeople quiet. Anyone who dares speak up finds themselves silenced—either through threats or worse."

I swallowed hard, the weight of his words sinking in. "So, what does that mean for me? I'm just trying to help with the festival."

"The festival is the perfect distraction," he said, his voice low and urgent. "While everyone's focused on balloons and parades, the real issues slip under the radar. You have to understand—Callahan controls the narrative. If you're asking questions, you're a threat."

A cold shiver ran down my spine. "You think I'm in danger?"

"Not just you. Anyone who gets too close to the truth finds themselves in precarious situations," he warned, his eyes narrowing. "You need to be cautious. I've seen good people lose everything because they dared to uncover the rot beneath this town's pretty surface."

The reality of the situation settled like a heavy fog, obscuring my judgment. But I wasn't ready to back down. "So what do we do? Just sit here and let him run amok?"

Elliot's expression hardened. "No. We gather evidence. We expose the truth. But it requires careful planning. We need allies—people who are willing to risk their comfort for what's right."

"Do you know anyone?" I asked, my mind racing with possibilities. The thought of uniting the townsfolk, rallying them against Callahan's hold, filled me with a fierce determination.

"There are whispers," Elliot replied, his gaze scanning the darkened shore. "But trust is hard to come by. You'll need to prove yourself before they'll join the cause. You might want to start by talking to Marjorie—she's more than just a librarian. She knows things, connections that could be invaluable."

I felt the rush of possibilities wash over me. Marjorie had always been a wealth of information, her passionate storytelling often threading history with the present. "I'll talk to her," I decided, the conviction in my voice surprising even me. "We'll start there."

"Good," Elliot said, nodding approvingly. "But tread lightly. The walls have ears, and Callahan's influence extends far and wide."

A sudden noise from behind startled us. My heart leapt as I turned to see a figure approaching in the distance, emerging from the mist like a specter. My gut twisted with apprehension as I squinted into the dark. "Is that—"

"Get down!" Elliot hissed, grabbing my arm and pulling me behind a stack of crates. The world around us fell silent, the rhythmic lapping of the waves replaced by the thumping of my heart.

From our hidden vantage point, I could see a group of figures moving closer, their silhouettes vague and menacing in the night. The air crackled with tension, and my mind raced as I tried to make sense of the situation. Were they working for Callahan? Or were they part of something else entirely?

"Stay quiet," Elliot whispered urgently, his breath warm against my ear.

I nodded, adrenaline coursing through me as I watched the figures draw nearer. Their voices were low and hushed, an ominous conversation slipping through the veil of the fog. One voice, gruff and commanding, rose above the others, sending a chill down my spine. “We can’t let anyone find out what’s happening. We need to take care of it tonight.”

My blood ran cold as the gravity of their words sunk in. “What do they mean?” I murmured, my heart racing.

“I don’t know,” Elliot replied, his eyes sharp with intensity. “But we can’t stick around to find out. If they’re here, it means we’re in danger.”

Before I could respond, the men shifted closer, their features emerging from the shadows, revealing faces marked by hard lives and dangerous intentions. I recognized one of them—a man often seen in town, chatting amiably with Callahan during events. I felt my stomach drop as the realization struck me. He was part of the mayor’s inner circle.

Elliot pulled me down lower, just as they stopped near our hiding place. I held my breath, every muscle in my body tense as I strained to hear their conversation, a sense of dread coiling tightly around me.

“We can’t afford any loose ends,” the man growled, his voice gravelly like the stones beneath our feet. “The mayor wants this wrapped up, and I’m not about to let some nosy newcomer ruin everything he’s worked for.”

I exchanged a glance with Elliot, fear etched on my face.

“Did you hear that?” I whispered, my voice trembling.

“We have to go,” he urged, a fierce determination burning in his eyes. “Now.”

But just as we began to move, the ground beneath us creaked ominously, the wooden planks betraying our position. The men turned sharply, eyes narrowing as they scanned the area. My heart pounded violently against my ribs as I realized we had been discovered.

“Hey! Who’s there?” one of them barked, stepping forward, his silhouette dark against the moonlit backdrop.

Panic surged through me, propelling me into motion as I grabbed Elliot's arm, both of us bolting down the dock, desperate to escape the encroaching danger. The footsteps behind us quickened, their shouts growing louder as we raced into the night, the weight of their intentions hanging heavily in the air.

In that moment, as we fled, I understood that this was no longer just a quest for answers; it had become a fight for survival. And as we plunged into the enveloping fog, I knew that uncovering the truth about Misty Shores was going to come at a cost far greater than I had ever anticipated.

Chapter 6: Shadows and Revelations

The night air was thick with salt and mystery, each breath tasting of the sea's secrets. I found myself at the cliffs, a place where the world seemed to teeter on the edge of reality. The moon hung low, a silver coin tossed into a deep blue sea, illuminating the jagged rocks below, their surfaces slick with the remnants of the tide. Shadows danced along the craggy edges, whispering stories I was only beginning to understand. A chill settled into my bones, not just from the cool breeze that swept through, but from the anticipation of what lay ahead.

Drawn by a force I couldn't name, I followed the path that wound like a serpent toward the flickering light I had spotted earlier. My heart thudded with each step, the rhythm a primal drumbeat that echoed the pulse of the earth beneath me. The lantern swung gently in the distance, casting playful shadows that flickered like spirits playing hide-and-seek with the night. As I drew nearer, I recognized the figure waiting for me. Gavin stood at the edge of the cave, his profile stark against the glowing light, a silhouette carved from the fabric of the night.

"Thought I'd find you here," he said, his voice a low rumble, filled with a warmth that cut through the cold. There was an edge of concern in his eyes, a flicker of something deeper that made my pulse quicken. "You shouldn't be alone out here. It's not safe."

"Safe?" I echoed, my lips curving into a teasing smile. "You've been in this town long enough to know that safety is a relative term, especially around here."

He let out a soft chuckle, a sound that rolled through the night like the waves crashing below us. It was oddly comforting, this moment between us, shared under the watchful eye of the moon. "I suppose you're right. But I'm here now, so at least you're not alone." He stepped closer, the lantern illuminating his features. The shadows sculpted his cheekbones, giving him an air of rugged handsomeness that sent a shiver of awareness through me. "What is it you're hoping to find?"

"Answers," I replied, suddenly serious. The cave loomed behind us, dark and mysterious, an invitation laced with danger. I had discovered those symbols etched into the rocks earlier, their meanings eluding me like a mirage just out of reach. "I feel like there's something buried here—something important."

Gavin's eyes darkened, and I saw a flicker of understanding pass between us. "You're right. There's more to this town than meets the eye. Let's see what we can uncover." He nodded toward the cave, the light casting a halo around his figure, igniting a spark of bravery within me. Together, we stepped into the darkness, where the air shifted, heavy with the weight of history.

Inside, the cave opened up like a hidden world, the walls glistening with moisture and adorned with strange markings that seemed to pulse in the light. My heart raced as we ventured deeper, the lantern illuminating relics of the past: broken pottery, rusted tools, and shards of glass glimmering like lost memories. Each item whispered tales of those who came before us, their laughter and sorrows echoing in the silence.

"Do you think this was a shelter?" Gavin mused, picking up a small, weathered stone. "Or maybe a place of worship?" His brow furrowed as he examined the etchings along the walls, lines that twisted and turned in patterns both beautiful and unsettling.

"Maybe both," I said, my fingers tracing the symbols. They felt alive under my touch, vibrating with energy. "These markings... they're not just random. They tell a story." The realization settled over me like a cloak, warming my skin despite the coolness of the cave.

Gavin stepped closer, his breath warm against my cheek as he leaned in to study the designs. "It feels like something... darker," he whispered, a shiver running through his voice. "What if these artifacts are tied to the stories the townsfolk have been avoiding?"

"What stories?" I asked, the curiosity igniting a fire within me. I leaned closer, drawn to the way his intensity lit up the space around us.

He hesitated, then spoke softly, as if the very walls might betray us. "About the disappearances. About the town being cursed. You know the legends."

I scoffed lightly, though a thrill of fear raced through me. "Legends are just stories people tell to scare kids. They're not real." But even as I said it, I felt the weight of truth behind his words. The town's shadowy history wrapped around us, thickening the air.

"Do you really believe that?" Gavin challenged, a flicker of mischief dancing in his eyes. "Or are you just trying to convince yourself?"

"I—" I faltered, unable to deny the truth in his gaze. "I want to believe that we're safe here. That it's just the sea and the wind we have to worry about."

He smiled, the warmth returning, but there was a deeper understanding behind it, a bond forming in the shared acknowledgment of fear. "Then let's uncover the truth together. If there's something lurking in the shadows, we'll face it. Together."

The echo of his words resonated in my heart, a promise stitched into the fabric of the night. Together. The word felt powerful, igniting a flame of courage within me as we continued our exploration, our shared resolve illuminating the darkness around us.

The lantern's glow flickered softly against the damp cave walls, creating shadows that danced like wraiths caught in a perpetual waltz. I marveled at the strange artifacts surrounding us, each one whispering a fragment of the town's hidden history. Gavin and I stood side by side, our breath mingling in the chill air, as the weight of what we'd stumbled upon settled over us like a thick fog. I could feel the electric tension crackling in the space between us, the urgency of our discovery igniting something deeper, something unspoken.

"Do you think we're the first ones to find this place?" I asked, my voice low, reverberating through the stillness. The air seemed to thrum with possibility, as if the cave itself was eager to share its secrets.

"Doubtful," Gavin replied, his brow furrowing in thought. He leaned closer to an ancient piece of pottery, the intricate designs hinting at stories lost to time. "People have lived here for generations. Someone must have known about this cave." He straightened, his gaze locking onto mine with an intensity that sent shivers down my spine. "But why did it remain hidden for so long?"

"Maybe they didn't want anyone to know." The notion sent a jolt through me, a mix of intrigue and fear swirling in my stomach. "What if there's something here that they were trying to protect?"

His eyes darkened momentarily, and the playful banter between us dulled. "Or something they wanted to keep buried."

The word 'buried' hung in the air like an uninvited guest, lingering between us as we continued our exploration. I could feel the pulse of the cave, its heartbeat echoing in the very marrow of my bones. Each artifact felt like a breadcrumb leading us deeper into the mystery, each marking on the wall a note in a long-forgotten symphony. I reached out to touch one of the symbols, tracing its path with my fingers. It felt alive, as if the stories it held were trying to break free, trying to be heard.

"What do you think it means?" Gavin asked, joining me, his breath warm against my cheek. The intimacy of the moment sent my heart racing in a way that had little to do with fear.

"Maybe it's a warning," I suggested, pulling back slightly, though I didn't want to lose the closeness we had found. "A cautionary tale about whatever darkness lies beyond."

"Or perhaps a call to action," he countered, his voice dropping to a whisper as if afraid to disturb the spirits that might linger in the shadows. "Inviting those brave enough to seek the truth."

I smiled at that, the tension between us shimmering like the lantern's light. "Brave? I think we're just curious fools stumbling into trouble."

"Curiosity might be the bravest thing of all," he said, his eyes sparkling with mischief. "And if trouble finds us, at least we'll have a good story to tell."

"Assuming we make it out alive," I teased, nudging him playfully, though the truth hung heavily in the air. There was an undercurrent of danger, a sense that we were dancing on the precipice of something far greater than ourselves.

As we delved deeper into the cave, the walls began to close in, the narrow passageways shifting our perceptions. The lantern cast strange, elongated shadows that seemed to twist and writhe, creating illusions that played tricks on my mind. I could feel a weight pressing down on us, as if the cave itself was holding its breath, waiting for something to unfold.

"Do you hear that?" Gavin suddenly asked, his voice tense.

I paused, straining to listen. A faint sound echoed through the cave—like whispers carried on the wind, though there was no breeze to be found. My skin prickled as I exchanged a glance with Gavin, our unspoken thoughts intertwining in that charged moment.

"Maybe it's just the cave settling," I suggested, but even I could hear the uncertainty in my voice.

"Maybe," he replied, though his eyes glimmered with doubt. "But I'd feel better if we had more light."

Nodding, I turned to the lantern, shifting its beam to illuminate the darker corners of the cave. The glow revealed more artifacts—a rusted dagger, shards of a cracked mirror, and what looked like a ceremonial mask, its eyes hollow and devoid of life. I swallowed hard as the mask seemed to stare back at me, a silent guardian of the secrets trapped within these walls.

"I don't like the way that thing looks at me," Gavin quipped, breaking the tension with a lighthearted laugh, though I could see the flicker of unease behind his smile.

"Maybe it's judging our life choices," I replied, trying to keep the mood light even as an unsettling thought crept into my mind. "Or warning us that we're not welcome here."

He chuckled, but his eyes drifted back to the mask, lingering as if drawn by some invisible thread. "It feels like it's waiting for something," he murmured, a hint of seriousness creeping back into his tone. "What if it's waiting for us?"

Before I could respond, the whispers grew louder, a cacophony of sound echoing off the walls like the cries of long-lost souls. My heart raced, and I stepped back, feeling the ground shift beneath me as if the cave itself was alive, reacting to our presence. Gavin reached for my hand, our fingers intertwining as we moved closer together, drawn into a cocoon of shared apprehension.

"Let's get out of here," I suggested, my voice trembling slightly. The atmosphere felt charged, an undercurrent of energy that made the hair on my arms stand on end.

"Agreed," Gavin said, squeezing my hand tightly. "But first, we need to find a way to silence those whispers."

"Or find out what they're saying," I countered, the adventurous spark igniting again within me.

"Are you always this reckless?" he asked, his eyes dancing with a mixture of admiration and exasperation.

"Only when it comes to uncovering secrets," I said, a playful grin creeping onto my lips. "And when it involves incredibly handsome companions."

His laughter rang through the cave, a bright note that chased away some of the shadows, even as the whispers grew more urgent.

We stood at the crossroads of curiosity and caution, the thrill of the unknown pulling us deeper into the labyrinthine mystery of the cave, where every shadow held a story and every whisper echoed the promise of revelations waiting to be unearthed.

The air thickened around us, saturated with a mix of excitement and foreboding as we moved deeper into the cave. Shadows slithered along the walls, shifting with every flicker of the lantern's light. Each artifact we passed seemed to vibrate with history, whispering tales of the past as if begging us to listen. Gavin and I exchanged glances, a silent understanding passing between us; we were on the precipice of something monumental, yet the darkness around us felt alive, as if it had eyes that watched our every move.

"Shouldn't we document this?" I asked, feeling a surge of urgency. "If we find something important, we need proof."

"Good idea," Gavin replied, reaching into his backpack. "I've got a notebook and a flashlight. Let's make sure we capture every detail." He pulled out the items, his fingers deftly flicking on the flashlight to illuminate the space further. The beam sliced through the shadows, revealing more artifacts tucked away in corners—an intricately carved bone, a leather-bound journal that looked as old as time itself, its cover cracked and weathered.

"Let's see what stories they can tell," I suggested, picking up the journal with reverence. It felt heavy in my hands, a tangible connection to the lives that once were. The spine creaked as I opened it, the scent of old paper wafting up, rich and musty. Words scrawled in elegant cursive filled the pages, faded ink barely legible, but enough to draw me in.

"'The tide brings more than shells and seaweed,'" I read aloud, my voice echoing through the cave. "What could that mean?"

"Maybe a metaphor for the secrets washed ashore," Gavin mused, leaning closer to peer over my shoulder. "Keep reading."

As I turned the pages, snippets of text began to unfurl a narrative steeped in mystique. Accounts of rituals, of storms that brought more than just rain, and of people who disappeared, leaving only echoes behind. Each word wove a tapestry of intrigue that wrapped around my mind, ensnaring my thoughts.

"'Those who seek shall find; those who find shall not return,'" I read, my voice faltering. The cave seemed to shudder in response, a palpable tension settling over us.

"What do you think it means?" Gavin's voice was steady, but I could sense the undercurrent of apprehension beneath his calm exterior.

"Sounds like a warning," I said, the implications hanging heavily in the air. "A curse, maybe? Or a prophecy?"

"Prophecies are usually shrouded in cryptic language," he replied, rubbing his chin in contemplation. "But this could be a guide as much as a warning. What if there's something here—something that needs to be unearthed?"

I glanced at him, his expression caught between thrill and fear, and I felt the same uncertainty gnawing at my insides. "Are we prepared to handle whatever that might be?"

"Honestly?" he said, a smirk playing on his lips. "I'm not sure we've ever been prepared for anything. But when have we ever let that stop us?"

"Point taken," I laughed, the sound echoing like music in the dim light. But as I chuckled, a faint sound echoed in the distance—scraping, almost like fingernails on stone. My heart stopped, the laughter dying on my lips.

"Did you hear that?" I whispered, my voice barely above a breath.

Gavin nodded, his eyes wide, the flashlight beam trembling as he trained it toward the sound. The light flickered, revealing the shadows that had grown darker, deeper, as if something was lurking just beyond our sight. "We should—"

Suddenly, the lantern flickered violently, casting us into a brief, disorienting darkness. I stumbled back, and Gavin grabbed my arm, pulling me close. When the light stabilized again, I could see the unease etched into his features, the laughter of moments before replaced by a steely resolve.

"We need to get out of here," he said, his voice low and urgent. "Now."

I nodded, the adrenaline coursing through me as we turned to retrace our steps. The shadows that once felt like a playful dance now felt like hands reaching out to ensnare us. The whispers morphed into murmurs, rising in pitch as if urging us to leave, and I quickened my pace, Gavin close behind.

As we navigated the narrow passages, a cold gust swept through the cave, snuffing the lantern's flame momentarily. In the ensuing darkness, I felt the weight of countless eyes on us, an oppressive presence that made my skin crawl. My instincts screamed at me to flee, to escape the oppressive grip of the cave, but curiosity tugged at me like a thread, urging me to explore deeper.

"Are you okay?" Gavin's voice cut through the darkness, pulling me back from the brink of panic.

"I'm fine," I lied, trying to sound steadier than I felt. "Just... let's keep moving."

We pressed on, our footsteps echoing eerily as we approached the mouth of the cave, but the whispers grew louder, drowning out our thoughts. I felt a rush of panic as a wave of darkness rolled over me, threatening to pull me under.

"Gavin!" I shouted, fear lacing my voice as we reached the entrance. "We need to hurry!"

But before we could escape, the ground beneath us trembled violently, sending shockwaves through the cave. Rocks crumbled from above, dust and debris raining down as the entrance threatened to collapse. My heart raced, fear clawing at my throat as I glanced back at Gavin, his expression a mix of determination and concern.

"Run!" he yelled, his hand gripping mine tightly as we dashed forward, adrenaline fueling our flight. The cave seemed alive, shifting around us, a living entity determined to keep us within its dark embrace.

Just as we neared the exit, the ground buckled again, a thunderous roar echoing in my ears. I glanced back one last time, and my breath caught in my throat. The shadows coalesced, forming a figure that loomed in the darkness, eyes gleaming like dying embers, a malicious grin stretching across its face.

"Those who seek shall find," it whispered, the words wrapping around me like chains, binding my feet to the ground.

"Keep moving!" Gavin shouted, pulling me back into the light of the cave's mouth. But I could feel the pull of the darkness, an insistent tug that threatened to drag me back into the depths.

With one last effort, I tore my gaze away from the figure and sprinted towards the light. The cave erupted behind us, the sound of falling rock and the chilling laughter echoing in the distance.

We burst out into the open air, gasping as the cool night wind hit our faces, but I couldn't shake the feeling that the darkness was still with us, lurking just beyond the edge of the moonlight, waiting for its chance to reclaim what it had lost.

Chapter 7: Unraveling the Pact

The cave's entrance loomed before us like a gaping mouth, dark and foreboding against the backdrop of an overcast sky. The air felt electric, tinged with the scent of damp earth and something ancient, almost metallic, lurking just beneath the surface. Gavin stood beside me, his shoulders tense, eyes scanning the mouth of the cave as if it were a portal to another realm. The faint sound of dripping water echoed from within, mingling with the whispers of the wind that seemed to carry a warning.

"What do you think we'll find in there?" I asked, trying to keep my voice steady. The anticipation bubbled inside me, a strange mix of dread and exhilaration. Gavin turned to me, his expression serious, but his lips quirked into a slight smirk.

"Probably a treasure map leading to the fountain of youth or maybe just a bunch of bats. Either way, it's going to be an adventure." His attempt at humor was just what I needed to lighten the heaviness hanging between us. I stepped forward, heart racing, and felt his hand grasp my arm gently, a reminder that I wasn't alone in this.

"Let's do this," I said, summoning all the courage I could muster. Together, we crossed the threshold into the cave, leaving the world behind, wrapped in an unsettling silence that swallowed our footsteps. The light from outside dwindled rapidly, replaced by the eerie glow of moss that clung to the damp stone walls. Each step deeper felt like we were peeling back the layers of a long-buried secret, the kind that could shatter lives if unleashed.

As we ventured further, the cave began to open up, revealing a vast chamber. The walls were adorned with carvings that danced in the dim light, depicting figures that resembled the townsfolk, their faces twisted in expressions of fear and despair. I traced one with my fingers, shivers racing down my spine as I read the familiar contours of Mayor Callahan's face among them, his features locked in a silent scream.

"Gavin, look at this," I whispered, beckoning him closer. "It's the mayor. He's... he's part of this."

His brow furrowed as he studied the wall, a realization dawning on him. "These aren't just random drawings. It's a story—our town's history, and not the kind they teach in school." His voice was barely above a whisper, reverberating through the stillness.

I could feel the weight of the truth pressing down on us. "What if the prosperity we've enjoyed has come at a cost? What if those people were sacrificed?"

The thought settled heavily in the air, a chilling reminder of the dark pact we had uncovered. The cave felt less like a discovery and more like a tomb, preserving the sins of generations past. I shuddered at the idea of our lives being built on the foundation of someone else's suffering.

Before I could voice my thoughts, Gavin's expression shifted, his protectiveness sparking to life. "We need to be careful. If this is true, there are those who will do anything to keep it buried. We can't let them know we're here."

I nodded, the adrenaline coursing through my veins. Just as I turned to explore further, my foot slipped on the slick stone, sending me tumbling. Gavin's quick reflexes caught me before I could hit the ground, pulling me back to safety, our bodies colliding with a softness that contrasted sharply with the harshness of our surroundings.

"See? I told you it was dangerous in here," he said, his voice laced with a teasing note, but the concern in his eyes was unmistakable. I found myself laughing, the sound echoing against the stone, breaking the tension just enough to remind me that we were still alive, still fighting.

"Maybe you should be the one looking out for me," I shot back, a playful spark igniting between us. But beneath the laughter, I could feel the gravity of our situation pressing closer, the threat of discovery looming like a dark cloud.

As we moved deeper into the cave, the atmosphere thickened with a sense of foreboding. The walls closed in, the air grew colder, and I could feel the weight of history pressing against us. At the far end of the chamber, a stone altar emerged, adorned with strange symbols and what appeared to be remnants of offerings—faded flowers and bones, long forgotten.

"Do you think this is where it happened?" I asked, unable to tear my eyes away from the altar.

Gavin stepped closer, studying it with a seriousness that sent a chill down my spine. "It could be. This place feels wrong, like it's soaked in fear and regret." His voice was low, reverent, as if acknowledging the lives that had been lost here.

Suddenly, the cave trembled, a low rumble that sent dust raining down from above. I stumbled back, instinctively reaching for Gavin. "What was that?" Panic surged in my chest, threatening to spill over.

"I don't know, but we should—" Before he could finish, the ground shook violently, and we both fell to the floor. The walls reverberated with a booming sound, echoing like a warning.

The light around us flickered, shadows dancing ominously as a crack formed in the stone, slithering like a serpent across the chamber.

"We need to get out of here!" I shouted, scrambling to my feet.

But Gavin, instead of retreating, took a step forward, eyes fixed on the altar. "Wait! There might be something here we need."

"Are you insane? This place is coming down!"

"Just give me a second." His tone was urgent yet calm, as if he could sense something I couldn't.

As I glanced back at the altar, an inexplicable pull tugged at me, a whisper in the back of my mind urging me to uncover the truth. The ground quaked again, more forcefully this time, and a sense of dread twisted in my stomach. I could feel the danger closing in around us, a noose tightening, and yet, there was a flicker of something else—hope, perhaps, that we could untangle this web of darkness if only we dared to delve deeper.

The cave loomed before us, a gaping maw nestled in the rugged hillside, its dark entrance inviting yet foreboding. The air was thick with a musty aroma, tinged with the whispers of time, as if the very stones held secrets waiting to be unearthed. Gavin stood beside me, his brow furrowed in contemplation, the flickering light of our lantern casting dancing shadows on the damp walls. I could see the trepidation etched on his face, an unspoken question hanging between us: What had we stumbled upon?

"Are you sure you want to go in there?" he asked, his voice low and steady, as if he were trying to anchor us both against the tide of uncertainty.

"Of course I do," I replied, trying to inject confidence into my tone despite the fluttering in my stomach. "If there's a chance to uncover the truth, we owe it to ourselves—and the town—to see this through." My words hung in the air, buoyed by adrenaline and a flicker of rebellion.

With a reluctant nod, Gavin stepped closer to the entrance, the lantern illuminating the jagged rocks and uneven ground. "Just promise me you'll stay close. I'm not losing you to whatever's lurking in the dark." There was a protective edge to his words, a reminder of the bond we'd forged in the face of our shared fears.

"Right back at you," I quipped, trying to lighten the mood, but the gravity of our situation was a tangible weight pressing down on us both. As we ventured inside, the sounds of the outside world faded, replaced by an eerie silence that enveloped us like a thick blanket.

The deeper we went, the more the cave revealed its hidden treasures. Ancient carvings adorned the walls, intricate symbols and figures etched into the stone, whispering tales of a time long past. I traced my fingers along the cool surface, feeling the history pulse beneath my touch. "These must be the records of the pact," I murmured, peering closer at the glyphs that seemed to swirl and twist in the dim light. "It's as if the walls themselves are warning us."

"Or inviting us," Gavin suggested, a hint of skepticism in his voice. "What if this is just a way to lure us into something we can't escape?"

His words sent a shiver down my spine, and I could sense the tension crackling between us, mingling with the dampness in the air. "I don't know, but we need to find out." My determination surged anew as we pressed on, deeper into the belly of the earth, where the air turned colder and the shadows grew thicker.

After what felt like an eternity of navigating the twisting passages, we stumbled into a cavernous chamber, the walls gleaming with an otherworldly sheen. In the center lay a stone altar, ancient and foreboding, adorned with relics that hinted at long-forgotten rituals. A chill crept up my spine as I approached, the weight of the past pressing heavily upon my shoulders.

"What do you think they did here?" Gavin asked, his voice barely above a whisper, as if the very act of speaking might awaken something slumbering in the dark.

"Something terrible, I'm sure," I replied, my gaze fixed on the altar, where a faded inscription caught my eye. It was written in a language I didn't recognize, yet the feeling it evoked was unmistakable—an echo of fear, a promise of doom.

As I translated the glyphs in my mind, piecing together their meanings, a sense of dread washed over me. The words spoke of sacrifices and offerings made in exchange for prosperity, a deal struck between Mayor Callahan and the malevolent forces that lurked beyond the veil of reality. "This is it," I breathed, the realization crashing over me like a wave. "This is the source of the town's misfortune."

Gavin's expression shifted, a blend of horror and disbelief. "You mean all those people who vanished? They weren't just lost—they were taken."

"Exactly." I felt my heart race, adrenaline coursing through my veins. "We have to warn the others. They deserve to know what their leaders have done."

But before we could move, a low rumble reverberated through the chamber, and the ground beneath us trembled. Gavin grabbed my arm, his grip firm as he pulled me closer. "What was that?" he asked, his eyes wide with fear.

"I don't know, but I think we've stirred something we shouldn't have," I said, scanning the darkness, the shadows seemingly shifting and swirling with a life of their own. The air grew thick, charged with an electric tension, and I felt a palpable sense of danger creeping into the cavern.

"Maybe we should head back," Gavin suggested, but the urgency in his voice spoke volumes. It wasn't just fear for our safety; it was the instinct to protect what we held dear.

Before I could respond, a figure emerged from the darkness, its form indistinct yet hauntingly familiar. My heart dropped as recognition washed over me, chilling my blood. "Mayor Callahan?" I gasped, the words escaping my lips before I could stop them.

He stepped forward, his eyes glinting with an unnatural light, a predator surveying its prey. "You should not have come here," he intoned, his voice a chilling melody that echoed off the stone walls. "You've uncovered things meant to remain buried."

Gavin's protective instincts surged, and he stepped in front of me, his body tense and ready for confrontation. "What did you do?" he demanded, his voice steady despite the trembling in his hands. "What did you sacrifice?"

A slow smile spread across the mayor's face, one that sent a wave of nausea through me. "Oh, my dear children, it's not what I sacrificed; it's what I gained. This town thrives because of the darkness we've embraced."

The weight of his words hung heavy in the air, a chilling reminder of the twisted bargain that had ensnared our community. I glanced at Gavin, our eyes locking in silent determination. Whatever fate awaited us, we would face it together, the bond forged in trust and defiance against the encroaching shadows.

In that moment, as the cavern trembled around us and the mayor's sinister laughter echoed in the dark, we understood the stakes were higher than we could have ever imagined. Our journey was no longer just about uncovering the truth; it was a battle for the very soul of our town, a fight against the darkness threatening to consume us all. And as we braced ourselves for the confrontation, I could feel the flames of resolve igniting within me, fierce and unyielding, a beacon in the encroaching gloom.

The air crackled with a tense energy as Mayor Callahan stepped into the faint glow of our lantern, his presence a jarring contrast to the musty darkness of the cave. Shadows danced across his face, accentuating the sharp angles of his jaw and the unsettling gleam in his eyes. "You really should have left well enough alone," he said, his voice smooth as silk, concealing a bitter edge that sent a shiver down my spine.

Gavin shifted beside me, a barrier of resolve between me and the mayor's insidious charm. "And what? Allow you to continue your twisted game? Not a chance." His tone was steady, but I could feel the underlying current of fear mingling with determination.

Callahan chuckled softly, the sound echoing eerily in the chamber. "Oh, how naïve. You think you can simply walk away from this? The pact is already woven into the very fabric of your town, entwining it with darkness. To expose it is to invite calamity—not just for me, but for everyone you love." He stepped closer, his gaze piercing, and I could see the shadows lurking behind him, waiting for the right moment to pounce.

"Then let me ask you this," I challenged, my voice gaining strength. "Is the prosperity of the town worth the lives you've sacrificed? The people you've doomed?"

His expression darkened, but he quickly masked it with a façade of indifference. "Ah, the idealism of youth. You presume to understand the complexities of power. Prosperity demands a price. This is merely the price I chose to pay."

As he spoke, I felt the weight of the truth crashing down around me. We were standing on the precipice of something monumental—a revelation that could alter the very course of our lives. I caught Gavin's eye, and in that moment, we shared an understanding that we couldn't back down now. The stakes were far too high.

"We're not afraid of you," Gavin declared, stepping forward, his body tense with resolve. "We're going to stop this, whatever it takes."

"Brave words," Callahan replied, a sly grin curling his lips. "But bravery has its consequences. You may think you can fight against the darkness, but it runs deep here. You are already entangled in its web, and to extricate yourselves will require more than mere will." His voice dripped with condescension, as if he were toying with us like a cat with a pair of mice.

Suddenly, the ground beneath us shook violently, sending a cloud of dust cascading from the ceiling. I stumbled, catching myself against the cool, damp wall, while Gavin steadied me with a firm hand. "What was that?" I gasped, my heart racing.

"It seems the cave doesn't take kindly to intruders," Callahan said, his tone almost gleeful, as if relishing our growing panic. "It's alive in a sense, fueled by the energy of the pact. Your presence here only strengthens it."

"We need to go," I urged Gavin, urgency lacing my words. "If this place is alive, it might be dangerous to stay."

He nodded, his jaw set in determination. "We can't leave without uncovering more. We need proof of this pact." As he spoke, the cave rumbled again, more ferociously this time, and I felt the walls tremble as if they were groaning under the strain.

Callahan's expression shifted, the amusement fading into something darker. "You're right. You need proof. But I'm afraid you won't find what you're looking for. You'll only find what I allow you to see."

With a flick of his wrist, a series of torches ignited along the walls, revealing hidden passages that branched off the main chamber like serpents winding through the earth. I squinted at the flickering flames, my breath catching at the sight of what lay beyond. Shadows flitted in the corners of my vision, and I couldn't shake the feeling that something watched us, biding its time.

"Come," Callahan beckoned, his voice almost melodic in its allure. "Let me show you the heart of this town's prosperity. You may just change your mind about what you think you know."

Gavin stepped forward, a reluctant curiosity mingling with caution. "You really think we'd trust you? After everything?"

"Trust is a fragile thing, isn't it?" Callahan mused, a glint of amusement in his eye. "But you're already here, aren't you? It would be a shame to waste this opportunity."

With a hesitant glance toward Gavin, I felt the gravity of the decision before us. We were standing at the intersection of truth and deception, our lives hanging in the balance. Yet the allure of unveiling the truth—the heart of the pact—was far too enticing to resist.

As we followed Callahan into the depths of the cave, the atmosphere shifted, becoming dense with anticipation. The walls pulsed with an eerie energy, and I could feel the air thicken as if the cave itself were holding its breath, waiting for us to unravel its mysteries.

We emerged into a vast cavern, and the sight stole my breath. In the center stood a colossal stone structure, its surface etched with more of the ancient glyphs we had seen earlier. The energy here was palpable, a dark force radiating from the stone, drawing me closer against my better judgment.

"Behold," Callahan declared, his arms spread wide, as if presenting a grand prize. "The altar of our town's salvation. The place where the pact was forged, and where souls are collected in exchange for prosperity."

My heart raced as I stepped forward, entranced by the intricate designs that seemed to shift and writhe beneath my gaze. I felt a compulsion to touch it, to understand the power it held, but Gavin's hand tightened around my wrist, pulling me back.

"Don't," he whispered, his voice thick with urgency. "We don't know what that thing can do."

Ignoring the warning, I took a step closer, my curiosity overpowering my caution. "What happens to those souls?" I demanded, forcing myself to look at Callahan, who watched me with an unsettling satisfaction.

He leaned closer, a smirk playing on his lips. "Ah, that is the true beauty of the pact. They become part of the town's very essence, ensuring its survival while sacrificing their freedom."

A sudden thought struck me, sharp and cruel. "And you? You're just fine with this? With the suffering of your own people?"

Callahan's laughter echoed off the cavern walls, a chilling sound that sent a ripple of dread through me. "I have made my peace with my choices. They are merely pawns in a grander game. This town thrives, and I thrive with it."

The ground shook once more, this time with a violent ferocity that sent us sprawling. I caught a glimpse of the cavern ceiling beginning to crumble, and panic surged within me. "We have to get out of here!" I shouted, scrambling to my feet.

Gavin grasped my hand, pulling me back as the earth trembled beneath our feet. "Follow me! We can't stay here!"

But as we turned to flee, the dark shadows that had lurked at the edges of the cavern surged forward, taking shape and form, coalescing into a mass of swirling darkness. My breath caught in my throat as I realized what we were facing—an embodiment of the very pact Callahan had forged, a swirling vortex of souls bound by his greed.

"Welcome to your demise," Callahan sneered, his eyes glinting with malice as the shadows rushed toward us, hungry and relentless.

In that moment, I understood the true cost of uncovering the truth. The darkness was alive, and it was coming for us. Desperation clawed at my chest as I and Gavin exchanged a glance, a silent vow passing between us. We would fight, we would resist, even as the shadows closed in, ready to claim us in the wake of the mayor's betrayal.

And just as I felt the pull of the darkness enveloping us, the cave erupted into chaos, the very ground splitting beneath our feet, sending us tumbling into the abyss, where nothing awaited but uncertainty.

Chapter 8: Tides of Emotion

The moon hung low over the jagged cliffs, casting a silver glow that danced upon the waves, each one a whisper of secrets long buried beneath the depths. I stood at the entrance of the cave, the salty breeze tousling my hair, a reminder of how small I was against the vastness of the ocean and the shadows that lurked within. It was here, amid the stones slick with sea spray and the echoing whispers of history, that Gavin and I discovered more than the town's mysteries; we unearthed the raw, unvarnished truth of ourselves.

Every night felt like a collision of worlds. The cave, with its intricate rock formations and damp, earthy scent, transformed into our sanctuary. It was a place where we shed our facades and bared our souls. I could feel the electricity crackling in the air, a vibrant tension that thrummed between us as I caught his eye. Gavin had a way of looking at me, piercing yet tender, that made the very marrow in my bones hum with anticipation. He wore his past like a weathered cloak, and every revelation he shared added another layer to the intricate tapestry of his being. The darkness clung to him, but so did the light, and I found myself irresistibly drawn to both.

"Do you think the ocean remembers?" he asked one evening, his voice a low rumble that sent shivers down my spine. We were seated on a rock, our legs dangling over the edge, the water frothing below like a restless beast. I turned to him, intrigued by the weight of his question.

"Remember what?" I prodded, pretending I didn't know. I had learned early on that sometimes it was better to let the other person draw out the truth, to unravel their thoughts like a thread from an old sweater.

"The lives lost, the promises made," he mused, his gaze fixed on the horizon where the water met the sky in a seamless blend of blue and gray. "Or do we just keep repeating the same mistakes?"

"Maybe it's a little of both," I replied, letting my words hang in the air between us. "Maybe it's like the tide—some things wash away, and some things just keep coming back."

He chuckled, a rich sound that wrapped around me like a warm blanket. "You think we'll keep coming back, then? Like barnacles on a boat?"

"Depends," I teased, leaning closer, the playful banter lightening the weight of the evening. "Are we the barnacles or the boat?"

Gavin shot me a sidelong glance, his lips quirking into a smile. "I'd like to think we're the boat—steadier than we appear."

"Steady, huh? I'll keep that in mind," I laughed, feeling the flutter of something sweet and dangerous swirl within me. It was a precarious dance we were engaging in, tiptoeing around the truth of our feelings while exploring the depths of our fears. I saw the shadows flickering behind his eyes, remnants of a life that had shaped him, but I also saw the fierce determination to keep those shadows at bay.

As we continued to explore the cave, the walls seemed to breathe with us, holding our secrets close. I discovered a hidden chamber, its entrance obscured by vines and thick foliage. The air inside was cool and fragrant, infused with the scent of damp earth and wildflowers. We stepped inside, our laughter echoing off the walls, and for a moment, the outside world faded away. The chaos of the town, the whispered warnings of danger, all dissipated, leaving just the two of us in our fragile haven.

"Why do you come here?" I asked, the curiosity bubbling up inside me. I could feel the atmosphere shift, the air thickening with unspoken truths. "What's your connection to this place?"

Gavin's expression darkened, a flicker of vulnerability flashing across his features. "It's where I learned to fight," he said softly, his voice barely above a whisper. "When the world seemed too heavy, I found solace here. I came to understand that sometimes you have to face your fears head-on."

"And what do you fear?" I pressed, my heart racing. The honesty in his eyes, the rawness of his admission, drew me closer, tethering us together in a way I couldn't quite comprehend.

He sighed, a deep, weary sound that resonated through the chamber. "Letting people in," he confessed. "And losing them. It's easier to stay distant, to keep my heart locked away."

"But you're not distant with me," I said, my voice firm. "You've let me in. We're not just two people wandering through a cave; we're navigating the wreckage of our pasts."

His eyes met mine, and I felt the air grow heavier with unspoken words. "You're different," he said, the intensity of his gaze wrapping around me like a protective barrier. "You make me want to fight for something worth keeping."

My heart thudded in response, a cacophony of hope and fear clashing within me. I had grown fond of the way his vulnerability juxtaposed with his strength, how it painted him as both a warrior and a lost soul seeking refuge. "Then let's fight together," I suggested, a flicker of determination igniting within me. "We can face whatever lies ahead, side by side."

For a moment, the world fell away. The air was electric, charged with the possibilities that lay before us. But even as I spoke those words, a shadow flickered at the edge of my mind—a reminder that our journey was fraught with peril, that the darkness we sought to escape was ever-present, waiting for a moment of weakness to slip in.

The cave around us felt alive, pulsating with our shared heartbeat, a reflection of the bond we were forging amid uncertainty. Each brush of our fingers, each stolen glance was a silent vow, a promise to venture into the chaos together. But the question lingered, like the lingering scent of salt and sea: could love truly blossom amid the storms of our pasts, or would it be swept away like grains of sand beneath the crashing tide?

The tide was shifting, ebbing and flowing in a rhythm as ancient as the rocks themselves, and I found myself caught in the undertow of Gavin's presence. We emerged from the cave into the twilight, the world transformed into a canvas of deep blues and purples. The horizon blazed with the last whispers of sunlight, casting a warm glow on Gavin's face, illuminating the sharp angles and soft curves that made up his striking features. I wanted to reach out, to trace the path of light across his cheek, but the moment felt too sacred, too fragile.

"Do you ever wonder if this is all some kind of cosmic joke?" he asked suddenly, his voice breaking the comfortable silence that enveloped us. "Like, we're just the punchline to a really bad story?"

"Only when I'm stuck in traffic," I replied with a playful smirk, but my heart was racing. There was something poignant in his words, a deep undercurrent of disillusionment that tugged at my heart. "But really, why do you think that?"

He shrugged, a gesture so nonchalant that it belied the intensity simmering beneath the surface. "It's just... this place, these secrets. It feels like we're all part of some elaborate riddle. The town, the cave, even us."

"What if the answer to that riddle is that we're supposed to find our own way?" I challenged, feeling a surge of boldness. "Maybe the joke is on those who refuse to see the magic in the chaos."

"Now you're just being poetic," he said, rolling his eyes playfully, but I caught a hint of appreciation in his gaze.

"Poetry is just another form of truth," I countered, stepping closer, my heart racing with each inch. "You've got to admit, it's more exciting than moping around."

Gavin chuckled, the sound rich and warm, yet it carried a weight that lingered in the air. "You have a way of making the absurd seem...

almost sensible," he mused, tilting his head slightly, his dark hair falling into his eyes. "You've got that knack for finding the light, even in the murkiest of waters."

"Maybe I'm just a good swimmer," I shot back, but as I said the words, a pulse of tension crackled between us, heavier than the humid night air. There was a moment of stillness, where time suspended itself, and I could feel the palpable attraction swirling around us like the very tides we had been discussing.

"I think you swim better than you give yourself credit for," he murmured, his voice dropping to that husky register that made my heart flutter. The world around us faded, leaving just the two of us suspended in a delicate balance of unspoken words and potential.

But just as I felt myself leaning in, willing to test the boundaries of that tension, the sharp ring of a phone shattered the moment, echoing ominously in the quiet. Gavin cursed softly under his breath, pulling his phone from his pocket. The light from the screen illuminated his face, casting shadows that danced across his features. I watched his expression shift from curiosity to something darker, a flicker of apprehension flashing in his eyes.

"Sorry, I need to take this," he said, turning slightly away, his tone clipped. The distance between us felt vast in that moment, and I couldn't shake the sensation of an impending storm brewing just beyond the horizon.

"Sure, take your time," I replied, trying to mask the disappointment threading through my voice. I wandered a few steps away, pretending to admire the view, while my mind raced. I couldn't help but feel a nagging sense of dread, like the ominous clouds gathering in the distance, threatening to unleash their fury.

Gavin's voice rose and fell, a mix of urgency and frustration that made me strain to catch the words. "No, I told you I'm done. I'm not getting involved in this anymore. You need to figure it out yourself."

A chill crept into the warm evening air, prickling my skin. There was something in his tone that spoke of a world I had yet to see, a web of entanglements I was not prepared to navigate. My heart sank at the thought of him being pulled back into whatever darkness haunted him, and I could feel the weight of my own insecurities pressing down on me.

When he hung up, I turned to face him, trying to mask my concern with a casual demeanor. "Everything okay?"

He ran a hand through his hair, a gesture of frustration that made my heart ache. "It's just... old business. Some people don't know when to let go," he replied, his voice heavy with unsaid words. "I thought I was clear, but it seems that's not the case."

I stepped closer, my resolve solidifying. "You don't have to face it alone, you know. I'm here."

"Yeah, but what if you get dragged into my mess?" he countered, a hint of defensiveness creeping into his voice. "I don't want that for you."

I could feel the pulse of emotion rising between us again, battling against the chaos outside our bubble. "Too late for that," I said lightly, though my heart was pounding. "You already have me tangled in your mess. And honestly? I'd rather face a mess with you than deal with it alone."

His gaze held mine, and for a moment, the night felt infinite, the world beyond us falling away. There was a spark of understanding, a silent agreement that perhaps we were both a little lost, both fighting our own battles while seeking refuge in each other. But then, as if summoned by the shadows lurking at the edges, the tension broke.

The distant sound of a siren wailed through the night, sharp and jarring. Gavin stiffened, the moment shattering like glass, reality crashing back in. "I should probably—"

"Go," I said, the word tumbling from my lips before I could stop it. "I mean, if you have to."

"No, I want to stay," he replied quickly, his eyes darting to mine, filled with urgency and something I dared to hope was desire. "But I can't just ignore this. Not now."

The ache of disappointment settled in my chest, but I nodded, a part of me understanding that some battles were his to fight alone. "Just... be careful, okay?" I managed, trying to sound brave even as the world around me dimmed.

He reached out, his fingers brushing against my arm, a fleeting connection that sent warmth flooding through me. "I promise I'll be careful," he said softly, his eyes searching mine, as if he were trying to memorize every detail.

And then, with one last lingering look, he turned and walked away, disappearing into the shadows that threatened to swallow him whole. I stood there, the night heavy with unfulfilled promises and untold stories, the echo of his footsteps fading against the distant roar of the waves. The cave behind me felt both inviting and haunting, a reminder of what we had shared and what lay ahead. The tides of our emotions were shifting again, leaving me stranded in a tumultuous sea, waiting for the next wave to crash upon the shore.

The night wrapped around me like a cloak, heavy with unspoken words and the bittersweet tang of anticipation. Gavin's absence gnawed at me, a palpable void that echoed through the stillness of the air. I kicked at the pebbles strewn along the shore, watching as they skittered away, disrupted by my restlessness. Each splash against the rocks felt like a reminder of the precariousness of the moment we had shared—an exhilarating kiss held back by the weight of his unspoken demons.

With a sigh, I turned back toward the cave, its entrance gaping like a mouth ready to swallow me whole. Inside, the shadows danced on the walls, teasing at memories of laughter and whispered promises. I felt as though I was an intruder in a sacred space, and yet I longed for the familiarity that came with being near Gavin, even in his absence. The damp air clung to my skin, mingling with the scent of salt and earth, wrapping me in a blanket of memories that pulled at my heart.

"What is it about this place that makes everything feel so... charged?" I murmured to myself, the echoes of my words bouncing back as if the cave were as curious as I was. My voice felt small against the vastness of the stone walls, but I could almost hear Gavin's reply, a teasing lilt in his tone.

"Maybe it's just you," I imagined him saying, and a smile tugged at the corners of my mouth despite the gravity of the situation. The thought of him made my heart race, a flicker of warmth in the chilled air.

Just then, a rustle broke the silence. My heart stuttered as I turned sharply, instinctively pulling my phone from my pocket, the screen illuminating my surroundings in a soft glow. Shadows darted between the rocks, and for a moment, my imagination ran wild with thoughts of specters and phantoms, remnants of the town's troubled past.

"Is anyone there?" I called out, my voice firm despite the flutter of nerves.

Nothing answered but the gentle lapping of the waves outside. I shook my head, dismissing my anxiety as nothing more than a trick of the dark. This was just a cave—nothing sinister about it. But the silence felt thick, as if it were holding its breath, waiting for something to happen.

As I moved deeper into the cave, the sound of water dripping echoed like a heartbeat, creating a rhythm that was oddly soothing. I ventured further, letting the flickering light from my phone guide me. The shadows shifted with each step, and I felt the weight of the cave pressing in around me, as if it had a pulse of its own.

And then, there it was—a soft glimmer reflecting off the damp walls, drawing me closer. Curiosity piqued, I approached cautiously, my heart racing with the thrill of discovery. The light danced before me, revealing a pool of water that shimmered with an ethereal glow. It was breathtaking, the way the bioluminescence pulsed in gentle waves, inviting yet mysterious.

"Gavin would love this," I whispered, kneeling beside the water, my fingers grazing the surface. It felt cool against my skin, a tantalizing contrast to the heat that lingered in my cheeks from our earlier encounter. My thoughts drifted back to him, to the laughter we shared, the glances that lingered a moment too long. The cave, which had once felt ominous, now cradled the warmth of our connection.

The moment was fleeting, though. The soft glow turned darker as clouds gathered outside, swallowing the moonlight. An eerie stillness settled in, the air heavy with something unnameable. I pulled back, an inexplicable sense of urgency overtaking me. Just as I stood to leave, a sharp sound sliced through the silence—a low rumble that vibrated beneath my feet.

"Okay, now that's new," I muttered, glancing around, the cave suddenly feeling less like a sanctuary and more like a trap. The rumbling grew louder, reverberating through the stones, shaking loose small pebbles that tumbled into the pool with soft plinks. Panic surged in my chest, and I instinctively took a step back, heart racing as the ground beneath me seemed to shift.

"Come on, not now," I breathed, darting for the exit, adrenaline propelling me forward. Just as I reached the mouth of the cave, the earth convulsed violently, sending me sprawling onto the damp ground. I pushed myself up, my palms slick with moisture and fear.

A voice rang out from behind me, familiar and strained. "What the hell are you doing in here?"

I turned to see Gavin emerging from the shadows, his expression a mix of concern and disbelief. "I was just—"

"Now is not the time to explore!" he interrupted, grabbing my arm, urgency radiating from him. The ground shook again, and I felt a wave of nausea roll through me as the cave groaned, the very walls seeming to tremble with the impending danger.

"I thought I heard something!" I protested, my heart racing, a wild mix of fear and exhilaration coursing through me. "What's happening?"

"I don't know," he said, eyes wide, scanning the cave as if it would divulge its secrets. "But it can't be good."

The rumble intensified, and suddenly, a cascade of rocks began to loosen from the ceiling, dust and debris swirling around us like a tempest. I lunged for him, and he pulled me close, shielding me as a larger rock fell perilously close, splintering against the ground with a deafening crack.

"Run!" he shouted, his voice cutting through the chaos, and we bolted from the cave, the dark maw behind us becoming a scene of pandemonium. The entrance seemed to narrow as we raced toward the mouth of the cave, the world outside bathed in eerie twilight.

As we burst into the open air, the ground continued to shake, and I stumbled, Gavin's grip tightening around my waist, steadying me. We barely made it out when a thunderous roar erupted from behind us, and I turned just in time to see the cave collapse in on itself, rocks and dust billowing into the sky like a violent storm.

"What the hell was that?" I gasped, breathless, my heart pounding as I clung to him, the reality of our narrow escape sinking in.

"I don't know," he said, still staring at the wreckage with a mixture of awe and dread. "But something is definitely not right."

Before I could respond, a low, guttural growl echoed from the depths of the cave, sending chills racing down my spine. The sound reverberated through the air, primal and hungry. My eyes met Gavin's, the shock of realization dawning between us. Whatever was hidden within those stones had awakened, and it wasn't done with us yet.

"Let's get out of here," I urged, but even as the words left my mouth, I couldn't shake the feeling that we had unleashed something far more dangerous than we had ever imagined. The shadows were stirring, and we were about to find out just how deep the darkness ran.

Chapter 9: The Gathering Storm

The salty tang of the sea mingled with the sweet, heavy scent of funnel cakes drifting through the bustling streets, weaving a tapestry of nostalgia that made my heart flutter with the kind of excitement only an annual festival could muster. Lanterns strung between the old oak trees swayed gently in the warm breeze, casting flickering shadows that danced playfully on the cobblestones. Children, their faces painted like the colorful fish that swam in the nearby harbor, darted between stalls with shrieks of joy, their laughter a bright counterpoint to the unease that settled around the adults like a thick fog.

Yet beneath this festive veneer, something darker stirred. I glanced at Gavin, who stood beside me, his brow furrowed as he surveyed the crowd. The way his jaw tightened revealed a tension that belied the cheerful atmosphere. We had spent the past few weeks piecing together the fragments of an ancient mystery that wrapped around our town like the ropes of a fishing net, and the weight of what we'd discovered pressed heavily on my chest. Mayor Callahan, once the charming face of our quaint little community, had transformed into a figure shrouded in shadows, his smile now a calculated mask.

"Do you think he'll show?" I asked Gavin, my voice barely above a whisper, almost drowned out by the jubilant music of the local band playing nearby. The sounds of accordions and fiddles filled the air, lively yet strangely discordant against the backdrop of our looming confrontation.

"He will. He always does," Gavin replied, his eyes darting to the makeshift stage where the mayor was expected to give his opening speech. "This is his moment to shine, to remind everyone of how lucky they are to have him."

I bit my lip, suppressing a smirk at the irony of his words. Gavin's sarcasm often masked his genuine concern. "Lucky, or oblivious?" I countered, scanning the sea of faces around us, noting the flickers of worry hidden behind forced smiles. "People don't just forget their history overnight. They're scared, Gavin. They know something's off."

He nodded, his gaze returning to me. "And it's our job to find out what that something is." The resolve in his voice anchored me, a steady reminder that we were in this together, no matter how tangled the web became.

The sun dipped lower, painting the sky in hues of orange and lavender, a breathtaking contrast to the brewing storm of secrets that threatened to unravel. The festival was a delicate balance of joy and tension, as if everyone was trying to hold their breath and pretend everything was fine while a storm gathered on the horizon.

Suddenly, the thrumming beat of drums crescendoed, drawing our attention. The mayor emerged, his figure silhouetted against the twilight sky. He wore a crisp white shirt, sleeves rolled up as if he was about to dig into the festival's activities, but there was an intensity in his eyes that belied his jovial demeanor. The crowd clapped politely, their cheers polite but subdued, like a wave washing over a beach only to retreat, leaving behind uneasy silence.

"Thank you, thank you!" Mayor Callahan boomed into the microphone, his voice rich and theatrical. "Welcome, my dear friends, to the annual Fisherman's Festival! Tonight, we celebrate our town's resilient spirit, our glorious history, and—" He paused, his smile faltering slightly, "—our bright future." The undertone of his words sent a ripple of apprehension through the crowd, and I felt it too, like a pebble dropped into still water, sending out concentric circles of unease.

I nudged Gavin, my heart racing. "This is it. We need to talk to him after this."

Gavin nodded, determination set in his features. “Let’s find out what he’s hiding.”

As the mayor continued his speech, extolling the virtues of our community and its fishing heritage, I felt the growing tension in the crowd. Their smiles were plastered, eyes darting towards each other, whispering behind cupped hands. It was a language I understood well—fear cloaked in facade.

“Something isn’t right,” I murmured, not entirely aware I’d spoken aloud. Gavin turned to me, his expression a mix of concern and interest.

“Yeah, no kidding. But what can we do? We can’t just waltz up there and demand answers,” he said, glancing nervously at the crowd.

“Maybe not waltz, but we can certainly walk,” I replied, a mischievous spark igniting within me. “Come on, let’s find out where he goes after this.”

As the mayor wrapped up his speech with a flourish, the crowd erupted into applause, but I barely heard it. My focus sharpened on the figure at the front. Gavin and I maneuvered through the throng, the chatter of the festival fading into a distant hum.

We slipped behind a row of stalls, my heart pounding in rhythm with the drums still echoing from the stage. The scent of fried food hung heavily in the air, but it was the acrid smell of something else that caught my attention—a sharp, metallic scent that turned my stomach.

“Julia, wait.” Gavin’s voice, low and tense, halted me in my tracks. His expression was grim as he gestured towards the alleyway that ran behind the stalls. “Look.”

I followed his gaze and froze. The flickering shadows of the festival seemed to retreat as a figure emerged from the darkness—slender, cloaked, and undeniably ominous. It wasn’t the mayor, but someone who moved with an unsettling grace, their presence electric in a way that sent shivers down my spine.

"What do you think he's doing?" I whispered, my breath hitching in my throat.

Gavin stepped closer, eyes narrowed, taking in the scene. "I don't know, but it's about to get interesting."

As the figure stepped fully into the light, the festival's joyous sounds faded into a haunting silence, like a choir turning to a single, dissonant note. The air crackled with anticipation, a prelude to the revelations that were about to unfold.

The figure that emerged from the shadows seemed to shimmer under the festival lights, an enigma wrapped in layers of darkness and intrigue. My heart raced as I struggled to decipher the silhouette before us, the flickering lanterns casting a dance of light and shadow across a face that remained tantalizingly hidden. Gavin and I exchanged glances, a silent understanding passing between us. Whatever was about to unfold, it was pivotal.

"Who are you?" I called out, my voice steadier than I felt, echoing off the brick walls of the narrow alley. The figure turned, and for a heartbeat, I thought I saw a flash of recognition in their eyes—a moment of connection that sent a jolt of energy through me.

They stepped closer, revealing a man dressed in a long, dark coat that flared slightly as he moved. His hair fell in waves around his shoulders, tousled by the wind, and his eyes sparkled like the depths of the ocean, deep and unfathomable. "Just a humble observer," he replied, his voice low and smooth, tinged with an accent I couldn't quite place. "But I believe you're not here to celebrate the festival, are you?"

"No, we're not," Gavin interjected, stepping slightly in front of me, protective yet curious. "We're looking for answers. About the mayor, about... everything."

The stranger's lips curled into a half-smile, one that spoke of secrets. "Answers, you say? In a town like this, you should know that answers come at a cost." His gaze flicked over the bustling festival beyond the alley, and for a moment, I caught a glimpse of something in his expression—was it longing? Regret?

"Right now, we're just looking to make sense of the chaos," I replied, emboldened by a sudden rush of frustration. "This festival is supposed to be a celebration, but all I see is fear and facade. What do you know about the pact?"

He tilted his head, a curious glimmer igniting in his eyes. "The pact? Ah, a tale as old as the tides. You're digging deeper than most dare to tread. But beware, dear girl—some truths are buried for a reason."

Gavin shifted closer, his brow furrowing. "What do you mean? What's the pact about?"

With an almost theatrical flair, the stranger stepped back, casting a glance toward the bright lights illuminating the festival. "This town has thrived on the balance of light and dark, prosperity and sacrifice. But when one side tips the scales, the storm begins."

"Storm?" I echoed, the word hanging in the air like a distant thunderclap. The metaphorical weight of it hung heavy between us.

"Indeed. The mayor, he plays both sides—a puppet master, perhaps, or merely a pawn. It's difficult to say." He paused, his eyes narrowing. "But you, you have the spirit to unravel it. You just need to be prepared for what you find."

Before I could respond, a loud cheer erupted from the festival, drawing our attention back to the stage. Mayor Callahan stood, flanked by the town council, an air of false joviality radiating from him as he waved to the crowd. The energy shifted, a new tension creeping in, more palpable than before.

"Let's not keep him waiting," the stranger said, and with a flick of his wrist, he gestured toward the alley's exit. "You might want to speak to him now before the storm breaks fully."

Gavin and I exchanged wary glances, the gravity of our situation weighing heavily upon us. "What's your name?" I asked, curious about this mysterious man who seemed to know so much yet revealed so little.

"Names can be burdensome. Call me Finn," he replied, a hint of amusement lighting his expression. "Now, go. The tide is turning, and you don't want to be caught in the undertow."

With that, he vanished back into the shadows, leaving us in the soft glow of the festival lights, the noise of celebration flooding back into my ears like a wave crashing onto the shore. My heart thudded in my chest as we approached the stage, a sense of urgency propelling us forward.

"Are you ready for this?" Gavin asked, his voice barely audible over the swell of the crowd.

"I'm not sure if we have a choice," I replied, determination settling in my bones. "We need to confront him now, while he's still under the spotlight."

The closer we got to the stage, the more the atmosphere crackled with an unsettling energy. The townspeople's faces, once bright with excitement, now wore a mask of unease, eyes flickering back to the shadows that surrounded us. It was as if they sensed the storm brewing, an invisible current threading through their laughter.

We finally reached the edge of the stage, a wooden platform adorned with ropes of colorful bunting. The mayor was mid-sentence, his voice smooth as honey, yet there was an undercurrent of something darker that seeped through. "And as we celebrate our past, let us not forget the sacrifices made for our future!"

The crowd applauded, but the clapping felt hollow, echoing off the walls of uncertainty. I took a deep breath and stepped forward, catching the mayor's eye. His smile faltered for just a moment, a flash of recognition mingled with something else—defensiveness? Guilt?

"Mayor Callahan," I called out, my voice rising above the murmurs of the crowd. "Can we speak with you? It's urgent."

A flicker of annoyance crossed his face before he replied, "Later, my dear. Can't you see the people need their celebration?"

"We need answers, not more distractions!" Gavin interjected, stepping up beside me, his tone unwavering.

The crowd shifted, a ripple of tension coursing through them. The mayor's smile tightened, the façade cracking ever so slightly. "I assure you, everything is under control. There's no need for alarm."

But I could see the fear lurking in the corners of his eyes, the way he avoided my gaze. "You're lying," I pressed, emboldened by the truth we had uncovered. "People are afraid. You know something you're not telling us. We deserve to know."

The laughter that had filled the air moments before evaporated, replaced by an uncomfortable silence, the crowd hanging on our every word. The mayor straightened, his posture becoming rigid, and I felt the atmosphere shift again, charged with a weighty tension that could snap at any moment.

"I can assure you that our history is complicated," he said finally, his voice low and deliberate. "But I will not let you tarnish our festival with unfounded fears. There are legends better left in the past."

His words hung in the air like a challenge, and the crowd's murmur grew louder, uncertain glances exchanged among the townsfolk. I sensed the shift in the mood, and with it, the tension thickened, coiling tighter around us, a spring ready to snap.

"We can't afford to ignore what's happening, Mayor," I insisted, feeling the urge to push forward despite the palpable fear in the crowd. "We can't afford to bury our heads in the sand. Not anymore."

The mayor's gaze hardened, a flash of something dangerous flickering behind his charming façade. "Sometimes, ignorance is bliss, Julia. Sometimes, it's safer."

And in that moment, I realized—this was no longer just about the pact or the symbols. This was about control, fear, and the lengths to which some would go to maintain the facade of safety. And if we were going to unveil the truth, we would have to be prepared for the storm that would surely follow.

The mayor's voice, once a confident rallying cry, now carried an edge of desperation, echoing off the festival tents like a warning bell. "You don't understand the risks, Julia," he said, his tone firm yet tinged with an undercurrent of urgency. The crowd shifted uneasily, caught between the spectacle of the festival and the unease that lingered in the air like a storm cloud threatening to burst.

"Then help us understand," I pressed, my heart racing. "Help us understand why you're keeping secrets from your own people."

"Secrets are necessary," he snapped, his eyes narrowing. "What you're stirring up isn't just history; it's a can of worms best left unopened. You think you want the truth, but you don't. Trust me, the past is a treacherous tide."

"Not knowing is worse," Gavin shot back, his voice steady and unwavering. "Your duty is to protect the town, not to hide behind a curtain of silence. You're creating more fear by not telling us the truth."

The crowd was restless now, whispers coursing through them like a ripple of wind on the water. I could sense the shift in their loyalty; no longer were they just passive observers to the mayor's theatrics. They were curious, agitated, waiting for a crack in the facade that would let the truth spill out.

"You're in over your head," the mayor warned, his demeanor darkening, his façade faltering as if a storm was indeed brewing beneath the surface. "There are forces at play that you can't even begin to comprehend."

"Like the symbols?" I pushed, emboldened by the crowd's growing unease. "Like the pact with whoever—or whatever—is out there?"

At that, he visibly stiffened, the flash of panic in his eyes revealing far more than his words could hide. "You must stop this," he insisted, his voice dropping to a low hiss. "If you don't, it won't just be your lives at stake. It's the entire town that will pay the price."

"Is that a threat?" Gavin asked, his tone sharp and accusatory, drawing a collective intake of breath from those around us.

"Consider it a warning," the mayor replied, his composure returning slightly as he straightened, puffing up as if to regain his authoritative stance. But the flicker of vulnerability remained in his eyes, a crack in the armor that told a story of fear and control.

Just then, a loud crash erupted from the direction of the harbor, followed by a collective gasp from the crowd. Heads turned in unison, and I felt a surge of anxiety course through me. What now?

"Stay here!" the mayor barked, his expression shifting to one of alarm as he headed toward the source of the noise. But it was too late; the air crackled with a new tension, drawing our attention away from the mayor and toward the darkening horizon.

"We can't just stand here!" Gavin shouted, tugging at my arm. "We need to see what's happening!"

As we pushed through the crowd, the atmosphere shifted again. The vibrant festival lights seemed to dim, the joyous music fading to a distant echo, swallowed by the murmur of apprehension. We arrived at the edge of the harbor just in time to witness a spectacle that would be etched in my memory forever.

A fishing boat, once sturdy and proud, lay on its side, debris scattered across the dock. The vessel had been torn apart, its timbers splintered like kindling. Smoke billowed up from below deck, a thick, ominous cloud that mingled with the salty air.

"What the hell happened?" Gavin breathed, horror etched across his face.

“I don’t know,” I said, squinting against the fading light, the chaos around us intensifying. Townsfolk rushed toward the boat, shouting for help, voices rising in a cacophony of fear and confusion.

Then, I spotted something else—a shadow moving just beneath the water’s surface, dark and serpentine, gliding with an unsettling grace. My heart raced as I pointed, my voice rising above the chaos. “Look!”

Gavin’s gaze followed mine, and for a moment, we stood frozen, mesmerized by the lurking shape beneath the waves. “What in the world is that?”

Before we could process what we were seeing, the shadow broke the surface, revealing a creature unlike anything I had ever encountered. Its scales shimmered in the dim light, a blend of emerald and deep blue, reflecting the chaos around us. The creature’s eyes glowed with an eerie luminescence, a haunting intelligence that sent chills skittering down my spine.

Then, as if sensing our presence, it turned toward us, its gaze locking onto mine. I felt an inexplicable connection, a mix of terror and intrigue, as if the creature was weighing my very soul.

“Get back!” a voice shouted, breaking the spell. It was Mayor Callahan, now sprinting toward us, his face pale and eyes wide. “Get everyone away from the water!”

But it was too late. The creature surged forward, breaking the surface with a rush of water that sent waves crashing over the dock. Screams erupted from the crowd, and people stumbled back, tripping over one another in their haste to escape.

I grabbed Gavin’s arm, adrenaline flooding my veins. “We have to warn everyone!”

The mayor reached us, breathless and frantic. “What have you done? You’ve awakened something you shouldn’t have!”

"What are you talking about?" I yelled back, my voice barely audible over the chaos. "This isn't our fault! We're not the ones keeping secrets!"

Before he could respond, the creature lunged again, its powerful tail splashing water everywhere. It let out a sound—a mix between a roar and a wail—that reverberated through the air, shaking the ground beneath our feet. Panic spread like wildfire, people fleeing in all directions, leaving chaos in their wake.

"Julia!" Gavin shouted, pulling me back as the dock shuddered underfoot. "We need to get out of here!"

But I couldn't move. The creature's eyes were locked on mine, and the world around us began to fade, the panic blurring into the background. "We need to help," I whispered, the words escaping before I could stop them.

"Help? It's a—" Gavin began, but I could barely hear him over the pounding of my heart.

With one final surge, the creature breached the surface, its massive form emerging fully from the water, revealing a sleek, serpentine body that glittered like the night sky. The air felt charged, alive with energy as if the very fabric of reality was about to unravel.

"Get back!" the mayor yelled again, but my gaze was fixed on the creature, a mixture of awe and fear gripping me.

In that moment, a realization hit me with the force of a tidal wave. The stories, the symbols, the pact—everything was woven together, and we had only just begun to scratch the surface. As the creature let out another haunting cry, echoing across the harbor, I knew one thing: the storm wasn't just coming; it was already here, and it was determined to reclaim what had been forgotten.

And in the middle of that chaos, I was caught between the depths of the sea and the secrets of the town, my fate intertwined with the shadows that danced at the water's edge.

Chapter 10: The Eye of the Storm

The night air hung thick with a salty breeze, mingling with the scent of roasted corn and caramelized sugar from the festival stalls that lined the waterfront. Vibrant banners danced overhead, their colors vivid against the deepening twilight. The chatter of families, punctuated by the laughter of children darting about like fireflies, created a facade of joy that barely concealed the undertow of unease running through Misty Shores. I leaned against the rough-hewn wood of a nearby railing, my eyes skimming the flickering lights of the festival. Gavin stood beside me, his jaw tense, a stark contrast to the merriment swirling around us.

"Do you think anyone else notices?" I asked, glancing up at him. The moonlight highlighted the angles of his face, making him look even more striking, like a figure carved from marble yet warmed by the pulse of life. "It's not just the mayor's speech, is it?"

His dark eyes held mine, an electric current zipping between us that sent a thrill up my spine. "No," he said softly, his voice barely rising above the distant strains of a fiddle. "There's something more. Something we don't understand yet."

I could feel the weight of his words, the gravity of our unspoken fears settling around us like a shroud. It was hard to reconcile the lively atmosphere with the foreboding that seemed to loom like a storm cloud overhead. The festival had always been a highlight of our small coastal town, a celebration of our community and the vibrant life that pulsed through it. But now, it felt like a masquerade, with the specter of the mayor's cryptic symbols lurking just beneath the surface.

"I can't shake the feeling that we're being watched," I murmured, glancing over my shoulder as if expecting someone to step out from the shadows. The laughter and music seemed to fade as my mind spiraled into darker thoughts. What if the mayor's symbols were more than mere art? What if they were a warning?

"Look." Gavin pointed toward a group of townsfolk gathered near the stage. "They don't seem worried. They're celebrating, forgetting about everything else. I wish we could do that."

I wished for that too, for the simplicity of joy unmarred by uncertainty. I imagined the comfort of being wrapped in a warm embrace, of not having to think about the weight of a town shrouded in mystery. But that comfort felt like a distant dream, replaced by the pulse of anxiety that raced through me.

"Maybe they just haven't connected the dots," I replied, a knot tightening in my stomach. "Or maybe they're too afraid to acknowledge it."

His brow furrowed, and I could see the muscles in his jaw work as he contemplated my words. I turned back to face the water, where the moon cast a shimmering path across the waves, creating a silver ribbon that danced with the ebb and flow. The beauty of it was almost surreal, as if nature itself were trying to soothe our fraying nerves.

"Should we tell someone?" Gavin's question cut through the moment like a sharp knife.

"Like who? The mayor? The council? They're the ones we can't trust." My frustration seeped through, mingling with the electric tension lingering between us. "We need proof, something concrete to show that this isn't just paranoia. Otherwise, we'll look like fools."

"I'm not afraid of looking foolish," he said, his gaze unwavering, a flicker of something fierce igniting in his eyes. "I'm afraid of doing nothing."

His words struck a chord deep within me. The quiet intensity that radiated from him was intoxicating, a siren call to my own courage, daring me to act when everything in my being urged me to retreat. I wanted to believe in the power of our shared determination, in the possibilities of what we could uncover together.

The festival music swelled, a lively tune that should have been contagious, yet all I felt was the heaviness of unspoken thoughts. "Okay," I said, a tremor of resolve threading through my voice. "What's our first step?"

Gavin hesitated, his eyes drifting toward the crowd. "We need to get closer to the mayor. If he's hiding something, it's probably somewhere in plain sight. Maybe we can catch him when he's off-guard."

The idea sent a thrill of apprehension through me. The thought of confronting the mayor, especially with the tension surrounding him, felt daunting. Yet the prospect of discovery beckoned like the luminous glow of the festival lights.

"Let's do it," I said, my pulse quickening. "But we need a plan. We can't just rush in."

"Right," he replied, a smile breaking through the tension that hung between us. "I'd hate to ruin my charming reputation by making a scene."

"Charming, huh? I must've missed that memo," I teased, feeling a lightness settle over me, even as the undercurrents of our mission lurked in the back of my mind.

He laughed, a genuine sound that momentarily lifted the weight of the world from my shoulders. "You're right, though. We need to be smart about this. No unnecessary risks."

We stood there, the festival a cacophony of life around us, yet our own world felt suspended in time. The shadows shifted, and I caught a glimpse of a figure watching from the edge of the crowd, their expression obscured by the flickering lanterns. An unease crawled up my spine, making my breath hitch. "Do you see that?"

Gavin turned to follow my gaze, his brow furrowing. "What?"

But the figure melted back into the throng, swallowed by the celebrations. I shook my head, convincing myself it was just the trick of the light, a figment of my anxious mind. “Nothing,” I said, brushing it off.

As the music played on, I felt the weight of the night’s mysteries pressing against my chest. With each heartbeat, the storm that raged within me mirrored the tempest that threatened to break outside.

The laughter and the music faded into a distant hum as we stood together, cloaked in shadows and uncertainty. Gavin leaned closer, his breath warm against my cheek. “If we’re going to confront the mayor, we need to do it smartly. It’s not just about what we find; it’s how we find it,” he said, his tone steady, yet a hint of mischief danced in his eyes.

“Are you suggesting we use stealth?” I quipped, trying to lighten the air thick with anticipation. “Because if it involves sneaking around, I’m afraid my ‘delicate footfalls’ might just give us away.”

He chuckled softly, his gaze unwavering. “More like a diversion. We can create a scene, draw him out. You know, like those classic spy movies, but with less drama and more potato salad.”

“Potato salad?” I raised an eyebrow, fighting a smile. “You mean we’ll whip up a feast and hope for the best?”

“Exactly! But let’s skip the potato salad. How about we grab some popcorn and create a distraction at the games booth? That should buy us some time to get close to him.”

I couldn’t help but laugh at his ridiculousness. “Popcorn? And what’s your grand plan? You throw it at him and hope for the best?”

“Hey, it’s a solid plan!” he replied, feigning indignation. “Distract with snacks, then swoop in like a hero in a romance novel.”

“Right, because nothing says ‘I’m a serious investigator’ like butter-soaked fingers and a half-eaten bag of popcorn.”

“Exactly! The mayor won’t know what hit him,” he grinned, the tension dissipating like mist in the morning sun.

As we laughed together, the warmth of the moment settled into me, reminding me that even in the face of uncertainty, I could find solace in his presence. I looked out over the water again, the moon shimmering like liquid silver, and felt a rush of determination swell within me. "Alright, let's do it. Let's make this happen."

With a newfound sense of purpose, we slipped away from our hiding spot, the crowd drawing us in like moths to a flame. The bright lights of the festival enveloped us, each booth bustling with laughter, the air thick with the scent of cotton candy and fried dough. I felt my pulse quicken, not just from the thrill of the festival but from the adrenaline of our mission.

"Alright, game plan," Gavin said, his tone shifting to a more serious note. "We need to create just enough chaos to grab the mayor's attention without raising too many eyebrows. Think you can handle some popcorn flinging?"

"Only if you can manage to be stealthy while I do it. I don't want anyone thinking I'm just some clumsy festival-goer," I shot back, the playful banter invigorating me.

We made our way to the games booth, where colorful lights blinked and the sounds of jubilant cheers filled the air. A group of teenagers were gathered around a ring toss, their faces lit with excitement as they vied for oversized stuffed animals. I felt a spark of nostalgia at the sight; these games had always been a highlight of the festival, and the sense of community was palpable.

"Looks like the perfect distraction," Gavin said, eyeing the booth where the mayor stood, conversing animatedly with a local vendor. "Just keep them occupied for a few minutes."

"Consider it done." I stepped forward, adopting a casual demeanor as I approached the booth. "Hey, everyone! Who wants to test their skills?"

The teenagers turned, momentarily distracted from their competition. "You? You think you can beat us?" one of them teased, crossing his arms.

"Of course! I challenge anyone here to a ring toss duel!" I declared, feigning confidence even as my heart raced.

Gavin snickered quietly behind me, clearly enjoying the spectacle. The teens accepted my challenge with laughter, and as we started tossing rings, I threw in exaggerated movements, determined to keep the crowd engaged.

"Come on, people! Are you really going to let me take you down?" I taunted, my competitive spirit igniting as I tossed the rings with newfound fervor. The laughter escalated, and before I knew it, several festival-goers had gathered to watch, their attention drifting from the mayor to our impromptu competition.

"Now's your chance," Gavin whispered from the sidelines, gesturing toward the mayor. "Go!"

I seized the moment, tossing my final ring with flair and spinning around to make my way toward the mayor, heart pounding in my chest. Gavin followed closely behind, keeping an eye on the crowd while we maneuvered through the throng of festival-goers. The music crescendoed, a joyful melody that felt incongruous against the tension simmering beneath the surface.

The mayor was oblivious to our approach, still engrossed in conversation with the vendor. I could hear snippets of their discussion about community projects and upcoming events, but my focus was laser-sharp, intent on uncovering the truth behind the symbols.

"Excuse me, Mr. Mayor!" I called out, injecting a playful lilt into my voice. The vendor glanced over, surprise flickering across his face, but the mayor turned with a practiced smile.

"Yes?" he asked, his expression shifting to one of curiosity.

"I just wanted to say that your speech earlier was...well, riveting!" I beamed, pouring on the charm. "But I couldn't help but notice those fascinating symbols. They've been the talk of the festival!"

His smile faltered for a brief moment, just a flicker of discomfort that was gone as quickly as it appeared. "Ah, yes. The symbols represent our community's growth and resilience."

"Growth and resilience, huh?" Gavin interjected smoothly, stepping forward. "They do have a unique aesthetic. Is there a story behind them?"

The mayor's gaze flicked to Gavin, a flicker of recognition crossing his features before he masked it behind a veneer of politeness. "Every symbol has its history, of course. It's important to reflect on our roots."

"Interesting," I said, my tone light, but the weight of his words hung heavy in the air. "It seems like there's more to them than meets the eye. I'd love to hear more about their significance sometime."

"Yes, well, perhaps in another setting," he replied, his voice tight, as if he were already sensing the direction of our inquiry. "Enjoy the festival."

With that, he turned back to the vendor, dismissing us with a wave of his hand. But the conversation lingered, a tension unspoken threading through the air.

"Did you catch that?" Gavin whispered as we stepped away, the crowd bustling around us, laughter and music fading into the background. "He's hiding something. I could feel it."

"I know," I replied, my heart racing with adrenaline and uncertainty. "But we're getting closer. He can't keep hiding forever."

Just then, a loud crash echoed from the nearby games booth, followed by a chorus of startled gasps. We turned to see one of the teenagers had knocked over a tower of plush toys, sending them tumbling across the ground. The laughter erupted anew, a raucous wave that swept through the crowd, leaving the mayor distracted and annoyed.

Gavin's eyes sparkled with mischief. "Looks like our diversion is working better than we thought."

"Or just making a mess," I said, shaking my head, but I couldn't suppress my smile. "Let's go see what other secrets we can uncover."

As we melted back into the crowd, the atmosphere shifted. The excitement surged around us like a tide, yet I could still feel the storm brewing just beneath the surface, waiting for the right moment to break free.

The vibrant chaos of the festival enveloped us as we stepped away from the mayor, still buzzing from our encounter. Laughter bubbled up around us, a symphony of joy that felt jarring against the backdrop of our secret mission. Gavin's eyes sparkled with the thrill of the chase, and I couldn't help but match his enthusiasm, even as an undercurrent of dread tightened my chest.

"Let's circle back to that booth," I suggested, gesturing toward the edge of the festival where the games were still drawing crowds. "We might be able to eavesdrop on the mayor or catch someone else who knows more about those symbols."

"Good thinking. Besides, I could use a few more rings to toss," Gavin replied with a playful smirk. "If we can distract them again, maybe we'll get more than just the mayor's pleasantries this time."

We navigated through the throng of festival-goers, the air rich with the scent of fried dough and the sweet tang of lemonade. Children darted past us, their faces painted with vibrant colors, embodying the carefree spirit of the evening. Yet, as we neared the games, I couldn't shake the feeling that our luck might not hold.

"Okay, on the count of three, let's create some chaos," I whispered, my pulse racing as I surveyed the crowd. Gavin nodded, his expression serious, but the playful glint in his eyes hinted at the mischief he always loved to embrace.

"One... two... three!" I shouted, launching a handful of loose change I had stashed in my pocket into the air. The coins clinked and scattered, capturing the attention of everyone nearby.

Gavin jumped in, waving his arms as if he were directing a circus. "Who wants to catch some free money?" he called, a wide grin splitting his face.

The effect was instantaneous. The crowd erupted into a frenzy, scrambling after the glinting coins that tumbled across the grass. Laughter mixed with surprised shouts filled the air, and I could see the mayor's head snap up, his brows furrowing in annoyance.

"Perfect distraction!" I said, slipping through the chaos and tugging Gavin along. We maneuvered past the booth and into a shadowy corner where the tents and stalls offered a momentary reprieve from the noise.

"There's the mayor," I whispered, spotting him just a few feet away, speaking to another town official, a woman I recognized from the council meetings.

"Let's listen in," Gavin murmured, inching closer, his eyes darting between the two. The tension thrumming in the air made my skin prickle, a mix of adrenaline and apprehension.

"I've told you before, we can't keep this under wraps much longer," the woman insisted, her voice low and urgent. "People are starting to ask questions."

The mayor's expression darkened. "They need to focus on the festival. This is not the time to stir the pot. Let them enjoy the festivities and forget about what lies beneath the surface."

"What lies beneath?" I whispered, leaning closer, my heart pounding. The woman's words hung in the air, heavy with implications.

Gavin's brow furrowed. "What do you think they're talking about?"

"Could be the symbols, the history. It's all connected somehow." I strained to hear more, but just as the mayor opened his mouth to respond, a sudden commotion erupted from the main stage.

"What now?" Gavin muttered, glancing toward the noise.

A voice boomed over the speakers, startling us. "Ladies and gentlemen, may I have your attention, please!" The announcer's voice cut through the laughter, urgency punctuating his tone. "We have a very special announcement!"

"Come on!" Gavin urged, pulling me along as we followed the crowd's curious buzz back toward the stage. The festival-goers, drawn in by the promise of something new, filled the space, their excitement palpable.

When we reached the front, I spotted the mayor standing by the stage, his demeanor now a mix of irritation and anxiety. The announcer was beaming, completely oblivious to the tension simmering beneath the surface.

"It's time for the unveiling of our new community initiative!" he proclaimed, his voice soaring with enthusiasm. "This year, we're launching a project that promises to transform Misty Shores for generations to come!"

Gavin leaned closer, his expression skeptical. "Great, just what we need—more vague plans wrapped in pretty words."

"Let's see what they have to say," I replied, half-hoping for something substantial.

The mayor stepped forward, flashing a rehearsed smile as he accepted the microphone. "Thank you all for joining us tonight. As we celebrate our community, we also recognize our future and the legacy we wish to leave behind."

The crowd clapped, but I could feel the air thickening, the unease settling like a dense fog. The mayor's words turned into a blur of jargon about growth and progress, but my focus was on his eyes, darting around as if searching for something—or someone.

Then, with a flourish, he revealed a large banner that was draped across a nearby wall, its colors vibrant but its design enigmatic. My breath caught in my throat as I took in the swirling shapes and symbols that mirrored those we had seen earlier. The same ones that haunted our conversations, now proudly displayed as if they were a badge of honor.

"What is he playing at?" Gavin's voice was barely audible over the murmurs of the crowd.

"I don't know, but it doesn't feel right." My gut twisted, sensing a deeper implication. "He's trying to sell something, and it's more than just a project. This is an invitation to questions we're not supposed to ask."

The crowd began to buzz, whispers of curiosity and confusion spreading like wildfire. "What do they mean?" "What's the story?" The questions floated around us, merging with the festival sounds, but the mayor stood resolute, a mask of confidence plastered across his face.

Suddenly, a commotion erupted to our right, pulling my attention away from the stage. A woman, her face pale and eyes wide, burst through the crowd. "Help! Someone's in trouble!"

The mayor's facade cracked, his gaze snapping toward her, fear etched in his features. "What do you mean?"

The woman pointed toward the edge of the festival, her voice trembling. "At the beach! I saw something... something strange!"

Gasps rippled through the crowd as the weight of her words settled like a lead balloon. "Gavin," I said, my heart racing. "We need to go."

"Wait—" he began, but I was already moving, drawn by the instinctive need to uncover the truth lurking just beyond our reach. As we pushed through the throngs of people, the murmurs of the crowd faded, replaced by the pounding of my heart and the sense that we were on the brink of something monumental.

We burst onto the sand, the festival lights dimming behind us, and there it was—a shape partially buried in the sand, unnatural and out of place. The waves lapped at its edges, a silent guardian revealing something we were never meant to find.

"Is that—" Gavin's voice faltered, his eyes wide with disbelief.

The figure was unmistakably human, a man lying motionless, the moonlight casting an eerie glow over his pale skin. The fear coursing through me morphed into urgency, but before I could take a step forward, a shadow loomed behind us, the unmistakable weight of something sinister shifting in the air.

And just like that, the night transformed from a celebration into a confrontation, the unknown now a tangible presence that threatened to engulf us both.

Chapter 11: A Secret Confrontation

The festival burst to life around me, vibrant banners flapping in the brisk autumn breeze, their colors dancing like flames against the azure sky. The air was thick with the sweet aroma of caramel apples and spiced cider, mingling with the sharp scent of wood smoke from nearby bonfires. Laughter echoed through the square, a jubilant chorus that seemed to push away any lingering shadows. Yet, in the heart of this celebration, I felt an undercurrent of anxiety tugging at my gut, a nagging sense that something was amiss.

Mayor Callahan stood at the center of it all, a beacon of warmth and charm. His broad smile could light up the gloomiest of days, and tonight, he played his part flawlessly, tossing out jokes and banter to an adoring crowd. But as I maneuvered through the throng, my heart pounded in sync with the beat of the festivities, every pulse urging me to confront him. I needed answers, and the weight of the truth pressed down on me like an invisible cloak.

"Mayor Callahan!" I called, pushing my way through clusters of people swaying to the lively music. The crowd parted, as if they sensed the gravity of my determination. He turned, the smile slipping from his face momentarily, replaced by a flicker of surprise. His eyes—usually twinkling with mischief—clouded over, and I caught a glimpse of something far deeper, a shadow lurking just beneath the surface.

"Ah, my favorite citizen!" he exclaimed, his voice as smooth as the silk ties he always wore. "What brings you here, my dear?"

I swallowed hard, feeling the vibrant atmosphere fade into a muted backdrop. "We need to talk. Now."

He raised an eyebrow, feigning nonchalance, but I noticed how the muscles in his jaw tightened. "Can't it wait? The festival is in full swing! Look at the smiles! The joy! Isn't that what matters?" His gaze swept over the crowd, but I could see the unease in the way his lips curled slightly.

"No, it can't wait." My voice was steady, though inside, I was an unraveling knot of nerves. "Not when I know what you've been hiding from us. Not when people's lives are at stake."

His laughter came too easily, a well-rehearsed performance. "Darling, you're letting your imagination run wild. There's nothing sinister lurking behind our little town's charm. Just... festive spirit!" He leaned closer, lowering his voice to a conspiratorial whisper that carried a sharp edge. "Don't make this harder than it needs to be."

As he spoke, I could see the glimmer of fear behind his facade, the truth rattling beneath the veneer of his charisma. The crowd around us, once vibrant and animated, began to shift, their joy morphing into a collective unease. I could feel their eyes on us, some curious, others wary, as if they sensed the electric tension crackling between the mayor and me.

"Then explain the whispers, the rumors about the land acquisitions," I pressed, heart racing. "Why are you buying up so much property? What are you planning?" Each word felt like a pebble tossed into a pond, sending ripples of doubt through the air.

"Property?" He laughed again, but this time it lacked warmth, and I could see the crowd bristle. "I assure you, it's just business. We're developing for the future, for progress." His eyes darted to the people milling around us, his mask slipping for just a moment. "But you wouldn't understand—this is above your pay grade, sweetheart."

"Above my pay grade?" My voice cut through the music, sharper than I intended, drawing more attention than I wanted. "If you think I'll just stand by while you make decisions that affect our entire town, you're sorely mistaken. People deserve to know the truth."

The laughter faded from his face, replaced by a hard glint of anger. "And what truth would that be? That I'm trying to make this town better? You think you're the only one who cares about these people?"

"Then let me in on your plans. Be transparent, Mayor." I took a step closer, fueled by the determination coursing through my veins. "What are you afraid of? Why hide behind this façade of merriment?"

A flicker of something dangerous sparked in his eyes, an emotion I couldn't quite place. Anger? Fear? I wasn't sure, but it sent a chill racing down my spine. "You're treading on dangerous ground, my dear. There are forces at play here that you cannot possibly comprehend." His voice lowered, and the warmth drained from his words, replaced by an icy edge. "This isn't just about you. This is bigger than us."

I hesitated, a million questions racing through my mind. What was he talking about? I could feel the energy of the crowd shift, their eyes darting between us like spectators at a tennis match. Whispers began to ripple through the festival, the joyful sounds muted beneath the tension hanging thick in the air.

"Then enlighten me," I challenged, my heart pounding in my chest. "What's so dangerous about the truth? What are you protecting?"

For a moment, the world around us blurred, the music fading into a distant hum as I searched his face for answers. There was a flicker of something—regret?—that crossed his features, but it vanished as quickly as it had appeared. He stepped back, the distance between us growing, the crowd sensing the shift in energy.

"I cannot help you," he said, his voice firm and resolute, but there was a tremor in his words that hinted at his uncertainty. "Some secrets are meant to remain buried."

I could feel the weight of his words, heavy and ominous, wrapping around me like a shroud. As I watched him retreat into the throng of revelers, his smile back in place, I was left standing in the midst of the festival, my heart racing and a cold dread settling in my stomach. The night had turned, and what had begun as a celebration now felt like a masquerade hiding the deepest fears of our town, with shadows lurking just out of sight.

The echo of the mayor's retreating footsteps reverberated through the festival grounds, a jarring reminder that I stood alone in a sea of laughter and light, yet felt more isolated than ever. People swirled around me, their faces painted with joy, but I was an outsider looking in, acutely aware of the shadows creeping at the edges of our perfect little town. I took a deep breath, inhaling the sweet and spicy notes of the evening, trying to drown out the anxiety that knotted in my stomach.

As the lively music picked up again, I noticed Claire, my childhood friend, weaving through the crowd toward me, her ponytail bouncing like a metronome. She was the embodiment of the festival spirit, her cheeks flushed with excitement, and her laughter a bright bell amidst the chaos. She spotted me and her smile faltered slightly as she registered my tense expression.

"Hey! Why do you look like you've just seen a ghost?" Claire teased, her voice playful but laced with concern. She slid her arm through mine, her warmth offering a semblance of comfort against the chill that still gripped my heart.

"I just had a rather enlightening conversation with Mayor Callahan," I replied, trying to keep my tone light but failing miserably. "Enlightening in a way that involves him dodging all my questions like a pro."

"Ah, classic Callahan. The man could sell ice to an Eskimo," she quipped, rolling her eyes. "What did he say?"

"Nothing," I sighed, the weight of my frustration escaping in a rush. "He danced around everything like he was at a ballet recital. But it's more than just him being evasive. It's about what's happening under the surface. I can feel it."

Claire's brow furrowed, her carefree demeanor slipping just a fraction. "You're not talking about the fireworks, are you? Because that would be an unfortunate way to ruin the mood."

"No, not the fireworks," I said, leaning closer, lowering my voice as if the celebration itself might overhear. "I mean the land he's been acquiring. There's something else going on, Claire, something that feels wrong. The way he deflected my questions... it's as if he's hiding something dangerous."

She considered my words, her bright eyes narrowing as she processed my revelations. "You really think there's something sinister at play? I mean, this is the mayor we're talking about. He's not exactly known for villainous schemes."

"Or maybe he's just very good at hiding it," I shot back, frustration creeping into my tone. "Look, I've been digging into the town's records, and it seems the mayor has been quietly purchasing properties around the old mill district. That's prime land for development, and I can't shake the feeling he's planning something that will benefit him and his wealthy friends rather than the community."

Her expression softened, and she nodded slowly. "Okay, I get it. But what do you want to do about it? Confront him again? With a mob of pitchfork-wielding townsfolk?"

"Not quite," I said, a smirk breaking through my anxiety. "But I do need to gather more information. Maybe if I talk to some of the local business owners who've been affected by these acquisitions, they can shed some light on what's really happening."

"Sounds like a plan," Claire replied, her eyes glimmering with mischief. "But you know what? We should probably look into it after we enjoy some festival food. I mean, the fried dough isn't going to eat itself."

I couldn't help but chuckle at her enthusiasm. "You're right. I'll think about the mayor's schemes while devouring something that will likely ruin my diet for a month."

The two of us navigated through the throng of festival-goers, laughter and chatter blending into a symphony of delight. The evening sky deepened into a rich indigo, studded with stars twinkling like diamonds scattered across velvet. We stopped at a booth selling fried dough, the sweet scent wafting through the air like a siren's call.

"Two, please!" Claire declared, her excitement infectious as she dug into her purse for cash. I couldn't help but smile at her enthusiasm. "The last thing you need right now is to stress over calories. Tomorrow is another day."

"Just remember, I'm not here to be a cautionary tale about fried food," I warned, playfully nudging her shoulder. We received our orders, and I took a huge bite, the sugary coating melting on my tongue.

"See?" she said, a mouthful of fried dough preventing her from articulating her point clearly. "Nothing like the fair to soothe the soul!"

As we moved away from the booth, laughter erupted nearby, and I turned to find a group of teenagers performing a goofy dance in front of the stage. Their carefree spirits lit up the evening, a stark contrast to the turmoil swirling in my chest. I took a moment to absorb the joy around me, letting it wash over me like a balm. But my thoughts were quickly interrupted by a sharp voice slicing through the laughter.

"There you are, you slippery eel! I've been looking for you!" It was Megan, the town's high-strung events coordinator, her eyes darting around with the intensity of a hawk. She marched toward us, her clipboard clutched tightly against her chest like a lifeline.

"Megan, what's the crisis?" Claire asked, her tone laced with playful sarcasm. "Did we run out of funnel cakes?"

"No, nothing so trivial," Megan snapped, the edges of her smile betraying her rising frustration. "I just spotted Mayor Callahan disappearing into the old mill area with a group of developers. Do you know anything about that?"

I exchanged a glance with Claire, our earlier conversation rushing back to the forefront of my mind. "We might have some theories," I said carefully, watching the color drain from Megan's face. "But why would they be there now?"

"Exactly!" she exclaimed, her voice rising in pitch. "And with all those plans he's been talking about? This doesn't feel right."

"Are you thinking what I'm thinking?" Claire asked, her excitement suddenly eclipsed by concern.

"That we need to find out what's happening before it's too late?" I replied, feeling the urgency bubbling to the surface. "Yes, we definitely need to investigate."

"Okay, let's be sneaky about it," Megan suggested, her demeanor shifting as she leaned in closer, her eyes glinting with determination. "We can't just let them plot behind closed doors. Let's go check it out."

In that moment, the festival, with its laughter and lights, transformed from a backdrop of merriment into a cover for our mission. We were no longer just revelers; we were a trio of unlikely detectives, ready to unearth whatever secrets the mayor and his corporate cohorts were keeping under wraps. As we slipped away from the revelry, a sense of purpose surged within me, illuminating the path ahead like the flickering lights strung overhead. Whatever lay in wait at the old mill, I knew one thing for certain: we were about to plunge into the depths of the mystery that surrounded our beloved town.

We slipped through the vibrant chaos of the festival, our laughter swallowed by the deeper shadows forming as we drew closer to the old mill. The distant sound of the band faded into a low hum, replaced by the rustle of leaves and the crunch of gravel beneath our feet. The air thickened with anticipation, every step laden with the weight of the unknown. I glanced over at Claire and Megan, their faces lit by a mix of excitement and apprehension, our little trio now entwined in a web of secrets and intrigue.

"This feels like something out of a mystery novel," Claire whispered, glancing around as if expecting someone to leap out of the bushes. "Only instead of a charming detective, we've got a trio of confused amateurs stumbling into a potential crime scene."

"Don't sell yourself short. You've got an impressive track record of detecting when the donut stand runs out of glaze," I shot back, unable to suppress a grin. The tension was palpable, but humor had always been our shield against the serious.

As we approached the old mill, the once lively festival behind us seemed to fade away, replaced by an oppressive silence that loomed over the dilapidated structure. The moonlight glinted off the weathered wood, casting ghostly shadows that danced in the night. It was as if the building itself was holding its breath, waiting for us to uncover whatever secrets it held within its rotting walls.

"Okay, so what's the plan?" Megan asked, pulling out her phone and illuminating the area with its screen. The glow revealed a scattering of debris around the entrance, remnants of long-forgotten festivities, and perhaps, darker dealings.

"Let's start by getting a closer look at the building," I suggested, my voice dropping to a hush. "We can peek through the windows and see if there's anything suspicious. If the mayor is in there with those developers, we'll want to know what they're discussing."

"Just remember, if we get caught, I'm blaming you," Claire joked, though I could sense a tremor of nervousness in her voice. She nudged me playfully as we crept toward the side of the mill, my heart thudding in my chest like a drum.

As we approached a broken window, I peered inside, careful not to make any noise. The interior was cloaked in darkness, but I could make out the faint outline of figures gathered around a table, illuminated by a flickering overhead light. My breath caught in my throat. There, unmistakably, was Mayor Callahan, leaning over the table, his face set in serious concentration. A group of men in suits surrounded him, their expressions stern and urgent.

"Do you see them?" Claire whispered, her breath brushing against my ear. "What are they doing?"

"I think they're discussing something important," I murmured, straining to catch snippets of their conversation. "But I can't hear what they're saying."

Suddenly, a loud bang echoed from within the mill, causing my heart to leap into my throat. The voices inside fell silent, and I jerked back, my pulse racing. "Did you hear that?" I asked, panic creeping into my voice.

Before either of them could respond, the door to the mill creaked open, and the figure of a man stepped out into the moonlight. My breath hitched—there was no mistaking it. It was Lucas, the mayor's right-hand man, his sharp features etched with an intensity that sent chills racing down my spine.

"What are we going to do?" Megan hissed, her eyes wide with fear. "We can't let him see us."

"Hide!" I whispered urgently, pushing us back into the shadows. We ducked behind a nearby pile of old crates, the splintered wood digging into my side as I strained to hear what Lucas might say.

He stood there for a moment, glancing around as if sensing the weight of our presence in the night. "It's not time yet," he murmured to himself, his voice barely audible but filled with tension. "If the mayor knew we were here... no, he can't find out."

"What does that mean?" Claire whispered, glancing at me with wide eyes. I could see the wheels turning in her head, and I felt a surge of determination.

"We need to get closer," I whispered back, a sense of urgency pushing me forward. "We can't let this opportunity slip away."

As we crept along the edge of the mill, we were careful to stay hidden. Every step felt like a tightrope walk between discovery and disaster. The moon hung low in the sky, casting a silver sheen across the ground as we reached the corner of the building. Peering around, I caught sight of the group through another grimy window.

The atmosphere inside felt thick, charged with an unspoken tension. Callahan was gesturing animatedly, his face lit with determination. "We've already invested too much for anyone to stand in our way," he said, his voice low but steady. "This town needs development, and we can't let a few rumors derail our plans."

"Exactly," Lucas chimed in, his tone smooth but laced with an edge. "If we push forward, the townsfolk will see the benefits. They'll come around. But we have to control the narrative. We can't let anyone expose our intentions."

"Control the narrative?" I muttered under my breath. "What narrative?"

Just then, a commotion broke out inside the mill. I squinted through the glass, trying to make sense of the chaos. A figure stumbled back, knocking over a stack of papers that fluttered to the floor like fallen leaves.

Callahan's face contorted with anger, and he slammed his fist on the table. "We can't afford any mistakes! Not now!" The passion in his voice resonated like a thunderclap in the stillness of the night.

"Maybe we should reconvene," one of the suited men suggested, his voice barely audible over the tension crackling in the air. "Before someone notices we're missing."

I could feel the world around me pulse with urgency. "We need to get those papers," I breathed, my heart racing at the thought of what secrets they might hold.

"What? Are you insane?" Claire's eyes widened in disbelief. "That's practically a death wish!"

"Maybe, but it's the only way we can get proof of what they're planning. We can't just stand here and do nothing," I replied, adrenaline coursing through my veins.

Megan's eyes darted between us, her expression shifting from fear to fierce resolve. "I'm in. Let's do it."

We crept closer to the entrance, hearts pounding like tribal drums in our chests. The adrenaline was intoxicating, heightening every sense, making the world around us feel surreal. I glanced back at my friends, and we shared a quick nod of determination.

As we approached the door, I spotted an old wooden crate stacked near the entrance, half-hidden in shadows. "If we can just get those papers before they leave..." I whispered, my voice trailing off as the door suddenly swung open, and the men inside spilled out into the night.

"Now or never!" I shouted, scrambling to duck behind the crate. My heart raced as I peered around it, the shadows of the men stretching long across the ground.

"Where are the damn papers?" Lucas barked, his voice rising. "I can't believe we lost track of them. We need to regroup. Now!"

I felt the chill of realization wash over me. They were leaving, and if we didn't act quickly, we'd miss our chance to uncover the truth. With a quick exchange of glances, we knew we had to make our move.

As I pushed forward, adrenaline fueling my every step, I heard a sudden, sharp crack. The sound resonated in the air, followed by a distant shout that sent a wave of panic surging through me.

"What was that?" Claire whispered, her eyes wide as we froze in place.

"I don't know, but we need to go!" I urged, my instincts screaming at me to get out of sight. But before we could retreat, the figures began to scatter, and I caught a glimpse of Callahan standing in the doorway, fury etched across his face.

And then I saw it—a flash of silver in his hand, glinting ominously under the moonlight.

"Get down!" I shouted, as the tension snapped like a taut wire, leaving us teetering on the edge of chaos.

Chapter 12: Beneath the Waves

The salt of the sea clung to my skin as Gavin and I adjusted our masks, the cold water wrapping around us like an icy embrace. With each inhale, the weight of the ocean pressed down, a constant reminder that we were not the masters here, merely guests in a realm of vibrant life and shrouded secrets. I could feel the heartbeat of the ocean thrumming beneath me, a pulse that urged us forward into its depths. The jagged cliffs above loomed like ancient sentinels, their shadows reaching down into the water, teasing us with hints of what lay beyond.

As we descended, the sunlight fractured above us, sending shimmering ribbons of gold and azure dancing through the water. Fish darted past, flashes of color against the darkening blue, their movements sharp and deliberate as if they were actors in an underwater ballet, rehearsed and refined. I turned to Gavin, his expression hidden behind the mask, but I could feel the thrill radiating off him. Together, we shared this journey, propelled by curiosity and the intoxicating lure of discovery. The deeper we ventured, the more I felt that the ocean had a story to tell, one that echoed through the ages.

Navigating the underwater caves was like wandering through an ancient cathedral, the formations of coral and stone weaving together to create a sanctuary that felt both sacred and eerie. The walls shimmered with bioluminescent algae, casting a soft glow that illuminated our path. I reached out to touch the coral, its texture rough and yet strangely beautiful, like the craggy hands of time itself reaching out to us from the past. Gavin's hand brushed against mine, a fleeting touch that sent a spark of warmth coursing through the cold water. In that moment, I could have sworn the ocean paused, holding its breath as if aware of the connection forming between us amid the wonders of the abyss.

Then we spotted it—an ancient shipwreck, half-buried in the sand like a long-forgotten memory. The hull, once proud and defiant, now lay twisted and broken, draped in seaweed like a tattered cloak. It was hauntingly beautiful, a ghost of a vessel that had weathered storms and time itself, and I felt a shiver of reverence as we approached. Gavin signaled for us to explore the wreck, and as we swam closer, I could see the way the sunlight danced through the cracks in the wood, illuminating the darkness within.

Inside, the air was thick with mystery. The ship's bones creaked softly, almost as if it were sighing under the weight of its own history. I peered into the captain's quarters, the remnants of a life once lived now scattered like forgotten dreams. A dusty compass lay abandoned on the table, its needle forever frozen in time. I picked it up, feeling the cool metal against my palm, and imagined the hands that had once held it, steering through treacherous waters, guided by stars long extinguished.

"Look at this," I whispered to Gavin, holding the compass up. His eyes widened behind his mask, and I could see the spark of intrigue mirrored in his expression. We shared a moment of silent understanding—this was no ordinary wreck. There was a weight to it, a significance that hung in the water like a low tide, drawing us further into its depths.

As we ventured deeper into the wreck, shadows danced along the walls, and I felt an inexplicable pull toward a small door at the back. It was ajar, creaking softly in the current, and the darkness beyond seemed to beckon. "Do you feel that?" I asked, my voice bubbling in the water. Gavin nodded, his eyes glinting with an intensity that sent a shiver down my spine.

We pushed the door open, and a rush of cool water greeted us. Inside, the air felt different—thicker, charged with energy. The walls were covered in strange symbols, carved into the wood as if marking a passage of time and significance. My heart raced as I traced my fingers over the engravings. They were unlike anything I had ever seen, ancient and cryptic, a language lost to the ages but echoing with familiar urgency.

"What do you think it means?" Gavin asked, his voice a low murmur against the sound of our bubbles. I shrugged, overwhelmed by the significance of the moment. "I don't know, but I feel like it's a warning—or a message."

Suddenly, the silence of the shipwreck was shattered by a low rumble, a sound that reverberated through the water like a distant thunderclap. The ocean seemed to shudder around us, a warning from the depths. I glanced at Gavin, fear and excitement mixing in the air between us. "We should go," I urged, instinctively knowing that whatever we had stumbled upon was far greater than either of us had anticipated.

As we turned to leave, a shadow flickered at the edge of my vision. My heart raced as I strained to see, but the murky water obscured whatever had moved. "Did you see that?" I whispered, my pulse quickening. Gavin nodded, his expression tense.

With a shared glance, we propelled ourselves toward the entrance, our hearts pounding in rhythm with the mysteries of the ocean. The shipwreck whispered its secrets as we swam back through the corridors, the walls now feeling less like a sanctuary and more like a warning. Whatever had lurked in those shadows was not ready to be uncovered, and as we broke through the surface, gasping for air, I couldn't shake the feeling that we had merely skimmed the surface of a far deeper tale—one that entwined us with the very heart of the ocean.

The moment we breached the surface, gasping for air, the sunlight felt almost foreign after the cool embrace of the ocean. It wrapped around us, warm and bright, illuminating the droplets cascading from my hair like a thousand tiny diamonds. I looked at Gavin, who was shaking the water from his head like a golden retriever, and couldn't help but laugh, the sound bubbling up, unrestrained and full of adrenaline.

"What do you think we found down there?" I asked, the thrill of the dive still coursing through my veins, a high I wasn't ready to let go of just yet. The fear that had gripped me in the wreck began to dissipate, replaced by the intoxicating rush of discovery.

Gavin squinted against the sunlight, his expression shifting from excitement to contemplation. "A shipwreck, obviously," he replied, his tone teasing. "But the symbols... they weren't just decoration. They felt important." He paused, a thoughtful look crossing his face. "Like they were warning us or guiding us."

"Or perhaps inviting us," I suggested, my imagination flaring to life. "What if we're meant to decode whatever mystery that ship holds? It could be something extraordinary, like treasure or..." My voice trailed off as a thought crossed my mind, heavy with implication. "Or something dangerous."

His brow furrowed, and I could see the spark of worry cloud his features. "You mean like a curse?"

"Curses have a way of creeping into the most innocuous places," I replied, leaning closer to him as we drifted on the surface, the waves gently rocking us. "Just look at the stories of this town. What's a ghost story without a little misfortune?"

Gavin rolled his eyes playfully, but the tension in the air was palpable. "Okay, so maybe we don't mention the word 'curse' too loudly. We wouldn't want to tempt fate." He grinned, but there was an edge to it, a knowing that echoed in our shared laughter.

The sun glinted off the water, and I couldn't shake the feeling that our dive had awakened something in the depths. My heart raced as we paddled back toward the shore, each stroke propelling me closer to the reality we had uncovered and the enigma that lay ahead. What secrets lingered within that shipwreck, and how were they tied to the history of our town?

As we reached the rocky beach, I glanced back at the ocean, shimmering under the sun, and felt an unexpected pang of longing. It was as if the sea was bidding us farewell, and I couldn't help but feel that we had entered into a pact with its depths. I could sense it—a connection that surged between us, urging us to return, to explore further.

Once on solid ground, we removed our gear, the air thick with the scent of salt and seaweed. I wrung out my hair, shaking it free from the clinging water, and watched as Gavin knelt to inspect the beach. His fingers sifted through the sand, pulling out small shells, each one a tiny, perfect marvel of nature.

"What are you doing?" I asked, amused.

"Just gathering evidence," he said, holding up a particularly smooth stone, glistening in the sun. "This one feels lucky. I think we'll need it."

"Lucky stone for a potentially cursed shipwreck? Perfect logic, as always," I teased, rolling my eyes.

"Hey, you never know. It could ward off evil spirits," he shot back, his eyes dancing with mischief.

Together, we strolled along the shoreline, our laughter mingling with the rhythmic crashing of the waves. But the lighthearted banter masked a deeper current swirling between us—an undercurrent of tension, unspoken thoughts that bubbled just beneath the surface. The day felt heavy with possibilities, and I could sense the weight of our shared adventure forging something new and uncharted between us.

As we reached a rocky outcrop, I spotted something half-buried in the sand—an old, weathered journal, its pages yellowed and frayed at the edges. I picked it up, brushing off the sand, and Gavin's curiosity piqued. "What's that?"

"I have no idea," I replied, flipping it open cautiously. The ink was faded, the handwriting almost illegible, but there were drawings that caught my eye. They resembled the symbols we'd seen in the shipwreck, intricately woven into a story that seemed to unfold across the pages. "It looks like it belonged to someone who was on that ship."

Gavin leaned closer, his eyes narrowing in concentration. "Let's take it back. We might be able to piece together what happened," he suggested, and I nodded in agreement, a sense of urgency bubbling within me.

Our excitement rekindled, we made our way back to my car, the journal clutched tightly in my hands. Once inside, I couldn't resist the urge to start decoding its contents right away. The leather cover felt warm against my palms, a promise of secrets waiting to be revealed.

The drive back was filled with the hum of the engine and the salty breeze wafting through the open windows. The ocean shimmered beside us, and I found myself glancing at Gavin, stealing glances at the way his hair caught the sunlight, the way his laughter echoed against the backdrop of crashing waves. It was easy to forget the deeper implications of our discoveries when he was around, his lightheartedness brightening the shadows lurking at the corners of my mind.

Once home, I spread the journal across the dining table, the pages flaring open like the wings of a great bird about to take flight. Gavin leaned over my shoulder, his presence a comforting weight as I tried to decipher the words. "It feels almost alive, doesn't it?" he murmured, and I could hear the wonder in his voice.

"Yeah, like it has a heartbeat," I replied, tracing the symbols with my finger. "These were drawn with purpose, not just doodles. Whoever wrote this had a message."

We began to piece together fragments of a story that felt like a dark whisper carried on the wind. Tales of betrayal, unfulfilled dreams, and a search for something lost in the tides. The words painted a picture of the past—a world that seemed as alive as the sea itself.

As I read, a chill crept down my spine, not from the eerie content but from the realization that our fates were intertwined with this narrative. The ocean was calling us back, and I knew, deep down, that our journey had only just begun. The thrill of the unknown ignited a fire within me, a spark that promised adventure but also danger. Whatever lay beneath the waves was no ordinary tale; it was a history waiting to be unraveled, and we were now players in a game much larger than ourselves.

The journal lay spread across the table like a treasure map, its pages a vivid tapestry of the past. Each line danced with stories, revealing fragments of lives once lived and lost in the embrace of the ocean. Gavin leaned in, his breath warm against my neck, a tantalizing reminder of how close we had grown during this adventure. The air was thick with tension as we absorbed the words, our fingers tracing over the symbols that seemed to shimmer under the dim kitchen light.

"I can't believe this was just lying there, waiting for us," I murmured, my heart racing at the sheer serendipity of it all. "What if this is the key to everything?"

Gavin chuckled softly, the sound rich and deep. "Or it could be a warning, like those 'don't go into the creepy forest' signs that kids ignore. You know, the kind that gets you chased by something terrible."

"Thanks for that delightful thought," I replied, rolling my eyes. "Let's focus on the treasure aspect, shall we? I'm much more interested in finding gold than getting chased by any terrifying ocean spirits."

His laughter filled the room, a comforting sound that pushed away the shadows lingering at the edges of my mind. I resumed my examination of the journal, my heart racing with anticipation. "Look at this part," I said, pointing to a particularly intricate drawing that resembled a map. "This could be where they buried something—or where they went after the shipwreck."

Gavin leaned closer, his brow furrowing as he scrutinized the lines. "If this is right, then it's not far from here. Just off the coast," he mused, a spark of adventure igniting in his eyes.

"What do you think? Should we check it out?" My pulse quickened at the thought, a thrill racing through me. The ocean had given us a taste of its mysteries, and I craved more.

"Are you kidding? We're diving again!" Gavin exclaimed, his enthusiasm infectious. "But this time, let's be smart about it. We'll plan, bring better gear, and maybe some snacks. Because who can resist a good beach picnic after diving into the unknown?"

I laughed, the lightheartedness of his suggestion contrasting sharply with the weight of what lay ahead. "Snacks while searching for potential treasure? Sounds like a solid plan. But if we find something valuable, I'm claiming first dibs."

"Deal, but you know I'm the better negotiator," he replied, a smirk playing on his lips. "You'll have to sweeten the deal if you want to keep me from claiming half."

We spent the next few hours poring over the journal, taking notes, and mapping out our next dive. As twilight approached, the room was filled with a warm glow, and the golden light cast playful shadows on the walls. Gavin's laughter rang out as he shared absurd theories about the ship and its crew, his humor a balm for the unease creeping into my thoughts.

Yet, beneath the laughter lingered an unshakable feeling—like a storm cloud gathering on the horizon. I couldn't ignore the sense of urgency that had settled deep in my chest. This journey was about more than treasure; it felt as though we were on the brink of awakening something that had long been buried.

That evening, after Gavin had left, I found myself alone in the kitchen, the faint sounds of the ocean crashing against the shore filtering through the open window. The journal lay before me, each word whispering secrets that felt both inviting and ominous. I felt a pull, a need to connect with the stories woven into its pages, as though they were reaching out to me.

As I leafed through the pages, one entry caught my attention, the ink darker and fresher than the others. It spoke of a storm—an impending tempest that would consume the ship and its crew. I could almost hear the thunder rumbling in the distance, echoing the fears lurking in the corners of my mind.

"Something isn't right," I muttered to myself, the words heavy with foreboding. The journal had felt like a key, but now it felt more like a warning.

Just then, my phone buzzed, shattering the silence. It was a message from Gavin: "Meet me at the cliffs at dawn. I think I found something."

A chill raced down my spine, anticipation mixing with dread. I texted back, "What did you find?" but he didn't respond. The unease wrapped around me like a tight coil, and I spent the night tossing and turning, the weight of the ocean's mysteries heavy on my mind.

Dawn broke in a wash of golden light, the sky painted in hues of pink and orange. I could feel the excitement and anxiety coursing through me as I pulled on my wetsuit, its tight embrace both comforting and claustrophobic. The cliffs loomed ahead, their rugged beauty casting long shadows over the sandy shore.

As I reached the meeting point, I spotted Gavin pacing back and forth, his brow furrowed in concentration. "You're late!" he exclaimed, his voice tinged with urgency. "You won't believe what I found. It's incredible!"

"What is it?" I asked, unable to hide my eagerness as I closed the distance between us.

He held up a small, intricately carved figurine, glistening in the early light. "I found this in the sand near the cliff's edge. It looks just like one of the symbols from the journal!"

I took it from him, examining the delicate etchings that mirrored the designs we had seen in the wreck. "This is amazing! It's like a piece of the puzzle falling into place."

"Exactly! But here's the catch," Gavin said, his eyes darkening with concern. "The moment I picked it up, I felt... strange. Like something shifted in the air. It was as if the ocean itself was watching us."

My stomach dropped. "What do you mean 'watching us'?"

He hesitated, looking out toward the water, a furrow forming on his brow. "I don't know how to explain it, but it felt like the ocean was reacting, like it was alive and aware."

"Okay, that's unsettling," I said, my heart pounding in my chest. "Are you sure you want to dive today?"

He met my gaze, determination flickering in his eyes. "We have to. If this figurine means something, we need to find out what. There's too much at stake now."

The adrenaline surged through me, battling with the unease tightening in my chest. "Alright, let's do this. But let's be careful. I'm not keen on any angry ocean spirits chasing us today."

With a shared look of resolve, we geared up once more, the waves crashing in anticipation. As we prepared to dive, a distant rumble echoed from the depths, a sound that sent shivers down my spine. The ocean churned beneath us, its surface shimmering with an ominous energy that prickled at the back of my mind.

We slipped into the water, the coolness enveloping us like a shroud, and as we descended, the light above faded, giving way to the dark embrace of the ocean. The pressure built around me, but the thrill of discovery overshadowed the unease.

Gavin signaled to follow him as we navigated back toward the shipwreck. The underwater world came alive around us, the fish swirling in vibrant colors, a stark contrast to the foreboding sensations creeping in from the edges of our adventure.

As we reached the wreck, the journal's symbols danced in my mind, guiding us deeper into the darkness. I could feel the weight of the figurine in my pocket, a heavy reminder of the stakes we were playing for.

But just as we were about to enter the wreck, a shadow loomed ahead, dark and ominous. My heart raced, a primal instinct screaming at me to turn back. Gavin glanced at me, eyes wide behind his mask, but before we could react, the water around us stirred violently. The ocean erupted with force, and in that moment, I understood—we weren't just exploring history; we were awakening something long buried, something that had been waiting for this very moment.

The shadows deepened, and as I struggled to regain my bearings, the realization hit me: the real mystery was just beginning, and we were far from prepared for what lay ahead. The darkness rushed toward us, and as the world blurred into chaos, I could only hope that we hadn't gone too far to turn back.

Chapter 13: Echoes of the Past

The salty breeze whipped through my hair, carrying with it the scent of brine and adventure as we stumbled onto the sun-bleached shore. The weight of the ocean's depths hung on our clothes like a second skin, each droplet shimmering in the golden light. My heart raced, not just from the thrill of discovery but from the sheer audacity of what we had unearthed. Clutching the weathered journal, its spine cracked and pages curling like the petals of an old flower, I felt an electric jolt of curiosity course through me. This wasn't just paper and ink; it was a bridge to a time long past, a time that had clearly been shrouded in shadows.

My best friend, Mia, sat cross-legged beside me, her eyes wide with a mix of apprehension and excitement. "Are you really going to read that thing?" she asked, arching an eyebrow playfully, the sunlight catching the golden strands of her hair. "What if it's cursed? You know how towns like this have a knack for drama."

"Cursed? Oh please, Mia, if it were cursed, I'd have felt it the moment I picked it up." I rolled my eyes, though a shiver ran down my spine. The legends surrounding Misty Shores were as thick as the fog that often draped over its cliffs. "Besides, I can't help but be intrigued. Who wouldn't want a little drama?"

With a smirk, I opened the journal, its scent a mix of salt and aged paper, an aroma that evoked the whispers of the past. The first entry was written in a careful hand, the letters flowing like the gentle waves that lapped at our feet. As I read aloud, the world around us faded, the rhythmic crash of the ocean providing a haunting backdrop.

"July 12, 1892," I began, my voice weaving through the air like a spell. "The darkness creeps in with the tide. The townsfolk speak in hushed tones, their eyes darting as if the shadows hold ears. I have seen the changes—the land, once bountiful, now lies cursed beneath a shroud of despair."

Mia leaned closer, her face pale but intrigued. "This is like something straight out of a gothic novel," she whispered, her enthusiasm bubbling beneath the surface.

"Just wait," I urged, flipping to the next page, my fingers trembling slightly. "It gets better."

"August 1, 1892," I continued, my voice steady. "Tonight, we gather at the old stone circle. They say the sacrifices must be made—offerings to the spirits who guard the sea. A blood pact must be formed."

Mia gasped, her eyes widening. "Sacrifices? Like, real ones? What, did they think the ocean would take them back if they threw a few goats in?"

"Looks like it. And it seems love doesn't escape the grip of darkness either," I said, flipping the pages as my pulse quickened with every word I spoke. "I found this next part especially gripping."

"Please, enlighten me!" Mia's tone dripped with mock seriousness, though she was leaning in closer, eager to hear more.

"August 15, 1892. The night was full of whispers. Clara, my beloved, slipped through the shadows, torn between loyalty to our people and her heart. She would pay the price to save me from the depths. In the light of the moon, we swore our love would transcend the darkness. But could love defy the forces that sought to claim us?"

I paused, the weight of the words hanging in the air. The journal was filled with an intensity that mirrored the crashing waves, each sentence punctuated by emotion, by a sense of foreboding that wrapped around us like a thick fog.

"Clara," Mia mused, biting her lip thoughtfully. "What a name. She sounds like someone who wouldn't take the darkness lying down."

"Or maybe someone who was foolish enough to challenge it," I replied, flipping another page. "She was brave but perhaps naïve. Just like us, diving into the unknown."

Mia chuckled softly, the sound like a gentle ripple against the roar of the sea. "I'm not naïve, just adventurous. There's a difference."

I laughed, her spirit infectious. But as I continued reading, the tone shifted. The entries became more frantic, the ink smudged as if the writer had penned them in haste. "September 3, 1892. Clara is gone. They took her to the stone circle. I cannot let her fate be sealed by the darkness. The pact will be broken, and I shall bring her back. I swear it."

"Wait, hold on," Mia interrupted, her brow furrowed. "What if he didn't bring her back? What if...?"

Her voice trailed off, but the implication lingered in the air, heavy and unsettling. My heart raced as I turned to the final entry, my eyes darting across the fading ink.

"September 15, 1892. I stand at the edge of the sea, the waves crashing with a ferocity that echoes my own. The darkness calls for my sacrifice. I will not go quietly, not while I still breathe her name."

With a final, breathless exhalation, I closed the journal, the finality of the words pressing against my chest like a weight I couldn't shake. "He didn't make it back, did he?" I murmured, staring out at the turbulent ocean, its surface roiling like the emotions within me.

Mia looked at me, her eyes bright with a mix of fear and fascination. "This is not just a story, is it? This feels... real."

I nodded slowly, my heart thumping in rhythm with the waves. We had stepped into a tale far beyond our expectations, one that seemed to stretch into the very marrow of Misty Shores. Each word resonated within me, echoing the struggles of love and sacrifice that were not bound by time, yet shaped by it.

As the sun dipped below the horizon, painting the sky in hues of violet and gold, I realized that we had not just uncovered a story;

we had unearthed a legacy, a haunting melody that would linger long after the tide had washed it away. The echoes of the past wrapped around us like a shroud, whispering secrets that dared us to dive deeper into the darkness that loomed just beneath the surface.

The sun dipped below the horizon, casting long shadows that danced on the sand like specters from the past. I closed the journal, its pages whispering of an era steeped in both dread and devotion. "What if," I began, my mind racing with the possibilities, "the dark forces still linger? What if they're not just tales spun to frighten children at bedtime?"

Mia, ever the skeptic, tilted her head. "You're not seriously considering that we might have awakened something, are you? Like some sort of supernatural sea monster?" She laughed lightly, but her eyes glimmered with an edge of concern, revealing a hint of the apprehension gnawing at her.

"Oh please," I shot back, nudging her playfully with my shoulder. "If I wanted to deal with monsters, I'd just confront my ex."

We shared a laugh, the sound mingling with the gentle surf, yet a tangible tension lingered. I could sense it in the air, like the moment before a storm. With the journal cradled in my lap, I peered into the depths of the ocean, its dark expanse mirroring the mysteries that lay ahead.

"Still, what if there's truth buried in those pages?" I mused aloud. "What if Clara and her lover weren't just figments of some long-lost imagination? What if they're part of a cycle that's repeating?"

"Let's not get dramatic," Mia replied, shaking her head but not entirely dismissing the notion. "It's a journal, not a prophecy. But—" She hesitated, her gaze flitting to the horizon. "But I can't shake the feeling that we're somehow tied to all this."

"Maybe we are," I said, my voice low, as if admitting a secret. "Maybe this is our chance to rewrite their story."

Mia raised an eyebrow, a mixture of intrigue and skepticism swirling in her expression. "Rewrite? Or just dig ourselves into a deeper hole?"

"Well, either way, it's bound to be more interesting than our usual Friday night binge-watching escapades," I retorted, my heart pounding with a mix of excitement and trepidation.

With a newfound determination, I stood, brushing sand off my legs. "We need to find out more. This town—its history—is calling us."

"Are you sure we're ready for that?" she asked, her voice tinged with concern, yet there was a spark of adventure in her eyes that I couldn't ignore.

"Ready or not, here we go," I declared, taking the first steps back toward the cliffs that loomed above us, a silent witness to all that had transpired in Misty Shores.

The path wound steeply up the rocks, twisting and turning until we reached the ancient stone circle where the journal had spoken of sacrifices. The stones stood like weathered guardians, their surfaces etched with age-old symbols that seemed to pulse with energy under the fading light. I could almost hear the echoes of whispered prayers and desperate pleas, a haunting reminder of lives forever intertwined with the whims of fate.

"What do you think happens here?" Mia asked, her voice barely above a whisper, as if speaking too loudly would shatter the solemnity of the place.

"I think it's where love was tested against the tides of fear," I replied, brushing my fingers over the cool, rough surface of a stone. "Where the courage to defy darkness was measured in blood and tears."

Mia stepped closer, her eyes wide, as if trying to unlock the secrets held within the circle. "Do you feel that?" she asked, her breath catching.

"What?"

"It's like... a pulse. A heartbeat."

I closed my eyes, straining to hear the rhythm of the earth beneath me. It was faint but undeniably present, a connection that bound us to something far greater than ourselves. "You're right," I said slowly. "It's like we're standing on the edge of a vast history. But what does it mean for us?"

"Maybe it means we need to dig deeper," Mia suggested, her voice filled with determination. "Let's find out what happened to Clara and her lover."

"Agreed," I replied, glancing around the clearing, my heart pounding with anticipation. "But we should be careful. If the stories are true, we might not be the only ones drawn to this place."

Just as I finished speaking, a chill swept through the air, raising the hairs on my arms. We both froze, exchanging uneasy glances. The wind howled, carrying with it the distant sounds of crashing waves, but there was something else beneath it—a low, rhythmic thrum that felt unsettlingly alive.

"What was that?" Mia asked, her voice barely above a whisper.

"I don't know," I admitted, my stomach knotting. "But we need to stay alert."

As we searched for clues, the fading light cast long shadows across the stones, transforming the circle into an ethereal world suspended between the past and present. The air crackled with tension, as if we were intruders in a sacred space where the line between the living and the dead blurred.

Mia knelt beside a patch of earth, brushing away dirt to reveal what appeared to be a shard of pottery, its surface painted with intricate designs. "Look at this!" she exclaimed, excitement lighting up her features. "This must be from the time of Clara and her lover!"

I leaned closer, studying the piece. "It's beautiful," I murmured, tracing the delicate patterns with my fingertip. "It's like a fragment of their world, a reminder that they existed, that they loved."

"Or a warning," Mia countered, glancing around the circle. "What if we're not supposed to be here?"

"Maybe," I replied, the weight of her words settling over me. "But then again, maybe we're here for a reason."

Before we could ponder further, a sudden rustle broke through the stillness, a sharp sound that cut through the air like a knife. We both whipped around, eyes wide, heartbeats drumming in sync with the unsettling rhythm that pulsed around us.

"Did you hear that?" Mia whispered, her face pale.

"Yeah," I said, scanning the perimeter of the stone circle. "What was it?"

A figure emerged from the shadows, a silhouette framed by the encroaching darkness. I squinted, straining to make out the details, but the face remained obscured, hidden by the gathering gloom.

"Who's there?" I called, my voice steady despite the apprehension gnawing at my insides.

The figure paused, a tension vibrating in the air. "You shouldn't be here," a low voice warned, dripping with an authority that sent chills down my spine.

"Neither should you," I shot back, my bravado surprising even me.

"Leave while you still can."

And just like that, the warning hung between us, an unspoken threat that suggested we were not only trespassing in the realm of the past but dangerously close to awakening something best left sleeping.

The figure stood just beyond the flickering light of the fading day, a shadow woven into the fabric of the encroaching night. The gravelly voice carried an unmistakable weight, as though it held the burden of secrets long hidden. My heart raced as I exchanged glances with Mia, her expression a blend of fear and fierce curiosity.

"Who are you?" I called again, my voice sharper this time, echoing off the ancient stones that seemed to lean in closer, eager to eavesdrop on our confrontation.

"Someone who knows this place better than you ever will," the figure replied, stepping closer, revealing a rugged silhouette. A tangle of dark hair framed a face that was both captivating and unsettling, shadowed but familiar. "You shouldn't have come here. It's not safe."

"Since when has 'not safe' ever stopped us?" I shot back, attempting to keep my tone light even as my insides twisted. "You sound like our mothers."

Mia snickered, breaking the tension momentarily, but I couldn't shake the feeling that we were on the precipice of something far darker than a typical adventure.

"What do you know about this place?" Mia asked, stepping closer to me, as if the strength of our friendship could fend off whatever menace lurked in the dark.

The stranger sighed, a sound heavy with a mix of resignation and pity. "I know that every generation thinks they can outrun the past, but it always catches up. You're not the first to seek answers here, and you won't be the last."

My mind raced. "What do you mean?"

"You'll understand when it's too late," he replied cryptically, his eyes narrowing as he scanned the horizon. The shadows deepened around us, the air thickening with an unseen tension that felt like static before a storm.

"Right, because ominous warnings are always the hallmark of a good time," I quipped, struggling to keep my voice steady. "What are you, the town's ghostly guardian?"

"Something like that," he said, a flicker of amusement crossing his lips, though it quickly faded. "You need to leave. This place isn't what it seems. The ocean has ears, and it remembers."

"Yeah, well, we're not the type to back down just because you give us a spooky warning," I said defiantly, crossing my arms, though doubt gnawed at my resolve.

Mia stepped forward, her curiosity unquenchable. "What happened to Clara? What's the real story?"

At the mention of Clara, a shadow flickered across the stranger's face, as if her name stirred memories best left undisturbed. "You really don't know what you're asking, do you? Some stories are better left buried."

"Too late for that," I interjected, unwilling to let him dismiss us. "We've already dug up one story; what's one more?"

"Fine," he snapped, the tension between us palpable, crackling like the air before lightning strikes. "But don't say I didn't warn you." He took a deep breath, as if bracing himself against the weight of a thousand untold secrets. "Clara was meant to be a sacrifice. A means to an end. The town has always believed that appeasing the darkness would keep it at bay, but it only grew stronger."

My heart sank at the gravity of his words. "You mean they offered her up? Just like that?"

"Desperation makes people do terrible things," he said quietly, glancing away, his expression pained. "Her love defied the odds, but in the end, love wasn't enough. She was taken, and the darkness claimed her. The town believed it had sealed the deal, that the ocean would be satisfied, but it only served to awaken something far worse."

"And what was that?" I pressed, feeling the chill of dread creep down my spine.

"The cycle of sacrifice never ends," he replied, his voice low, almost a whisper. "You might think you can break it, but it will always find a way to reclaim what's owed."

"What does that mean for us?" Mia asked, her eyes wide.

"Everything," he said, and in that moment, the shadows around us seemed to pulse, alive with an ancient energy that pressed in on us from all sides. "If you're here, it means you've been chosen."

"Chosen?" I echoed, incredulous. "Chosen for what? A misguided attempt at historical reenactment?"

"No," he said, shaking his head, his voice suddenly serious. "Chosen to either end it or become part of the story. And trust me, it's not as glamorous as it sounds."

Before I could respond, the earth beneath our feet trembled, a low rumble that echoed through the stones, vibrating in my bones. Mia grabbed my arm, her grip vice-like, as we both stared in horror.

"What the hell is happening?" she shouted over the rising cacophony.

"It's the town's reckoning," the stranger said, his eyes wide with urgency. "You need to get out of here!"

But before we could move, a sharp crack sounded above us, and I looked up just in time to see one of the ancient stones wobbling precariously, as if it had awakened from centuries of slumber, angry and restless.

"Run!" I yelled, pulling Mia with me as the stone toppled, crashing down where we had just stood. We sprinted away from the circle, adrenaline coursing through my veins.

The wind howled, an otherworldly scream that echoed through the trees, and I could feel the very fabric of the air shifting, as if something unseen was pushing back against us, wanting to drag us down into the depths of the ocean.

"Why is this happening?" Mia panted, fear threading through her voice as we raced down the path.

"I don't know!" I gasped, dodging another falling stone. "But we can't stop now!"

As we reached the edge of the cliff, my heart raced with a mix of panic and exhilaration. The waves below roared, foaming with a wild energy that matched the chaos in our hearts. I glanced back at the figure, still standing in the stone circle, his face now a mask of grim determination.

"Don't look back!" he shouted, the wind carrying his voice like a warning. "The past doesn't want to be disturbed!"

And then, just as the last rays of sunlight vanished, plunging us into darkness, the ocean surged upward, a colossal wave rearing back, poised to crash down upon us. Time stretched, and for a fleeting moment, I felt suspended between the echoes of the past and the uncertainty of our future.

"Julia!" Mia screamed, and the sound of my name cut through the chaos like a knife.

In that instant, I made my choice. I stepped forward, heart pounding in rhythm with the ocean, ready to confront whatever lay ahead. But as the wave broke, cascading toward us with the force of a thousand storms, I knew that this was only the beginning of a much darker story.

Chapter 14: Unraveled Threads

The musty air of the town library wrapped around me like a cozy quilt, a stark contrast to the chill of the revelations Gavin and I had unearthed. Wooden shelves towered overhead, laden with tomes that whispered secrets of centuries past, their spines cracked and dusty, as if each held a memory waiting to be unfurled. I stepped deeper into the labyrinth of knowledge, the faint glow of the overhead lights casting long shadows that danced along the walls. Each step echoed, mingling with the soft rustle of pages, creating a symphony of suspense that quickened my heartbeat.

Gavin lingered just behind me, his presence a steady anchor in the storm of uncertainty swirling in my mind. He was a force of nature, all rugged charm and quiet intensity, his brows knitted in concentration as he studied the faded photographs littered across the table. My fingers grazed the spines of the books, tracing the letters that had endured the passage of time, each title a tantalizing invitation to explore further. I felt the weight of history around us, the ghosts of those who had come before hovering just out of sight, urging me to uncover their truths.

"Look at this one," Gavin called softly, his voice low but charged with excitement. He held up a photograph that looked like it had been taken in a different century. A group of townsfolk posed stiffly, smiles frozen on their faces, their eyes reflecting a shared burden that seemed to transcend time. "What do you think they were hiding?"

I leaned closer, peering at the faces in the image, searching for clues in their expressions. "Maybe the same thing we are," I mused, my gaze landing on a woman with deep-set eyes and a familiar tilt to her chin. "She looks like me," I added, barely above a whisper.

Gavin shifted beside me, the warmth of his arm brushing against mine, sending an unexpected jolt through my core. "You're right. It's uncanny." His eyes narrowed slightly as he studied the photo. "If she was involved in the pact, maybe there's more to her story. What if your connection to this place runs deeper than we thought?"

The thought sent a thrill of adrenaline coursing through my veins. As I pulled the photograph closer, I could almost feel the woman's spirit rising from the pages, urging me to listen to her silent screams. "We need to find out who she is," I declared, my resolve strengthening. The path ahead was tangled, but I could no longer ignore the signs that intertwined my fate with the history of this town.

The air shifted, a whisper of something dark brushing against the edges of my consciousness. "What if the mayor knows more?" Gavin proposed, his voice laced with a hint of mischief. "He's been acting shady lately, and this whole pact thing could be his way of keeping a tight grip on the town. Maybe he's protecting his own interests."

I couldn't shake the feeling that we were onto something big, a web of deceit that stretched far beyond what we could see. "Let's not waste time," I said, my heart pounding with urgency. "We need to talk to him, find out what he's hiding. And I want to learn more about her."

The plan was reckless, but it thrummed with the kind of electricity that made my skin prickle with excitement. Gavin met my gaze, a spark of understanding passing between us. There was something intoxicating about this journey we were on, a dance on the edge of danger that drew us closer together.

As we made our way to City Hall, the streets felt alive with tension, the fading light casting long shadows that twisted and turned like the secrets we were chasing. The smell of damp earth mingled with the sweet scent of late-blooming flowers, creating a strange harmony that underscored the turmoil brewing in my gut. "You think he'll even see us?" I asked, trying to mask the uncertainty in my voice.

"He'll see us," Gavin replied, confidence radiating from him like the warmth of the sun. "We'll make him see us."

As we approached the imposing brick building, its façade loomed above us, a reminder of the authority it held. The air thickened with anticipation, and I found myself drawing in a deep breath, my lungs filling with the weight of what lay ahead. Gavin pushed open the heavy door, and the hinges creaked ominously, as if the building itself were groaning in protest.

Inside, the dimly lit foyer was sparsely decorated, a stark contrast to the opulence one might expect from a mayor's office. A receptionist glanced up, her expression a mix of curiosity and annoyance, as if we were intruders in her quiet sanctuary.

"We need to see Mayor Callahan," I stated, surprising myself with the firmness of my voice.

Her brow arched, skepticism dripping from her tone. "Do you have an appointment?"

I opened my mouth to respond but was cut off by Gavin. "We don't need an appointment. This is urgent."

A silence fell, heavy and expectant, before the receptionist sighed and picked up the phone, relaying our request in a tone that suggested we were more annoyance than necessity. I leaned against the counter, my heart racing as I exchanged glances with Gavin. He gave me a subtle nod, a promise that we were in this together, no matter what awaited us on the other side of that door.

Minutes felt like hours as we waited, the tension coiling tighter in the air, a prelude to the storm we were about to unleash. Finally, the receptionist hung up and gestured for us to enter, her expression a blend of reluctance and resignation.

"Good luck," she muttered under her breath as we crossed the threshold into the mayor's office. The room was plush but sterile, the walls adorned with photographs of Callahan shaking hands with various dignitaries. I could feel the weight of his gaze as he looked up from behind a grand mahogany desk, a mixture of surprise and irritation crossing his features.

"What is this about?" he demanded, his voice a low growl that hinted at the power he wielded.

I took a deep breath, ready to unleash the truth. This was it—the moment we had been waiting for, the unraveling of threads that had bound this town in secrecy for far too long. "We know about the pact, Mayor Callahan," I said, my voice steady, unwavering. "And we know you're involved."

His expression shifted, a flicker of something akin to fear flashing across his face before it was masked by a veneer of indifference. "You don't know what you're talking about."

But I could see it—the cracks in his facade, the underlying tension that betrayed his calm exterior. The air grew electric with the potential for revelation, and I could almost taste the truth on the tip of my tongue.

The mayor's office felt like stepping into a lion's den, each detail designed to inspire both respect and trepidation. From the ornate carvings on the desk to the plush, maroon chairs that practically screamed authority, everything in the room bore the weight of power. I swallowed hard, the air thick with tension as Mayor Callahan's icy demeanor washed over us like a wave, momentarily stifling my resolve. Gavin shifted beside me, his presence a reassuring balm against the suffocating atmosphere.

"You don't know what you're talking about," the mayor repeated, but there was a hint of uncertainty in his voice, a quiver that betrayed the bravado he was attempting to project.

"Oh, I'm pretty sure we do," I replied, my tone light, as if we were discussing the weather rather than the dark undertones of a town shrouded in secrecy. "There's this lovely little journal," I continued, the corners of my mouth twitching with the thrill of confrontation, "filled with delightful stories of a pact and some rather unsettling symbols. Care to enlighten us?"

His steely eyes narrowed, and the moment stretched like taffy, thick with unspoken threats. The silence was pregnant with possibilities, and I could feel Gavin's muscles tense beside me, ready to spring into action if necessary. I leaned forward slightly, trying to pierce through his façade. "You see, I believe our interests align here. The town deserves to know the truth, don't you think?"

"Align?" he scoffed, dismissing my words as if they were a pesky fly buzzing in his ear. "Your naivete is astonishing. This town's history is nothing but a collection of myths and legends. You're chasing shadows, and I won't have you dragging others down this rabbit hole with you."

Chasing shadows. The phrase echoed in my mind, rattling around like loose change. How easy it would be to dismiss what lay beneath the surface, to turn away from the darkness creeping in from the edges. But I wouldn't be so easily deterred. "This isn't just folklore, Mayor. Lives are at stake—my life, my family's life," I countered, the urgency in my voice rising like a tide. "We need to understand what happened to those who came before us, to learn from their mistakes."

The mayor's expression hardened, but I could see the gears turning behind his eyes. Perhaps the shadows I was chasing were more tangible than he wished to admit. "You're playing a dangerous game," he warned, a thread of menace woven into his tone. "You have no idea what you're up against."

"Then enlighten me," I challenged, a spark of defiance igniting within me. "You're the one with the keys to the past, aren't you? The one with all the answers?"

He leaned back in his chair, his posture relaxed yet predatory, as if he were sizing me up like a cat observing a mouse. "You really think you can handle the truth? There's a reason these stories are buried. They're not pretty."

Gavin stepped forward, his presence amplifying the tension in the room. "We're not afraid of the truth, Callahan. What we fear is your silence." His voice was steady, and I marveled at how he seemed to draw strength from my own resolve, a partner in this unfolding drama.

A flicker of surprise crossed the mayor's face, and for a fleeting moment, I could see the wall cracking, a chink in his armor revealing a glimpse of vulnerability. "You should," he finally said, his voice low and threatening. "There are some things that can't be undone once you've unearthed them."

With those words hanging heavily in the air, I felt a shiver dance down my spine, a warning that whatever lay ahead would be more dangerous than I had anticipated. "So, you admit it," I said, my tone sharp. "There is a truth to uncover. You're scared of it, aren't you?"

"Fear is an overrated emotion," he retorted, but his eyes betrayed him, darting to the window, as if searching for an escape. "What you're meddling with is far beyond your comprehension."

Gavin and I exchanged a glance, the silent communication passing between us solidifying our shared purpose. "We'll decide what we can comprehend," I said, my voice firm, even as doubt began to creep in around the edges of my confidence. "You're the one standing in the way of progress. What are you hiding, Mayor?"

Callahan sighed, rubbing a hand across his temples as if to ward off a headache. "You think you can just walk in here, demand answers, and leave unscathed? You have no idea of the consequences that come with prying into things that are best left buried."

"Then let's discuss the consequences together," I pressed, trying to match my determination to his imposing presence. "Because I refuse to leave this office until I know the truth."

He studied me, the tension palpable, and for a heartbeat, I thought I saw a flicker of respect cross his face. "You're more tenacious than I anticipated," he admitted reluctantly. "But know this: your quest for truth could cost you dearly."

"I'm already in too deep," I replied, the weight of my family's legacy pressing down on me like an anchor. "And it's not just about me anymore. There are others who deserve to know the truth—those who have been affected by this pact, this silence. The town deserves more than whispers and shadows."

Callahan leaned forward, his steely gaze boring into mine. "Fine. If you must know, there are fragments of truth hidden in our past, some intertwined with my own family history. But this isn't a game, and it's certainly not a fairy tale. The truth is a dangerous thing to wield."

Gavin placed a hand on my shoulder, grounding me amidst the swirling storm of revelations. "We can handle it," he assured, his voice a steadying force. "We're prepared for whatever comes next."

"Very well," the mayor said, his voice suddenly resigned, as if he were a man backing into a corner, ready to show his cards. "You want to know about the pact? You'll need more than just curiosity. You'll need the heart to face what you find, and I warn you, it won't be pretty."

As the words hung in the air like a storm cloud ready to burst, I felt the thrill of dread and anticipation curling around my heart. We were on the precipice of something monumental, the air electric with the promise of discovery. I could sense that our lives would never be the same again, and as daunting as that thought was, a small part of me was exhilarated. I was finally unearthing the truth that had been buried too long, and alongside Gavin, I was ready to face whatever came next, no matter the cost.

"Let's get to it then," I said, summoning the courage that surged within me. "Tell us everything."

The mayor's gaze shifted momentarily, and in that brief flicker of vulnerability, I seized the opportunity, plunging deeper into the heart of the matter. "You mentioned your family's history is intertwined with the pact," I prompted, my voice steady, but inside, a storm of emotions swirled. "What exactly does that mean?"

Callahan leaned back, folding his arms, a practiced gesture that exuded control. "It means my family has carried the burden of that pact for generations, a legacy woven into the fabric of this town's existence," he said, his voice low and gravelly, each word heavy with significance. "You're not just stirring up old ghosts; you're threatening to unravel the very foundation of this place."

"Why would you want to protect a foundation built on deception?" Gavin interjected, his voice steady, but there was an edge that suggested he was ready for whatever Callahan might throw our way. "If there are lies at the core, don't you owe it to the town to set the record straight?"

The mayor's lips twisted into a grimace, as if the very thought of exposing the truth tasted bitter on his tongue. "You think you understand the stakes? The town has thrived on its secrets for too long. Uncovering the truth might unleash chaos. People fear what they don't understand."

"Fear doesn't have to dictate how we live," I shot back, feeling the adrenaline surge through my veins. "And if this town is living in the dark, then it's time for a little illumination."

He stared at me, calculating, as if trying to gauge whether I had the resolve to handle the storm that was about to break. "Fine," he finally said, letting out a breath that seemed to weigh a ton. "You want the truth? It began over a century ago, when the town was just a fledgling settlement. A group of founders, desperate to ensure prosperity and security, struck a pact with forces beyond their comprehension."

"Like some sort of dark magic?" Gavin quipped, raising an eyebrow, but there was a seriousness in his tone that underscored the gravity of Callahan's admission.

The mayor shot him a warning look before continuing. "You could call it that. They made sacrifices—offers of loyalty and blood in exchange for protection and wealth. It worked, for a time, until the cost became too high. The pact demanded more than they could give, leading to tragedies that reverberate to this day."

A chill crept down my spine as the implications began to sink in. "Tragedies? What kind of tragedies?"

"People vanished," Callahan admitted, his voice barely above a whisper, as if the very act of speaking it would summon the specters of the past. "Those who tried to break the pact, or those who simply knew too much. They were never seen again, their families left to mourn without closure."

Gavin shifted slightly, his brow furrowing. "And you're willing to let this continue? To let it haunt generations?"

"It's not that simple," Callahan snapped, frustration flashing across his face. "I am not the enemy here. I'm trying to protect this town from itself. You two think you can just waltz in and change things? You have no idea what you're dealing with!"

"And yet, here we are," I said, determination coursing through my veins. "It's not just about us; it's about everyone who has suffered because of this pact. We deserve to know the truth, even if it's messy. Especially if it's messy."

Callahan seemed to wrestle with his thoughts, the weight of history pressing down on him. "Very well. But understand this: there are consequences. The deeper you dig, the more you risk losing."

"We're already lost," I replied, the words escaping before I could stop them. "If uncovering the truth is the only way to reclaim our lives, then we're all in."

For a moment, silence enveloped us, the air thick with unspoken agreements and the shared weight of a past we were determined to unravel. The mayor's eyes narrowed, and I could sense the battle waging within him—an internal struggle between loyalty to the town and a desire for truth.

"Then we need to go to the place where it all began," he finally said, the gravity of his words hitting me like a physical blow. "The old church. It's where the pact was first made, and it's where you'll find the answers you seek."

"The church?" Gavin asked, skepticism mingling with intrigue. "Isn't it abandoned?"

"It is, but it still holds the remnants of that dark history," Callahan replied, a note of reluctance creeping into his voice. "The symbols, the writings...they're all there. But be warned: not everything can be explained through logic. Some truths can only be felt."

"What do you mean?" I pressed, the tension in my chest tightening.

"There are those who guard the secrets of the past," he said, his voice lowering as if conspirators might be lurking in the shadows. "And they won't take kindly to trespassers. You must be prepared for anything."

Gavin and I exchanged glances, a silent agreement forming between us. We had come this far; turning back now wasn't an option. "We'll go," Gavin said resolutely, the determination in his voice echoing my own resolve.

"Just remember," Callahan cautioned, "the line between truth and myth is thin, and you may not like what you find. Be careful what you wish for."

With a nod, we exited the mayor's office, the oppressive atmosphere lifting slightly as we stepped back into the hallway. The air felt charged with anticipation, as if the town itself were holding its breath, waiting for us to take the next step.

"Did he mean what he said about the guardians?" I asked, my heart pounding with a mix of excitement and dread. "What kind of guardians?"

"I don't know," Gavin replied, glancing back toward the office door as if expecting Callahan to emerge and stop us. "But we need to prepare. Whatever lies in that church isn't going to just roll over and tell us its secrets."

The sun dipped below the horizon as we walked, the sky streaked with hues of purple and gold, casting an ethereal glow over the town. Shadows danced in the fading light, whispering stories of what lay ahead. The church stood at the edge of town, a relic from another time, its steeple piercing the sky like a finger pointing to the heavens—or perhaps, to the past.

"Are you ready?" Gavin asked, his voice low, filled with a mix of excitement and trepidation.

I took a deep breath, the weight of our mission settling heavily on my shoulders. "I've never been more ready for anything in my life."

As we approached the church, an ominous silence enveloped us. The doors, heavy and weathered, creaked as I pushed them open, revealing a cavernous interior cloaked in darkness. Dust motes floated through the air like tiny ghosts, and the musty scent of old wood and forgotten prayers enveloped us.

"Welcome home," Gavin joked, a wry smile breaking through the tension, but the lightness of his words couldn't pierce the shroud of unease hanging over us.

We stepped inside, the echo of our footsteps swallowed by the silence. Shadows flickered along the walls, dancing as if they were alive, a reminder of the secrets buried within this sacred space. The air crackled with anticipation, and I could feel the pulse of history thrumming beneath my skin.

"Look," I said, pointing to the far wall where faded symbols glimmered faintly in the dim light. "Those must be the markings from the journal."

Gavin nodded, stepping closer to inspect the intricate designs etched into the stone. "It's hard to believe this place has been hidden away for so long. There's something almost...sacred about it."

"Or sinister," I countered, my voice barely above a whisper.

As we approached the wall, I noticed a flicker of movement in the corner of my eye. My heart raced as I turned, scanning the shadows for any sign of life. "Did you see that?" I asked, a tremor of fear creeping into my voice.

"See what?" Gavin replied, his expression shifting from curiosity to concern.

Before I could answer, the church doors slammed shut behind us with a deafening thud, the sound reverberating through the hollow space like a gunshot. Panic surged through my veins, and I spun to face the door, but it was as if an unseen force had sealed it shut.

"What the hell?" Gavin exclaimed, his eyes wide as he tested the handle, only to find it unyielding.

A low rumble echoed through the church, and the very air around us seemed to thicken. Shadows flickered and shifted, morphing into shapes that danced just beyond the periphery of my vision. My heart pounded in my chest, a primal beat of fear and adrenaline, as I turned back to Gavin, who was staring at the wall with a mixture of awe and dread.

"Did you feel that?" he asked, his voice barely above a whisper.

Before I could respond, the symbols on the wall began to glow, pulsating with an eerie light that illuminated the darkness around us. The air crackled with energy, and I felt a deep vibration resonate within my bones, as if the very essence of the church were awakening.

"Something's happening," I breathed, my voice trembling with anticipation.

The glow intensified, casting flickering shadows that danced wildly, and in that moment, I realized we were no longer alone. Figures began to emerge from the shadows, their faces obscured but their

Chapter 15: The Weight of Choices

The old church loomed before us like a relic from a forgotten age, its crumbling facade partially obscured by twisting vines that seemed to reach for the earth as if attempting to anchor themselves against the gusts of an unforgiving wind. A slate-gray sky cast a muted light over the structure, illuminating the shattered stained glass that still clung desperately to the wooden frames, resembling shards of a long-lost mosaic now reduced to scattered dreams. Each piece that flickered in the sparse light told stories, whispered secrets of weddings and baptisms, of community and belief, now dulled under layers of neglect.

Gavin's hand brushed against mine as we stepped over the threshold, the heavy wooden door creaking in protest, as if warning us to turn back. The chill inside was palpable, wrapping around me like a shroud. Dust motes danced in the air, swirling in the beams of dim light that filtered through the broken windows. The scent of damp wood and mildew hung heavily, a reminder of how time could claim even the most sacred spaces. As we moved further in, I could almost hear the echoes of laughter and the soft murmurs of prayers, weaving a tapestry of longing that enveloped us.

"Can you believe this place?" Gavin asked, his voice low, reverberating against the stone walls. I could see the way his brow furrowed, a mixture of fascination and sadness playing across his features. The man had a way of immersing himself in every moment, his enthusiasm for our little adventures infectious.

"It's haunting," I replied, my words barely breaking the stillness. I stepped forward, drawn to the altar at the front, its surface marred with age and neglect. The intricate carvings, once proud and detailed, were now obscured by layers of dust and decay. It felt like stepping into a world where time had ceased to matter, where the past lingered in the air, heavy with unfulfilled promises.

As I traced a finger along the altar's edge, a shiver coursed through me. The symbols etched into the worn wood mirrored those I had seen on the cliffs—a connection I couldn't ignore. It was as if the very essence of this place intertwined with the ominous feelings I had felt since arriving in town. "These markings... they're the same as the ones we found," I murmured, glancing back at Gavin, whose eyes sparkled with the thrill of discovery.

"Maybe this was a place of power for them," he speculated, stepping closer to me. His breath was warm against my cold skin, grounding me amidst the encroaching unease. "Like a shrine or a gathering place."

"Or a hiding spot," I countered, a wave of apprehension washing over me. It was strange, but I could almost hear the whispers of the townspeople, their fears and hesitations echoing through the ruins. They had turned their backs on this place, shrouding it in silence, and perhaps in doing so, they had allowed something darker to take root.

Just then, a sudden gust of wind rattled the broken windows, sending a cascade of dust swirling around us. I recoiled instinctively, and Gavin grabbed my arm, steadying me. "You okay?"

"Yeah, just... it's like this place has a heartbeat," I said, shaking off the unease. "I can feel it pulsing under my skin."

He raised an eyebrow, a teasing smile playing on his lips. "You've been reading too many ghost stories, haven't you?"

I scoffed, my heart racing for reasons I couldn't quite pinpoint. "Maybe it's not just stories. Maybe it's a warning."

With a determined breath, I stepped back towards the altar, drawn to its secrets. My fingers brushed against a rough-hewn stone nearby, and as I pressed against it, a low groan echoed through the church. My heart leaped, and I exchanged a glance with Gavin that spoke volumes of shared disbelief.

"Did you hear that?" he whispered, eyes wide.

"I did." I was almost afraid to breathe, the air thick with anticipation. What were we uncovering? It felt as though the church was alive, as if it bore witness to our every move. The thought sent chills down my spine, yet I felt an undeniable urge to uncover whatever lay hidden beneath its somber exterior.

"Maybe we should—"

"No." I interrupted him, the decision surging through me like an electric current. "We came here to find answers, and I won't back down now."

He nodded, a look of admiration flashing across his face. "Alright, lead the way, fearless leader."

I couldn't suppress a smile at his playful tone. With each step toward the altar, the weight of the moment pressed down on me. The air crackled with anticipation, and as I drew closer, the markings on the altar shimmered ever so slightly, catching my eye. They seemed to pulse, calling out to me, begging for recognition.

"What if it's a trap?" Gavin's voice broke through the silence, his playful demeanor replaced by concern.

"Then we'll spring it together," I replied, grinning back at him, trying to inject a semblance of humor into the tension that hung between us.

I pressed my palm against the cool wood, and a shudder coursed through me. The altar vibrated beneath my hand, sending ripples of energy up my arm. Suddenly, I felt a rush of memories flood my mind—visions of ceremonies long past, laughter, joy, and then an undercurrent of fear that left me breathless.

"We shouldn't be here," I gasped, the realization washing over me in a wave of urgency. "This place... it holds too much."

Gavin stepped back, his expression darkening. "What do you mean?"

Before I could respond, the air around us shifted, growing heavy with unspoken words and lingering shadows. The once-familiar surroundings of the church transformed, revealing fragments of its history—a flicker of candles, the rustling of ceremonial robes, the sound of laughter replaced by echoes of despair. Each vision spiraled into a haunting tableau, and the very fabric of this place tightened around me, leaving me gasping for breath as I grappled with the weight of the choices that had led us here.

The church seemed to pulsate with an energy all its own, the air thickening around us as the visions faded and the oppressive silence reigned once more. I leaned back, steadying myself against the altar as if its ancient wood could somehow absorb the turmoil churning inside me. Gavin stepped closer, his eyes searching mine, an unspoken question lingering in the space between us.

"What did you see?" he asked softly, his voice a soothing balm amidst the confusion.

I shook my head, trying to shake off the remnants of those haunting images. "It was... like stepping into someone else's nightmare," I admitted. "There were moments of happiness, but they were so quickly overshadowed by something darker. It's as if this place was a battleground of emotions."

"Sounds like a perfect backdrop for a horror movie," he replied, trying to inject a note of levity. His grin was infectious, a brief flicker of brightness in the dim light of the church. "Maybe we should start a film project."

"Right, because what every haunted church needs is a documentary crew," I shot back, unable to suppress a smile. The tension lightened slightly, but the weight of the atmosphere still pressed down on us like a heavy blanket.

"Seriously though, do you think those markings are part of a ritual? Like, maybe they sacrificed something?" His voice lowered, and the teasing glint in his eyes was replaced by a hint of genuine curiosity.

I considered his question, the fluttering in my stomach returning as I recalled the symbols. "It's possible. Or maybe they're meant to ward off something. It's hard to tell with places like this. Legends have a way of twisting the truth."

His brow furrowed, and he glanced around, as if the walls themselves might offer a confession. "You know, this isn't just a relic of the past. It's a part of the town's history. We need to figure out what it all means."

The urgency in his voice struck a chord within me. "Yes, but how? The townspeople seem content to ignore it, hoping it will disappear if they don't talk about it."

"They're scared," he said, running a hand through his hair in frustration. "And that fear has festered. If we dig too deep, we might unearth something that's better left buried."

"Like an ancient curse? Or perhaps a hidden treasure?" I teased, but the reality of our situation was becoming increasingly clear. The very air in the church seemed to thrum with the secrets of those who had come before us.

"Maybe it's both. A treasure cursed by secrets." His voice dropped to a conspiratorial whisper, and we both laughed, the sound echoing through the crumbling walls. But our amusement was short-lived, as the seriousness of our mission returned, settling around us like a fog.

"Let's search the place. Maybe we'll find something that ties it all together," I suggested, my resolve hardening.

"Together," he echoed, his tone matching mine, infused with determination.

We began to explore the dim recesses of the church, moving cautiously among the pews, their wood warped and splintered. Each creak beneath our feet sounded like a warning, as if the very structure was warning us against uncovering too much. Gavin pulled aside a tattered old hymn book lying open on the floor, its pages yellowed and brittle.

"Here's a fun little read," he quipped, holding it up. "'How to Summon a Demon: A Beginner's Guide.'"

"Just what I always wanted," I said, laughing as I nudged him with my shoulder. "I can see the bestseller list now."

"Don't laugh. You could be the next great horror author."

"Yeah, right. If this town has taught me anything, it's that horror stories aren't meant to be written—they're meant to be lived."

I moved toward a narrow doorway leading to a small room at the back, the frame sagging as if it were weary from holding the weight of the past. The door swung open with a hesitant creak, revealing a space filled with dust and shadows. Inside, the remnants of what looked like an old storage room spilled out—broken furniture, tattered cloths, and a single, solitary candle flickering weakly in the corner.

"Gavin, come here," I called, curiosity lacing my voice. I stepped further in, brushing aside cobwebs that hung like delicate lace curtains. The candle was unlike any I had seen, ornate and covered in intricate designs that echoed the symbols from the altar. "This is... strange."

He joined me, his eyes widening as he examined the candle. "This looks like it was used for something significant. A ritual, maybe?"

I nodded, entranced. "What if it was meant to seal something? Or perhaps to summon it?" My pulse quickened at the thought. The candle's wax, still slightly warm, suggested it had been lit not long ago. "We need to figure out why it's here."

Gavin reached for it, lifting it carefully from the dusty shelf. As he did, the air around us thickened, and a low hum vibrated through the room. I gasped, instinctively stepping back.

"Did you feel that?" I asked, my heart racing.

"Yeah. It's like the candle has its own... energy," he replied, his voice low.

Just then, the sound of footsteps echoed outside the church, drawing our attention. They were hurried, heavy—like a storm barreling toward us. My heart sank as the reality of being caught in this forsaken place hit me.

"Gavin, someone's coming!" I whispered urgently, panic rising within me.

He dropped the candle, and we quickly moved to the shadows, hearts pounding in unison. The footsteps grew louder, and as the door creaked open, the figure that entered seemed shrouded in darkness. I held my breath, every instinct telling me to retreat deeper into the shadows.

"Why do I feel like we're the main characters in a horror movie?" Gavin muttered under his breath, the humor a thin veneer over the tension crackling in the air.

"Because we are," I whispered back, my eyes glued to the figure emerging into the dim light. The person moved cautiously, their silhouette revealing nothing, just the glimmer of eyes scanning the room with palpable intent.

"Stay quiet," I urged, gripping Gavin's arm. The figure paused, a tense moment stretching between us as we held our breath, each heartbeat a drumbeat in the silence. Something in the air shifted, heavy with unspoken secrets, as if the very walls conspired to keep us safe from whatever shadows lurked beyond our vision.

I pressed back against the cool stone wall, heart racing as the figure stepped deeper into the church. The shadows danced across the room, twisting and writhing like serpents eager to swallow us whole. Gavin held his breath beside me, the tension thick enough to slice through. The figure was cloaked in a long, dark coat, the kind that seemed to swallow light rather than reflect it. A hood obscured their face, and for a moment, I felt a primal instinct to run. But curiosity, that persistent little gremlin, held me in place.

"Who's there?" the figure called out, voice echoing off the walls. It was low and gravelly, tinged with authority. I exchanged a glance with Gavin, his eyes wide with uncertainty.

"Great, we've stumbled into the lair of the town's resident ghost," I whispered, a nervous chuckle escaping my lips despite the gravity of the situation.

"Shhh!" Gavin hissed, eyes darting around, clearly weighing our options.

The figure turned, the hood falling slightly to reveal a sharp jawline and a pair of intense, piercing eyes that glimmered even in the dim light. There was something hauntingly familiar about them, an unsettling recognition that curled in my gut.

"Are you lost?" the figure asked, stepping closer. "This place isn't safe for you."

My heart raced as I tried to gauge their intentions. "Define 'safe,'" I muttered under my breath, half to myself, half to Gavin.

"Please," the figure continued, voice firm yet laced with a hint of concern. "You don't want to be here when it gets dark."

"We're not scared," Gavin shot back, and I couldn't help but admire his bravery, even if it bordered on reckless.

The figure chuckled softly, the sound almost disarming. "You should be. Darkness brings out things that are best left undisturbed."

"Thanks for the heads-up," I replied, stepping forward despite the warning bells ringing in my head. "But we're not here for a ghost tour. We're looking for answers."

The figure paused, eyes narrowing as if weighing my words. "Answers can be a heavy burden, you know. Sometimes it's better to let the past lie."

"Isn't that exactly what everyone in this town has been doing?" I shot back, my frustration bubbling to the surface. "Pretending it doesn't exist. That's why we came here."

The figure regarded me with a curious intensity. "And what makes you think you can handle the truth? People have tried before. They didn't fare well."

I opened my mouth to retort but faltered under the weight of their gaze. Gavin stepped in, his voice steady. "We're not afraid of the truth. We want to help—"

"Help?" The figure interrupted, disbelief etched across their features. "You're just kids playing in a haunted house. You don't understand the forces you're toying with."

I could feel my heart pounding against my ribcage, the tension rising like a storm about to break. "And what makes you the authority on this place?" I challenged, my pulse racing with each word. "You don't know us."

"You're right. I don't," they conceded, their tone shifting to something softer. "But I've seen too many lives lost to this place. It's a parasite, feeding on fear and ignorance. You two are mere snacks in its banquet."

The gravity of their words struck me, resonating in the hollow chambers of the old church. I exchanged a glance with Gavin, who was equally taken aback. "So, what are you saying?" I pressed, unwilling to let the conversation slip away.

"I'm saying," the figure said, stepping into the flickering light of the candle, "that there's more at play here than you realize. The markings you found, the candle, they are all pieces of a puzzle that no one wants to solve."

"Then help us solve it," Gavin urged, stepping forward. "If you know something, you need to tell us. We can't just walk away."

A flash of something—fear?—crossed the figure's face before they quickly masked it with resolve. "You truly don't understand.

Knowledge has its price. The moment you uncover the truth, you'll unleash forces you cannot control."

"Then we'll figure out how to control them," I declared, defiance bubbling within me. "We didn't come this far just to walk away."

The figure paused, weighing our determination against the shadows that whispered around us. "Very well. But understand this: once you step onto that path, there is no turning back."

With that, the figure reached into the folds of their coat and pulled out a small object. It glinted in the low light—a key, ancient and ornate, seemingly alive with history. "This will lead you to the truth, but use it wisely."

"What's it for?" I asked, my pulse quickening.

"The church's hidden chamber. You'll find the answers you seek within." The figure hesitated, their expression wavering between hope and dread. "But be warned: the truth is a double-edged sword. You may not like what you find."

Before I could respond, the figure spun on their heel, retreating into the shadows. I blinked, trying to process the whirlwind of revelations and warnings, but the space where they had stood felt empty, their presence lingering like a fading echo.

"Did that just happen?" Gavin asked, his brows knit in confusion.

"Apparently, we've entered the realm of supernatural intrigue," I replied, the thrill of adventure coursing through me. The key felt heavy in my palm, its weight a promise of discovery. "We need to find this hidden chamber."

"Just a casual stroll through a haunted church to uncover ancient secrets, right?" he said, trying to lighten the mood even as the weight of the moment hung in the air.

"Exactly," I quipped, the thrill of uncertainty igniting my resolve. "What could possibly go wrong?"

As we turned to leave the storage room, I felt an inexplicable tug at my heart—a sensation that this was only the beginning of something much larger than ourselves. The atmosphere shifted, growing thick with tension as we stepped back into the main hall, the flickering candlelight casting dancing shadows on the walls.

Then, a deafening crash echoed from somewhere within the church, rattling the very foundations beneath our feet. The floorboards creaked ominously as the lights flickered erratically, plunging us into intermittent darkness.

"What was that?" Gavin's voice rose above the chaos, laced with a mixture of excitement and fear.

"I don't know, but we need to go—now!" I shouted, adrenaline spiking through my veins as the walls seemed to close in around us.

Just as we turned to escape, the hooded figure reappeared, blocking our way, their eyes blazing with urgency. "You shouldn't have come here!" they warned, voice urgent. "You've awakened something—something that wants to be free."

Before we could react, the ground trembled beneath us, and I felt the air rush out of my lungs as the shadows erupted into a swirling vortex, engulfing the room in darkness. The last thing I saw was the terrified look on Gavin's face as everything spiraled into chaos, leaving us teetering on the edge of the unknown.

Chapter 16: The Awakening

The wind picked up, swirling leaves in a chaotic dance as we stepped into the heart of Maplewood. It was a quaint town with a façade of friendly smiles and cozy porches, yet the air crackled with unspoken tension. Shadows elongated across the cobblestones, stretching like fingers grasping at the fading warmth of the day. I could almost hear the whispers weaving through the trees, secretive and sharp, as if the very branches conspired to keep us at bay.

Gavin walked beside me, his tall frame casting a long shadow. The autumn sun dipped lower, igniting the sky in hues of orange and crimson, yet the warmth felt distant, eclipsed by an undeniable chill that crept into my bones. I caught a glimpse of his expression—a mixture of determination and concern. His dark hair tousled by the wind, he glanced at me, and for a moment, the world around us faded, leaving just the two of us and the weight of what we were about to uncover.

"Are you sure about this?" he asked, his voice low, just above a whisper, but heavy with the gravity of our quest. I could feel the heat of his gaze on my face, a mix of encouragement and worry, and it stirred something inside me.

"I have to be," I replied, squaring my shoulders as I stepped onto the path leading to the old library. It loomed before us, an ancient structure wrapped in ivy, its wooden doors painted a deep, weary green that seemed to sag under the weight of history. The townspeople had their secrets tucked away in those dusty shelves, and I was determined to unearth them.

As we approached, the sound of laughter broke the stillness, a sharp contrast to the unease that had settled like fog over Maplewood. A group of children chased each other, their bright laughter ringing out like tiny bells, unaware of the shadows lurking just beyond the glow of their innocence. I paused, captivated by their joy. I had once been like them, innocent and free, running through fields with my hair streaming behind me like a banner of rebellion. But that was before reality became a relentless storm, eroding the simplicity of childhood.

Gavin's hand brushed against mine, a subtle reminder of our shared purpose. "Let's go," he urged, leading the way inside. The library creaked in protest as we pushed open the door, the scent of old paper and polished wood enveloping us like a familiar embrace.

Inside, the dim light cast long shadows, and dust motes floated lazily in the air, dancing in the fading sun. Rows of books towered around us, their spines lined like sentinels guarding secrets long forgotten. I moved cautiously, running my fingers along the shelves, feeling the texture of the leather bindings and the brittle pages that whispered tales of the past.

"Look," Gavin said, pointing to a section at the back marked "Local History." His brow furrowed with concentration as he plucked a heavy tome from the shelf. "This could have something about the festival."

I stepped closer, intrigued. "Or the legends that haunt this place."

He grinned, a flash of mischief lighting up his eyes. "You mean the 'haunted by the vengeful spirits of Maplewood' legends?"

I smirked, shaking my head. "More like the ones that have made people disappear."

As I leaned over to peer at the book, a sudden noise echoed through the library—a loud thud, followed by a hushed murmur. My heart raced, and I straightened up, scanning the room. An older woman stood at the entrance, her eyes narrowed, lips pressed into a thin line. The sight of her sent a shiver down my spine. She looked like the embodiment of every ghost story I had ever heard, draped in layers of dark clothing that seemed to absorb the light around her.

"What are you doing here?" she croaked, her voice gravelly as if she hadn't spoken in years.

Gavin stepped protectively in front of me. "Just doing some research," he replied, the warmth in his tone belying the tension in the air.

"Research?" she echoed, skepticism dripping from her words. "You won't find what you seek. Best leave it buried."

I couldn't suppress the urge to challenge her. "What if we want to dig it up? The truth deserves to be uncovered, doesn't it?"

Her eyes flashed with an intensity that sent a jolt of fear racing through me. "Truth can be a dangerous thing, girl. Sometimes it's best left undisturbed."

With that, she turned and swept away, her long skirt trailing behind her like a dark cloud. I exchanged a look with Gavin, our shared apprehension thickening the air.

"Dangerous?" I mused aloud. "What does she know?"

Gavin sighed, running a hand through his hair. "It's a small town. People like her don't take kindly to outsiders stirring up trouble."

"Or digging up the past," I added, my determination hardening. "But we can't back down now. There's something here, and we're going to find it."

The library, once a haven of knowledge, now felt like a battleground, and I was ready for whatever came next. The stakes were rising, and with every turn of the page, the shadows deepened, beckoning me closer to the heart of Maplewood's darkest secrets. And as I prepared to dive into the abyss, I felt a thrill of excitement course through me, igniting a fire that refused to be extinguished.

"Let's get to work," I said, my voice steady and resolute, as I gestured toward the open book. The search for truth had begun, and I would not rest until every stone was overturned, every secret unveiled, no matter the cost.

The musty scent of old paper clung to the air like a memory, both familiar and unsettling, as I delved into the heart of the library's archives. Sunlight trickled through the high windows, casting a golden hue over the dust motes that danced in the beams. It felt surreal, almost as if the place were alive, each book a living entity, eager to share its secrets, yet wary of the hands that sought to pry them open. I brushed my fingers across the spines, glancing over titles that promised histories filled with both glory and despair.

"Do you think we're really going to find anything here?" Gavin asked, flipping through an ancient ledger, its pages yellowed and fragile. His brow furrowed in concentration, but I could see the hint of a smile tugging at the corners of his mouth, as if he were trying to lighten the oppressive atmosphere.

"Of course we will," I replied, matching his playful tone. "All great mysteries begin with dusty books and a bit of stubbornness." I paused, arching an eyebrow. "Though I'll admit, a little ghostly intervention wouldn't hurt."

He chuckled softly, the sound breaking the heavy silence. "Well, if we run into any spirits, I'll let you do the talking. You have a way with the supernatural."

Ignoring the way my heart raced at the thought, I dug deeper into a nearby stack of books. My fingers traced the edges of a volume labeled "Local Legends," its spine creaking as I pulled it toward me. The title seemed innocuous enough, but I could sense something charged beneath the surface, an energy that beckoned me closer.

As I flipped through the pages, I stumbled upon an illustration that made my breath hitch—a drawing of the very festival we had attended just days prior. The colors were faded, yet vibrant enough to convey the spirit of celebration, with townsfolk dancing in the streets beneath lanterns strung up like stars. Yet beneath the surface of merriment lay a shadow, a dark figure lurking at the edge of the illustration, its features indistinct but unmistakably sinister.

"Gavin, look at this," I said, my voice barely above a whisper. He leaned over, his shoulder brushing against mine, sending a spark of warmth through me that was almost distracting.

"What do you see?" he asked, his breath warm against my ear.

I pointed to the figure. "This. It's... it's there, lurking. Like it knew something would happen during the festival." My mind raced, weaving possibilities together, each thread pulling tighter. "What if the festival isn't just a celebration? What if it's a cover-up for something darker?"

His eyes widened, a spark igniting in them that mirrored my own enthusiasm. "You mean like a ritual? A way to appease whatever it is that haunts this place?"

"Exactly," I said, excitement bubbling up within me. "If the townspeople believe it's tradition, they might ignore the signs. They could be unwitting participants in something far more sinister."

Before we could dig deeper into the implications, the door swung open with a creak, and a sudden gust of wind rushed through the library, swirling around us like a whirlwind. My heart skipped a beat as I turned to see the older woman again, her silhouette framed in the doorway.

"I thought I told you to leave," she said, her voice low and steady, sending chills down my spine.

"Really? Because we're just getting to the good part," I replied, channeling every ounce of bravado I could muster. The air was charged with unspoken tension, and I felt Gavin's presence at my side, steady and reassuring.

"Good can be deceiving," she shot back, her eyes narrowing, flickering with something ancient and unyielding. "You dig too deep, and you may find more than you bargained for."

"Why do you care?" I shot back, unable to hide my frustration. "What's so important about keeping the past buried?"

Her lips twisted into a thin smile, a hint of something dark lurking just beneath the surface. "Some truths are better left forgotten. Innocence is a fragile thing, and curiosity has a way of leading to ruin."

With that ominous warning hanging in the air, she turned on her heel and left, the door slamming shut behind her, leaving a suffocating silence in her wake. I exchanged a glance with Gavin, the weight of her words settling between us like a fog.

"Curiosity leading to ruin?" he murmured, disbelief evident in his voice. "Sounds like a challenge to me."

"Good," I replied, gritting my teeth. "I wasn't looking to back down."

We turned back to the books, but I could feel the unease creeping back in, wrapping around me like a tightening noose. Each word on the page seemed to pulsate with warning, yet I was undeterred. I had come too far to retreat now.

After a few more minutes of frantically flipping through pages, I found something that made my heart race again—a series of newspaper clippings dating back decades, chronicling mysterious disappearances in the town. Names blurred together like a haunting litany, and the dates converged around the festival time, their stories shadowed in tragedy. Each article spoke of a life snuffed out, a family shattered, and a community that moved on as if nothing had happened.

"What if the festival isn't just a celebration?" I whispered, piecing it together in my mind. "What if it's a way to bury the truth under layers of joy and festivity?"

Gavin leaned closer, his eyes scanning the articles, the gravity of the situation settling over us like a heavy cloak. "We need to find out what these families have in common. There has to be a thread connecting them."

"Agreed," I said, my determination hardening. "And if the town is trying to silence us, we need to tread carefully. We might be on the brink of something explosive."

The thrill of discovery coursed through me, and for a fleeting moment, the shadows receded. Yet, even as I felt the adrenaline surge, the weight of the town's gaze pressed on my shoulders. I glanced toward the windows, half-expecting to see the townspeople watching us, their expressions a mixture of suspicion and disdain.

As we settled into our research, the library became our sanctuary, a place where whispers of the past beckoned us forward. But I couldn't shake the feeling that time was running out, that the deeper we delved, the more dangerous our path would become. I needed to uncover the truth before the shadows could reclaim what was theirs, and before we became just another forgotten story in Maplewood's haunting tale.

The shadows grew longer as the sun sank lower, surrendering the day to twilight's embrace. Gavin and I sifted through the remnants of the past in that musty library, surrounded by tomes that seemed to hum with secrets. Each rustle of paper was a reminder that we were not alone in our quest. The atmosphere felt thick with the weight of unwritten histories, and I could almost hear the faint echoes of those who had come before us, their stories trapped within the pages we turned.

I spotted a particularly worn-out book, its spine cracked and pages frayed. "This looks promising," I said, extracting it from the shelf. The title was embossed in gold but barely legible. "It seems like it hasn't seen the light of day in years."

Gavin leaned in closer, his breath warm against my cheek as he read over my shoulder. "What does it say?"

"'The Histories of Maplewood,'" I murmured, intrigued. "Let's hope it's not just a collection of dusty old anecdotes." I opened it carefully, revealing delicate sketches that depicted the town's founding families, their smiles frozen in time, concealing layers of complexities beneath.

As I flipped through, one particular image caught my eye—a family portrait surrounded by a wreath of autumn leaves. "Gavin, look! This family... they were involved in the first festival. And their names keep coming up in the articles about the disappearances."

"Do you think they could be connected?" he asked, his voice barely above a whisper, filled with both excitement and trepidation.

I nodded, piecing together fragments of a puzzle that had eluded us for far too long. "What if this family played a role in whatever ritual happens during the festival? Maybe they're the reason the town keeps the past hidden."

As we continued to flip through the book, a folded piece of parchment slipped out, fluttering to the floor like a ghostly whisper. My heart raced as I picked it up, the paper yellowed and brittle beneath my fingers. I unfolded it slowly, revealing a handwritten note scrawled in an elegant, flowing script.

"Listen to this," I said, my voice trembling slightly. "'To remember is to invite the darkness. What was buried must remain hidden; otherwise, the past will awaken and claim what is rightfully theirs.'"

A shiver ran down my spine. Gavin's expression shifted from curiosity to concern, a shadow crossing his face. "That sounds like a warning, not just some old ghost story."

"Or a threat," I replied, my voice low as I folded the note back into its original shape. The air in the library seemed to tighten around us, as if the walls themselves were closing in.

We exchanged worried glances, both realizing we were standing at a precipice. The weight of our discoveries pressed down on us, and the vibrant threads of hope I had felt just moments before began to unravel, replaced by a gnawing dread.

"I think we should take this to the town's historian," Gavin suggested, breaking the heavy silence that enveloped us. "He might know more about this family and what they were involved in."

I nodded in agreement, though a part of me hesitated. "What if he's in on it? What if the whole town is protecting something?"

Gavin leaned closer, his voice dropping to a conspiratorial whisper. "Then we'll have to be clever about how we approach him. We don't want to tip our hand too soon."

The plan formed in my mind, and with each step, I could feel the pulse of the town quickening. We returned the book to its shelf, leaving behind the ghosts of the past that now felt more alive than ever.

As we exited the library, the crisp air enveloped us, invigorating yet charged with an undercurrent of tension. The streetlights flickered on, illuminating the cobblestones in pools of soft yellow light, yet I couldn't shake the sensation that unseen eyes were tracking our every move.

"We should be careful," Gavin warned, scanning the street. "The locals are watching us."

I chuckled softly, despite the fear clawing at my insides. "Let them watch. I'd rather face their disapproval than live in ignorance."

"Or worse," he added, his expression darkening. "What if we find ourselves in danger?"

My heart thudded at the thought, but I pushed it aside. "Danger has never stopped us before, has it? We'll just have to be smart about it."

As we made our way through the dimly lit streets, the festival remnants scattered about like lost dreams. Banners fluttered in the breeze, and the aroma of leftover treats wafted through the air, a bittersweet reminder of what had transpired.

But my thoughts were elsewhere, trapped in the web of mysteries we had begun to unravel. We rounded a corner and found ourselves in front of a quaint building adorned with wooden signage that read "Maplewood Historical Society."

"Here we go," I said, determination flooding through me.

We stepped inside, and the bell above the door tinkled, echoing into the quiet space. Dust motes floated in the air, catching the dim light, creating a cozy, yet eerie atmosphere.

An elderly man with round spectacles perched precariously on the bridge of his nose sat behind a cluttered desk, surrounded by stacks of papers and artifacts. He looked up, his eyes narrowing as if assessing us. "Can I help you?"

"Actually, yes," Gavin replied, taking the lead. "We're looking for information about the first festival and its connection to the recent disappearances."

The man's demeanor shifted instantly. He set his pen down, folding his hands together, his gaze sharp. "That's a sensitive topic. You might not want to dig too deep."

"What do you mean by that?" I interjected, a mix of curiosity and caution flooding through me.

He hesitated, glancing around as if expecting to see someone listening. "There are things you don't understand. Maplewood has its traditions, and some things are better left untouched."

"Like what? The families involved? The history of the festival?" I pressed, my determination growing stronger in the face of his reluctance.

The man sighed, the weight of years etched into his features. "The past can be a dangerous thing. If you're not careful, it will come back to haunt you."

"What if we can help? What if we can protect this town from whatever it is that's lurking in the shadows?" Gavin offered, his voice earnest.

Just then, a loud crash echoed from outside, rattling the windows. My heart raced as we exchanged worried glances, the sudden noise pulling us from our conversation and into the heart of the chaos.

Without thinking, I dashed to the window, peering outside. The street was awash with commotion, the townspeople gathering in clusters, their faces twisted with fear and confusion.

"What's happening?" I whispered, dread pooling in my stomach as a figure appeared at the edge of the crowd, cloaked in darkness, its presence radiating an eerie stillness.

Gavin joined me, his eyes wide with alarm. "We need to find out."

But just as we turned to make our way outside, the lights flickered ominously, plunging the room into darkness for a heartbeat before a deafening crash resounded through the historical society, shaking the very foundations of the building.

I stumbled backward, and in that instant, something cold and heavy wrapped around my heart. We had ventured too far into the depths of Maplewood's secrets, and the shadows were ready to reclaim what was theirs.

Chapter 17: The Night of Reckoning

The fog wrapped around me like a cloak, shrouding everything in a ghostly embrace as I approached the abandoned farmhouse. Each step stirred the dust of years gone by, a soft whisper of stories that lingered long after the last occupant had departed. The air was heavy with the scent of damp earth and decaying wood, mingling in a way that made the hairs on my arms stand on end. I clutched the flashlight tightly, its beam cutting through the thick gloom, illuminating the warped wooden planks of the porch, each creak beneath my feet echoing like a specter's lament.

Inside, the darkness enveloped me, a tangible entity that seemed to breathe alongside the house. The walls, once painted in cheerful hues, had succumbed to layers of grime and peeling wallpaper, the patterns now mere ghosts of their former vibrancy. I let out a breath, the sound muffled by the oppressive stillness. It was as if the house had held its breath all these years, waiting for someone brave—or foolish—enough to disturb its slumber.

A chill skittered down my spine as I scanned the room, my flashlight sweeping across a collection of broken furniture, each piece telling its own silent story of neglect. A shattered mirror leaned against the wall, its jagged edges catching the light, reflecting fractured images that mirrored my own unease. It was in this fragmented reality that I sensed it: the remnants of a life long forgotten but steeped in the secrets of those who once inhabited this space.

The tip we received had hinted at something significant hidden within these walls, something that might finally unravel the tangled web woven by Mayor Callahan's machinations. My heart raced as I moved deeper into the house, compelled by a mixture of dread and determination. I could no longer remain a passive observer in the drama that had consumed our town; it was time to take control of my own narrative.

The beam of my flashlight landed on a dusty wooden table, its surface strewn with papers yellowed by age. I approached cautiously, brushing away the cobwebs that draped like veils over the artifacts of the past. Among the scattered papers, my pulse quickened as I recognized the elegant script of the mayor himself, the ink still dark and legible despite the years. Each word felt like a knife, slicing through the veil of respectability he had carefully crafted over the years.

"Looks like your secrets are not as well hidden as you thought, Callahan," I murmured to myself, an ironic smile tugging at the corners of my mouth. The audacity of it all, the sheer arrogance with which he believed he could control everything and everyone, infuriated me. I imagined his smooth, practiced smile crumbling as I laid this evidence bare, exposing the man behind the façade.

Just as I was about to gather the documents, a sudden noise broke the silence—a soft scuffle outside, accompanied by the crunch of gravel underfoot. My heart leaped into my throat. Was I alone, or had someone followed me here? I stilled, straining to listen, the whispers of the house seeming to echo my own apprehension.

"Great, just what I need," I muttered, rolling my eyes at the irony of the situation. The thrill of discovery was rapidly being overshadowed by the reality that I might not be the only one interested in these secrets. I crept toward the window, heart pounding in time with the distant echo of my own breath. Outside, shadows danced, flitting in and out of view, each movement sending adrenaline coursing through my veins.

The door creaked open slowly, and I instinctively ducked behind a dilapidated armchair, its upholstery worn and faded like the memories of its former life. A figure stepped inside, silhouetted against the moonlight spilling through the door. It was a man, tall and broad-shouldered, the outline familiar. My heart sank as recognition hit me like a freight train.

"Callahan," I whispered, irritation and disbelief coiling within me. What was he doing here? Did he know I was onto him? My thoughts raced as I watched him move through the dimly lit room, seemingly unfazed by the decay surrounding him.

"Searching for ghosts, are we?" His voice was low, dripping with sardonic charm as he paused to inspect the scattered papers. "How poetic."

I couldn't help but admire his audacity, even as anger bubbled to the surface. "You might want to be careful where you tread, Mayor. This place is crawling with secrets you can't bury," I shot back, stepping out from my hiding spot, my resolve sharpening into something akin to a blade.

He turned, surprise flashing across his features before it was quickly masked by his practiced smile. "Ah, I see you've become quite the detective, haven't you? Perhaps you should consider a different line of work. This one seems too... hazardous for your health."

"Health is the least of my concerns," I retorted, my voice steadier than I felt. "What I'm concerned about is the good people of this town who've trusted you with their lives. I've seen the pain you've caused, the shadows you've cast over us all."

He stepped closer, and I could see the flicker of menace in his eyes, the charming veneer cracking just enough to reveal the predator beneath. "You have no idea what you're meddling with, my dear. Some secrets are best left buried. For your own sake, I suggest you turn around and forget this little adventure."

My heart raced, a mix of fear and defiance igniting a fire within me. "And what if I refuse? What if I decide that the people of this town deserve the truth? Your days of manipulating us are over, Callahan."

A tense silence stretched between us, thick with unspoken threats and unyielding resolve. I felt the weight of the moment settle on my shoulders, a reckoning in the making. The air crackled with anticipation, the promise of conflict lurking just beneath the surface. In that instant, I realized I was no longer just a bystander in this twisted narrative; I was the author, and I intended to write my own ending.

He chuckled, a low, almost sinister sound that echoed off the crumbling walls, and my skin prickled with an uncomfortable mix of fear and indignation. "Such fire. It's almost admirable, really. But passion alone won't change anything, my dear." His words dripped with condescension, and I fought the urge to roll my eyes.

"Passion has a way of lighting the path, Callahan. It's desperation that blinds." I stepped forward, defiance spurring me on, even as I felt the adrenaline coursing through my veins, urging caution. "You think you can intimidate me? You think I'll just waltz out of here, pretending I didn't see anything?"

"Let's not get dramatic," he said, waving a hand dismissively, but there was an underlying tension in his posture, a slight shift that suggested I had struck a nerve. "I'm merely trying to protect you from the fallout of your own curiosity. After all, a good little citizen shouldn't go digging in places best left alone."

"Ah, the classic 'for your own good' line. I suppose you'll add it to your campaign slogan next year?" My voice was sharper than I intended, but the absurdity of his arrogance ignited a firestorm of indignation. "You think people will blindly follow you? You've done enough to this town to fill a novel of bad decisions."

He stepped closer, and I could feel the weight of his presence like a storm pressing against the air. "Be careful, my dear. You're treading dangerous waters. Those who get too close to the truth often find themselves drowning."

His eyes darkened, and for a fleeting moment, I saw the wolf beneath the tailored suit, a predator ready to pounce. I took a breath, grounding myself in the moment. My mind raced with thoughts of the people I cared about—the townsfolk who had placed their trust in him, the friends I had grown up with, their lives tangled in the web he spun.

"Drowning isn't my concern," I shot back, holding my ground. "It's being too blind to see what's right in front of me. You've played this game long enough, Callahan. It's time for a new player to take the lead."

For a heartbeat, the tension between us hung heavy, and I could almost hear the gears grinding in his mind. I knew I was taking a risk, pushing him like this, but there was an exhilaration in standing my ground.

"Your bravado is impressive," he finally said, his tone betraying a hint of grudging respect. "But you should know that this isn't a game for the faint-hearted. You might discover things about yourself that you're not quite ready to face."

"Like your connection to the past?" I countered, my pulse quickening at the thought of the papers still scattered on the table. "Or perhaps your involvement in a pact that's cost this town so much? I'm ready to face those truths, Callahan. Are you?"

He stepped back, a mask of amusement slipping into place, though the tension still crackled in the air. "Ah, there it is—the righteous indignation. It makes for a good story, doesn't it? But do you really think anyone would believe you?"

In that moment, I saw the perfect opening, a chance to flip the script. "Maybe it's time to show them, then." I gestured to the papers, my voice steady. "You've hidden behind your power for too long. What if I were to share these findings? What if I exposed you for what you truly are?"

His expression darkened, the friendly veneer eroding. "You wouldn't dare."

I stepped closer, my heart racing, the thrill of danger palpable. "Try me. You may have pulled the strings for years, but I'm done being your puppet. The people deserve the truth, and I won't let you stifle that anymore."

He narrowed his eyes, and for a moment, I feared he would lash out, but then he smiled—a predatory, chilling smile that sent a shiver through me. "Very well. You've made your choice, and now you'll face the consequences."

Before I could react, he pivoted, moving toward the door with an unexpected swiftness. Panic flared in my chest. I had to act. I darted forward, grabbing the nearest chair and flinging it in his direction. It collided with the door just as he pushed it open, the loud crash reverberating through the house.

"Do you really think you can escape this?" I shouted, my heart pounding as I watched him stumble, momentarily disoriented. "You've underestimated me."

His eyes flashed with anger, but the moment of chaos had given me the edge I needed. I lunged for the papers on the table, grabbing a handful of documents that might hold the evidence I desperately needed.

"Go ahead," he spat, regaining his composure, anger etched in every line of his face. "But remember, you can't unring the bell. Once you've crossed this line, there's no going back."

I met his gaze, fear mingling with fierce determination. "Maybe that's just what this town needs—someone willing to burn down the old for the chance to build something new."

With that, I turned, bolting toward the back of the house, the weight of the papers clutched tightly to my chest. The wooden floors creaked beneath my feet, the sound echoing like a heartbeat, urging me to move faster. The back door was my only escape, and I pushed it open with a force that sent it swinging wide, the night air hitting my face like a breath of freedom.

I could hear his footsteps behind me, the soft thud of his shoes striking the ground with a growing urgency. The fog swallowed me whole as I dashed into the night, adrenaline coursing through my veins. I had to get to my car, had to get away from this nightmare.

The night felt alive, each shadow and whisper amplifying the fear that had taken root within me. I glanced back, catching a glimpse of Callahan, his silhouette breaking through the fog, determined and relentless. A part of me trembled at the thought of his reach, the power he wielded in our town, but another part flared with defiance.

I sprinted towards my car, the familiar sight of it a beacon of hope amid the chaos. The engine roared to life with a satisfying growl, a sound that reverberated through me like a rallying cry. I glanced in the rearview mirror, Callahan's figure growing smaller, but I knew this wasn't over. Not by a long shot.

As I sped down the darkened road, the papers still clenched in my hand, I could feel the weight of what lay ahead. The stakes had never been higher, and the path to the truth was fraught with peril. But as the lights of the town flickered in the distance, I felt an undeniable resolve take root within me. I was ready to fight for what was right, and I wouldn't back down until the truth was laid bare for all to see.

The tires of my car screamed against the gravel as I raced away from the farmhouse, the adrenaline in my veins surging like a runaway train. The night was still thick with fog, each swirl of mist curling around the headlights, creating an otherworldly haze that felt more like a cloak than an obstacle. I had escaped Callahan, but I could still feel the weight of his presence, that ominous promise lingering in the air like the scent of rain before a storm.

Glancing in the rearview mirror, I expected to see him hot on my tail, but instead, the road behind was empty, swallowed by the darkness. Relief surged through me, but it was quickly overshadowed by the gravity of the evidence I had gathered. My heart raced with the realization that I now held the key to unearthing the truth. The papers, still clasped tightly in my hands, were a blend of the mayor's own words and incriminating details that could shatter his carefully constructed empire.

I turned onto Main Street, the familiar sights of my hometown blinking back at me through the mist. Everything felt surreal, like a dream that straddled the line between nightmare and reality. The streetlights flickered, casting long shadows that danced in sync with my thoughts. I needed a plan—a way to unveil the truth without losing everything in the process.

The urge to drive straight to the police station clawed at me, but instinct told me I needed allies who wouldn't flinch in the face of danger. I needed Ava. My best friend, with her fiery spirit and unwavering loyalty, would stand by me no matter what. I could almost picture her now, her wild curls bouncing as she paced in my kitchen, phone in hand, ready to launch into a tirade about the latest town gossip.

Pulling into my driveway, I dashed inside, heart pounding. I grabbed my phone, my fingers trembling as I dialed her number. "Pick up, pick up," I whispered, pacing the living room, the familiar walls suddenly feeling too constrictive.

"Hello?" Her voice crackled through the line, laced with a hint of sleep but quickly shifting to alertness. "Is that you? What's going on?"

"I need you to come over. Now. It's urgent," I urged, the gravity of my words hanging in the air like a dark cloud.

"On my way," she replied without hesitation. I felt a flicker of gratitude amidst the chaos, knowing she wouldn't ask questions until she was there.

As I waited, I paced the room, the shadows twisting around me, amplifying my growing anxiety. The papers I had taken from the farmhouse lay spread out on the kitchen table, their edges crumpled from my grip. I could almost hear Callahan's voice in my head, a sinister echo reminding me of the danger I was courting.

Just as I was about to run through the evidence again, the door swung open, and Ava burst in, her vibrant energy lighting up the dim room. "What's happened? You look like you've seen a ghost!"

"I might have," I shot back, biting my lip as I gestured toward the table. "I found something at the farmhouse. Something big. And it's about Callahan."

Her expression shifted from concern to curiosity as she approached the table, her eyes widening as she scanned the papers. "What did you find? Spill it."

"His secrets—everything he's been hiding. There's a connection to the pact, Ava. We can't let him keep this buried." My voice trembled with urgency, and I felt the weight of the truth pressing down on me.

Ava picked up a document, her brow furrowing as she read. "This is... explosive. Are you sure you want to do this?"

I nodded, determination setting my jaw. "I can't walk away. Not now. If we don't act, he'll continue to manipulate everyone. We need to go public."

She glanced at me, her fierce gaze steady. "Then we do it together. But we need a plan. If Callahan is as powerful as you say, he won't take kindly to this."

The room hummed with tension as we strategized, my mind racing with possibilities. We would need evidence, more than just these papers. The community had to see the truth, feel its weight.

Ava's voice pulled me back to the present. "What if we gather more evidence? Something concrete? We could visit the old town records office; they might have more on this pact."

"That's a great idea," I replied, heart racing with newfound hope. "And if we can find any witnesses—people who've been hurt by his decisions—this could rally the townsfolk."

Just as the excitement began to swell between us, a loud knock shattered the moment, echoing through the quiet house like a harbinger of doom. I exchanged a wary glance with Ava, the thrill of our plans abruptly dampened by the ominous sound.

"Who could that be?" she whispered, eyes wide.

"I don't know. Maybe it's just a neighbor," I said, though my voice lacked conviction. The hairs on my neck prickled as I approached the door, unease settling in my stomach like a stone. I peeked through the peephole and froze.

It was Callahan, flanked by two men in dark suits, their presence imposing and ominous. My heart dropped, the weight of the evidence still in my hands suddenly feeling like a noose tightening around my neck. "Ava, it's him," I whispered, panic rising in my throat.

"Don't open it!" she hissed, stepping back as if the door itself might spring to life.

His voice came through the door, smooth yet cold, like ice cracking beneath pressure. "I know you're in there, and I suggest you open this door. We need to talk."

"Talk? You've got some nerve," I muttered, adrenaline flooding my veins.

"We don't have time for this," Ava urged, glancing toward the kitchen window. "We have to get out of here."

But I hesitated, torn between fear and a desperate need to confront him. "What if we don't? What if we face him now?"

"Facing him means giving him the upper hand. We need to protect the evidence. He can't know what we have," she insisted, her voice urgent but calm.

Another knock echoed, louder this time, the door rattling on its hinges. "You have until the count of three," Callahan's voice was smooth, almost charming. "Then I will come in, whether you like it or not."

My heart raced. "What do we do?"

Ava's eyes darted around the room, panic and resolve colliding. "We need to hide the papers. Now!"

In a frenzy, I shoved the evidence into a drawer, slamming it shut just as the count reached two. "Get back," I whispered, pushing Ava toward the kitchen.

The door burst open, and Callahan stepped inside, flanked by his imposing companions, their eyes scanning the room like hawks searching for prey.

"Well, well," he said, an unsettling grin spreading across his face. "I see you've been busy."

The atmosphere crackled with tension, and I felt the ground shift beneath me. I was standing on the edge of a precipice, one wrong move away from everything crumbling into chaos.

"Do you really think you can intimidate us?" I managed to say, though my voice quivered.

He stepped closer, an unsettling calm in his demeanor, as if he had all the time in the world. "You have no idea what you're playing with. And I suggest you hand over what you've found before things get... unpleasant."

As the weight of his words settled, I felt my pulse quicken, the room closing in around me. In that moment, I realized I was caught in a dangerous game, and the stakes were higher than I had ever imagined.

"Unpleasant for whom?" I challenged, even as doubt gnawed at me.

"Unpleasant for you, my dear," he replied, his smile widening into something predatory. "You see, this town has a way of taking care of its own, and I have no intention of letting a little thing like evidence ruin my carefully orchestrated plans."

As he spoke, I felt the shadows in the room stretch and shift, and in that moment, the air thrummed with the promise of confrontation. The weight of the truth pressed down on me, and I knew there was no turning back now.

With a defiant breath, I squared my shoulders, ready to face whatever darkness awaited us. The dance of secrets and lies was far from over, and I was determined to take my place in this twisted narrative. But as I stood there, heart racing, a chilling thought crossed my mind—what would happen if the truth never saw the light of day?

Chapter 18: The Trap is Set

The air in Misty Shores was thick with an electric tension, each breath I took mingling with the faint scent of saltwater and the sharp tang of anxiety. The townspeople shuffled into the community center, their faces a tapestry of emotions—curiosity flickered in some eyes, while fear gnawed at the edges of others. They had come not just for another routine town hall meeting, but for the promise of truth, the possibility of change, and perhaps a little bit of drama, too. I stood at the back of the room, my heart pounding a chaotic rhythm that matched the murmurs of the crowd.

Gavin, my partner in this audacious scheme, stood by the podium, his broad shoulders squared and his jaw set with determination. He had transformed from the charming guy with a disarming smile to the steadfast ally I needed in this moment. The way his eyes scanned the room told me he was as aware of the stakes as I was. Today was not just about exposing the mayor; it was about confronting the shadows that had loomed over Misty Shores for far too long.

With each passing moment, the room filled with a diverse cast of characters, each with their own stories woven into the fabric of this tight-knit community. Old Mrs. Pennington, with her ever-present knitting needles, sat in the front row, her eyes darting nervously between Gavin and the door, as if expecting a villain to burst through at any moment. The young couple from the bakery, faces flushed with the excitement of recent engagement, leaned closer together, whispering sweet nothings, unaware that today's revelations could put their bright future at risk. And then there was Tommy, the local bartender, his usually jovial demeanor replaced by a pensive frown, as he exchanged knowing glances with his friends seated beside him.

As the meeting began, I felt the weight of every gaze directed toward us. The mayor, slick and polished, strode into the room like a king claiming his throne. He wore his confidence like a well-tailored suit, but I could sense the undercurrent of fear beneath his bravado. Today was a game-changer, and he knew it. The murmurs quieted as he took his place at the front, greeting the crowd with his trademark charisma.

"Good evening, everyone! I trust you're all ready for another productive session?" His voice was smooth, but I noticed the slightest tremor as he spoke, a crack in his facade that did not go unnoticed by me. The audience clapped half-heartedly, many clearly torn between loyalty and doubt.

The minutes ticked by as we navigated through the usual agenda, a charade of normalcy while the real drama simmered just below the surface. As the mayor began his usual spiel about community progress and upcoming events, I felt the adrenaline coursing through my veins. Each phrase he uttered felt like a betrayal, a lie that wrapped itself around my heart and tightened its grip. I glanced at Gavin, who nodded slightly, a silent agreement that the time for our reveal was nearing.

Finally, the moment arrived. The mayor opened the floor for questions, his eyes scanning the room for familiar faces ready to toe the party line. My stomach twisted with anticipation, but it was now or never. I raised my hand, my voice cutting through the thick atmosphere like a knife. "Mr. Mayor, I think it's time we talked about the development plans for the old lighthouse."

The room fell silent, every pair of eyes swinging toward me. The mayor's smile faltered for just a second, a flicker of something—fear, perhaps?—crossing his features before he masked it with a rehearsed grin. "Ah, yes, the lighthouse. A grand old structure, isn't it? We have big plans for it."

"Plans that have left many of us feeling uneasy, especially considering the discrepancies in the budget allocations," I pressed, my voice steady despite the tremor in my heart. "There have been whispers—no, truths—about the funds disappearing, used for purposes other than what you claimed."

Gasps rippled through the audience, a wave of disbelief washing over them. I locked eyes with Gavin, who stepped forward, his presence commanding the attention of the room. "We've gathered evidence, Mr. Mayor. Evidence that ties you directly to the misuse of funds for personal gain."

The mayor's smile evaporated, replaced by a grimace that sent chills down my spine. "You're making baseless accusations," he barked, but his voice lacked the conviction it usually held.

"Are they baseless, though?" Gavin countered, pulling out a folder and holding it high for all to see. "Or are they the very truths that you've tried to bury?"

A hush fell over the room, broken only by the faint sound of pages flipping as Gavin revealed documents, photographs, and statements that painted a vivid picture of corruption. I felt a surge of triumph as I saw the shock etch itself onto the faces of my neighbors, the very people I had grown up with. This was not just about exposing the mayor; it was about unveiling the truth that had long been hidden.

But as the atmosphere shifted from anticipation to outrage, a new fear crept in. The mayor's composure shattered completely. He turned pale, his eyes darting around as if searching for an escape. "You think you can just walk in here and ruin everything?" he hissed, his voice low and dangerous. The threat was unmistakable, and I could almost feel the energy in the room change, a predator watching its prey.

"Ruin everything?" I replied, my voice unwavering despite the threat. "Or are we finally fixing what's broken?"

In that moment, the stakes had never felt higher. I sensed danger lingering in the air, and the realization struck me like a cold wave. As the townsfolk began to murmur among themselves, some in disbelief, others in anger, I knew that I had lit a fire that could consume us all.

The air crackled with an electric mix of fear and exhilaration, each murmur among the townsfolk igniting the flames of unrest that flickered just beneath the surface. The mayor's face twisted into a mask of anger and denial, but I could see the sweat beading on his brow, the slight tremor in his hands. It was as if the walls of the community center had become a pressure cooker, the tension building with every heartbeat, ready to explode.

"What evidence?" he barked, his voice rising in pitch, a desperate attempt to regain control over a situation spiraling wildly out of his grasp. "You can't just accuse someone without proof."

I stepped closer to the podium, my heart thundering like a drum in my chest. "We have proof, and it's time the people of Misty Shores saw it." I gestured to Gavin, who stepped forward with that air of confidence that always seemed to settle my nerves. The papers in his hands fluttered slightly, each one a tiny testament to the deception that had seeped into our town like an insidious fog.

"What's happening here?" someone shouted from the back, a young man whose face I vaguely recognized as part of the local fishing community. "Are you saying the mayor's been lying to us?"

The collective gasp that followed was a living entity, swelling and contracting, a palpable wave of disbelief that crashed against the mayor's facade. He opened his mouth to speak, to smooth over the growing dissent, but Gavin seized the moment, holding up a photograph. The picture showed the mayor standing on the steps of the old lighthouse, a stack of cash nestled conspicuously in his hands, accompanied by a developer known for shady dealings and backdoor negotiations.

"Looks like our mayor has been caught red-handed," Gavin quipped, a smirk playing on his lips, his eyes sparkling with mischief. "And here I thought all he was doing was saving the lighthouse."

Gasps erupted around the room, faces shifting from shock to anger. The elderly lady in the front row clutched her pearls, her eyes wide. "I knew there was something off about him!" she exclaimed, her voice quavering with indignation.

The mayor's cheeks flushed crimson, anger and panic warring for dominance. "You're all being led astray by these two troublemakers!" he shouted, desperation oozing from every word. "They want to tear this town apart!"

"On the contrary," I replied, forcing calmness into my voice even as my pulse raced. "We want to build it up. You've been lining your pockets while the town has crumbled around us. We're done with the secrets, the lies." The crowd shifted restlessly, murmurs rising again, this time a tide of support for our cause.

As the meeting spiraled into chaos, the mayor's bluster crumbled. "You'll regret this," he hissed, leaning closer to me, his eyes narrowing dangerously. There was something in his tone that made my skin crawl, a promise wrapped in threat. "You think you can just waltz in here and expose me? You have no idea what I'm capable of."

I felt a chill settle deep within me, an instinctual warning that this battle was far from over. The room around us erupted into heated discussions, voices rising and falling like the waves outside the window. I wanted to scream, to drown out the noise and tell everyone to listen to reason, but reason felt distant in this boiling cauldron of emotion.

Gavin, ever the optimist, turned to me, a glimmer of mischief still in his eyes despite the gravity of the situation. "You know," he said with a crooked grin, "if we make it through this, I'm going to take you out for the best dinner Misty Shores has to offer. Think of all the fresh seafood."

"Gavin," I said, my heart both fluttering and sinking at his humor, "I'm not sure there will be a town left to enjoy dinner in after this."

"Sure there will," he replied, his tone unwavering. "Once they realize how much better off they'll be without the mayor, they'll rise up. Just watch." His optimism, like a warm blanket in the midst of chaos, wrapped around me, bolstering my courage as the room continued to shift and shake with anger and disbelief.

Suddenly, the mayor leaned over and grabbed the microphone, his voice cutting through the tumult like a knife. "You're all making a terrible mistake!" he shouted, desperation spilling from his lips. "I'm the one who brought funding into this town. I'm the reason the schools are better. You think these two are going to save us? They're trying to tear down what we've built!"

"Built on lies!" a voice from the crowd shouted back. "You've been stealing from us, and we won't stand for it anymore!" The defiance in that voice struck a chord, igniting a spark of rebellion that spread through the room like wildfire.

The mayor's bravado faltered as he realized he was losing his grip. He turned, glancing around the room, and in that instant, I saw the panic set in, a flicker of realization that he had underestimated us all. In that moment, he looked less like a mayor and more like a cornered animal, wild-eyed and desperate, ready to lash out.

"Enough!" he roared, but the power in his voice was waning, like a balloon losing air. He turned back to me, and for a brief second, the fear in his gaze matched my own. "You have no idea what you're getting into," he warned, his tone low, dripping with malice. "I'll make sure you regret this."

I swallowed hard, the weight of his threat pressing down on me. "We'll see about that," I shot back, trying to inject my voice with confidence I didn't fully feel. But somewhere deep within me, a flicker of defiance ignited. I wouldn't back down. I couldn't.

As the meeting raged on, fueled by revelations and outrage, I caught sight of Tommy in the back, his brows furrowed in concentration. He suddenly stood up, his voice booming above the crowd. "I have something to say!" His boldness commanded attention, and all eyes shifted to him, curious about what this local bartender might contribute.

"Let's not forget that Misty Shores has always been a place of community," Tommy began, his voice steady but passionate. "We can't let one man's greed destroy what we've built together. We need to stand united, now more than ever."

A ripple of agreement spread through the audience, and for the first time, I felt a real sense of hope fluttering in my chest. The mayor's grip on power was slipping, and as more voices joined Tommy's, a chorus of resistance grew, drowning out the mayor's frantic attempts to regain control.

As the crowd rallied together, I felt an unexpected warmth bloom within me—a sense of belonging and purpose that had long been overshadowed by doubt. This was our moment, and I was determined to see it through, to stand beside my friends and neighbors as we faced the storm together.

But as the uproar continued, I couldn't shake the feeling that the real battle was still ahead, lurking just beneath the surface, waiting for the right moment to strike. The mayor may have been cornered now, but I could sense the darkness behind his eyes, the desperation that could lead him to make dangerous moves in retaliation. Whatever he had planned, it would be a fight for our lives, our town, and our future.

The energy in the room pulsed like a living organism, a tangible wave of emotion that swelled and receded with each new revelation. Gavin and I stood at the forefront of this storm, adrenaline coursing through us as Tommy's rallying cry had set the tone for defiance. The crowd, emboldened by his words, seemed to shift like the tide, a collective swell of resolve rising up against the mayor's tyranny. Yet, amid the fervor, a gnawing unease churned in my stomach, a whisper that the mayor would not go down quietly.

"Let's be clear," the mayor retorted, trying to claw back control. "I've brought this town jobs, I've funded our schools. These two are trying to destroy that for their own gain!" His voice was strident, but I could hear the cracks, the desperation creeping in like a chill wind through a broken window.

"Your so-called funding came with strings attached," Gavin shot back, voice steady, the anger in the room turning the air electric. "You can't just throw money around and expect everyone to look the other way while you profit off our misfortunes."

Someone from the back called out, "Yeah, we've seen the impact! Our community's in shambles, and you've been lining your pockets!" The truth hung in the air, heavy and undeniable, as the townsfolk began to rally, murmurs of support rising like a choir of discontent.

Just then, the mayor's assistant, a young woman with a penchant for pastel blazers and sharp nails, stepped forward, her face pale but fierce. "You're all being manipulated," she cried, her voice trembling but clear. "This isn't what you think. You're about to ruin everything!"

"Are you sure it's not you who's being manipulated?" I countered, my heart racing. "It takes a special kind of courage to stand up for what's right, even if it means going against your boss." The crowd murmured again, the words igniting a flicker of courage in those who had sat silent for too long.

The mayor, visibly sweating now, seemed to be unraveling before our eyes. "This isn't over," he hissed, his voice dripping with menace. "I've spent years building my career, and I won't let you take it from me."

"Then you should've thought twice before betraying the very people who put you in that chair," Gavin replied, stepping closer, his posture unyielding. "You've been playing a dangerous game, and we're not going to let you win."

But the mayor's eyes, wild with a mixture of fear and fury, scanned the room. It was as if he was calculating his next move, weighing the consequences of his desperation. "You think you've won? You have no idea what I'm capable of," he spat, the bravado fading to a quiver of vulnerability that sent a shiver down my spine.

Before I could respond, the doors burst open, a cacophony of footsteps heralding the arrival of several uniformed officers. The crowd parted as they strode in, the tension palpable as they moved toward the front. I glanced at Gavin, confusion etched across his face, and a creeping sense of dread began to settle in the pit of my stomach.

"Mayor Dawson," one of the officers said, voice firm but respectful, "we have a warrant for your arrest. You're to come with us immediately." The shock in the room was electric, as gasps filled the air, and eyes darted between the mayor and the officers.

"Arrest? For what?" the mayor blustered, though the fight in his eyes had dimmed significantly. "You can't do this! I'm the mayor!"

"Not for long, you won't be," one of the officers replied, unfazed by his bluster. "You're under investigation for corruption, misuse of funds, and conspiracy. We have evidence."

The crowd erupted in a mix of disbelief and exhilaration, a wave of emotion surging through them. I felt my heart race, a cocktail of fear and hope swirling within me. This was what we had fought for, but the uncertainty gnawed at me like a persistent itch.

Gavin turned to me, a smirk on his lips. "Looks like we might actually have a shot at cleaning house."

"Let's not celebrate too soon," I cautioned, my instincts prickling. The mayor's eyes glinted with something dark, something that suggested he wasn't ready to capitulate just yet. "He won't go quietly."

"Not without a fight," Gavin agreed, his expression turning serious. "But at least we have the law on our side now."

Just then, the mayor raised his hands, palms out in mock surrender, a sinister grin spreading across his face. "You think this is a victory? You have no idea what I've set in motion. The web I've spun is far bigger than any of you can imagine. You've only scratched the surface."

The officers exchanged wary glances, unsure of how to proceed with this sudden shift in the atmosphere. The crowd, caught between exhilaration and apprehension, seemed to hold its breath, sensing the tension thickening like the fog that often rolled in from the sea.

"Mayor Dawson, I suggest you come quietly," one of the officers said, taking a cautious step closer. "Resisting arrest will only make this worse for you."

The mayor laughed, a low, menacing sound that echoed around the room. "You really think you can take me down? You have no idea what I've planned. This isn't just about me; it's about everything I've built! You're all in over your heads."

I felt a chill run down my spine as he spoke, the implications of his words hanging heavy in the air. What had he done? What kind of damage could he unleash before he was dragged away?

The officers moved in, ready to handcuff him, but the mayor stepped back, a sudden wildness igniting in his eyes. "You think you've got it all figured out? I'm just getting started. Enjoy your little victory while it lasts!" With that, he lunged toward the nearest window, shattering the glass with a loud crash.

Gasps erupted from the crowd as the mayor dove through the broken glass, disappearing into the fog that hung thick over Misty Shores. The officers rushed after him, but the fog swallowed him whole, leaving only the echoes of his manic laughter behind.

I stood frozen, heart racing, breath catching in my throat. The room fell silent, the air heavy with uncertainty and fear. What had he meant by everything he'd built?

Gavin turned to me, eyes wide. "What just happened? Where did he go?"

"I don't know," I whispered, dread pooling in my stomach. "But we can't let this end here. If he's still out there, he'll come back with a vengeance."

A rumble of thunder rolled outside, almost in response to my fears, and I knew deep down that this wasn't over. Not by a long shot. The fight was far from finished, and as I stood there, surrounded by the remnants of shattered glass and broken trust, I couldn't shake the feeling that Misty Shores was about to be swept into a storm far more dangerous than any of us had anticipated.

Chapter 19: The Unveiling

The town hall, a weathered building cloaked in years of secrets and unspoken grievances, buzzed like a beehive disturbed by an intruder. The air crackled with tension, a mixture of anticipation and dread. I stood at the front, clutching a battered journal in one hand, the other holding a handful of photographs that seemed to pulse with a life of their own. Each picture was a portal into the past, a testament to the dark corners of our town's history that had long been buried under layers of silence.

"Let me show you what I've discovered," I said, my voice rising above the discordant murmur. The room fell into an uneasy hush, and for a moment, I could hear my heart pounding, a wild drumbeat against the backdrop of the mounting tension. A dozen pairs of eyes, some wide with curiosity, others narrowed with suspicion, turned toward me.

With a deep breath, I opened the journal. The pages were yellowed and frayed, the ink faded yet still legible, each line a confession, a whispered truth waiting to be heard. "This is a record of events," I began, the words tasting both foreign and familiar on my tongue. "A record of decisions made in the shadows, a pact that sealed our fate." As I flipped through the pages, the crowd leaned closer, drawn in by the gravity of the moment.

The first photograph I held up revealed a timeworn gathering, townsfolk clustered in grim faces, their expressions etched with a mixture of resolve and fear. "These people," I pointed to the figures frozen in time, "made a choice that day. They believed it would protect us." My voice quivered slightly, but I pushed through, the adrenaline surging through me. "What they didn't foresee was the cost."

A murmur rippled through the audience, a low hum of disbelief and intrigue. My best friend, Nora, stood at the back, her eyes wide as she processed the revelations. I could see the gears turning in her mind, the same fiery determination that had always driven her to uncover the truth.

"But the truth doesn't protect us from our past," I continued, urgency threading my words. "It chains us to it." I could feel the weight of the mayor's presence behind me, looming like a thundercloud ready to unleash a storm. I had expected resistance, but the intensity of Mayor Callahan's glare sent chills down my spine. He was a man who had thrived on power, and the flicker of panic in his eyes told me he was all too aware of the storm brewing.

"Enough of this nonsense!" he shouted, his voice booming over the gathering like a clap of thunder. "This is nothing but slander and lies!"

The crowd gasped, and I felt a surge of defiance. "Lies?" I retorted, my voice steady now. "These are truths you would prefer to remain hidden, truths that can no longer be ignored. Your reign of silence is over." I could see whispers darting through the audience, and for a moment, I relished the notion that the tide was shifting.

Mayor Callahan stepped forward, his face a storm of fury and indignation. "You think you can tear this town apart with your fantasies? We have built a community here, one based on trust and unity!" His words dripped with irony, the warmth of his bravado chilling under the weight of my evidence. "You're nothing but a fool chasing shadows."

"Chasing shadows?" I echoed, my tone sharper than intended. "What's truly foolish is pretending we can sweep our history under the rug while we dance around in ignorance. This 'unity' you speak of is nothing but a thin veneer covering years of deceit."

The room was thick with tension, the energy shifting from anticipation to confrontation. Nora, sensing the undercurrents, took a step forward. "This isn't just about the mayor, everyone. This is about us—about our families and our future. We owe it to ourselves to confront the truth, no matter how painful."

Her words resonated, igniting a spark of rebellion among the townsfolk. Faces that had once appeared blank now mirrored my determination, a shared awakening flickering in their eyes. "We deserve to know what's been done in our name," I added, feeling the swell of courage in my chest. "What happened here isn't just history; it's part of us, and it will continue to haunt us until we face it."

The mayor's expression darkened, the mask of authority slipping as he clenched his fists. "You think this is a game? You're meddling with things you don't understand!" His voice was a low growl, threatening and primal, echoing through the hall like a warning bell.

"And you're right, Mayor," I shot back, adrenaline fueling my resolve. "I don't understand everything yet, but I'm determined to find out. If we have to unravel this mess, then so be it. We owe it to those who came before us and to those who will come after."

The crowd's murmur grew into a chorus, voices blending into a collective heartbeat that seemed to resonate in the very walls of the building. The fear that had once paralyzed us began to dissolve, replaced by a shared determination to uncover the truth. I glanced at Nora, whose expression mirrored my own resolve, and I felt a rush of gratitude for her unwavering support.

But Mayor Callahan's eyes gleamed with malice, a predator cornered but not yet defeated. "You're playing a dangerous game, my dear," he warned, his tone smooth yet laced with menace. "And the consequences could be far worse than you imagine."

With a defiant glare, I straightened my posture, feeling the journal's rough edges dig into my palm, grounding me. "Then let the game begin. I'd rather face the truth, no matter how dark, than live in the shadow of a lie."

The crowd erupted in a mix of gasps and murmurs, the energy shifting once more. It was a fragile victory, but it was a victory nonetheless, one that lit a fire within us all. The stakes were high, but I was ready to fight for the truth, no matter the cost.

The air thickened with tension as Mayor Callahan stepped back, the defiance in my voice lingering in the space between us like a challenge thrown into the wind. The crowd shifted, a mass of uncertain faces caught in a whirlwind of emotions—fear, anger, hope—all tangled together. It was as if the very foundation of our small town, one built on whispers and hidden truths, was cracking before my eyes. I could sense the shift, a wave of energy pulsing through the room as if we were on the brink of something monumental.

"Do you truly believe you can just tear down what we've built?" Mayor Callahan's voice dripped with incredulity, but there was a tremor beneath the bravado. "You think those who made that pact didn't have their reasons?"

I felt the weight of the journal pressing against my side, the words within it like a ticking clock, counting down the moments until the truth would either set us free or bury us deeper in the shadows. "Reasons? Or excuses?" I shot back, the challenge igniting a fire within me. "What you've called progress has merely been a mask for oppression. And every one of us in this room has paid the price."

Behind me, the townsfolk began to murmur, their voices blending into a chorus of agreement, a tide slowly rising against the mayor's authoritarian grip. I could see the faces of those who had once stood by him, those who had trusted him without question, now flickering with uncertainty. There was Nora, her fingers fidgeting nervously, but her eyes were bright, urging me on. "We have a right to know," she mouthed, and I could almost hear her echo in the hearts of the others.

"Listen to her!" a voice called from the back, strong and unwavering. It was Old Man Thompson, the town historian, who had spent decades piecing together the fragments of our past. "We've been living in fear for too long, afraid to confront the darkness that lurks behind our façades."

The shift in the crowd was palpable, a collective inhalation that held the promise of rebellion. I took a deep breath, trying to steady my racing heart. This was it—this was our moment. "We are not here to condemn the past," I said, my voice rising again, firm yet resonant. "We are here to understand it, to break free from the chains that bind us."

Mayor Callahan's face darkened, his brows furrowing in frustration. "And you think you're equipped to handle the truth? You, a child playing with fire?" He turned to the crowd, his voice oily with manipulation. "What she's offering is chaos. A return to the very fears we sought to escape."

The crowd shifted uneasily, wavering like candle flames caught in a draft. "If we bury our heads in the sand, we'll just be stepping into the same trap," I pressed on, determined to reclaim their attention. "You may have lived your life without questioning, but I refuse to accept ignorance as safety. We deserve to know what sacrifices were made in our name."

The mayor glared at me, his expression a tempest of fury and desperation. "You're just a kid with big dreams. You think this journal holds answers, but all it does is sow division." His voice dripped with condescension, each word calculated to sting.

A man in the front row rose to his feet, his voice booming. "And what do you propose instead? To keep us in the dark? To continue living under your thumb? We have a right to decide our future!" The conviction in his tone reverberated through the hall, a rallying cry for those yearning for change.

"Exactly!" I chimed in, grateful for the support. "Every one of us deserves the chance to choose our own path, not be led by someone who cloaks himself in authority while hiding the truth behind closed doors. What's the worst that could happen? We might actually find out who we are."

The room seemed to vibrate with shared energy, a sense of unity building as the murmurs shifted into a chorus of agreement. I could see it in their eyes—the flicker of recognition, the dawning realization that together, we could confront our past and reclaim our future.

But the mayor wasn't finished. "You think this is all a game?" he sneered, stepping closer. "You think that exposing what's hidden won't have consequences? This is more than just our town; it's our lives, our families. Do you think they'll thank you for unraveling the delicate fabric we've woven?" His voice dripped with false concern, but the tremor betrayed his fear.

I refused to flinch. "What's more dangerous: a life built on deceit, or the potential for a fresh start, even if it means facing uncomfortable truths? If we can't confront our history, we are doomed to repeat it."

The room fell into silence, the weight of my words settling over us like a thick fog. A few people exchanged glances, uncertainty still etched on their faces, but others nodded slowly, a hint of understanding breaking through the doubt. I could feel the tide turning, the momentum shifting as the crowd began to lean in, captivated by the possibility of change.

"Let's choose to rise together," I urged, my voice softer now, drawing them in. "We can't rewrite history, but we can rewrite our future. Imagine a place where we're no longer haunted by our past, where we can live without the specter of fear looming over us."

The murmurs grew louder, a palpable sense of resolve igniting the air around us. "What do we want?" someone shouted from the back.

"Truth!" another voice chimed in.

"Unity!" came the response.

"Freedom!" echoed another, the chant rising like a tide.

"Then let's stand together," I called out, my heart racing as I realized we were forging something powerful. "Let's commit to understanding our past, to reclaiming our narrative, and ensuring that the dark corners of our town can no longer dictate our lives."

As the crowd erupted in applause and cries of agreement, I locked eyes with Mayor Callahan, who stood rooted to the spot, fury etched across his features. The room buzzed with renewed energy, each heartbeat a promise of change. We were no longer merely individuals—together, we were a force, ready to confront whatever shadows awaited us.

The applause faded, replaced by a tension so thick it felt like a living thing, curling around us as we held our collective breath. I could sense the mayor's fury boiling beneath the surface, a tempest waiting to erupt. "You think this is a victory?" he spat, venom dripping from his words. "You're just opening a door to chaos, and once it's open, there's no going back."

The crowd, once a sea of faces filled with uncertainty, now shifted to one of resolve. The energy surged, electric and palpable, igniting a spark of defiance that shimmered in the air. "And what have we been living in? A façade?" I challenged, my voice steady as I faced him head-on. "You call it order, but it's nothing but oppression masked in civility. We can't afford to be blind any longer."

Old Man Thompson, still standing strong, interjected, "What's the truth behind the pact, Mayor? Why was it hidden? We deserve to know!" His voice boomed through the hall, stirring the restless murmurs of agreement among the crowd.

Mayor Callahan's expression hardened, and I could see the gears of his mind turning, weighing the potential fallout. "Fine. If you want the truth, then prepare yourselves for what it truly means," he said, his voice dropping into a low, almost conspiratorial tone that sent chills down my spine. "You think this is just about a simple agreement? The past is a web woven tightly. Pull one thread, and you'll find it's all interconnected. You might unleash something you're not ready to face."

A ripple of unease passed through the audience. "What do you mean?" someone shouted from the back. "What are you hiding?"

"Ah, hiding is such a lovely word," he said with a tight smile, the corners of his mouth twitching as if he were trying to contain something monstrous beneath. "What I'm saying is, sometimes the truth is more dangerous than ignorance. It's not just our past that's at stake. It's our future."

Nora leaned closer to me, her voice barely a whisper. "What's he talking about? Do you think he knows more than he's letting on?" Her eyes flickered with worry, a stark contrast to the fire ignited in my heart.

"I don't know," I murmured, feeling the weight of the moment pressing down. The air felt thick and heavy, laden with anticipation. "But we can't back down now."

The mayor took a step closer, his presence looming, a dark silhouette against the flickering lights of the hall. "What if I told you that the pact was never meant to protect you? What if it was always a means to an end?" His words dripped with malice, each syllable echoing like a distant drumroll, beckoning the chaos that lay just beneath the surface.

"What end?" I pressed, a mixture of dread and determination swelling within me. "If it was meant to protect us, then what could possibly be so threatening?"

He smiled then, a smile that didn't reach his eyes. "You've seen only fragments, my dear. You think history is just a collection of events? It's a living, breathing entity. And some things—some truths—were buried for a reason. If you dig too deep, you may awaken the very horrors that lie beneath."

A gasp rippled through the crowd, and I could feel the fear tightening around us like a noose. "Are you threatening us?" I demanded, anger surging through me. "This isn't about you. This is about us taking our power back."

"You're treading on dangerous ground," he warned, his voice dropping to a low growl. "I've lived in this town longer than most of you. I know what can happen when the past refuses to stay buried. People can get hurt."

Hurt. The word hung in the air, a specter looming over our heads. "We've already been hurt!" I shouted, the frustration bubbling over. "What more can you possibly threaten us with? We have to face this together, or we'll be forever chained to your secrets."

Nora stepped forward, her eyes bright with a fierce determination that seemed to galvanize the crowd. "We're done being afraid! If we're going to face the darkness, we need to know the truth, whatever it may be."

The murmurs grew again, the crowd shifting toward her, caught in the wave of her conviction. I could feel the hope swelling, pushing against the despair that had long clung to our town. But I also felt the mayor's simmering anger, a dangerous heat that threatened to boil over.

With a sudden move, he raised his hand, silencing the crowd. "You don't understand what you're asking for," he said, his voice low and intense. "You think this is just about the past? What if I told you there are forces at work here that are far beyond your comprehension? Those photographs, that journal—it's not just a history lesson. It's a warning."

"What do you mean?" I pressed, desperation tinging my words.

"Those involved in the pact didn't just promise to keep the darkness at bay; they made sacrifices," he said, his voice chillingly calm. "Sacrifices that could come back to haunt us all if disturbed."

A cold shiver raced down my spine as I considered the implications. "What kind of sacrifices? What are you hiding?"

His gaze flickered across the room, taking in the faces of the townsfolk who had stood with me, who had begun to challenge him. "You're digging deeper than you should, and it may very well cost you your lives," he warned, his eyes narrowing as if he were assessing each of us, weighing our resolve against the darkness he hinted at.

Suddenly, the lights flickered, casting erratic shadows on the walls, and a sharp crack echoed from somewhere outside, as if the very heavens were responding to the storm brewing within the hall. Gasps erupted, and I felt the ground tremble beneath us, as if the earth itself were reacting to the truth we were on the brink of uncovering.

"See?" Mayor Callahan said, his voice rising above the chaos. "Do you think this is just coincidence? This is only the beginning. What you're stirring isn't just history; it's a curse that can reach far beyond this town. You might awaken something that has been sleeping for generations."

"Then let it awaken," I said, heart racing as I faced him down. "If that's the price we must pay to uncover the truth, then I'm willing to risk it. We all are."

But before the crowd could respond, the doors of the town hall burst open with a resounding crash, and a figure stepped inside, drenched in shadows, eyes glinting with a fierce light that cut through the dimness. "Stop!" the figure shouted, voice laced with urgency. "You don't know what you're dealing with!"

As the figure stepped into the flickering light, I recognized them instantly—a face I had thought lost to time, one that held secrets that could alter everything we had just begun to uncover. A gasp rippled through the crowd, and the tension shifted again, the atmosphere charged with fear and confusion.

"Who are you?" I demanded, my heart pounding in my chest as the weight of the moment settled in.

But the answer hung heavy in the air, unresolved, and in that moment, it was clear: we were not just fighting for our past, but for our very lives.

Chapter 20: The Mayor's Wrath

The wood-paneled walls of the town hall loomed around us, a monument to tradition now transformed into a stage for the unfolding drama. Shadows danced across the faces of the townspeople, reflecting their confusion and fear, swirling like the autumn leaves outside the tall windows. The scent of old books mingled with the acrid smell of sweat and tension, suffocating in its intensity. Mayor Callahan, with his sharply tailored suit and an expression etched with fury, stood at the dais like a dark cloud about to unleash a storm. His voice thundered through the hall, a booming reminder of the power he wielded in this small town.

"You dare to question my authority?" His tone was laced with incredulity, and I could see the veins throbbing at his temples, an alarming indication of his escalating rage. The townspeople, a mix of familiar faces—Mabel from the bakery with her flour-dusted apron, and Mr. Jenkins, the elderly librarian whose spectacles teetered precariously on his nose—shifted uneasily in their seats. They had once looked to him for guidance, but now I sensed a flicker of doubt creeping into their eyes.

"Your authority is built on lies, Mayor," I said, my voice trembling only slightly as I stepped forward. Gavin's grip on my hand was a steadying force, grounding me in this whirlwind of conflict. "I'm not here to destroy, but to reveal the truth that has been buried beneath your misdeeds. The safety of this town depends on it."

"Safety? You think you can protect them by spreading chaos?" He stepped down from the dais, his presence looming larger, as if he could intimidate me back into silence. "You're no hero, Emily. Just a misguided girl playing with matches in a house of cards."

His words stung, igniting a familiar flame of determination within me. The stakes were higher than ever. Behind me, the townsfolk whispered among themselves, their murmurs growing louder, punctuated by the rustling of their chairs as they leaned in closer. They were hungry for the truth, just as I was desperate to unveil it.

"It's not chaos; it's clarity," I retorted, my pulse quickening. "The real danger lies in the shadows you've created. The missing funds, the neglected roads, the broken promises. You think this is just about you and your pride, but it's about every single person in this room who has trusted you."

At that moment, I felt the weight of my words settling into the air, wrapping around us like a suffocating fog. Gavin's thumb brushed over my knuckles, a silent reminder that I wasn't alone in this fight. I stole a glance at him, his blue eyes filled with quiet resolve that mirrored my own. Together, we had pieced together the evidence—years of corruption hidden behind the guise of civic duty.

Mayor Callahan scoffed, the contempt dripping from his lips. "You really think you can make a difference? You think people will believe a disgruntled employee over their beloved mayor?" His voice dripped with sarcasm, but I could see the crack in his facade. The longer I spoke, the more I peeled back the layers of his arrogance, revealing the vulnerability beneath.

The murmurs among the townsfolk began to crescendo, igniting a flicker of hope within me. I took a deep breath, feeling the weight of their collective gaze pressing down, urging me forward. "They deserve to know the truth, Mayor, even if you don't want them to. I've gathered evidence, testimonies from those who've suffered under your rule. You've silenced dissent for too long, but no more."

The tension shifted palpably in the room as some townspeople nodded, emboldened by my words. Mabel's hand rose, trembling but determined. "Emily's right! We've been afraid to speak up, but that doesn't mean we haven't noticed. The roads are falling apart, the schools are underfunded, and you keep smiling while we suffer!"

A ripple of agreement swept through the crowd, a wave of realization crashing over them. The mayor's face paled, his confidence faltering as he realized he was losing his grip. The echo of voices filled the hall, each one a small act of rebellion against the power he wielded.

Callahan's eyes narrowed, fury transforming into a desperate attempt at control. "You will regret this, Emily. I will make sure of it. You think this is a game?"

"Perhaps you're the one playing games, Mayor," I shot back, the words spilling from my lips with unexpected ferocity. "This isn't a game for me or for anyone in this room. This is our home, and we deserve better than the lies you've fed us."

Gavin squeezed my hand, an anchor in the tumult. "Emily, they're starting to see through the fog. Don't stop now." His encouragement was like a balm, soothing the tension coiling within me.

I turned back to the townspeople, their faces a canvas of hope and fear. "We have the power to change things. Together, we can reclaim our town. We can hold him accountable!" My voice rang out, strong and clear, resonating with the heartbeat of the room.

In that moment, the air crackled with energy, a shared conviction igniting a fire in their hearts. The mayor, once a towering figure of authority, now seemed smaller, cornered by the tide of dissent that had risen in the wake of my defiance.

"Enough!" he barked, his face flushed with rage. "You're playing with fire, and I will make sure you get burned!"

The threat hung in the air, heavy and oppressive, but I felt a surge of courage wash over me. I had stepped into the light, and there was no turning back. This was more than a battle for truth; it was a fight for the very soul of our town. I couldn't falter now—not when the stakes had never been higher.

Gavin's grip was warm against my palm, a steady anchor as the tide of doubt and uncertainty ebbed and flowed among the townsfolk. The murmurs intensified, rising and falling like waves crashing against a rocky shore, each voice a small ripple in the growing current of dissent. I could sense their collective heartbeat, pulsing with trepidation but also a flickering spark of courage. It was intoxicating, this blend of fear and resolve.

"Emily, you've crossed a line," Callahan spat, his voice slicing through the air like a knife. The sweat glistened on his forehead, and I could almost see the gears turning in his mind as he scrambled to regain control. "Do you really think the people will follow you? You've lost your grip on reality."

"Oh, I'm afraid you're the one losing grip, Mayor," I replied, my voice rising above the din. "Your grip on power is slipping through your fingers like sand, and you know it. You can shout all you want, but the truth has a way of surfacing, even in the murkiest waters."

The crowd shifted, their uncertainty teetering on the edge of transformation. Mabel stepped forward, her apron fluttering like a flag of rebellion. "We've all seen the discrepancies in the budget. It's time we stop pretending everything is fine. How many more lies do we have to swallow before we take a stand?"

Her words ignited a spark in the room, and I felt the atmosphere shift, like a storm cloud gathering momentum. It was electric, the kind of tension that could erupt into something beautiful or something disastrous. I was counting on the former.

"Do you really want to be remembered as the mayor who let corruption fester?" I continued, my voice steady now, bolstered by the support of my friends and neighbors. "This isn't just about me. It's about all of us—the families struggling to make ends meet, the children who deserve better schools, the roads that are practically impassable. We deserve a leader who will fight for us, not against us."

Callahan's face contorted, his lips curling into a sneer. "And you think you're that leader? A little girl playing dress-up in a big city? This is laughable!"

Laughter erupted from the back of the room, a harsh sound that cut through the tension like a knife. It was Jimmy, the town mechanic, who had always had a flair for the dramatic. "Well, Mayor, if Emily's just a little girl, then what does that make you?" he shot back, his voice dripping with sarcasm. "A big fish in a tiny pond? Or just a little fish that's grown too big for its boots?"

Laughter rippled through the crowd, a wave of energy washing over them, and I felt a rush of hope. Even the mayor couldn't ignore that. His face flushed a deep crimson, and I could see the anger boiling just beneath the surface, ready to explode.

"Enough of this nonsense!" he bellowed, his hands clenching into fists at his sides. "I will not allow you to tear this community apart with your delusions! You think this is easy? You think leading a town is just about waving a magic wand and making everything perfect? It's hard work! It requires sacrifices!"

"Sacrifices?" I echoed, incredulous. "What sacrifices have you made besides our trust? You've built your empire on our backs, while we scrape by and you line your pockets! That's not sacrifice; that's betrayal!"

The room fell silent, the gravity of my words hanging in the air like an uninvited guest. I could feel the shift in the atmosphere, a collective breath held in anticipation. Mayor Callahan was on the defensive now, and I was not about to let him regain his footing.

"I've sacrificed my personal life for this town," he shot back, desperation creeping into his voice. "I've given everything! My family, my time... for what? So you can tear it all down?"

"Your family? Your time?" Mabel scoffed, stepping closer, emboldened. "You don't get to use that as a shield. You've sacrificed nothing but integrity and trust. We deserve a leader who actually cares about this community, not one who thinks they're untouchable!"

A murmur of agreement rippled through the crowd, and I felt Gavin's hand tighten around mine once more, as if he were channeling all his strength into me. My heart raced, pounding like a drum in my chest, urging me to keep going.

"Emily is right," he said, his voice steady. "This town deserves more than empty promises and threats. We can do better. We must do better."

Callahan's eyes darted between us, calculating, his façade cracking under the pressure of our unity. "You think this is a joke? You think you can just waltz in here and challenge my authority? I've been mayor for fifteen years! I'm the only reason this town hasn't gone completely under!"

"And yet here we are," I said, stepping forward, challenging him with a fierce gaze. "If you were so great, why are we drowning? You've lost the trust of the people, and you know it."

A crack in his armor appeared, a flicker of uncertainty that made my heart surge with hope. The tension was palpable, a thick fog of emotions that filled the hall. The townspeople were no longer just spectators; they were participants in a story that had long been dictated by fear.

"Let's put it to a vote," I proposed, my voice ringing clear through the air. "Let's see who really has the support of this town. Are we willing to accept the status quo, or do we demand change?"

A ripple of surprise coursed through the crowd, and I saw the glimmer of hope in their eyes. The mayor's face paled, but I could sense his anger boiling just beneath the surface. This was the moment of truth, the point of no return.

"Are you willing to risk your future on this?" Callahan spat, his eyes blazing. "Do you think the grass is greener on the other side? You have no idea what you're asking for!"

"Oh, but I think I do," I replied, my voice steady. "We're asking for honesty, for accountability, for a chance to rebuild our town without the weight of corruption hanging over us. We've suffered long enough, and it's time to rise above it."

The tension shifted again, and I could feel the crowd leaning in, their collective energy swirling around us, a vortex of determination and hope. I locked eyes with Gavin, and in that moment, I knew we were on the brink of something monumental, something that could redefine the very fabric of our community. The die was cast; now all that remained was to see how it would unfold.

The room was a battleground, each breath filled with the scent of heated arguments and the electric thrill of defiance. The townsfolk were no longer mere spectators; they were co-conspirators in this volatile moment. My heart hammered in my chest, a wild drumbeat urging me forward. "Let's take a vote," I repeated, my voice stronger this time, piercing through the oppressive atmosphere. "Let's see if the mayor still has the support he claims, or if the truth is finally stronger than his lies."

The mayor's expression morphed from disbelief to fury, his brow furrowing deeply as he processed the implications of my challenge. "A vote? You think you can orchestrate a coup in a matter of minutes? You're delusional!" His laughter was a harsh bark, but it faltered against the tide of murmurs swelling in the crowd.

"Delusional or not, the truth is in front of you, Mayor," I pressed, emboldened by the crowd's shifting loyalty. "The question is, are you willing to let the people decide their future? Or will you continue to hold them hostage to your reign of fear?"

A silence fell, thick and suffocating, broken only by the rustle of chairs as townspeople leaned in, drawn by the drama unfolding before them. My pulse raced, the anticipation almost intoxicating. A hand shot up at the back of the room, trembling but determined. It was Mrs. Henley, the retired schoolteacher, her voice quaking yet resolute. "I vote for change," she declared, her words ringing with conviction.

As if ignited by her bravery, others began to follow suit. "Change!" shouted Jimmy again, his voice a rallying cry. "We've had enough!"

With each new declaration, the momentum swelled, the very air crackling with a newfound energy. Callahan's face darkened, an ominous storm cloud brewing above him. "You're all fools! You don't understand what you're asking for!" He stepped forward, his voice rising in desperation. "Do you think another mayor will solve anything? You'll end up with worse!"

I could feel the crowd's resolve solidifying. "Maybe," I said, matching his intensity. "But we can't go on like this, pretending everything is fine while you line your pockets and leave us to fend for ourselves. At least give us a chance to choose!"

The mayor faltered, caught in the tempest of dissent that he had created. I watched the gears in his mind turn, a mix of anger and fear playing across his face. The reality of losing his power was a palpable threat, and I could see it weighing heavily on him.

"Let's take a vote!" Gavin's voice cut through the mounting chaos, his tone authoritative yet encouraging. "A show of hands! All those in favor of calling for a new leadership, raise your hands!"

I looked around as hands hesitantly shot up, rising like saplings seeking sunlight. Mabel's hand shot up proudly, followed by Jimmy's and Mrs. Henley's. One by one, more hands joined the chorus, my heart swelling with hope.

With every hand that raised, the weight of fear began to lift, replaced by a sense of agency I hadn't felt before. Callahan stood frozen, a wild animal cornered, his bravado crumbling under the weight of reality. "You're making a grave mistake," he warned, but the tremor in his voice betrayed the bluff.

The hall erupted into applause and cheers, a symphony of voices echoing off the walls, their unity forging an unbreakable bond. But amidst the elation, a chill crept into my heart, a whisper of doubt that settled like ice in my veins. What would happen when the dust settled? Would the mayor retaliate in ways we hadn't foreseen?

Suddenly, the doors of the town hall burst open, slamming against the wall with a thunderous crash. All heads turned, the raucous noise falling into stunned silence as a figure stepped inside. It was Greg Thompson, the mayor's right-hand man, his face pale and strained, eyes wide with urgency.

"Emily! You need to come with me, now!" he shouted, panic coloring his voice, cutting through the euphoria. "It's not safe. The mayor—he's not taking this well. You need to leave before—"

Before he could finish, the mayor exploded into action, his voice rising in fury. "Get her! Don't let her escape!"

In an instant, the air shifted, a palpable sense of danger hanging heavy as Greg grabbed my arm, pulling me toward the exit. "Come on!"

The crowd erupted into chaos, the applause turning to shouts of confusion and fear as the mayor's men—his enforcers—began to swarm. Gavin's hand slipped from mine as I was yanked away, his blue eyes wide with alarm. "Emily!" he yelled, desperation lacing his voice.

"Gavin!" I screamed back, but I was already being pulled away, the crowd parting like the Red Sea, confusion and fear filling the air. "You can't—"

Before I could finish, Greg dragged me through the doors, the weight of the mayor's wrath crashing behind us. "We have to move! Now!"

Outside, the cool evening air hit me like a slap, but there was no time to breathe it in. The sounds of chaos erupted from within, the shouts of the crowd mixing with the threat of authority. I felt like a marionette with its strings cut, flailing in the storm of uncertainty.

"Where do we go?" I gasped, my heart racing, the pounding echoing in my ears as we sprinted down the street.

"There's a car waiting! We can't stop!" Greg urged, pulling me along. My mind was a whirlwind of thoughts, images of Gavin's worried face flashing through my mind. Would he be safe? Would he follow?

As we rounded the corner, I caught a glimpse of something moving behind us—dark figures emerging from the town hall, urgency and anger etched into their faces. They were coming after us, and I could feel the dread clawing at my throat.

"Faster!" Greg shouted, his urgency driving me forward, but my legs felt like lead.

I glanced back just in time to see the mayor himself, a towering figure of rage, charging into the street, eyes blazing with fury. "Emily! You can't run from me!"

My heart lurched, a visceral panic propelling me onward. "We have to get to the car!" I gasped, my breath quickening as we rounded another corner.

But the way was blocked ahead—a group of men waiting, their expressions hard as stone, arms crossed and bodies tense, a wall of confrontation ready to crash down. I skidded to a halt, panic clawing at my insides.

"Greg, what do we do?"

He hesitated, eyes darting, searching for an escape route, but the realization hung heavy in the air—we were trapped.

Then, like thunder cracking in a clear sky, a gunshot echoed, the sound sharp and shocking. The world stilled, time suspended in a breathless moment as my heart stopped.

And just like that, everything changed.

Chapter 21: Dark Alliances

The air in the old church was thick with a tension that clung to my skin like a damp fog. Shadows danced across the stained glass, their kaleidoscopic colors flickering ominously as the sunlight struggled to penetrate the darkened corners of the room. I stood at the front, my heart racing as I faced the gathering crowd, their murmurs rippling through the space like a restless tide. Gavin, ever the steady presence beside me, held my gaze, a reassuring anchor amid the tempest brewing around us.

"Is this true, Emily?" A voice broke through the murmur, sharp and incredulous. It was Mrs. Granger, her hands clasped tightly in front of her, the rings on her fingers glinting like tiny stars. "What you're saying about the mayor... it can't be right. He's always been good to us."

Her words hung in the air, a thread pulling taut between loyalty and doubt. I could see the conflict churning in the eyes of those around her, a mixture of fear and curiosity that mirrored my own unease. "He has a reputation," I replied, my voice steadying, "but reputation is often just a mask, isn't it? What I've uncovered suggests there's more lurking beneath the surface."

I could feel the heat of the room rising, the subtle shift in energy as the townsfolk wrestled with the implications of what I was saying. Gavin stepped forward, his presence commanding. "Look, we're not here to tear this town apart," he said, his tone calm yet firm. "But if we don't confront the truth now, it'll only fester and grow. We owe it to ourselves—and to the future of this town—to dig deeper."

A low murmur rippled through the crowd, but Mrs. Granger shook her head, her expression a mix of confusion and disbelief. "And what exactly are we supposed to do with this information? The mayor has always looked out for us. You're asking us to turn against him without proof."

Her words stung, each syllable a dagger in my resolve. I could almost hear the wheels turning in the minds of the onlookers, the gears of loyalty and betrayal grinding against one another. I opened my mouth to respond, but before I could find the right words, a chill swept through the room, as if the very air had turned to ice.

"Emily," a voice called from the back, cutting through the rising tide of dissent. It was Jake, his presence like a beacon in the gloom. "What do you know about the old quarry?"

The question hung in the air, dense and heavy. I could feel the crowd shift, their attention pivoting toward me, curiosity woven with apprehension. "The quarry?" I repeated, trying to mask the flicker of surprise. "What does that have to do with anything?"

"It's where the mayor had that deal with the developers," Jake explained, stepping closer, his brows furrowed in concentration. "I heard they were planning to turn it into a luxury complex, but something fell through. Something that made him... desperate."

My mind raced, the pieces of the puzzle clicking into place. "Desperate enough to go to extremes?" I mused, the realization dawning like the first light of dawn breaking through a long night. The quarry, a place steeped in history and whispered tales of betrayal, was the crux of it all.

Gavin shifted beside me, his expression sharpening. "If he's desperate, then he might have something to hide. We need to look into this."

I nodded, adrenaline coursing through my veins. "If there's corruption tied to that deal, it could unravel everything. But how do we convince them?" I glanced at the townsfolk, their faces still wrestling with doubt.

"Let's start by showing them," Gavin suggested, his voice steady as granite. "We'll investigate the quarry, dig up the facts, and present the truth. The mayor can't hide behind his charm forever."

With that spark igniting in my chest, I turned to the crowd again, my voice clear and resolute. "We can't let fear keep us silent. We have a choice: to stand by and let one man's greed dictate our future, or to uncover the truth, no matter how dark it may be."

A murmur of agreement rippled through the crowd, gaining strength. Hope flickered in the air, battling against the shadows of doubt. Mrs. Granger looked at me again, the war in her eyes beginning to shift toward understanding. "And if you're wrong?" she asked, her voice softer now, almost hesitant.

"If I'm wrong, I'll admit it," I replied, feeling the weight of her gaze. "But if I'm right, we'll have saved our town from the very thing that could tear it apart."

The air crackled with tension, and for a moment, it felt as though we were all suspended in time. I held my breath, waiting for the tide to turn, praying that the currents of change were finally in our favor.

Just then, the doors of the church swung open with a creak, and in stepped Mayor Callahan himself, the embodiment of charm wrapped in a cloak of authority. His smile was disarming, but I felt the undercurrents of unease ripple through the crowd like an electric charge. "What's all this commotion?" he asked, his eyes sweeping over us, assessing, calculating.

I straightened, heart racing, suddenly acutely aware of how our fragile alliance hung in the balance. This was the moment. "We're talking about the quarry," I said, my voice stronger than I felt. "And your plans for it."

His smile faltered, just a fraction, but it was enough. In that instant, I knew we were standing on the edge of something monumental, a precipice where truth and deception would clash in a battle for the soul of our town.

The tension in the air thickened as Mayor Callahan stepped further into the church, his presence a dark cloud that loomed over our fragile gathering. The flickering light cast shadows that danced ominously on the walls, and for a heartbeat, I could almost hear the whispers of the past echoing through the rafters. He was dressed impeccably, as always, in a tailored navy suit that seemed to absorb the light, enhancing the aura of authority that surrounded him. The way he moved, with that easy confidence, sent a ripple of unease through the crowd.

"Emily," he said, his voice smooth like velvet, yet underscored with steel, "I hope you're not spreading rumors that could harm our community." His smile, tight-lipped, was the kind that sent shivers down my spine.

"Rumors?" I shot back, refusing to shrink under his gaze. "I prefer to call them revelations." The room held its breath, a collective gasp nearly palpable. Gavin's hand brushed against mine, a silent affirmation of our resolve.

"I think we can all agree that your enthusiasm is commendable," Callahan replied, his tone dripping with condescension. "But let's not forget that unfounded accusations can lead to unwarranted fear." He turned to the townsfolk, a practiced orator skillfully playing the crowd. "This is a good town. We've built it together, brick by brick. Why would we want to destroy it over wild fantasies?"

A murmur of uncertainty spread through the crowd, and I felt a surge of frustration. "What's wild about asking questions?" I challenged, stepping forward. "What's wild about demanding transparency from our leaders? You've built this town on trust, Mayor. Shouldn't we hold you accountable for the truth?"

He raised an eyebrow, an amused smirk tugging at the corners of his mouth. "And I suppose you think you're the arbiter of that truth? What exactly do you think you've uncovered?"

My heart raced as I sensed the crowd's shift, their gazes flitting between us like a flock of startled birds. I needed to rally them, to remind them why we were here. "I've uncovered connections—dealings that put profit over our community's wellbeing. The quarry isn't just a piece of land; it's a battleground for power, and it's time we claim our voice in this."

With every word, I felt the weight of their doubts begin to lighten, the veil of fear lifting just a fraction. Mrs. Granger's expression softened, her previous defensiveness giving way to curiosity.

"Maybe we should hear her out," Jake interjected, a spark of defiance lighting his eyes. "If there's something to this, we owe it to ourselves to look deeper."

Callahan's smile faltered, the façade cracking. "You'd risk everything for a story?" he said, his voice low, menacing. "What if it's all a lie? Are you prepared to bear the consequences of that?"

"Yes," I asserted, the conviction in my voice growing bolder. "Because living under the shadow of deceit is a far greater consequence."

The room was alive with murmurs, the townsfolk stirring as the tide began to turn. But just as I felt the momentum shift, Callahan's eyes narrowed. "You don't know what you're getting into, Emily. Some things are better left buried."

The warning sent a chill racing down my spine, but I met his gaze, unwavering. "What are you afraid of, Mayor? That the truth will come to light?"

He took a step closer, the tension palpable, like a string stretched to its breaking point. "Be careful, my dear. Truth has a way of twisting itself into something unrecognizable."

Before I could respond, a loud crash echoed through the church, causing everyone to jump. The doors swung open violently, and a figure stumbled in—Clara, breathless and wild-eyed. "You need to see this!" she exclaimed, her voice urgent, cutting through the heaviness like a knife.

The crowd shifted, eyes wide with curiosity and concern. Clara had always been the town's unofficial historian, a keeper of secrets tucked away in the folds of our shared history. She approached me, her hands trembling slightly. "I found something at the library. Documents—records about the quarry."

"Documents?" I echoed, my heart racing anew. "What kind of documents?"

"Come on!" Clara urged, glancing nervously at Callahan, whose expression darkened. "They're in the back. You won't believe what I uncovered."

Gavin took my hand, his grip firm, and we followed Clara, the crowd parting for us like the Red Sea. As we made our way to the back of the church, I could feel the weight of the mayor's gaze on my back, a predator sizing up its prey.

Clara led us to a small room filled with old, dusty books and scattered papers, the scent of aging wood mingling with the musty aroma of forgotten knowledge. "I was organizing some old records and stumbled across these," she said, her fingers riffling through a stack of papers. "It's all about the town's dealings with the quarry—plans, correspondence, even a few financial reports that suggest some shady dealings."

My pulse quickened as she handed me a crumpled piece of paper. I scanned it quickly, my heart thudding as I absorbed the implications. "This... this outlines a deal with a company from out of town. They were set to develop the quarry, but it looks like they backed out last minute. Why?"

Clara shook her head, her expression troubled. "That's the question, isn't it? But there's more. If you dig deeper, you'll find names—people connected to Callahan. Friends, business partners..."

A feeling of dread settled in my stomach as the pieces started to connect. "He wasn't just trying to build a new development; he was trying to cover something up."

"Exactly," Clara said, her voice barely above a whisper. "But we need to be careful. If Callahan catches wind of this..."

"Then we'll make sure he doesn't," I replied, determination surging through me. "This town deserves the truth, no matter what it takes."

The sound of footsteps echoed in the hallway, drawing closer. Callahan's voice, smooth yet menacing, floated through the air. "Emily, I trust you'll reconsider your approach. You don't want to make an enemy of me."

A glance exchanged between Gavin and me ignited a silent pact, a shared understanding that we would not back down. As the footsteps drew nearer, the tension hung thick in the air, every moment pulsing with uncertainty, yet igniting a fire within me that demanded to burn brighter. The truth was waiting to be uncovered, and I was ready to face whatever shadows lay ahead.

As the footsteps drew closer, I felt a tension knotting in my stomach, a visceral instinct warning me that the game was about to escalate. Clara and I exchanged a glance, her eyes wide with both anticipation and dread. Gavin's grip on my hand tightened, grounding me in the moment even as the shadows deepened around us. The mayor's smooth voice resonated from the doorway, laced with a threatening undertone that sent chills skimming down my spine.

"Emily, I truly hope you're not considering reckless actions. It's not wise to poke your nose into affairs that don't concern you," he said, stepping into the room like a wolf among sheep. The way the light played off his slick hair and polished shoes gave him an almost supernatural quality, a predatory elegance that made my skin crawl.

I steeled myself, forcing my voice to remain steady. "This does concern me, Mayor. It concerns all of us. We deserve to know what's happening with our land and our future." The truth resonated in my chest, a pulse of righteousness that I could no longer ignore.

He chuckled, a sound that was both charming and dangerous. "You see, that's where we differ. You view it as a matter of justice; I see it as a matter of discretion." He leaned against the doorframe, his posture relaxed but his eyes sharp, darting between Gavin, Clara, and me as if sizing up our resolve. "Discretion has kept this town thriving. It's a delicate balance we've maintained, and I would hate to see it disrupted by rumors and unfounded fears."

"Rumors?" Clara shot back, her voice rising. "These are documents, Mayor. Evidence. You're the one who should be worried about what people will think if they find out about your dealings."

His smile faded, and for a split second, I glimpsed something darker beneath the surface—a flicker of anger that momentarily unmasked the charm he so carefully wore. "Careful, Clara. You might not like the consequences of your words."

The warning hung in the air, heavy and foreboding, but it only fueled my determination. I stepped forward, my voice ringing out with newfound courage. "You think you can intimidate us into silence? You're wrong. This town deserves transparency, not threats."

Gavin moved beside me, his presence a steadfast reassurance. "We won't back down, Callahan. If you think this is going to end here, you're mistaken."

The tension in the room crackled like static before a storm, the air thick with unresolved conflict. Callahan's lips twisted into a smirk, his bravado unwavering. "Very well, but don't say I didn't warn you. The truth can be a dangerous thing, especially when it's not the whole truth." With that, he pushed himself off the doorframe, his retreat smooth and calculated.

As the door closed behind him, I felt the room exhale, the oppressive weight of his presence dissipating, leaving behind a lingering tension that seemed to pulse in the stillness. Clara let out a breath she hadn't realized she'd been holding. "What do we do now?" she asked, her voice shaking slightly.

"Now," I said, glancing at the papers scattered across the table, "we dig deeper. We find out everything we can about those documents and about Callahan's connections. If we can expose his lies, maybe we can finally break the grip he has on this town."

Gavin nodded, his determination matching mine. "I'll help however I can. We need to act quickly before he figures out we're onto him."

Just as I began to sort through the papers, trying to piece together the connections Clara had hinted at, a loud thump echoed from the main hall. My heart raced as I exchanged worried glances with Clara and Gavin. "What was that?" I whispered, the weight of dread settling in my stomach.

Clara stepped closer to the door, straining to listen. "I don't know, but it didn't sound good."

Before I could respond, the door swung open again, this time with such force that it rattled on its hinges. A figure burst into the room, panic etched across her face—Mary Thompson, the local journalist who had always been one step ahead of the town's gossip mill. "You won't believe what I just saw!" she exclaimed, her breath coming in quick bursts.

"Mary, what is it?" I asked, my curiosity piqued, yet dread creeping back in.

"I was at the old quarry," she said, words tumbling out in a frantic rush. "I thought I'd gather some information, you know, for a piece on local history. But when I got there, I saw something. Something big."

"What did you see?" Gavin pressed, his voice firm, encouraging her to keep going.

She hesitated, her eyes darting around the room as if expecting eavesdroppers. "There were trucks—huge trucks, and they were unloading equipment. I thought they'd stopped working on the site, but now it looks like they're gearing up for something major."

"Are you sure?" I asked, the implications dawning on me like a storm cloud gathering overhead. "What were they unloading?"

Mary swallowed hard, her hands trembling. "I couldn't get too close, but it looked like machinery for drilling. And there were men in hard hats, not the usual crew. They seemed... different."

Gavin and I exchanged a look that spoke volumes. "We need to go," I said, adrenaline surging through my veins. "If they're starting work again, it could mean Callahan is planning something big—and if it's shady, we need proof."

Mary nodded, her determination mirroring mine. "I'll drive. I know a way to get close without being seen."

As we hurried out of the church, I felt the urgency of the moment enveloping us, the weight of our mission pressing down with every step. The sun had dipped low, casting long shadows that stretched like fingers across the path as we rushed to the car.

Once we were inside, Mary turned to me, her eyes wide with anxiety. "Are you really sure we should be doing this? What if we get caught?"

"If we don't do anything, Callahan wins by default," I replied, my voice steady but my heart racing. "We have to take this chance."

The engine roared to life, and as Mary navigated the winding roads toward the quarry, I couldn't shake the feeling that we were heading into the belly of the beast. The trees blurred past us, shadows shifting in the dying light, and I realized how much was at stake.

As we approached the quarry, the sight that greeted us sent a shiver down my spine. The sprawling site was lit up with harsh floodlights, illuminating a scene that felt all too surreal. Heavy machinery loomed like giants against the night sky, and a flurry of activity swirled around us, voices raised in urgent chatter.

"Look," Mary whispered, pointing toward a cluster of men huddled together, their hard hats gleaming under the lights. "They're all wearing the same logo. That can't be good."

I squinted into the darkness, trying to make sense of it all. Just then, a sharp cry sliced through the air, and we froze. A figure stumbled from the shadows, staggering backward, hands raised in a panic. "Help!" he shouted, eyes wide with terror. "They're coming!"

Before I could react, the ground beneath us trembled, a distant roar building into a crescendo. The floodlights flickered ominously, casting an eerie glow over the chaos unfolding at the quarry.

"Get out!" I yelled, adrenaline surging as I realized we had stumbled into something far more dangerous than we anticipated. The roar grew louder, the air thickening with the unmistakable scent of smoke and fear.

And then, out of the shadows, figures emerged—menacing shapes, their intentions clear as they closed in around us, the night suddenly feeling more hostile than ever. In that moment, I understood the depths of Callahan's machinations and the stakes we had unwittingly stepped into. We had crossed a line, and the dark alliances we were unraveling were about to respond.

Chapter 22: Unmasking the Shadows

The moon hung high, a silver coin tossed into the velvet sky, casting an ethereal glow over the dilapidated church that had been a witness to secrets far darker than the shadows that clung to its crumbling walls. Gavin and I had ventured into this sanctuary of history, determined to unearth the truths buried beneath layers of dust and deceit. I pulled my cardigan tighter around my shoulders, the chill seeping in through the cracked windows and the echo of our footsteps reverberating like whispers of ghosts long forgotten.

The scent of mildew mingled with that of ancient wood, creating a heady perfume that felt almost sacred. I could almost hear the stories woven into the fabric of this place, the prayers and fears of those who had sought solace within its weathered confines. Gavin, a tall figure beside me, his brow furrowed in concentration, was equally captivated. His fingers danced over the ledgers we'd discovered, each page crackling softly under the pressure of his touch. I glanced at him, taking in the way his dark hair fell slightly over his forehead, the hint of a smile playing at the corners of his lips despite the gravity of our task. There was something disarming about him, a warmth that soothed my unease.

"Are you sure this is where we'll find anything?" I asked, breaking the silence that had settled between us like a heavy blanket. My voice felt small against the backdrop of our search, but it was also laced with determination. I had learned that even in the most unlikely places, truth could flicker to life like a candle in the dark.

Gavin looked up, his blue eyes sparkling with mischief, even in this gloomy sanctuary. "You underestimate the power of history, my dear. These ledgers are like breadcrumbs leading us to the truth." He paused, his lips curving into a smirk. "And maybe a few more than just breadcrumbs. I'm betting there are whole loaves of scandal here, just waiting for us to slice them open."

I chuckled, the sound bouncing off the walls, and for a moment, the tension that had coiled tightly in my chest began to loosen. It was moments like these that reminded me of why I found him so compelling—a mix of charm and intellect wrapped in a package that was surprisingly endearing. The fact that he was risking everything to stand by my side made the hairs on the back of my neck stand up, but not in fear. No, this was a different sensation—one of exhilaration, a thrill that promised change was within our grasp.

As we sifted through the papers, the flickering candlelight danced across the pages, illuminating faded ink that told tales of deals struck in the dead of night, of shady transactions with dubious figures, all orchestrated by a man who was supposed to be our protector. The mayor's name appeared more than once, a ghost haunting the records we unearthed. The deeper we delved, the more it felt like we were peeling back layers of an onion, each revelation bringing tears to my eyes, though these were not tears of sorrow, but of disbelief.

"Look at this," Gavin said, his voice barely above a whisper as he turned a page, his fingers trembling slightly with anticipation. "It mentions an alliance with the old mining company—back when the town was nearly bankrupt. They accepted a deal that turned their fortunes around but at what cost?"

I leaned closer, my heart racing as I scanned the text. "It's like they sold their souls for a quick profit," I murmured, my mind racing with the implications. "How could they do this? How could they let themselves be drawn into something so... so sinister?"

Gavin's gaze met mine, a fire igniting between us, a shared understanding of the weight of the truth we were unearthing. "Because sometimes, desperation makes us blind to the darkness lurking beneath our desires." His words resonated deeply, a reminder of the human fragility that often led us astray.

We continued to scour the records, my fingers brushing over the pages, feeling the stories embedded in the paper. Each ledger we uncovered seemed to pulse with its own heartbeat, a reminder of the lives that had been forever changed by choices made in shadows. I felt an unshakeable urge to do something—anything—to bring this truth to light, to help the townspeople reclaim their power from the hands of a man who thrived in the darkness.

Gavin leaned back against a dusty bookshelf, crossing his arms as he watched me with a bemused expression. "You look like you're about to launch into a revolution."

"Maybe I am," I replied, a spark igniting in my chest. "If we can gather enough evidence, we could expose the mayor's corruption. We could give the people back their hope."

He chuckled, the sound a low rumble that echoed in the hushed space. "And if we get caught? This isn't just a matter of exposing someone's bad choices; it's a fight against a man who won't hesitate to silence us."

A chill ran down my spine, and I couldn't shake the feeling that we were being watched, the very shadows around us twisting with the weight of our conversation. "Then we need to be careful. If we tread lightly, we might just make it out alive."

His expression shifted, and I saw a flicker of something—fear, perhaps? Or was it a deep-rooted commitment to our cause? Either way, I could see that my determination was beginning to seep into him. Together, we were building a fragile alliance, one rooted in truth and rebellion, and I was sure we'd need every ounce of courage we could muster for the battle ahead.

As we dove deeper into the archives, I could feel the pulse of the town's history vibrating around us, a melody of struggles and triumphs that had gone unheard for too long. The dusty papers became our armor, the knowledge within them our weapon, and with each revelation, I knew we were inching closer to the heart of the darkness that had gripped our town for too long. The night was far from over, and with every moment, we were weaving our own story into the tapestry of this place—a tale of courage, defiance, and hope that would one day light the way for others lost in the shadows.

As dawn's first light filtered through the cracked stained glass, splashing colors across the dusty floor like spilled paint, I felt an uneasy thrill settle in my bones. The atmosphere was thick with unspoken possibilities and latent danger, yet a flicker of hope ignited within me. Gavin, still engrossed in the musty ledgers, barely noticed as I traced the patterns on the floor with my fingertips, feeling the coolness of the stone beneath. Each heartbeat echoed the rhythm of the past, a reminder that we were standing on the precipice of something monumental.

"Hey, you think the mayor has a secret lair down here?" Gavin's voice broke through my reverie, rich with playful skepticism. He flipped through another brittle page, his eyebrows raised in mock seriousness. "I can picture it now—a hidden door behind the altar, a dark chamber filled with money, secrets, and maybe even a pet tarantula named Edgar."

I snorted, half-laughing, half-sighing. "If that were true, I'd like to think Edgar would be the one calling the shots." I leaned against the wall, crossing my arms, feeling the wood splinter slightly under my weight. "But let's face it, if he had a lair, it would probably be filled with more paperwork than nefarious plans."

A glimmer of mischief danced in Gavin's eyes, and I felt a warmth spread through me. It was moments like this that grounded me, made the gravity of our situation a little lighter, if only for a heartbeat. The seriousness of our quest could easily crush a person under its weight, yet here we were, weaving humor into the threads of danger.

As I resumed my search, the musty aroma of paper seemed to intertwine with my thoughts, pulling me deeper into the tangled web of our town's history. Each ledger unveiled a world of conspiracy and compromise, revealing names and dates I'd never expected to see linked together. I felt a twinge of anger bubbling beneath the surface. How could the townsfolk have trusted him? A man who'd traded their future for power and profit.

"Look at this." Gavin's voice, suddenly serious, drew me back to the present. He held a ledger page aloft, his expression a mix of triumph and disbelief. "This entry shows funds being funneled into renovations for the mayor's mansion from the mining company. They're literally using taxpayer money to fix up his digs!"

My heart raced as I leaned closer, the reality of it washing over me like ice water. "That's unbelievable. He's robbing from the very people who put him in power." The anger in my voice surprised me; it had a depth that felt unfamiliar yet empowering. "We need to find a way to expose this."

Gavin nodded, his eyes narrowing as he flipped to another page. "Here's the kicker. Look who signed off on these funds—none other than our dear Mayor Thompson himself." His finger traced the ink as if hoping to extract some hidden truth from the curls of the letters. "If we can gather enough evidence, we could bring him down."

The gravity of our discovery settled heavily in the air between us. My heart raced with both excitement and apprehension, like I was standing at the edge of a cliff, peering into the unknown depths below. What would it take to challenge the man who had wrapped our town in shadows for so long? A pang of doubt fluttered in my chest, but I pushed it aside. I wouldn't let fear dictate my choices.

"I don't know how much longer we have," I said, my voice steadier than I felt. "If he catches wind of what we're doing, he won't hesitate to bury us." I paused, biting my lip. "We need a plan. We can't just wander around digging up dirt without thinking it through."

Gavin's gaze was steady, and I saw a flicker of understanding there. "You're right. We need to be tactical. Let's document everything, then devise a strategy for getting the information into the right hands. The press, maybe? Or even someone in law enforcement we can trust?"

"Or someone who's already got a foot in the door," I suggested, my mind racing. "What about Marissa? She's always been a staunch advocate for transparency in the local government. If anyone can make a splash, it's her."

Gavin's brow furrowed slightly. "But can we trust her? The last thing we need is to tip off someone who might run straight to the mayor. She's got connections, but those connections might not work in our favor."

I considered his words, feeling the tension of the decision creeping in. "I know her well enough to trust her. Besides, what's the alternative? Sitting on this evidence while he continues his reign of deceit? I refuse to stand by while he manipulates everyone in this town."

Gavin rubbed the back of his neck, a gesture I had come to recognize as a sign of his internal debate. "Alright, let's move forward with caution. We can approach her discreetly and gauge her reaction. If she's on board, we can plan our next steps."

With renewed determination, we returned to our search, each page revealing more of the mayor's treachery. The ledger records spoke of dark deals made under the guise of economic growth, manipulations that left many in our community suffering while he filled his pockets. Each line felt like a knife, slicing through my faith in the very institutions meant to protect us.

A soft creak echoed from the shadows, and I froze, every instinct screaming that we were no longer alone. Gavin's eyes darted to the door, a silent communication passing between us as he gestured for me to stay low. My heart hammered against my ribcage, a frantic rhythm that echoed the uncertainty of our predicament.

"Do you think it's him?" I whispered, trying to keep my voice steady as I scanned the dimly lit room.

"Let's not assume anything until we know for sure," he replied, his voice low and calm, but I could see the tension in his jaw.

Just then, a figure stepped into the doorway, silhouetted by the early morning light. My heart dropped as the outline became clearer, and a familiar face emerged from the shadows—Marissa, her expression a mixture of concern and curiosity. "What are you two doing in here at this hour?"

Relief washed over me, but it was quickly replaced by a new kind of tension. "We're, uh, doing some research," I stammered, trying to gauge her reaction.

Her eyes narrowed slightly, picking up on our unease. "Research? In the church archives? That doesn't seem very... conventional."

"Maybe unconventional is what we need," Gavin interjected smoothly, a flicker of his earlier mischief returning. "You know how boring town meetings can be. Thought we'd spice things up a bit."

Marissa crossed her arms, a knowing smile tugging at her lips. "If you're looking for a little excitement, I hope you've come across something worth sharing."

The spark of possibility ignited again, but this time it felt different. We weren't just sharing a joke; we were standing on the edge of revelation, ready to pull back the curtain on the truth that had long been hidden. And as we exchanged glances filled with unspoken understanding, I knew we were no longer just three individuals bound by circumstance; we were allies, each of us willing to take risks in the pursuit of justice.

With a deep breath, I prepared to dive into the story that was unfolding, knowing that the path ahead would be fraught with peril, yet promising the kind of adventure that transformed lives. In that moment, I felt the weight of history shift, as if the town itself was leaning closer, eager to witness what we might uncover together.

The tension in the church was palpable, a living entity that seemed to wrap itself around us as Marissa stepped further into the room, her expression shifting from curiosity to concern. "What do you mean by research?" she pressed, her tone a mixture of playful suspicion and genuine interest. "Are you two diving into the town's murky history without me?"

Gavin leaned against the dusty bookshelf, arms crossed, a lopsided grin forming. "You caught us, Marissa. We're forming a secret society dedicated to unearthing all the town's dirty laundry. Interested?"

Marissa arched an eyebrow, her lips curving into a smile that suggested she was well aware of his charm. "As tempting as that sounds, I prefer my laundry to be washed and folded. What's really going on here?"

I exchanged a glance with Gavin, who gave me a slight nod. I could sense the delicate balance we had to maintain, a trust that hung in the air like the dust motes swirling in the early morning light. "We've come across some records," I said, my voice steadying, "that detail some troubling financial dealings involving Mayor Thompson and the mining company. We believe there's corruption at play."

Marissa's demeanor shifted immediately, seriousness eclipsing her earlier amusement. "Corruption? That's a bold accusation." She stepped closer, the confidence radiating from her compelling. "What kind of dealings are we talking about?"

With a quick exchange of glances, Gavin began to summarize the key points while I rifled through the ledgers for the most damning evidence. "It looks like taxpayer funds were diverted to the mayor's personal projects under the guise of 'community development,'" he explained, his voice steady but laced with urgency. "If we can prove it, we could take him down."

Marissa leaned in, absorbing every word, her eyes widening slightly with each revelation. "If this is true, we need to act fast. The mayor has a lot of influence, and he won't take kindly to anyone prying into his affairs." She paused, her lips pressing into a thin line. "Do you have a plan?"

"Not yet," I admitted, feeling the weight of our recklessness settle on my shoulders. "But we thought you might have some ideas on how to approach this without putting ourselves at risk."

Marissa's gaze flicked from Gavin to me, a thoughtful expression crossing her face. "We can't just march into the local news office waving these documents around. That'll tip him off immediately. We need to be strategic." Her eyes gleamed with determination. "What about gathering more evidence? If we can find witnesses or additional records, we'd have a stronger case."

"Exactly," Gavin chimed in, enthusiasm creeping into his voice. "We need to build a solid foundation before we make our next move."

I nodded, feeling a renewed sense of purpose surge within me. "What if we set up meetings with key people in town who might be privy to what's been going on? If we can get them to talk, we might uncover more dirt without drawing too much attention."

Marissa's eyes lit up, a spark of excitement igniting. "That's brilliant! We could start with those who've been affected by the mayor's decisions. There's bound to be a few disgruntled residents willing to share their stories."

Gavin clapped his hands together, breaking the tension that had settled around us. "Looks like we have ourselves a plan, then. Operation Unmask the Mayor is officially in motion."

As we huddled together, plotting our next steps, I felt an unexpected sense of camaraderie enveloping us, a bond forged in the heat of a shared mission. The anticipation coursed through me, mingling with the underlying fear that gnawed at the edges of my resolve. The path ahead was fraught with uncertainty, but for the first time in a long while, I felt empowered. The shadows that had haunted our town no longer felt insurmountable; we were ready to drag them into the light.

We spent the next hour poring over the ledgers, documenting key findings, and drawing up a list of potential contacts. The more we uncovered, the more it became clear that the mayor's grip on our community was far more sinister than we'd initially thought. He wasn't just a corrupt politician; he was a puppet master, manipulating the strings of fear and ignorance to maintain his façade of power.

When the sun began to rise higher, spilling golden light through the broken stained glass, we decided it was time to leave the sanctuary of the church. The air outside was fresh, a crispness that felt like a promise of new beginnings. I took a deep breath, inhaling the scent of damp earth and blooming flowers that seemed to embody the hope we were trying to cultivate.

"Let's reconvene later," Marissa suggested as we stepped outside, the weight of the ledgers in our hands feeling lighter in the brightness of day. "I'll reach out to a few people I know and see if I can line up some meetings. Meanwhile, you two should try to gather as much information as you can."

"Sounds like a plan," Gavin agreed, a smile tugging at his lips. "And hey, if we find anything juicy, I promise to save you the best bits for our big reveal."

Marissa laughed, a sound like bells tinkling in the air. "You know I'll expect nothing less. Just don't get yourselves into too much trouble while I'm gone."

"Trouble is our middle name," I shot back, a playful challenge in my voice. "Just wait and see what we can dig up."

As we parted ways, I felt the excitement building within me, an electrifying buzz that made my heart race. With each step, the reality of our mission settled deeper into my bones. We were on the brink of something significant, and I could almost taste the freedom waiting just beyond the horizon.

Hours later, Gavin and I met at our favorite café, a cozy little place with mismatched furniture and the rich aroma of coffee that filled the air. As I sipped my espresso, I couldn't shake the feeling that we were on the cusp of discovery. We shared our findings, piecing together the fragments of information that might serve as the final pieces to the puzzle.

"Okay, so what's our next move?" I asked, my mind racing with possibilities.

Gavin leaned back in his chair, his brow furrowing in thought. "I think we should pay a visit to the old community center. There might be records there that could provide more insight into the mayor's dealings with the mining company."

"Great idea," I agreed, my excitement bubbling over. "The community center has always been the heart of our town. If anything is amiss, it'll be buried in those archives."

As we finalized our plan, the café door swung open, and a gust of wind swept through, rattling the loose papers on our table. My heart skipped a beat as I spotted a figure stepping inside, a tall silhouette cloaked in shadows. The moment I laid eyes on him, I felt my stomach drop. It was Mayor Thompson himself, his sharp gaze scanning the room like a predator on the hunt.

Gavin must have sensed my sudden tension because he turned to follow my gaze, his face paling as he recognized the man who had been at the center of our storm. "What do we do?" he whispered urgently, his voice barely audible above the hum of conversation.

Before I could respond, the mayor's eyes locked onto ours, a sinister smile creeping across his face that sent shivers down my spine. "Well, well, what do we have here?" he drawled, the smoothness of his voice laced with condescension. “Looks like you two have been busy.”

My heart raced, panic and adrenaline surging through me as I realized we had been found. In that instant, I knew we were teetering on the edge of danger. The atmosphere shifted, and the world around us faded into a blurred backdrop, leaving only the tension between us and the man who had ensnared our town in darkness.

Gavin and I exchanged a frantic glance, the gravity of the situation hitting us like a tidal wave. The mayor had arrived, and it was clear he wasn’t about to let us walk away unscathed. My pulse raced, adrenaline flooding my veins as I prepared for whatever confrontation lay ahead. Would we be able to stand our ground, or would we crumble beneath the weight of his power?

With a steadying breath, I steeled myself for the impending showdown, ready to face the storm brewing between us, my heart pounding in time with the uncertainty of what would come next.

Chapter 23: The Gathering Storm

The salty tang of the sea hung in the air, wrapping around me like a familiar embrace. I strolled along the weathered boardwalk, my feet crunching on the scattered remnants of seashells, each crackle echoing the rising tumult in my heart. Misty Shores, with its picturesque charm, had always felt like a slice of paradise. Now, however, it was a powder keg of secrets just waiting for a match. The laughter of children playing near the tide was a stark contrast to the urgent whispers I had overheard just moments ago. It felt as if the ocean itself was holding its breath, waiting for the tide to change.

Gavin walked beside me, his expression a mirror of my apprehension. His tousled hair caught the wind, sending curls dancing playfully above his forehead. The sight made me want to smile, but the gravity of our situation grounded my thoughts. He brushed a hand through his hair, glancing sideways at me. "You know, for a town that prides itself on its tight-knit community, it sure is full of loose lips," he quipped, attempting to lighten the mood.

"True, but in this case, I think the lips are better left sealed." I shot him a pointed look. "Especially if they lead straight to the mayor."

His brow furrowed, the lightness of his previous comment evaporating. "We need to find something concrete before he decides to make us disappear, or worse, frame us as the culprits."

The thought sent a shiver down my spine, the very notion of being hunted by the very man sworn to protect us igniting a fire within me. I had always been a fighter, but this was different. The stakes were higher, and the risks were more profound. I couldn't help but think of the hidden dangers lurking just beneath the surface of our idyllic town. What lay behind the charm of the white picket fences and blooming hydrangeas?

"I heard some talk about the old lighthouse," Gavin continued, his voice barely above a whisper, as if the wind might carry our plans away. "They say it hasn't been used in decades, but it's rumored to hold some secrets."

The lighthouse. My mind raced with possibilities. It stood at the edge of town, looming like a ghost from the past, forgotten yet full of stories begging to be uncovered. "Do you think the mayor knows about it?" I mused aloud, images of dusty staircases and salty air swirling in my imagination. "What if he's been hiding something there?"

"Only one way to find out." His resolve sent a flicker of hope through me. I had always admired Gavin's determination. It was infectious, a steady anchor when my own thoughts threatened to drift into despair.

As we made our way toward the lighthouse, the sky darkened, heavy clouds rolling in like the town's buried secrets rising to the surface. The air grew thick with anticipation, the wind whipping around us, tugging at my hair and urging us forward. The landscape changed, the cheerful sounds of the boardwalk fading into an eerie silence.

The lighthouse stood tall against the encroaching storm, its paint peeling, a sentinel against the elements. It had seen better days, much like our little town, but it still possessed a certain charm. As we approached, a sense of foreboding enveloped me. I glanced at Gavin, his determined stance a stark contrast to the unease creeping into my bones.

"Ready?" he asked, his voice steady despite the turbulence brewing in the sky.

"Only if you are," I replied, a hint of bravado threading through my words. Together, we pushed the heavy door open, the creaking sound echoing in the silence like an ominous welcome.

Inside, dust motes danced in the fading light, swirling like forgotten memories. The air was thick with the scent of aged wood and salt, a testament to the years spent battling the elements. Each step we took sent a plume of dust spiraling into the air, disturbing the tranquility that had settled here.

"Look at this," Gavin said, his voice reverberating off the walls as he crouched to examine an old lantern resting on a table, its glass cracked but still gleaming faintly. "This hasn't seen light in years."

"Just like the truth," I muttered, my thoughts racing ahead. "What if the mayor's hiding something here? Something that could expose his lies?"

His eyes met mine, a spark of determination igniting between us. "Let's split up and look for anything that could help. If he's hiding something, it's bound to be here."

We moved in tandem, scanning the room for clues, the walls echoing our footsteps as we tread softly on the worn floorboards. The tension in the air crackled, each creak and groan heightening our senses. I caught glimpses of rusted tools and forgotten trinkets, relics of a time when the lighthouse had been a beacon of hope. Now, it felt more like a tomb of secrets.

Suddenly, a noise echoed from the upper levels, a sharp scuffle that sent adrenaline racing through my veins. I shot a look at Gavin, who nodded, the unspoken agreement solidifying our resolve. We crept up the narrow, spiraling staircase, the walls closing in around us, shadows dancing as we ascended.

At the top, the lantern room welcomed us with a dim light, filtering through the dusty glass. My heart raced as we stepped into the vastness of the room, but what greeted us was not what I expected. An old journal lay open on the floor, its pages yellowed with age, filled with the scrawled handwriting of a long-forgotten keeper.

I knelt down, the scent of ink and paper wrapping around me. The words blurred together at first, but then they struck me like a bolt of lightning. Hints of hidden treasures, whispers of deceit, and a name I recognized all danced across the page, pulling me deeper into the mystery. I glanced at Gavin, who was poring over a set of old maps pinned to the wall.

"Gavin," I breathed, excitement surging through me, "I think we're onto something."

But before I could elaborate, a loud crash echoed from below, cutting through the fragile threads of our discovery. The sound sent us both reeling, instincts flaring. I exchanged a quick glance with Gavin, my heart pounding in sync with the chaos that threatened to engulf us.

The moment the crash echoed through the lighthouse, I felt the ground beneath me shift, not just from the sound but from the palpable fear that prickled at the back of my neck. Gavin's eyes widened, the once playful spark now replaced by a serious intensity that made my heart race even faster. "We should check that out," he whispered, his voice low, careful, as if we were in the midst of a heist rather than a simple search for the truth.

"Right, because lurking in a dark, creaky building with a potential criminal makes total sense," I shot back, my sarcasm a thin veil over my anxiety. But the adrenaline pulsed through my veins, propelling me forward. If there was danger lurking, I needed to confront it, and I was damned if I'd let fear dictate my actions.

We crept down the narrow staircase, my breath hitching as each step creaked underfoot. I couldn't shake the feeling that we were stepping into a spider's web, each movement drawing us closer to a sticky, dangerous trap. The ground floor loomed before us like a gaping mouth, ready to swallow us whole.

As we reached the bottom, the crash turned into a flurry of activity, muffled voices penetrating the walls, a cacophony of anger and urgency that made my stomach churn. I exchanged a glance with Gavin, who raised an eyebrow in question. We moved toward the door leading to the lighthouse's entrance, our bodies pressed against the wall, trying to catch snippets of the chaos unfolding outside.

"Do you think it's the mayor's goons?" I whispered, my voice trembling slightly. The idea of being caught up in something so big, so dangerous, sent a chill down my spine.

"Or maybe it's just a seagull with a vendetta," Gavin replied with a teasing smirk, though I could see the tension etched across his face. His attempt at humor fell flat in the face of the escalating turmoil outside.

With a nod, I pushed the door open just a crack, the rusty hinges groaning in protest. A narrow slit of light spilled into the dim room, and I squinted through the opening, my heart hammering in my chest. Below, a small group of figures surrounded a fallen crate, arguing vehemently. The sight was surreal—men in dark jackets gesticulating wildly, their voices rising and falling like the tide outside.

"What are they doing?" I breathed, straining to hear over the rushing sound of my pulse.

"Looks like they've stumbled upon something." Gavin leaned closer, his forehead nearly touching mine. "We need to get a better look."

I hesitated, the thrill of adventure warred with the instinct to retreat. "And if they see us?"

"Then we'll have a much more interesting story to tell." His smile was infectious, igniting a spark of courage in my chest. I pushed the door wider, and we slipped outside, shadows cloaking us as we inched closer, using the crates as makeshift cover.

"Hey, what do you mean it's not here?" one of the men bellowed, frustration lacing his tone. "The intel was clear—there was a shipment, and we need it before he finds out!"

"Calm down, all right?" another voice snapped back, barely audible over the whistling wind. "We're not leaving empty-handed. We'll check the old warehouse. If we don't find it there, we'll—"

"Find it where? In the mayor's office?" the first man retorted. "You think he's just going to hand it over? We're running out of time. He'll bury us all if we don't get that shipment."

Gavin and I exchanged worried glances, the implications of their conversation hanging heavy in the air. The mayor was involved in something far more sinister than I had ever imagined, and whatever it was, it was about to blow up in Misty Shores.

"Let's follow them," Gavin suggested, his voice urgent.

I hesitated for a moment, weighing the potential danger against the thrill of uncovering a hidden truth. "Do you have a plan?"

"Just stay close and don't let them see you," he whispered, his eyes glinting with excitement.

I nodded, adrenaline coursing through my veins, and we darted into the shadows. We trailed behind them, our footsteps muffled against the damp ground as we made our way through the maze of crates. The air was thick with the scent of brine and rust, each breath reminding me of the ocean's relentless power.

The group moved toward the old warehouse at the edge of the docks, the structure looming like a ghost against the darkening sky. The paint was peeling, the windows cracked, but it had an undeniable air of secrets hidden within its walls. I felt a thrill of anticipation—this was the heart of the mystery, the place where everything might converge.

Once inside, we pressed ourselves against a wall, barely daring to breathe as the men began to argue again, their voices rising in a fever pitch. "You don't understand how deep this goes! If we can't get that shipment, it's not just our heads on the chopping block—he'll come for everyone. The mayor isn't just any politician; he's a kingmaker. And we're pawns in his game."

My heart raced at the mention of the mayor's name. What kind of operation was this? The pieces began to fall into place, but the puzzle was far from complete.

"We need to find out what's in that shipment," I whispered to Gavin, who nodded, his gaze fixed on the men.

"Let's get closer," he replied, glancing around for an opening.

With a quick nod, we maneuvered through the shadows, inching toward a half-open door leading to the back room of the warehouse. The closer we got, the more I could hear the men's heated discussion.

"This is about more than just us," one of them said, his voice tense. "The mayor's dealing with some powerful players. If he gets cornered, who knows what he'll do? We have to get the shipment before he decides to cover his tracks."

I turned to Gavin, my heart pounding with a mix of fear and determination. "We have to record this," I murmured, pulling out my phone, knowing full well how shaky my hands were.

Gavin nodded, his expression grave. "Let's move quickly before they catch wind of us."

As I hit record, the tension in the air grew thicker, as if the very walls were leaning in, eager to catch every word. I could almost feel the secrets swirling around us, whispering promises of revelation that sent chills down my spine.

But just as I thought we might learn something crucial, the door to the warehouse swung open, revealing a tall figure silhouetted against the fading light. The breath caught in my throat as the unmistakable outline of the mayor stepped into view.

"What are you doing here?" he barked, his voice a low growl that sent a shiver of dread coursing through me.

The words hung in the air like a thunderclap, sending a jolt through my body. The mayor's presence loomed large, more threatening than the gathering storm outside. I felt Gavin stiffen beside me, his hand instinctively reaching for mine, anchoring me as

I fought the instinct to bolt. The shadows of the warehouse seemed to thicken around us, and the whispering voices of the men inside fell silent, each pair of eyes darting toward the intruder with a mix of fear and respect.

"What are you doing here?" the mayor repeated, his voice laced with irritation. He stepped fully into the dim light, his expression a mask of cold authority. His tailored suit, impeccable as always, did little to conceal the menace that radiated from him.

Gavin and I exchanged a quick, frantic glance, our minds racing. We were cornered, and our options were dwindling faster than the fading light outside. I could hear the faintest thud of my heart echoing in my ears, drowning out everything else. We were exposed, the walls closing in with every second.

"Um, we were just..." Gavin started, but the words tumbled out unconvincingly. The mayor's piercing gaze cut through our flimsy excuse like a knife.

"Spying?" he offered with a cynical tilt of his head. "That's rich, coming from a couple of kids playing detective. Do you think you can unearth secrets that have eluded far more capable people?"

The tension was so thick I could taste it—metallic and bitter, a warning of the danger that lay ahead. I could see the muscles in Gavin's jaw clench, a mix of defiance and fear bubbling beneath the surface. He had always been brave, and I admired that about him.

"We're just trying to help," I blurted, desperate to reclaim some semblance of control. "If something shady is happening, people deserve to know."

The mayor's laugh was a low rumble, almost mocking. "Help? How noble. But let me tell you something, sweetheart: the truth is often murky, and the people of Misty Shores are better off not knowing what lurks beneath the surface."

"Or maybe they'd be better off with someone who actually has their best interests at heart," Gavin shot back, his voice rising, emboldened by the urgency of our situation.

The mayor's eyes narrowed, a flash of irritation cutting through his composed facade. "You think you're the heroes in this story? You're merely children playing with fire. And I assure you, fire burns."

Before I could respond, the group of men shifted restlessly, the tension escalating like a dormant volcano ready to erupt. One of them took a cautious step forward, glancing between the mayor and us, his brow furrowed in uncertainty. "Sir, we need to—"

"Shut it!" the mayor snapped, his tone silencing the room. "This doesn't concern you. Get rid of them."

The command hung in the air, and I felt my stomach drop. This was it. We were outmatched, outnumbered, and unprepared for the consequences of our reckless curiosity. As the men approached us, their intentions evident in their advancing steps, panic clawed at my throat.

"Run!" Gavin shouted, his voice slicing through the chaos as he yanked me back toward the door.

We sprinted, adrenaline surging as we dashed past the men who hesitated, caught off guard by our sudden escape. The warehouse doors swung open with a creak, and the salty sea breeze met us like a welcome friend, urging us onward. But we had barely stepped outside when a figure blocked our path—another man, larger than the others, his arms crossed and a glare that could curdle milk.

"Going somewhere?" he growled, taking a menacing step forward.

I could feel my heart pounding in my ears, drowning out the sounds of the ocean. I glanced at Gavin, whose expression was a mixture of determination and desperation. "We need to distract him," I whispered urgently.

"On it," he replied, his voice steady despite the fear lacing it.

Before I could question his plan, he turned to the larger man. "Hey, why don't you ask the mayor what he really thinks of you? I hear he's not too happy about your little 'dealings' with his shipment!"

The man's brow furrowed, confusion flickering across his face. "What are you talking about?"

It was the opening we needed. Gavin took a step back, feigning innocence, while I edged around to find an escape route. "You know," I called out, "he's been calling you guys incompetent. Bet he wouldn't be too upset if you got caught doing something illegal."

The man's eyes narrowed, a mix of anger and suspicion swirling as he turned to glance back at the warehouse. It was the distraction we needed.

"Come on!" I urged Gavin, and we bolted past the man, adrenaline coursing through our veins. We raced toward the trees lining the edge of the property, their leaves rustling like a crowd of spectators urging us on. The sound of shouting followed us, a chaotic symphony of anger and confusion, but we couldn't stop now.

Once we reached the cover of the trees, I turned to Gavin, panting heavily, trying to catch my breath. "What now?"

"Head to the beach," he suggested, his eyes scanning the darkening landscape. "We can circle around and—"

But before he could finish, the unmistakable sound of footsteps on gravel drew closer, the crunching echoing ominously in the silence that enveloped us.

"Hide!" I hissed, pulling him down behind a cluster of bushes. We crouched low, our breaths quieting to muted whispers as we watched a pair of headlights sweep across the clearing.

"Damn it," Gavin muttered, frustration etched across his face. "They're coming after us."

I bit my lip, fear coiling tight in my stomach. "What if they find us?"

“Then we need to make sure they don't,” he replied, his voice steady, but I could see the flicker of worry behind his eyes.

The vehicle pulled up just beyond the trees, the headlights illuminating the warehouse and casting long shadows. We held our breath, our hearts pounding as the engine turned off, plunging us into a tense silence.

A door slammed, and the unmistakable sound of footsteps approached. “They can't have gone far,” the voice was familiar—it was the mayor, his tone filled with frustration. “I want them found. Now.”

As I looked at Gavin, a sudden thought struck me, an idea so crazy it might actually work. “We can't let them see us. We need to create a distraction, something big enough to draw them away.”

Gavin's eyes widened, the gears in his mind clearly turning. “What did you have in mind?”

I smiled, adrenaline surging once more. “You still have that old firecracker from the Fourth of July, right?”

“What? Are you out of your mind?” he laughed nervously, but there was a glimmer of excitement in his eyes.

“Do you have a better idea?” I shot back, determination coursing through me.

He shook his head, the playful spark returning. “No, but it better not blow us up in the process.”

I grinned, feeling that familiar thrill of rebellion. “We'll make it work. Trust me.”

As he rummaged through his bag, the footsteps drew nearer, the mayor's voice carrying an ominous promise. “They can't hide forever. They think they can meddle with my plans, but I'll show them the consequences.”

We exchanged one last glance, our resolve solidifying as the weight of the moment bore down on us. Time was running out, and so was our chance to uncover the truth. The night felt electric, filled with the tension of unspoken threats and hidden dangers, and as we prepared to set our plan in motion, a shadow loomed at the edge of the trees—a figure emerging from the darkness, watching us with eyes that sparkled with malice.

"Looks like your little adventure is about to come to an end."

Chapter 24: Nightfall's Embrace

The salty breeze whipped through my hair, each gust a reminder of the storm brewing both outside and within. The cliffs rose sharply behind us, jagged sentinels against the horizon, while the ocean below crashed relentlessly against the rocks. Each wave seemed to echo my inner turmoil, the rhythmic crash and retreat mirroring the tumult in my heart. I had always found comfort in the wildness of the sea, but tonight it felt different, more ominous, as if it were warning me of the tempests yet to come.

Gavin stood beside me, his silhouette a stark contrast against the silver light of the moon, which hung heavy in the sky, illuminating the world in an ethereal glow. He was a steady presence, his broad shoulders relaxed yet alert, embodying the calm I so desperately sought. I turned to him, catching the glint of vulnerability in his eyes. "What if we're chasing something that isn't even there?" I asked, my voice barely rising above the roar of the ocean. "What if this quest of ours leads to nowhere?"

He didn't answer immediately, his gaze fixed on the horizon where the water met the sky in an indistinguishable line of dark. The tension stretched between us, palpable and thick, like the air before a summer storm. I shifted my weight, the sharp edge of the cliff pressing against my back, grounding me as I awaited his reply.

"I know how you feel," he finally said, his tone low and contemplative. "I've been there before. The world can seem so dark sometimes, as if the light is just out of reach." His words hung in the air, heavy with shared understanding. "But I've learned that even in the shadows, there's always a glimmer of hope, something worth fighting for."

A shiver ran through me, not from the chill of the wind, but from the depth of his confession. Gavin had always been a pillar of strength, but tonight, I sensed the cracks beneath his sturdy facade.

"What happened to you?" I ventured, curiosity woven with concern. "What made you this way?"

He turned to me, and for a fleeting moment, the wall he had built around his past seemed to waver. "I lost someone once," he said, his voice barely above a whisper. "Someone who believed in me when I didn't believe in myself. I thought I could protect them, but I failed. And I've been running from that failure ever since."

The weight of his words settled over us like a thick fog. I could almost feel the air grow heavier, each breath laden with the unspoken stories of his heart. "Gavin..." I began, unsure of how to offer comfort without pushing him further into the shadows. "You can't carry that alone."

A flicker of something—regret, perhaps—passed through his eyes, but he quickly masked it with a soft smile, one that didn't quite reach the depths of his gaze. "I learned that the hard way," he admitted, his lips curving in a wry grin. "But I've also learned to lean on others. And you... you make it easier to open up."

His honesty ignited a fire in my chest, an urge to peel back the layers of his heart and share my own fears in return. "I've been scared too," I confessed, my heart racing as I stepped closer to him, feeling the warmth radiate from his body. "Every step we take feels like we're walking a tightrope. What if we fall?"

"Then we'll fall together," he said, his voice steady, his hand reaching out to intertwine with mine. The contact sent a jolt of electricity through me, grounding and sparking all at once. "We'll find a way to stand back up. We'll figure it out together."

The tide surged, a massive wave crashing against the rocks below, sending sprays of saltwater into the air, mingling with the sound of our laughter. I marveled at how easily the atmosphere shifted, how the darkness felt less daunting with him by my side. It was as if the moonlight had cast a spell over us, illuminating the hidden corners of our souls, and in that moment, the chaos of our quest felt surmountable.

As the laughter faded, a deeper silence settled in, allowing the weight of our words to linger. I glanced sideways, studying the contours of his face, the way the moonlight accentuated his strong jaw and the slight furrow in his brow as he stared out at the restless sea. There was a yearning in his expression, an unvoiced question that hung in the air between us.

"What if we actually succeed?" I mused aloud, the thought both thrilling and terrifying. "What if we find what we're looking for?"

"Then we'll change everything," he replied, his voice low and fervent. "We'll change ourselves, and maybe even the world around us." His gaze met mine, and in that moment, the vastness of the ocean felt like a mere reflection of the boundless possibilities that lay before us.

The silence that followed was charged with unspoken dreams and fears, a tapestry woven from our hopes and doubts. I could feel the weight of the unknown pressing against us, but Gavin's presence felt like a lifeline. It was strange how, in this vast expanse of the world, we had carved out a small sanctuary on this cliff, where everything else faded into the background, leaving only us and the shadows that danced beneath the moonlight.

"What if the journey is the destination?" I asked, my voice a mere whisper, uncertain yet hopeful. "What if it's about finding each other along the way?"

He chuckled softly, the sound warm and inviting, melting away the chill that had crept into my bones. "You always did have a knack for turning the bleak into something beautiful," he teased, his thumb brushing lightly over my knuckles. "But you might be onto something. Maybe it's not just about the end, but the moments that lead us there. And these moments... they're worth fighting for."

The world around us faded into a hazy backdrop as our connection deepened, drawing me closer to him. The moon hung high above, a silent witness to our unraveling truths, as if it too understood the weight of our fears and the promise of our bond. In the embrace of nightfall, we stood together on the precipice of uncertainty, not just facing the darkness but daring to explore it together, one heartbeat at a time.

The night air crackled with unspoken promises as I stood there, heart racing, captivated by Gavin's unwavering gaze. The world around us faded, and the sound of the waves crashing against the cliffs became a soothing backdrop to the chaos of our thoughts. I marveled at how we had carved out this little pocket of time amidst our swirling lives, a sanctuary where our vulnerabilities could intertwine.

"What if we're too late?" I murmured, the words escaping before I could catch them. The festival had left behind more than memories; it had unearthed expectations, shadows that loomed larger than life. I felt the weight of my concerns settle like stones in my stomach. "What if we've missed our chance to discover whatever it is we're searching for?"

"Then we create our own chance," Gavin replied, his voice steady as the lighthouse that stood sentinel on the farthest edge of the cliffs. "Every moment we've spent searching, questioning, even doubting, has brought us here. Together."

I caught his eye, a flash of mischief darting through his expression. "You're sounding almost poetic. Are you sure you're not a secret author?"

He chuckled, the sound rich and deep, resonating within me like a favorite song. "Only if you promise not to critique my metaphors. I've had enough of those in my life."

"Deal," I shot back, matching his grin. It felt good, exchanging banter that pushed away the dark clouds of uncertainty hovering above us. Still, beneath the surface, the gravity of our quest weighed heavily on my mind. "But seriously, Gavin, what if we don't find the answers? What if this is all for nothing?"

His expression softened, and the playfulness of our exchange faded like the setting sun. "What if it is?" he asked, tilting his head as if he were weighing my words on a scale of importance. "Sometimes, the search itself holds more significance than the outcome. It's about what we discover along the way."

He had a point. I considered the friendships we'd forged, the laughter shared, the moments of vulnerability that had woven our lives together. But there was still a lingering doubt, a whisper of fear that gnawed at me. "I guess, but what if we're not enough?"

"Not enough?" His brows knitted together, and I could see the challenge sparking in his eyes. "What does that even mean? Are you saying you think you lack something?"

My heart raced at the intensity of his gaze. "Maybe I'm not brave enough. Not as brave as you."

"Bravery is subjective," he said, stepping closer, our bodies nearly touching, the tension thickening the air between us. "You're not afraid to confront your fears head-on. You may feel small next to them, but you still face them. That's what makes you brave."

My breath hitched. He had an uncanny ability to see through my defenses, peeling back layers I didn't even know existed. "I guess I just don't want to let you down."

Gavin's laughter was light, the sound like a burst of sunlight piercing through storm clouds. "You could never let me down, trust me. Even if we find absolutely nothing, just being here with you makes it worth it."

His words washed over me, warm and comforting, and I felt a sense of belonging bloom in my chest. "Okay, Mr. Poet. But if we find nothing, you owe me a drink."

"Deal," he replied, extending his pinky as if sealing an ancient pact. "And I'll make sure it's the best drink you've ever had. Something extravagant."

"Like a piña colada?" I teased, wiggling my eyebrows. "I'm not above tropical drinks, you know."

"Let's save the umbrellas for when we win," he replied, his tone light, but I noticed the flicker of determination in his eyes.

We stood there, caught in a moment that felt both fleeting and eternal, and I realized how much I wanted this—him, us—together against the world. The night had wrapped us in its embrace, the stars twinkling like a million tiny hopes above us.

As we gazed out at the horizon, the ocean's surface shimmered with light, and for the first time in days, I felt a flicker of optimism ignite within me. The darkness might encroach, but the light within us could break through.

Just then, a loud crash broke the tranquility, sending my heart racing. I turned to see a group of revelers wandering dangerously close to the edge of the cliffs, their laughter echoing through the night, oblivious to the peril they flirted with. "What are they doing?" I whispered, my instincts flaring.

Gavin followed my gaze, his expression shifting to concern. "They're playing with fire. Or, in this case, the ocean."

As if on cue, a sudden wave surged higher than the rest, crashing violently against the rocks, sending sprays of water into the air, glistening like stars in the moonlight. The group shrieked, laughter turning to gasps of shock as one of them stumbled too close to the edge.

"Gavin, we need to help!" I exclaimed, adrenaline surging through me.

"Stay here!" he instructed, his voice firm. "I'll go."

"No! I'm coming with you." My resolve solidified, the need to protect those foolish souls outweighing my fear.

Together, we rushed toward the group, calling out for them to move back from the edge. "Hey! It's not safe!" I shouted, my voice cutting through their laughter like a knife.

As we approached, I could see the intoxicated joy on their faces, their recklessness infuriating and terrifying me all at once. They turned to us, wide-eyed and stumbling, the momentary thrill of danger blinding them to the reality of their situation.

"What's the matter? You scared?" one of the girls jeered, a wild grin plastered on her face, her hair whipping around her like a storm.

"Scared? No, just practical," Gavin shot back, stepping forward, his presence commanding. "You're too close to the edge. Back away!"

"But the view is amazing!" another one protested, teetering dangerously.

"Trust me," I interjected, heart pounding as I reached for the girl, pulling her back just as another wave crashed, sending water cascading over the rocks. "The view won't be worth it if you fall."

They exchanged glances, some hesitant, others still caught in the thrill of the moment. "We're fine," one of them insisted, the bravado cracking under the weight of reality.

Gavin took a step closer, his voice low but firm. "You might think you're invincible, but the ocean doesn't care about your confidence. It will take you, and then it will forget you."

The truth in his words silenced their laughter, and slowly, one by one, they began to back away from the edge, the gravity of their recklessness settling in. As the tension in the air lightened, I felt the adrenaline begin to fade, leaving behind a rush of relief.

"Thanks for the save, I guess," one of the guys mumbled, sheepishly avoiding our gazes.

"No problem," I replied, though my heart still raced. "Just be smarter next time, alright? Life's too precious to play games like that."

They nodded, and as they wandered back toward the festival lights, I felt a wave of satisfaction wash over me. I turned to Gavin, catching his eye, and we exchanged a knowing look that spoke volumes about the bond we had forged.

"Maybe we are enough," I said quietly, feeling the truth settle in my bones.

He smiled, the warmth of it wrapping around me like a soft blanket. "Together, we're more than enough."

In that moment, I understood: it wasn't just about the answers we sought; it was about the journey we were on, the strength we found in each other, and the unexpected turns that made life beautifully unpredictable.

With the ocean's roar still echoing in my ears, I turned to Gavin, the thrill of our earlier encounter still pulsing through me. The cool breeze tousled our hair, and the faint scent of salt and adventure hung in the air, mingling with the undeniable chemistry that crackled between us. The group of revelers had retreated, their bravado deflated like a popped balloon, leaving us in the comforting glow of moonlight and the weight of our shared vulnerability.

"What do you think they'll remember from tonight?" I asked, leaning against the rough stone of the cliff, the texture grounding me. "The laughter or the sheer stupidity of it all?"

Gavin laughed softly, the sound rumbling deep in his chest. "Probably the laughter. It's easier to forget the close calls when you're too busy reminiscing about the fun." He glanced sideways at me, a teasing glint in his eye. "Like that time you almost tripped over your own feet back at the festival."

I feigned indignation, playfully nudging him with my shoulder. "That was one time! And I would argue it was more of a strategic maneuver than a trip."

"Sure, if strategic means losing your balance while trying to dance." He grinned, the lightness of our banter allowing us to shed the weight of the night.

"Hey, some of the greatest performers started out with two left feet," I shot back, laughing at the absurdity. "Just think of me as a diamond in the rough. A very, very rough diamond."

"More like a rough, uncut rock with potential," he said, his tone teasing yet affectionate. "But seriously, you shine when you let loose. You should embrace that side more often."

His encouragement warmed me, threading a comforting ribbon through the fabric of my insecurities. But just as I was about to respond, the air around us shifted. The joyful sounds of the festival seemed to fade, swallowed by the inky darkness that spread over the cliffs like a shroud.

"Do you feel that?" I asked, instinctively moving closer to him, my heart racing with a mix of apprehension and anticipation.

Gavin's expression shifted, his smile fading as he turned his gaze toward the horizon, where the ocean met the sky in an indeterminate haze. "It feels... different," he admitted, his brow furrowing. "Like something is lurking just beneath the surface."

My stomach churned, unease settling in. "What do you think it is?"

"I'm not sure, but I think we should be cautious." His tone was serious now, the playful banter swept away by an undercurrent of tension.

As if in response to our apprehension, a low rumble echoed from the depths of the ocean, vibrating through the ground beneath our feet. The air thickened, charged with electricity, and I felt a chill race down my spine. "Gavin..."

Before I could finish my thought, a series of bright flashes illuminated the night sky, striking out across the ocean like veins of silver lightning. They flickered and danced, casting eerie shadows across the water, each burst more vibrant than the last.

"Is that...?" I stammered, trying to comprehend what I was seeing.

"It looks like bioluminescence," Gavin breathed, his eyes wide with wonder. "I've heard of it happening, but I never thought—"

"Never thought we'd get to see it?" I interrupted, awed by the beauty unfolding before us. The waves shimmered with electric blue and green hues, the sea alive with an otherworldly glow. "This is incredible!"

"Breathtaking, yes," he agreed, but I noticed the way his shoulders tensed, the excitement battling with an underlying fear. "But there's something unsettling about it."

"Unsettling? Or magical?" I teased, attempting to lighten the mood, though the uncertainty gnawed at my insides.

"Maybe both," he replied, taking a step closer, his eyes scanning the horizon as if seeking answers in the undulating waves. "But I can't shake this feeling that it's a warning, not just a spectacle."

A sudden swell of the ocean surged forward, crashing violently against the cliffs, sending salty mist swirling around us. I stumbled back, the ground beneath me quaking as a surge of energy pulsed through the atmosphere. "Gavin!" I called, grasping his arm as I fought to keep my balance.

"Stay close!" he shouted, his voice cutting through the roar of the sea, but there was no time to think as the waves began to swell higher, crashing harder against the rocks.

Then, without warning, a colossal wave rose in the distance, a towering wall of water that seemed to swallow the moonlight, casting everything into shadow. "Get back!" Gavin urged, pulling me toward the more stable part of the cliff, his grip firm yet reassuring.

Panic surged through me as I glanced back at the oncoming wave, its crest frothing and churning like a living thing. "Is it going to—?"

"Hold on!" he shouted, his voice barely audible over the cacophony as he shielded me with his body. The world around us blurred, and in that heart-stopping moment, time stretched, each heartbeat echoing in my ears like a countdown.

The wave crashed against the cliffs, sending a spray of saltwater cascading over us, soaking us to the bone. I gasped as icy water engulfed me, the shock rattling through my core. As I blinked the salt from my eyes, I saw Gavin's expression—determination mixed with a fierce protectiveness.

The wave receded just as quickly, but the world had shifted. The bioluminescence pulsed more fiercely, the ocean alive with energy. I could feel the vibrations in the air, a tingling sensation that coursed through my body, heightening my senses.

"Gavin, look!" I pointed toward the water, my heart racing as a shadow darted beneath the surface, moving with an unsettling speed. "Something's out there."

"What do you mean?" His voice was strained, his focus narrowing as he searched the dark water.

Before I could respond, the shadow broke through the surface, a creature unlike anything I had ever seen. Its scales glimmered with bioluminescent hues, shifting colors in the moonlight as it leaped into the air, crashing back down with a splash that sent ripples across the water.

"What in the world is that?" Gavin whispered, his voice a mix of awe and dread.

"I... I don't know," I stammered, my heart racing as the creature swirled back into the depths, leaving behind a sense of unease. "But it doesn't seem friendly."

As we stood there, breathless and stunned, the world felt off-kilter, as if the fabric of reality was fraying at the edges. The creature circled back, its massive form emerging from the depths once more, glistening under the moonlight, and in that moment, I realized we had awakened something ancient, something that thrived in the depths of the sea, and it was coming for us.

"Gavin!" I cried, instinctively backing away, heart pounding with a mix of fear and adrenaline. The tension coiled tightly in my chest, and as the creature broke through the waves again, its eyes locked onto mine, a thrill of terror coursed through me.

What had we unleashed upon ourselves?

Chapter 25: A Desperate Gambit

The café was a sanctuary of sorts, the walls lined with faded photographs that whispered stories of laughter and heartbreak. Mabel, the proprietor, had a knack for brewing a coffee so rich it could charm the devil himself, and tonight, the scent enveloped us like a warm embrace. As the small group settled around the round table in the corner, I could feel the weight of our mission pressing down like the storm clouds that loomed just outside the window. I glanced at each face illuminated by the soft, trembling glow of candlelight: Sam, the burly mechanic with grease-stained hands that spoke of long hours and hard work; Clara, the librarian whose glasses perched on the bridge of her nose like a quizzical bird; and Tom, the quiet artist whose sharp gaze belied a passion for change.

"Are we really doing this?" Clara's voice trembled slightly, and I could see her fingers fidgeting with the hem of her sweater, a nervous habit that was as familiar to me as my own.

I nodded, my heart racing as I leaned forward, eager to convey the urgency that had propelled us into the depths of this shadowy world. "We have to. If we don't take a stand now, we'll lose everything. The mayor is playing a dangerous game, and we can't let him win."

The coffee cups clinked softly as Mabel refilled our mugs, her expression a mixture of concern and fierce loyalty. It was the sort of place where bonds were forged over steamy cups of courage and whispered dreams, and tonight felt more pivotal than ever. The outside world faded away, leaving us cocooned in a sense of purpose that electrified the air.

"Tell us everything," Sam said, his voice steady despite the turmoil swirling around us. He was a gentle giant, his demeanor usually calm, but the fierce glint in his eye hinted at the storm brewing beneath his surface.

Taking a deep breath, I shared the details of our investigation, the mayor's secret pact with the developers that threatened to pave over our beloved park. The land that had cradled our childhood memories—picnics under the oak tree, laughter echoing as we chased fireflies—was on the verge of being erased. The mayor's greed had entwined itself around our town, and it was time to cut those strings before we suffocated under his ambitions.

As I spoke, I watched the shift in my companions' expressions, the way determination seeped into their bones. "But we need more than just anger," I cautioned. "We need a plan. We need to rally the town. If we're going to stand against him, we can't be divided."

Tom, who had been sketching absently on a napkin, looked up. "What if we held a town meeting? Invite everyone, put the facts out there. People need to know what's at stake." His suggestion hung in the air, shimmering with possibility.

"Sure," Clara chimed in, a spark igniting in her eyes. "But we'll need to make it more than just a meeting. We need to show them what they stand to lose."

Mabel leaned closer, her voice low but steady. "I can help. The café has always been a gathering place. We could host it here, provide refreshments. Make it feel like a celebration, rather than a confrontation."

A flicker of hope blossomed in my chest. The idea of rallying the townsfolk, transforming our anger into action, felt electric. "That's it! A community gathering, a chance for everyone to voice their concerns, to come together as one."

We bounced ideas off each other, our voices rising and falling like a lively symphony. Every suggestion brought us closer, tightening the bond between us like the warm threads of a knitted blanket. It was exhilarating, seeing how each of us brought our unique strengths to the table, a patchwork of skills that could weave a tapestry of change.

But as the caffeine coursed through our veins, an underlying tension lingered. The threat of the mayor loomed larger than the shadows that danced around us. With every laugh and every spark of enthusiasm, I could almost hear his disdainful laughter echoing in my mind. He would not take kindly to our rebellion.

"What if he finds out?" Sam's voice cut through the excitement, and I could see the flicker of worry behind his steely facade. "What if he tries to silence us?"

The room fell silent, each of us lost in the implications of his words. The very idea sent chills down my spine, yet I felt the fire of defiance rising within me. "Let him try," I replied, surprising even myself with the steadiness of my voice. "We're stronger together. If we can get enough people on our side, he won't be able to ignore us."

"But we need to be careful," Clara added, her brow furrowed. "If he catches wind of this too soon, he'll use everything in his power to crush us."

Mabel interjected, her voice resolute. "Then we keep it under wraps for now. We'll plan the meeting, spread the word quietly. We can't be afraid of him. We have to show the town that there's strength in numbers."

We nodded, a sense of unity blossoming amidst the uncertainty. The café felt charged, a clandestine headquarters for our nascent revolution. The challenges ahead were daunting, but the flickering candlelight cast a soft glow over our determined faces, illuminating the path forward.

As the conversation flowed like the coffee that filled our cups, I felt a sense of hope unfurling in my chest, a fragile but persistent thing that whispered of possibilities yet to come. This was just the beginning of our fight, and together, we would rise to meet it head-on.

The following days felt like a delicate dance between urgency and secrecy, each step we took meticulously calculated. Our plan took root, sprouting tentative branches of optimism amidst a landscape of looming danger. Mabel's café transformed from a quaint gathering spot into our headquarters, its familiar warmth now laced with an undercurrent of rebellion. The laughter that usually echoed off the walls was replaced by hushed discussions about strategy and solidarity, our whispers swirling with the fragrant steam of Mabel's coffee.

We decided on a date for the town meeting, careful to choose a night when the stars would shine bright, a cosmic reminder that even in darkness, light persisted. With each passing day, more townsfolk expressed interest, drawn in by the fervor we exuded. Clara became our unofficial organizer, her meticulous nature turning our ideas into actionable plans. She created flyers that looked like they had sprung from the pages of an old-timey newspaper, announcing our gathering with bold letters and an inviting warmth that invited curiosity rather than fear.

"Look, if we're going to stir the pot, we might as well do it with style," she said, her glasses slipping down her nose as she squinted at the layout. "No one wants to show up to a dull meeting, right?"

Sam laughed, a rich, deep sound that echoed in the café. "Style? Is that your secret weapon? I thought we were counting on passion and maybe a touch of dramatic flair."

"I'll take both," Clara shot back, a playful grin lighting up her face. The camaraderie that grew among us was palpable, a balm against the uncertainty that clung to our mission.

As the day of the meeting approached, a sense of excitement buzzed through the town, yet an undercurrent of anxiety crackled in the air like static before a storm. I found myself tossing and turning at night, haunted by visions of the mayor's wrath, imagining him standing at the front of the room, eyes narrowed and voice dripping with contempt. What if he used his influence to discredit us? What if our allies turned tail when faced with his threats?

On the day of the meeting, the sky hung heavy with clouds, a brooding gray that seemed to echo the weight in my chest. Mabel's café bustled with energy as we prepared. The tables were rearranged to form a semicircle, creating an intimate space for discussion. I took a moment to breathe in the scent of fresh pastries wafting from the kitchen, grounding myself amid the chaos.

"Remember," I said to the group as we stood huddled around the makeshift podium, "this isn't just about the park. It's about our community, our future. We need to show them the strength we have when we come together."

Just then, the door swung open with a creak, and a few brave souls trickled in. The buzz of conversation began to rise, weaving a tapestry of voices filled with curiosity and concern. Mabel moved through the crowd, serving steaming mugs and slices of pie, her smile radiating reassurance. She had always known how to make people feel at home, and tonight, her warmth felt like armor against the chill of impending confrontation.

As more townsfolk gathered, I felt a thrill of hope rise within me. My heart raced, and I could almost hear it echoing in my ears. This was it. This was our moment.

When the clock struck seven, I climbed onto a chair to get a better view of the crowd. I took a deep breath, steadying my nerves as I scanned the sea of faces looking back at me. "Thank you all for coming tonight," I began, my voice trembling slightly but gaining strength with each word. "We're here because we believe in our community and our right to protect it."

As I spoke, I could feel the energy shift in the room, the tension morphing into a collective determination. I shared our findings about the mayor's pact, detailing the dangers it posed, not just to the park, but to the heart of our town.

"What he's trying to do is not just a betrayal; it's a full-on attack against everything we cherish," I urged, gesturing to the window where the park lay just beyond. "We have to stand up for our home, for our memories, and for the future of our children."

Clara, standing beside me, took over seamlessly, sharing her vision for what the park could become if we united to save it. Her passion spilled over like the coffee Mabel served, warm and inviting. "Imagine a place where families gather, where children play, where art thrives. We have the power to protect that!"

The crowd murmured in agreement, eyes sparkling with determination. But just as I felt the momentum building, a shadow darkened the doorway. The mayor stood there, his presence a palpable force that sucked the air from the room. He surveyed us, a thin-lipped smile curling his mouth, but it didn't reach his eyes. "What a charming little gathering you have here," he drawled, his voice smooth like oil but dripping with menace.

The room fell silent, tension thickening the air until it felt almost suffocating. I felt my heart lurch in my chest, but the fire of defiance ignited once more. "We're here to discuss the future of our town," I said, trying to keep my voice steady.

He stepped forward, and I could see the disdain etched on his face, a mask of authority slipping into place. "This town doesn't need your meddling, my dear. You should know your place."

His words hung in the air like a challenge, a gauntlet thrown at our feet. But I could feel the collective strength in the room, the whispers of solidarity weaving through the crowd. It was as if we all shared a silent pact, a promise to rise against the threat looming before us.

"Actually," I said, my voice gaining strength, "we're taking back our town, one way or another. You may think you can bully us, but we're not backing down."

The tension crackled, and for a moment, the mayor's eyes narrowed in surprise. Perhaps he hadn't anticipated such resolve from a group he deemed easily intimidated. The townsfolk around me straightened, shoulders squared, emboldened by the confrontation.

As he opened his mouth to retort, Clara jumped in, her voice cutting through the tension like a blade. "We're here to protect what's ours, and we'll fight tooth and nail to ensure our voices are heard. You underestimate us, but we're done being afraid."

In that moment, I realized our unity was our strength. The mayor might be powerful, but together, we were an unstoppable force. I couldn't predict what would happen next, but I felt the tide shifting, a wave of courage rising in our hearts. The battle had only just begun, and we were ready to stand and fight.

The atmosphere in Mabel's café shifted palpably, the air crackling with the tension between our small group and the looming figure of the mayor. His presence was like a storm cloud, dark and foreboding, casting shadows over our carefully laid plans. But the resolve in the room was a powerful antidote to his intimidation. We stood united, a wall of strength forged from shared beliefs and hopes. I could see it in the determination etched on Clara's face, the defiance radiating from Sam's sturdy frame, and the fierce glimmer in Tom's eyes.

"Now, now, don't you all look cozy," the mayor drawled, leaning casually against the doorframe, arms crossed. "I didn't realize you had formed your little club. How quaint." His condescension dripped from his words, but as I looked around, I sensed that our group was anything but quaint. We were a tapestry of resilience, and his sarcasm merely fueled the fire within us.

"Cozy isn't the word I'd use," I replied, my voice steady despite the tremor of adrenaline coursing through me. "We're here to discuss the future of our town, and you are not welcome to dictate that."

The townsfolk stirred at my words, their eyes flickering with a blend of uncertainty and fierce loyalty. The mayor's brow furrowed for a moment, as if trying to gauge whether he could extinguish our flames with mere words. But tonight, we were emboldened by our shared purpose, and I was determined to push through.

"I think it's adorable," he continued, stepping closer, the glint in his eyes sharper now. "You think your little meeting will change anything? I've been in politics long enough to know that talk is cheap, and you, my dear, are in way over your head."

A low murmur spread through the crowd, a wave of tension and determination. "You may have influence, but you don't own us," Sam declared, his voice booming. "This is our town, and we won't let you ruin it."

The mayor's smile faltered, and for a fleeting moment, I saw the slightest crack in his veneer of confidence. "Is that so?" he retorted, his tone turning icy. "Then let's see how much you value your little park when the truth comes out."

Before I could process his words, he turned on his heel and strode out, the door slamming behind him with a finality that echoed through the café. The sudden silence was deafening, punctuated only by the rustle of our anxious breaths.

"What does he mean?" Clara asked, her voice barely above a whisper. The fear in her eyes mirrored the worry creeping into my mind.

"I don't know," I admitted, a cold shiver racing down my spine. "But it can't be good."

Sam's brow furrowed as he exchanged glances with the others. "We need to find out what he's planning. He wouldn't just threaten us for no reason. He has something up his sleeve."

I nodded, determination hardening in my chest. "We need to dig deeper. We have to get ahead of whatever he's concocting."

As the evening wore on, we brainstormed strategies, fueled by adrenaline and coffee. Clara began drafting a plan to gather more intel on the mayor's dealings, while Tom sketched out ideas for flyers that would spread awareness of our cause. Every suggestion was met with enthusiasm, a testament to the bond we had forged through this shared fight.

But my mind couldn't shake the unease that had settled in my stomach like a lead weight. The mayor was not a man to be underestimated, and I couldn't help but wonder what lengths he might go to protect his interests.

When the meeting finally concluded, we exchanged hurried goodbyes and promises to meet again the next day, a sense of urgency electrifying the air. As I stepped outside into the cool night, the streets were eerily quiet, the stars blinking down like silent witnesses to our rebellion. I glanced over my shoulder, half-expecting the mayor to emerge from the shadows, his shadowy figure looming behind me, but the road was empty.

"Let's meet back at Mabel's early tomorrow," I said, my voice barely more than a whisper, as if saying it too loudly would summon the specter of our adversary.

"Agreed," Clara said, pulling her jacket tighter around her. "We'll need a plan, and we can't afford to be caught off guard."

As I walked home, the moonlight cast an ethereal glow over the quiet streets, illuminating my path but doing little to dispel the shadows lurking in my mind. The mayor's words echoed, chilling my resolve: "When the truth comes out." What truth? What had he concealed that could unravel our fight before it even began?

Once home, I tried to shake off the ominous feeling. I brewed a cup of tea, hoping its warmth would calm my frayed nerves. As I settled onto the couch, the rhythmic ticking of the clock filled the silence. I closed my eyes, letting the steam from the cup envelop me, but sleep eluded me. Instead, my mind churned with the possible implications of the mayor's threat.

Just when I thought I could breathe easy, the sharp trill of my phone cut through the stillness. I grabbed it, expecting a message from Clara or Sam, but the number was unfamiliar. A sinking feeling settled in my stomach as I swiped to answer.

"Hello?" I ventured, my voice steady but my heart racing.

"Is this the girl who's causing trouble?" The voice on the other end was low and gravelly, sending a chill down my spine. "You've stirred up quite the hornet's nest."

My grip on the phone tightened as my pulse quickened. "Who is this?"

"Let's just say I'm someone who knows things. Things about your friend the mayor." There was a pause, the silence stretching between us like a taut wire. "And if you don't want your little revolution to blow up in your face, you should meet me tomorrow night. I have information that could change everything."

The line went dead, leaving me breathless, the weight of uncertainty crashing over me like a wave. I stared at my phone, the screen illuminating my face in the dark, my mind racing with questions. Who was this mystery caller? Did I dare to trust them?

As I leaned back against the couch, a sense of foreboding settled around me, thick as fog. The stakes had just been raised, and I knew that whatever lay ahead would test not just my courage, but the very foundations of the bonds we had forged. This was no longer just about the park; it was about our lives, our futures, and the very essence of our town. I would have to make a choice, and soon.

Chapter 26: The Web Tightens

The rustling leaves whispered secrets in the dim light of the evening, a stark contrast to the simmering tension that wrapped around our small town like an unwanted fog. Each breath I took felt thick with unease, yet the scents of autumn—a mingling of damp earth and distant woodsmoke—carried a bittersweet comfort. It was as if the world was both vibrant and dying, a reflection of the struggle we faced. Gavin stood beside me, his jaw clenched and brows furrowed, a living embodiment of the turmoil swirling around us.

We had gathered in the old community center, its walls a tired yellow, faded from years of neglect but still echoing with laughter and camaraderie from times long past. Tonight, it felt like a battleground. The townspeople shuffled in, faces etched with worry and defiance. I had always thought our community was strong, knit together by shared histories and dreams, but Mayor Callahan's ruthless tactics had begun to fray those seams. He had unleashed an army of intimidation, sending shadows to cast doubt and fear into our hearts.

"Remember when this place was just a little sleepy town?" Gavin murmured, his voice barely a whisper over the cacophony of murmurs. "Now it's like a pressure cooker, waiting to explode."

I turned to him, feeling the warmth radiate from his presence, a solid rock in the swirling sea of uncertainty. "We can't let him win," I insisted, my voice steady even as my heart raced. "We owe it to everyone to stand our ground. They need to see that we won't be intimidated."

"Easier said than done," he replied, eyes scanning the room. "Look at them. They're scared."

As if on cue, the door swung open, and the mayor strode in, flanked by his loyal followers. A murmur of discontent rippled through the crowd. Callahan's tailored suit gleamed under the flickering fluorescent lights, and he wore a smile that didn't reach his eyes. The air shifted, thickening with tension, like the moment before a storm.

"Good evening, citizens!" he called, his voice smooth as silk but cutting like glass. "I'm delighted to see such enthusiasm for our community's future." His gaze swept over us, and for a fleeting moment, I felt the weight of his scrutiny—like a predator assessing its prey. "Tonight, I'll be discussing the plans for revitalization. Your concerns have been heard, and I assure you, I am here to listen."

"Listen?" someone shouted from the back, a wiry man with a gray beard who had always been known for his outspokenness. "You mean to dictate! You're tearing our town apart, Callahan!"

The room erupted in murmurs, and I could feel the electricity in the air—the palpable fear and anger mingling together like a storm waiting to break. Gavin squeezed my hand, a reminder of our shared resolve. I looked around, catching glimpses of familiar faces twisted in fear, some whispering to each other, others standing rigid with defiance. It was a motley crew, but in that moment, they were family.

"Let's not forget," Callahan continued, raising his voice to drown out the dissent. "I am the one fighting for jobs, for progress! You'd all rather stay in the past, wallowing in nostalgia instead of embracing change."

Nostalgia. The word hung in the air, taunting us. This wasn't merely about progress; it was about preserving the essence of who we were. A small-town charm that had weathered storms and triumphs, rich in memories that had shaped our lives.

"Change doesn't have to mean losing ourselves!" I blurted out, my voice rising above the din. All heads turned to me, a mix of surprise and admiration flickering in their eyes. "We can evolve without erasing our history! We're not just a project to you; we're a community!"

Callahan's eyes narrowed, and I felt a shiver travel down my spine. "And who might you be, young lady, to lecture me about progress?" he shot back, his tone dripping with condescension.

"I'm someone who cares," I retorted, emboldened by the murmurs of agreement rising around me. "Someone who believes in this town and its people, not just in profits and development."

The crowd erupted into applause, a small yet fierce wave of unity. For the first time, I saw something flicker in Callahan's eyes—anger? Fear? It was difficult to discern, but it ignited a spark of determination within me. If he could feel threatened by our collective voice, then we had a chance.

"Enough of this nonsense!" Callahan bellowed, raising a hand to silence the crowd. "This isn't a democracy; it's a business. And I won't tolerate any more interruptions. If you can't support progress, then perhaps you should consider moving elsewhere."

A gasp rippled through the room, and I felt the air grow cold. There it was, the thinly veiled threat. People exchanged nervous glances, doubt creeping in like a thief in the night. Gavin's grip on my hand tightened, his expression a mixture of anger and fear.

"Is that what you want?" he shouted back, his voice strong and steady. "To turn this place into a ghost town? To drive out those who've built their lives here? We won't let you."

In that moment, I realized we weren't just fighting for our town; we were fighting for our lives—the lives we had built, the love and laughter shared in every corner of our community. We were not going down without a fight.

Callahan's eyes flickered with something akin to rage. "You'll regret this," he warned, his voice a low growl. "I promise you that."

As he stormed out, the atmosphere shifted, a strange blend of triumph and terror enveloping us. My heart raced with adrenaline and fear, but I felt alive—more alive than I had in weeks. The fight was far from over, but for the first time, we had dared to stand against the tide. And in that act of defiance, I could feel the tide beginning to turn.

The following day dawned with a reluctant sun, its rays struggling to pierce through a veil of ominous clouds. I stood at my kitchen window, cradling a mug of steaming coffee, the rich aroma wrapping around me like a comforting embrace. Yet, the serenity of my morning ritual felt hollow, overshadowed by the urgent buzz of anxiety that had settled into my bones. Each sip tasted bitter, a reminder of the escalating conflict gnawing at our town.

Gavin entered, rubbing sleep from his eyes, his hair tousled in that adorably reckless way I had come to love. "You're up early," he said, voice raspy, as he poured himself a cup. "Planning a revolution before breakfast?"

I smirked, but the heaviness in my heart dimmed my light. "Something like that. More like trying to figure out how to convince everyone that we can't let Callahan silence us."

He leaned against the counter, the warmth of his presence a small balm against the rising dread. "You really think we can sway them? People are scared, Anna. They're afraid of losing their homes, their jobs... their lives."

"Exactly," I replied, my voice steadying as I spoke. "But we can't let that fear paralyze us. We have to show them that we're stronger together. Callahan wants us divided, but if we stand united..."

Gavin's eyes sparkled with that fierce determination I admired. "Then we can take him down."

With our resolve renewed, we made plans for the evening's meeting. The air buzzed with whispers of what might transpire, but we couldn't allow fear to quench our hope. As the sun set, painting the sky in fiery hues of orange and pink, we made our way to the community center once again, hand in hand.

Inside, the atmosphere was charged. People filled the folding chairs, their faces a mix of anticipation and apprehension. I took a deep breath, the weight of their expectations settling on my shoulders like a heavy cloak. Gavin squeezed my hand, a silent promise that I wouldn't face this alone.

I stepped forward, feeling the energy of the room shift as eyes turned toward me. "Thank you all for coming tonight," I began, my voice unwavering despite the tremor of nerves. "We're facing a challenge like no other, but if we stand together, we can protect our home."

A murmur of agreement rippled through the crowd, igniting a flicker of hope within me. "We've all seen what happens when fear takes control," I continued, glancing at familiar faces etched with worry. "But we have power, and that power lies in our unity. Let's not forget the reasons we fell in love with this town. It's our shared history, our relationships, our dreams."

Gavin stepped up beside me, his presence a steady anchor. "We need to strategize," he added, his voice steady. "We can organize rallies, door-to-door visits, and even social media campaigns. We must ensure every single voice is heard."

"Social media?" A voice piped up from the back, its owner a wiry woman named Martha who was known for her shrewd insights. "Is that really effective? It feels like shouting into the void sometimes."

"True," I replied, meeting her gaze. "But it can also amplify our voices. Every story shared, every post liked, can reach someone who feels the same way. We have to try."

As the discussion flowed, ideas began to blossom, and the room transformed from a quiet, fearful space into a vibrant hub of hope and determination. The energy was electric, each voice building on the last until it crescendoed into a symphony of resolve. I could feel my heart swell with pride as we spoke, laughed, and even cried together, forging connections in the crucible of our shared struggle.

Yet, just as the atmosphere turned jubilant, the door swung open, and Mayor Callahan entered, his presence casting a shadow over our gathering. The room fell silent, the air thick with tension as he surveyed us with an almost predatory gaze.

"Looks like the rebels have convened," he said, a smirk tugging at his lips. "I hope you're all prepared for the consequences of your insurrection."

Gavin stepped forward, his expression fierce. "We're not afraid of you, Callahan. We're here to protect our town."

"Protect it? Or destroy it?" The mayor's voice dripped with sarcasm. "You think you're saving it by fighting change? You'll only bring ruin upon yourselves."

"You can't silence us!" I shouted, my voice ringing out defiantly. "This is our home, and we refuse to let you take it from us."

A tense silence stretched, and I could see the uncertainty in the eyes of some of the townsfolk. Would they back down? Would the fear he instilled swallow them whole?

"I hope you all realize what you're getting into," Callahan sneered, his eyes glinting with malice. "I've seen towns like yours crumble under the weight of rebellion. Your quaint little lives could easily be turned upside down."

"That's a threat," I said, feeling the weight of every gaze on me. "But threats won't work anymore. We're done cowering."

The crowd erupted in murmurs of agreement, fueled by newfound courage. Callahan's face darkened, but before he could retort, a commotion broke out near the back of the room. A figure pushed through the crowd, breathless and wide-eyed.

"Anna!" It was Tyler, my neighbor's son, his voice cracking with urgency. "You have to come quickly! It's about your father!"

My heart dropped, and the room fell silent once more. "What about him?" I gasped, dread pooling in my stomach.

"He's been taken," Tyler blurted, fear lacing his words. "The mayor's goons— they were at the shop. They said he was interfering."

The world tilted on its axis, a thunderous roar drowning out everything else. My father, the man who had instilled in me the very values I clung to, had always been my anchor. The realization sank like a stone in my chest.

"Callahan," I hissed, rage boiling within me. "This is his doing."

Gavin stepped closer, his expression a mask of fierce determination. "We won't let him get away with this. We need to rally everyone."

As the crowd stirred, unease morphed into a potent mixture of fear and resolve. We had to act quickly, before Callahan's intimidation tactics turned our town into a ghost of its former self. I glanced at Gavin, our eyes locking in a silent understanding. We were in this together, ready to fight not just for our town, but for my father's freedom and our future.

The cacophony of voices swelled around me as the reality of my father's abduction settled like a dark cloud, thick and suffocating. Tyler's frightened eyes seemed to pull me back into the present, and I focused on him, trying to parse through the chaotic swirl of thoughts racing through my mind. I could feel the palpable tension in the room, the murmurs rising and falling like the tide, each wave lapping at the shore of our collective fear.

"Where are they holding him?" I demanded, gripping the back of a nearby chair to steady myself. "We have to find him!"

"They— they didn't say," Tyler stammered, panic etched across his youthful face. "But they drove off toward the old mill. I think they were going to—"

"Enough!" Callahan interjected, his voice slicing through the gathering like a knife. "This is clearly a misguided attempt to disrupt the peace."

Gavin stepped forward, brimming with righteous fury. "You're the one disrupting the peace, Callahan! Let's not pretend you're innocent here. If anything happens to my father, it'll be on your head."

With every word, I felt my anger boiling over, a fierce fire igniting within me. "You think you can intimidate us into submission? We're not afraid of your threats or your goons. We're done cowering in fear!"

"Fear?" Callahan chuckled darkly, though it held no trace of humor. "You've not yet seen fear, my dear. But you will."

Before I could respond, Gavin's hand shot out to catch my arm, pulling me back as a flicker of fear crossed his face. "Anna, let's focus. We need to get to your father before it's too late."

With a heavy heart, I nodded, gathering my thoughts like a lifeline thrown into turbulent waters. The community center, once a refuge of laughter and hope, now felt like a cage closing in around us. I glanced around, seeking out familiar faces—Martha, her expression steely; Tyler, his eyes wide with fear; and others, hearts pounding in a shared rhythm of defiance.

"Alright, everyone," I called out, voice steady despite the tempest brewing inside me. "We need to rally together. If Callahan thinks he can pick us off one by one, he's sorely mistaken. Let's show him what we're made of!"

A roar of approval erupted from the crowd, a wave of solidarity washing over us. It was a moment of clarity amid the chaos; we were no longer individuals, but a unified front ready to push back against the darkness threatening to engulf our lives.

Gavin turned to me, eyes sparkling with determination. "We can't waste any time. If they're at the mill, we need to move."

"Do we take the trucks?" I asked, my heart racing at the thought of the confrontation that awaited us.

"Better than that," he replied, a devilish grin spreading across his face. "I've got my motorcycle. It's faster."

As he led me outside, the cool evening air hit my face like a refreshing splash of water, invigorating me. The sun was slipping below the horizon, leaving behind streaks of crimson and gold. The world felt electric, charged with possibilities and dangers alike.

Within moments, we were straddling his motorcycle, the engine purring beneath us. I wrapped my arms tightly around his waist, pressing my cheek against his back, feeling the steady rhythm of his heartbeat. There was an adrenaline-fueled thrill in the air, mingled with the fear of what lay ahead.

"Hang on tight," he said, a teasing lilt to his voice that helped to ease the weight of anxiety pressing down on me. "This ride's going to be a wild one."

With a swift twist of the throttle, we shot off into the twilight, the wind whipping through my hair, stealing away my worries like magic. The world blurred around us as we raced down familiar roads, each turn taking us closer to the abandoned mill, an old relic of our town's industrial past.

As we approached the mill, the sky darkened further, casting shadows that seemed to dance menacingly around us. We parked the motorcycle behind a dilapidated building, slipping off with a sense of urgency that matched the pounding of my heart.

"Stay close," Gavin instructed, and I could see the intensity in his eyes, a mix of determination and concern.

Moving quietly, we approached the entrance of the mill, the air thick with the scent of damp earth and rust. The old structure loomed before us, its windows dark like empty eyes watching our every move. With each cautious step, I could hear the distant echoes of our footsteps bouncing off the walls, a reminder that we were entering a place fraught with uncertainty.

"Over there," Gavin whispered, pointing toward a sliver of light peeking through a jagged opening. "That looks like it could lead inside."

I nodded, my heart racing as we edged toward the entrance, every fiber of my being urging me to turn back. But the thought of my father, held captive, pushed me forward. We squeezed through the opening, entering a dimly lit interior that was both haunting and eerily beautiful.

Dust motes floated lazily in the air, illuminated by the shafts of light filtering through the cracks. The sound of dripping water echoed like a metronome, marking the passage of time in this forsaken place. Shadows danced along the walls, creating a haunting tableau that made my skin crawl.

We crept deeper into the mill, and I strained to hear any signs of life. Suddenly, a low murmur reached my ears, the unmistakable timbre of voices discussing something just out of sight. My heart pounded, adrenaline surging through me as I exchanged a glance with Gavin, his eyes wide with unspoken fear.

"Should we split up?" I whispered, the thought both exhilarating and terrifying.

"Not a chance," he replied, his voice resolute. "We stick together."

As we rounded a corner, I caught sight of two figures standing in the shadows, their backs turned to us. The flickering light from a nearby lantern cast an eerie glow, illuminating the contours of their faces just enough for recognition to hit me like a punch to the gut.

"Callahan's men," I breathed, dread pooling in my stomach.

"Do you think they have him?" Gavin asked, his voice barely above a whisper.

Before I could respond, a clattering sound echoed from deeper within the mill, and the figures turned sharply, their eyes narrowing as they spotted us. Panic surged through my veins, and I could feel the weight of the moment pressing down on us.

"We need to go, now!" I hissed, backing away as quietly as I could, but the sound of heavy footsteps approaching from behind us sent a chill down my spine.

"Too late," one of the men snarled, advancing toward us with a predatory grin. "You really thought you could play hero? This is where your little rebellion ends."

As the darkness closed in around us, I felt the ground shift beneath my feet, my heart racing as we prepared to fight—or run. But before I could make a decision, the lights flickered ominously, plunging the space into darkness.

And then, a sharp scream pierced the air, echoing through the mill, leaving us frozen in place. My pulse thundered in my ears as I turned to Gavin, my eyes wide with terror and disbelief.

"Anna!" his voice called out, but before he could say anything more, the world around us erupted in chaos, leaving only the harrowing sound of my father's desperate cry reverberating in the silence.

Chapter 27: The Turning Tide

The sun had begun its descent, casting a warm golden hue over the town square, illuminating the weathered cobblestones beneath my feet. People gathered, their faces illuminated by the evening light, a sea of expressions ranging from anxious curiosity to steely resolve. I could hear the low murmur of voices, the blend of anticipation and trepidation weaving through the crowd like a fragile thread, binding us together in our collective desire for change. The scent of blooming lilacs wafted through the air, a delicate reminder of the beauty we were fighting to preserve, and I inhaled deeply, channeling that fragrance into my resolve.

Gavin stood a few paces behind me, his presence a steady anchor in the swirling tide of emotion that threatened to engulf me. He adjusted his glasses, the sunlight catching the lenses just right, making his blue eyes gleam with determination. "You ready?" he asked, his voice low, almost drowned out by the growing crowd. There was a flicker of concern in his expression, but beneath it lay a fierce loyalty that had grown over the months we had spent unraveling the mayor's web of deceit.

"More than ever," I replied, straightening my shoulders. The warmth of his belief in me steadied my nerves. I had always been the girl who blended into the background, whose opinions were often overlooked in a room full of louder voices. Yet here I stood, poised to challenge the very heart of our town's governance. As I glanced at the gathering before me, I saw familiar faces—neighbors who had shared meals with me, kids I had watched grow up, and even the elderly couple who'd frequented my parents' shop since I was a child. Each of them had their stories, their lives woven into the fabric of this community, and today, we were united in our purpose.

As I stepped up to the makeshift podium, the whispers hushed into an expectant silence, as if the very air had thickened with our shared anticipation. I cleared my throat, the rasp echoing in the stillness. "Thank you for being here," I began, my voice steadying with each word. "Today, we stand not just for ourselves but for every family, every child, and every future that could be affected by the choices made in this town. We have gathered not only to present our case against Mayor Grant but to reclaim the voice that has been silenced for too long."

A ripple of agreement coursed through the crowd, and I could see nods of affirmation, glimmers of hope sparking in the eyes of those gathered. The memories of countless conversations echoed in my mind—late-night debates in the diner, whispered discussions at the local barbershop, and the urgency that had seeped into our gatherings as we pieced together the truth. It wasn't just about the recent corruption allegations; it was about the manipulation, the neglect of our town's needs, and the undercurrent of fear that had silenced dissent.

"Our town deserves better than this," I continued, the fire in my belly igniting. "We deserve a leader who values transparency over deception. Someone who prioritizes community over greed." I gestured to Gavin, who stood at my side, a symbol of the quiet yet fierce resistance that had blossomed alongside me. "Together, we've uncovered documents, testimonies, and evidence that show the extent of Mayor Grant's betrayal. This is not merely hearsay; this is truth, and today we present it to you."

As I revealed the first piece of evidence, a crisp document outlining questionable land deals that had favored the mayor's friends, the gasps rippled through the crowd. I could see the disbelief etched on faces that had once been loyal to the mayor, and in that moment, I knew we had struck a chord. I continued with fervor, detailing testimonies from residents who had suffered from the mayor's negligence, painting a vivid picture of the impact his actions had on our community. The air thickened with emotion, anger and determination coiling around us like a living entity.

"And this," I said, pulling out a photograph that captured the dilapidated state of our town's only playground, overrun with weeds and broken swings, a stark contrast to the vibrant laughter that used to fill the air. "This is what he has allowed to happen. Our children deserve better than this!" My voice rang with fervor, punctuated by the rising claps and cheers that erupted from the crowd. Each cheer fueled my confidence, and I found my rhythm, building momentum as I wove through the narratives of despair and resilience, crafting a tapestry of our town's struggle.

In the back, I spotted Clara, the fiery-haired woman who had long been the backbone of our community, her fists clenched in righteous indignation. She raised her hand, beckoning me to pause, and when the crowd quieted, she shouted, "What are we going to do about this? We can't just stand here and listen!" Her voice, tinged with urgency, resonated in the gathering dusk, igniting a spark of action that had been dormant for too long.

"Together," I replied, feeling the weight of her gaze. "We can demand accountability. We can rally together to challenge the mayor at the upcoming town hall meeting, ensure that our voices are heard, and insist that he answer for his actions. We deserve a town that thrives, not one that languishes under the weight of betrayal."

The fervor in the crowd ignited a fire within me, and I pressed forward with fervent passion. This was not just a confrontation; it was a rallying cry for justice, a testament to the resilience of a community ready to fight for its future. I could see the determination blooming in the faces around me, the embers of hope transforming into a blazing resolve. The tide was turning, and we were ready to ride it together.

The applause that erupted felt like a wave crashing against the shore, sweeping me up in its force. Encouraged by the murmurs of support and the unmistakable spirit of unity, I knew this was just the beginning. People leaned in closer, faces lit with a mix of hope and determination, as if the very act of gathering together had breathed new life into our weary hearts. I took a deep breath, letting the energy of the crowd infuse my words with urgency. "But we can't stop here," I implored, my voice rising above the excitement. "What we do next is just as important as what we've done so far."

In the back, Clara stood resolute, her arms crossed defiantly. "What do you propose?" she shouted, her voice cutting through the chatter. "We can't just shout our frustrations into the wind and hope it carries to his ears."

I nodded, acknowledging the weight of her question. "We need a plan," I said, glancing over at Gavin, who nodded in silent agreement. "We need to organize a coalition—one that spans every corner of our town. We need representatives from each neighborhood, families, and local businesses. This isn't just about us; it's about our children, our future." The conviction in my words resonated, and the atmosphere buzzed with a collective spark of inspiration.

"Count me in," Gavin chimed in, stepping forward, his enthusiasm infectious. "If we gather more testimonies, form a petition, maybe we can gain enough momentum to call for a special town meeting. We can't let this go unnoticed."

The crowd murmured approval, and I felt a swell of pride. "Exactly! We can organize meetings, distribute flyers, and even set up a social media campaign. We need to make it clear that we're not backing down. We're not afraid of his power because together, we are more powerful." The enthusiasm in the air swelled, a palpable sense of purpose threading through the gathering like an electric current.

Just as the ideas began to crystallize, a familiar figure emerged from the throng—Mayor Grant himself, flanked by a couple of his loyal supporters. The collective gasp that rose from the crowd was like a sudden gust of wind, chilling the warmth that had been building. His presence was like a dark cloud, and I felt my stomach twist with unease. What was he doing here?

"Ladies and gentlemen," he called out, his voice dripping with feigned sincerity. "It seems we have a little town meeting in progress. Isn't this adorable?" His smirk sent a shiver through the crowd, and I felt a simmering anger bubbling just below the surface. "But let's not forget who has been leading this town, making decisions for your best interests." He stepped closer, as if to physically overshadow us, his bravado unyielding.

"Leading?" I couldn't help but blurt out, surprising even myself. "You mean leading us straight into chaos. We're done being misled by your so-called 'leadership.'" The crowd erupted into a chorus of cheers, a tidal wave of support crashing against the mayor's facade. I could see him stiffen, the playful glint in his eyes turning cold, as if he had just realized he had underestimated us.

"Your little protest won't change anything," he shot back, his voice suddenly sharp. "You think this gathering gives you power? You're just a group of disgruntled townsfolk clinging to fantasies of change. I have the resources, the connections." He gestured grandly, as if to encompass everything he believed was his domain.

"Resources?" Clara countered, stepping forward with an intensity that had the crowd buzzing again. "You mean the connections that line your pockets? We're not buying your empty promises anymore. We want accountability, not more spin." The boldness in her tone was infectious, and I felt the energy in the crowd shift once again, a collective unity hardening into resolve.

"Enough!" Grant barked, but the laughter from the crowd erupted again, a release of tension that felt liberating. His façade was cracking, and I could see the frustration etched into his features. He was losing control, and we were gaining ground.

"What we want," I said, my voice calm yet insistent, "is for you to step aside and allow someone who truly cares for this town to lead us. Your time is up."

He took a step back, and for a fleeting moment, I thought I saw uncertainty flicker across his face. "You're making a grave mistake," he warned, though his tone lacked the conviction it had earlier. "You don't know what you're messing with."

"I think we do," I replied, my heart racing, but I refused to let fear seep in. "You're the one who doesn't realize the strength of this community. We're not just going to roll over."

With that, the crowd surged forward, a living, breathing entity fueled by our shared history and determination. I felt a surge of exhilaration, a heady rush that coursed through my veins, pushing aside any doubt that still lingered. Together, we were an unstoppable force, and the energy in the square was electric.

As the mayor stumbled backward, losing his grip on the narrative, I caught Gavin's eye. He grinned, a spark of mischief lighting up his features. "Looks like someone's not as invincible as he thought."

"Or as clever," I replied with a sly smile. "We may have underestimated the impact of a united front." The thrill of rebellion ignited a fire within me, and I relished the warmth of camaraderie enveloping us all.

With our momentum building, I knew this was just a skirmish in a much larger battle. The road ahead was fraught with challenges, but as I looked around at the faces of my friends, neighbors, and newfound allies, I realized that we had the courage to confront whatever lay ahead. This was our home, our community, and we would not let it be dismantled by greed and deceit.

I took a deep breath, allowing the excitement of the moment to fuel my passion. "Let's show him what we're made of!" I shouted, and the crowd erupted in applause, a rallying cry that echoed through the twilight, a promise that our fight was far from over.

The crowd surged around me, a collective heartbeat pulsating with newfound resolve. As Mayor Grant retreated, the laughter and cheers enveloped us, and I felt the weight of our shared purpose propelling us forward. Yet, the air was thick with tension, the kind that foreshadows a storm. I caught a glimpse of Gavin, his brow furrowed in concentration, the playful glimmer in his eye replaced with something sharper—an awareness that we were entering dangerous territory.

"Do you think he'll actually back down?" I asked, leaning closer to Gavin, my voice just above a whisper, as if saying it aloud would make it more real. The exhilaration of the moment felt fragile, like glass teetering on the edge of a table.

Gavin shrugged, his expression thoughtful. "He might try to twist this in his favor. Power rarely goes quietly." His words hung between us, a reminder that the battle was far from over.

Before I could respond, Clara elbowed her way back to us, her cheeks flushed with adrenaline. "We need to capitalize on this momentum. Let's get the word out, gather even more testimonies, and ensure everyone knows what he's up to." The fervor in her voice was infectious, igniting a fire in the belly of the crowd.

"Absolutely," I agreed, my own enthusiasm rekindled. "Let's set up a community forum—somewhere we can strategize, share ideas, and rally more support. We can't allow his threats to intimidate us." The idea took root, blossoming in my mind like the early spring flowers pushing through the last remnants of winter.

As we moved to disperse, ready to take action, a figure appeared at the edge of the square—Maggie, the town's newspaper editor, her notebook clutched tightly in one hand. She pushed through the throng, determination etched on her face. "You all are creating quite the buzz," she said, her tone equal parts admiration and caution. "I'd like to cover this, but we need to tread carefully. The mayor's got friends in high places who won't take kindly to this."

"Let them try," Clara replied defiantly, crossing her arms. "We have truth on our side."

Maggie nodded, her expression softening. "Truth is powerful, but so is fear. Just remember, the mayor has a way of twisting narratives to suit his needs. I want to help you, but we need to be strategic."

"Right," I said, feeling a mixture of excitement and apprehension. "If we can control the narrative, we might just stand a chance."

Gavin chimed in, "Let's schedule a meeting tonight. We can draft a press release and outline our next steps."

The crowd began to disperse, energized chatter filling the air like a lively melody, but I couldn't shake the feeling that our confrontation had not gone unnoticed. As people shuffled away, I felt a prickle of unease dance along my spine. We were drawing attention, and not all of it would be friendly.

Night fell, wrapping the town in a velvety darkness punctuated by twinkling stars overhead. The hum of anticipation lingered, but as I arrived at the community center, the atmosphere shifted. Inside, the fluorescent lights buzzed overhead, illuminating a group of familiar faces—Clara, Gavin, and a handful of others who had stepped forward to lend their voices.

"Alright, let's get to work," I said, my heart pounding with both excitement and trepidation. As we gathered around a table scattered with papers and coffee cups, I felt a sense of purpose solidifying among us, as if we were crafting a shield against the chaos that lay ahead.

Maggie pulled out her notebook, ready to take notes. "What do we want to accomplish in the next few days?"

Gavin leaned forward, his brow furrowed in thought. "First, we need to solidify our coalition—reach out to everyone we can, especially those who have been directly affected by the mayor's decisions."

"Agreed," Clara added, her voice strong. "And we need to ensure we have testimonies ready to go. Personal stories resonate, and they'll help illustrate the real impact of the mayor's actions."

As the conversation flowed, the energy in the room shifted. Ideas bounced off the walls, each suggestion sparking enthusiasm. We discussed tactics for approaching local businesses for support, strategizing how to use social media effectively, and drafting a list of potential allies who might join our cause. It felt like a whirlwind of hope and ambition, each word stitching our resolve tighter.

Just as we were getting into a rhythm, the front door swung open, and a figure stepped inside. It was Tom, the mayor's most loyal supporter, a man whose presence instantly dampened the atmosphere. "Thought you'd keep this little gathering a secret?" he sneered, his tone dripping with mockery.

"Tom," I said, my voice steady despite the tension curling in my stomach. "What are you doing here?"

"Just came to remind you that not everyone shares your... enthusiasm for change." He stepped closer, the smirk on his face a stark contrast to the warmth of our camaraderie. "The mayor won't take kindly to this little rebellion of yours."

"Rebellion?" Clara scoffed, crossing her arms defiantly. "This is about accountability. Something your precious mayor knows nothing about."

Tom laughed, the sound low and threatening. "You think you're in control? You're playing a dangerous game. The more noise you make, the more you draw attention to yourselves. And not all attention is good." He leaned against the wall, crossing his arms as if he owned the place.

"Is that a threat?" I challenged, stepping forward, feeling the heat of anger rising within me. "Because it sure sounds like one."

"Just a friendly warning," he replied, his smirk widening. "You may want to reconsider your approach. You wouldn't want anything... unfortunate to happen, now would you?"

I exchanged glances with Gavin and Clara, an unspoken understanding passing between us. This was more than a political skirmish; it felt personal, as if the stakes had just been raised dramatically.

As Tom sauntered out, I felt the chill of his presence linger in the air, a shadow that clung to my skin. "He's trying to intimidate us," Gavin said, his expression grave.

"Let him try," Clara said, her voice steady but her eyes betraying a flicker of concern. "We won't back down."

"Right," I agreed, though unease gnawed at me. I could feel the weight of our decision pressing down like a heavy cloak. This was no longer just about the mayor's wrongdoings; it was about standing up against a force that could threaten everything we held dear.

As we settled back into our strategy session, the energy shifted. Laughter faded, and a tangible tension filled the room, an uninvited guest. Suddenly, the lights flickered ominously overhead, and I felt my heart race. Then, just as quickly as the lights dimmed, they surged back to life, but the moment of uncertainty left an imprint on my mind.

"Did you see that?" I asked, my voice barely above a whisper. "That felt... strange."

Before anyone could respond, the door swung open again, this time with a force that sent a chill racing through me. The mayor stood there, flanked by a couple of his supporters, their faces dark with intent. "What's this? Planning your little coup?" he demanded, his eyes glinting with malice.

The air thickened, and I could feel the weight of the moment settling in, the kind of heaviness that precedes a storm.

"Maybe it's time for us to settle this once and for all," he continued, stepping inside, the door swinging shut behind him.

The room felt smaller suddenly, the walls pressing in as the realization hit me: we were at a precipice, and there would be no turning back.

"Are you ready to face the consequences of your actions?" he asked, his voice dripping with menace, as the tension coiled tighter, every heartbeat echoing in my ears.

Just as I opened my mouth to respond, the lights flickered again, plunging us into darkness. And in that moment of uncertainty, the unmistakable sound of shattering glass echoed through the room, leaving us teetering on the edge of fear and defiance.

Chapter 28: Confrontation

The town square pulsed with life, a vibrant canvas of voices and colors weaving together under the late afternoon sun. Banners fluttered above us, the faded remnants of celebrations long past, their colors dulled by time and neglect. I could feel the rough wooden podium beneath my palms, a makeshift platform crafted from old crates, but it was my lifeline today, the only thing separating me from the storm of whispers and wary glances that churned in the crowd. The scent of fresh-cut grass mingled with the pungent aroma of roasted chestnuts from a nearby vendor, wafting tantalizingly in the air, while the faint rustle of leaves added an undertone of anticipation, almost as if the very town itself was holding its breath.

As I glanced out over the sea of faces, I noted the familiar contours of neighbors, friends, and those I had known since childhood, their expressions a tapestry of hope, fear, and disbelief. Mrs. Turner, with her ever-present floral apron and wild hair, clutched her grandson's hand tightly, her knuckles white against his small, soft palm. And there was Mark, the burly blacksmith, his arms crossed over his chest, frowning deeply, the lines on his forehead deepening with every word I spoke. It was all too much; the stakes had never felt so high.

"Fifty years ago," I began, my voice steady despite the tremor in my heart, "this town made a choice—a pact cloaked in shadows and secrets, binding its future to a darkness we dared not acknowledge." The words tumbled out, the truth of our town's history surfacing like flotsam in a murky pond. "You thought it was for the greater good, but you were misled. Misguided by fear and the comforting words of a man who thrived on power."

The murmurs grew louder, an undercurrent of disbelief rippling through the crowd. My gaze fell upon the mayor, his face twisted in a mask of anger that made him look more like a caricature than a leader. He was a man who had thrived in shadows, his hair slicked back with an almost desperate precision, as if the sheen of it could reflect away the accusations I hurled. He stood off to my left, the veins in his neck bulging like angry serpents, a pitiful attempt to reassert control.

"You think you can stand there and distort our history?" he shouted, his voice harsh and strained. "This is nothing but slander!"

But the crowd shifted, an electric pulse of uncertainty coursing through them. I could see the doubt creeping into their eyes, like shadows in the twilight. "I'm not here to slander," I countered, a defiant edge sharpening my tone. "I'm here to reveal the truth. The truth that has shackled this town for too long."

As I recounted the tales of the past—how the town's founders had made a desperate deal with forces unknown, trading peace for silence—I felt a wave of urgency wash over me. The sun hung low in the sky, casting long shadows that danced at our feet, and I feared time would slip away from me like grains of sand in an hourglass. Each sentence felt like an incantation, drawing forth ghosts from our history that threatened to break the fragile hold of complacency.

It was then that Gavin stepped forward. He was always the quiet one, lurking in the background, but today he carried an aura of resolve that surprised me. His presence cut through the tension like a blade. "Let me speak," he said, his voice steady yet soft, carrying a weight that belied his unassuming nature.

The mayor bristled, his mouth a thin line of contempt, but the crowd was willing to listen. Gavin took a deep breath, his hands trembling slightly as he began to share his own experiences, his voice breaking through the cacophony like a ray of sunlight piercing through dark clouds. "I grew up hearing whispers," he said, his eyes scanning the crowd, locking onto familiar faces as if seeking connection in their shared histories. "My father worked in the mines, and he told me stories of strange happenings—how people vanished, how shadows lingered just beyond the edges of our sight."

I held my breath, realizing the truth in his words. Gavin was no longer just a backdrop to my story; he was woven into the very fabric of it. "I thought it was just folklore," he continued, "but the more I learned, the more I understood the toll it took on our families, on our lives. This town has been living under the weight of its secrets for too long."

His honesty struck a chord. I could see the people around us shifting, their postures softening, heads nodding as they began to connect the threads of their own experiences to his. Gavin's vulnerability was disarming, a balm against the tension that had filled the air just moments before. "The mayor wants us to believe this is all in the past, that we should let it go," he said, his voice rising above the murmurs. "But if we let it go, we are destined to repeat it."

In that moment, the crowd turned toward the mayor, eyes blazing with a mixture of anger and betrayal. The atmosphere shifted, the air thick with the smell of something electric—revolution, perhaps. "You can't silence us anymore!" someone shouted from the back, and a cheer erupted, echoing around the square, the sound swelling like a rising tide.

The mayor's bravado crumbled, and I could see the fear lurking behind his eyes. This was the moment I had been waiting for—the pivotal moment where the tide would turn, where truth and courage would emerge from the depths of despair. Together, we were a force to be reckoned with, a tapestry of resilience woven from shared stories and hard-won truths.

I looked at Gavin, a newfound respect blooming in my chest, knowing we were bound together in this struggle. His courage had sparked something within me, igniting a flame that had been flickering in the darkness for far too long. As the crowd erupted into voices demanding change, I realized we were no longer just individuals standing alone; we were a community, united by a shared purpose.

The energy in the square crackled like static electricity, surging through the crowd and making the hairs on my arms stand on end. As Gavin spoke, his voice resonated with an unexpected authority, compelling even the most skeptical townsfolk to lean in, straining to catch every word. The mayor's bluster faded, leaving him to fume silently, his bravado dissolving like sugar in hot tea.

"Don't you see?" Gavin continued, his hands gesturing emphatically. "We've been kept in the dark, blind to the reality that our lives have been dictated by fear and manipulation. The stories your parents whispered to you at night were not mere tales; they were warnings. They were meant to keep you compliant and silent. We've all felt the consequences of that silence."

A ripple of agreement flowed through the crowd, and I could see a transformation taking place. Faces once shadowed with doubt now glowed with realization, their eyes lighting up as if they were seeing the town through a new lens—one free of the suffocating veil of secrecy. Murmurs of recognition turned into shouts of solidarity.

"Gavin's right!" someone yelled from the back, an older woman whose name I couldn't recall but whose face I recognized from the market. "We deserve to know the truth!"

The air grew thick with a mix of tension and hope, a concoction that set my heart racing. I could feel the shift in momentum, the collective determination brewing like a storm on the horizon. I stepped forward, emboldened by the response to Gavin's plea. "For too long, we've let the past dictate our present," I declared, my voice rising to match the swell of the crowd's energy. "We owe it to ourselves—and to those who came before us—to break this cycle. Together, we can uncover the truth that's been buried beneath layers of deception."

I searched the crowd for familiar faces, locking eyes with Mark the blacksmith, who nodded vigorously. The trust and camaraderie that had been forged in the fires of shared history now burned brightly between us. "We're all in this together," I continued, feeling the weight of every person present, their hopes and fears swirling around us like autumn leaves caught in a gust of wind. "This isn't just about one man's greed; it's about reclaiming our lives, our stories, and our future."

Just as the crowd began to chant my name, a thunderous voice interrupted, booming through the air with the authority of a king addressing his subjects. "You think you can sway these people with lies?" The mayor stepped forward, his face mottled with rage and desperation, his eyes darting from one familiar face to another, as if seeking allies in this unexpected rebellion. "They don't want the truth; they want the comfort of ignorance. Don't you all understand that? It's safer this way!"

But safety, as I had come to learn, was merely an illusion—one that could vanish in an instant when faced with the harsh glare of reality. "Is it safe to live under the shadow of lies?" I shot back, the words spilling out with a ferocity that surprised even me. "Is it safe to allow one man's greed to dictate our lives? We are stronger than this, and together, we can forge a new path!"

With every passing moment, the tide shifted further away from the mayor. The people around me surged forward, their voices rising, each cry mingling with the fervor of hope and change. It was intoxicating, this sense of power we had reclaimed together. Just as I thought the mayor would crumble under the weight of our unity, he drew himself up to his full height, his face contorting into a twisted mask of fury.

"You will regret this," he spat, pointing a finger at me, as if he could summon fear with a mere gesture. "You have no idea who you're up against."

A shiver of unease ran through me, but I pushed it aside. I had to remain focused, to keep my heart steady even as it raced with the adrenaline of the moment. "I know exactly who I'm up against," I replied, locking my gaze onto his. "A man afraid of losing his grip on power. But fear no longer rules us. We choose to stand for something greater—our freedom."

Just as the crowd began to echo my sentiments, a figure broke through the throng, a young girl whose bright red hair shone like a beacon. It was Lily, the mayor's daughter, her eyes wide with a mixture of confusion and rebellion. "Dad," she called out, her voice trembling but resolute. "Is this true? Have we been living a lie?"

The crowd quieted, every eye turning toward the mayor, who looked as if he'd been struck. "Lily, this isn't the place for you," he stammered, but there was a crack in his voice that revealed his uncertainty.

"No!" she shouted, her voice cutting through the tension with a clarity that rang true. "I deserve to know the truth! We all do!"

The weight of her words hung in the air, a palpable challenge that dared the mayor to deny his own daughter. I could see the gears turning in her father's mind, a mixture of anger and fear etched into the lines of his face.

"Lily, you don't understand what you're asking," he growled, but his bluster lacked conviction. The crowd began to shift restlessly, and it was as if they sensed the ground beneath the mayor was crumbling.

"I understand enough!" she replied fiercely, stepping forward with a bravery I could only admire. "We can't live in fear any longer. It's not just your decision to make anymore."

Her words hung heavy in the air, igniting a fresh wave of support from the townspeople. The mayor's facade shattered, revealing a man struggling to maintain control of a situation spiraling beyond his grasp. With every heartbeat, I felt the town pulling together, a living organism pulsating with the promise of change.

Then, just when it seemed the mayor would concede, a sharp voice sliced through the air. "And what do you propose, then?" It was the voice of Mr. Anderson, the town's oldest resident, his face weathered like an ancient map, lined with the tales of countless years. "What do we do with this truth once it's out? How do we mend the fractures it's caused?"

The crowd stilled again, the question hanging in the air like a pendulum, swinging between hope and trepidation. I opened my mouth to respond, feeling the weight of their anticipation, but it was Gavin who stepped forward, his eyes fierce with determination. "We start by holding those responsible accountable," he said, his voice steady. "We begin with the mayor and then we rebuild. Together, we can create a future where honesty reigns, where we reclaim our town from the clutches of fear."

The chant of support rose again, swelling like a tidal wave, drowning out the remnants of the mayor's power. I could feel the heat of their passion coursing through me, an intoxicating elixir that filled my veins with possibility. In that moment, everything shifted. The mayor's power had begun to wane, and as we stood united in our resolve, I knew we were ready to confront whatever lay ahead.

As Gavin's words echoed in the square, the crowd began to morph into a living tapestry of emotions, vibrant and restless, fueled by hope and a hint of rebellion. I could see Mrs. Turner, her floral apron still dusted with flour from her baking that morning, clenching her fists as if preparing for battle. Mark's arms were crossed tightly, but the way his jaw clenched suggested he was ready to act. The atmosphere was thick with the scent of possibility and something sharp—anticipation, perhaps.

"Are we really going to allow a man who has manipulated us for so long to dictate our future?" Gavin's voice rose again, cutting through the murmur of the crowd. "I refuse to let my children grow up in a town where fear is our guiding light. We deserve to live in the truth!"

His passion ignited something within me. "We deserve to thrive!" I shouted, stepping closer to the edge of the podium, my heart racing. "No more secrets, no more shadows. It's time to reclaim our lives!"

In that moment, the square erupted into a chorus of agreement, the sound reverberating through the cobblestone streets like a battle cry. People surged forward, eager to add their voices to the fray, a rising tide of unity against the mayor's once-unassailable grip. The air crackled with excitement and defiance, as if the very ground beneath us was ready to split open and reveal the truth buried beneath decades of silence.

But the mayor, his face mottled with a mixture of anger and disbelief, fought to regain control. "You're all fools!" he bellowed, his voice strained. "You don't understand what you're doing. If you unravel this, if you dig too deep, you won't just lose your comfort—you'll lose everything!"

"What is 'everything' worth if it's built on lies?" I challenged, the words spilling out before I could second-guess myself. "You're right; we might lose what we have, but what we gain will be so much greater. We'll gain our dignity, our freedom, and a future we can be proud of!"

With every word I spoke, the crowd's enthusiasm surged. Faces lit with determination, and hands reached out to one another in solidarity, creating a web of support that spread across the square. I could see the mayor's facade beginning to crack, the self-assuredness replaced by panic as he realized the ground was shifting beneath his feet.

"You'll regret this," he hissed, his voice low and venomous. "You think you know the truth? There are forces at play that you cannot comprehend! You think your unity will protect you? It won't."

Gavin took a step closer to the mayor, defiance in his stance. "What forces? What are you hiding? We're not afraid of the truth, and we won't be cowed by threats." His voice rang clear, steady against the mayor's desperate attempts to regain authority.

A murmur rippled through the crowd, a blend of curiosity and concern. The mayor's eyes darted from face to face, and in that fleeting moment, I saw a flicker of vulnerability, a glimpse of the man who had hidden behind the mask of power for so long.

Then, as if summoned by some unseen hand, a figure emerged from the back of the crowd—a tall, striking woman with hair the color of midnight and eyes that glinted like sharp glass. It was Elena, a name that had been whispered in hushed tones among the townsfolk for years, a woman said to be a seer, one who could navigate the unseen threads of fate. The crowd parted, and she strode forward with an authority that silenced even the mayor.

"Enough," she said, her voice low and resonant, as if it belonged to the earth itself. "You think you are fighting against the past, but it is the future you should fear." Her gaze swept across the crowd, landing finally on me, pinning me in place with an intensity that made my heart race. "There are forces much older than you realize, and the truths you seek are not without their consequences."

The mayor's lips curled into a twisted smile, as if he had been waiting for her arrival, his façade now half-masked with a sinister glee. "See? Even the seer knows you're playing a dangerous game," he said, his voice dripping with mockery.

"Dangerous, yes," she replied, undeterred, her eyes never leaving mine. "But change often is. You seek to expose the darkness of your town, but know this—what you uncover may be more than you bargained for."

"What does that mean?" I shot back, frustration boiling within me. "Are you trying to intimidate us into silence?"

She stepped closer, her presence commanding yet unsettling. "I speak only of the truth. The truth you are so eager to uncover may not be the one you want. It may unravel not only the mayor but everything you hold dear."

Just then, a gust of wind whipped through the square, sending a shiver down my spine and stirring the banners that hung limply in the afternoon sun. The atmosphere felt charged, alive with an energy that suggested we were on the precipice of something monumental. I exchanged a glance with Gavin, and in that shared moment, we understood the gravity of her warning.

"Maybe that's what we need," Gavin said, his voice steady despite the whirlwind of emotions swirling around us. "Maybe the only way to truly live is to confront the worst parts of ourselves."

Elena's lips twitched into a semblance of a smile, but her eyes remained sharp, assessing. "Then you will need more than just courage. You will need allies. The past is not merely behind you; it is woven into the very fabric of your town. Unraveling it will take strength, unity, and sacrifices that you cannot yet fathom."

As the crowd simmered with a mix of excitement and apprehension, I felt a tremor of uncertainty creep into my heart. I had expected a fight, a clash of wills, but now it felt as if we were stepping into an abyss. "What sacrifices?" I asked, my voice trembling slightly despite my resolve.

Before she could answer, the ground beneath us shook, a low rumble that felt like the town itself protesting against the weight of our secrets. Gasps erupted from the crowd, eyes wide with fear and confusion. The mayor's expression morphed from smug superiority to pure panic as he stumbled back, trying to regain his footing.

"This is what happens when you disturb the past!" he shouted, his voice cracking as the rumble intensified, resonating through the cobblestones beneath our feet. "You don't understand what you're meddling with!"

Just then, the sky darkened, heavy clouds rolling in as if summoned by the mayor's words. The air thickened, charged with an ominous energy, and I felt a pulse of fear race through me. I exchanged another look with Gavin, who seemed equally alarmed yet resolute.

And then, amidst the chaos, a deafening crack sounded, followed by a flash of lightning that split the sky, illuminating the square for a brief heartbeat. The crowd erupted into chaos, people shouting and scrambling, fear gripping their hearts as they sought shelter.

But I stood frozen, eyes locked on Elena, who was now staring directly at me, her expression inscrutable, a mix of urgency and something darker lurking behind her gaze.

"Are you ready for the truth?" she asked, her voice barely audible above the tumult.

Before I could respond, the ground trembled violently, and I stumbled, feeling the world tilt around me. The moment hung suspended, an electric current crackling through the air, and in that instant, I realized we were no longer just battling for our town's future; we were on the brink of uncovering something far more profound—something that could shatter the very foundations of our lives.

And as the darkness closed in around us, I knew that whatever lay ahead would demand everything we had—and more.

Chapter 29: The Reckoning

The air in Misty Shores was thick with tension, a palpable force that coiled around us like the encroaching fog, heavy and damp. I stood shoulder to shoulder with Gavin, my heart racing as I surveyed the scene unfolding before us. The square, once a place of laughter and community, had transformed into a cauldron of discontent. Voices that had previously murmured in hushed tones of discontent were now rising in a collective roar, drowning out the soft whisper of the wind and the faint crackle of the streetlamps struggling to pierce the gloom.

Mayor Callahan had been the undeniable king of this castle, his reign built on a foundation of charm and false promises. But now, that throne was crumbling under the weight of his deceit, and the townsfolk—our friends, our neighbors—had finally begun to see him for what he was: a puppet master with strings tangled in greed. I could see Mrs. Hargrove, her frail frame trembling with indignation, brandishing her knitting needles like weapons as she yelled at the mayor to step down. Beside her, old Mr. Kline, usually the epitome of stoic restraint, waved a sign hastily scrawled with "Enough is Enough!" in bold, furious letters.

As the crowd surged forward, I felt a spark of hope ignite within me, warming the icy tendrils of fear that had crept into my heart. This was the moment we had all been waiting for, the climax of the unease that had gripped us for far too long. I turned to Gavin, whose eyes mirrored my determination, a fire igniting within them that made my heart race even faster. "Are you ready?" I asked, my voice barely audible above the cacophony.

"Ready as I'll ever be," he replied, his smirk tinged with a hint of mischief, a testament to his courage even in the face of chaos. I appreciated that about him; even in the darkest times, he found a way to keep my spirits buoyant.

With the fog swirling like a wraith around us, we pushed our way through the throng, a tide of bodies surging with energy. My senses sharpened as I felt the warmth of my community around me—the scent of the salt from the nearby ocean, the tang of the rain-soaked earth, the bitter edge of adrenaline that electrified the atmosphere. Every shout, every passionate plea resonated within me, a drumbeat echoing our collective anger.

"Callahan!" someone shouted, their voice slicing through the din. "You owe us the truth!" The crowd roared back, a swell of agreement washing over us like a wave crashing on the shore. I caught sight of Callahan, his face a mask of shock and desperation. He was no longer the man who had so easily swayed our hearts with his polished speeches and grand gestures. Now, he was cornered, a rat exposed in a trap of his own making.

"Ladies and gentlemen," he called, his voice strained and shaky, "let's not let our emotions take control. I assure you, I've always acted in your best interests." The words, meant to soothe, only ignited further outrage. Gavin snorted, a sound of disbelief that I found oddly comforting amid the chaos.

"Oh, he's good," Gavin said, rolling his eyes. "When the smoke clears, I bet he'll say he was just misunderstood, a victim of circumstance. A real classic."

"Or he'll say we're overreacting," I shot back, though a smile tugged at my lips. We both knew the man was about to face the reckoning he so richly deserved.

The energy in the square shifted, the fog swirling more aggressively, as if it were a living entity stirred by our fervor. The townsfolk pressed in closer, emboldened by the solidarity that thrummed in the air. I could feel it too, an intoxicating mixture of fear and hope that made me giddy. I glanced around, catching snippets of conversations fueled by both rage and laughter. The camaraderie in our rebellion was intoxicating, an unbreakable bond that connected us, stitched together by the shared dream of a better Misty Shores.

Suddenly, Callahan's bravado cracked as he attempted to back away, but the crowd surged forward, blocking his escape. "Wait! You don't understand!" he stammered, desperation creeping into his voice as the realization of his impending downfall set in. "I did everything for you! You'll regret this!"

"We've already regretted it," Mrs. Hargrove yelled back, her voice steady and fierce. "You played with our lives like they were mere pawns on a chessboard."

I couldn't help but admire her courage. The square erupted with chants, echoing her sentiments, each voice layering upon the other until it became a symphony of defiance. We were no longer passive spectators in this game; we were players, ready to reclaim our agency.

As the tension thickened, the fog swirled ominously, transforming the square into an otherworldly arena where the past collided with the present. It felt as though the spirits of Misty Shores, long silenced by neglect and betrayal, were rising alongside us, their whispers fueling our resolve.

Then, just as the atmosphere reached its boiling point, a sudden flash of lightning split the sky, illuminating Callahan's terrified face for a heartbeat. It was a stark reminder of the power he had once wielded, but also a prelude to the storm we were about to unleash. With my heart pounding and the crowd rallying behind me, I took a step forward, ready to confront the man who had betrayed us all. The reckoning was upon us, and I was determined to see it through to the end.

The tension in the square was electric, crackling with the unspoken hopes and fears of a community long overshadowed by complacency. As I stepped forward, I felt the weight of the crowd behind me, a swell of energy ready to break free. Gavin nudged me gently, his expression a mix of admiration and mischief. "Just remember, if things go south, I can outrun you. You've seen my track record on the field," he teased, his voice low but laced with warmth.

"Ha! You think I'd let you leave me to face him alone?" I shot back, playfully shoving him. The lighthearted banter felt like a lifeline amidst the rising storm, a reminder that even in the darkest moments, we could find humor to guide us.

The mayor was still trying to extricate himself from the crowd, his face a canvas of confusion and fear. "This isn't how it was meant to be!" he blurted, stumbling over his own words. His usual charm had evaporated, leaving only the desperate man behind. The crowd grew restless, their anger transforming into a palpable force that seemed to ripple through the very ground beneath our feet.

"Then how was it meant to be, Callahan?" someone shouted, cutting through the din. "Because it sure as hell wasn't meant to look like this!"

The words hung in the air, heavy with accusation. I could see Mrs. Hargrove shake her head, her white hair catching the flickering streetlights as she rallied her fellow neighbors. "We trusted you! We believed in your promises! Look where that got us!"

Every shout, every roar echoed back to the mayor like a drumbeat of retribution. The fog thickened, swirling around our feet like a living entity, and I could almost hear the ghosts of Misty Shores whispering through the mist, echoing our frustrations and dreams. In this moment, I was reminded of the stories that had been told about this town, tales of its founding, of resilience and hope. We were here to reclaim that legacy.

As I took another step forward, I could see a flicker of recognition cross Callahan's face. It was as if he suddenly realized the tide had shifted, and he was no longer the captain steering the ship. "You don't know what you're doing!" he yelled, his voice tinged with panic. "If you go against me, you'll only create chaos!"

"Chaos is what we're living in, you fool!" Gavin shot back, his voice ringing with an authority that was almost surprising. I turned to him, a grin breaking through my tension. "Who knew you had a flair for drama?"

"Just practicing for my upcoming career as a politician," he replied, raising an eyebrow. "But I think I'll steer clear of your charming mayor."

Before I could respond, the crowd surged forward, demanding answers and justice. The spirit of unity enveloped us, a shared resolve rising like steam on a cool morning. I felt my pulse quicken, the thrill of confrontation mingling with fear. This was not just about the mayor; it was about us, about the reclamation of our power, about standing up for what we believed in.

"Enough!" Callahan's voice rose above the cacophony, and for a moment, silence fell as the crowd hesitated, caught in the web of his authority. "I've given you everything! This town was built on my vision! You're all just too blinded by your emotions to see it!"

"Your vision? Or your pockets?" a woman shouted back, her voice dripping with disdain. Murmurs rippled through the crowd, igniting a firestorm of agreement. I could feel the heat of their anger rising, a palpable wave that threatened to engulf the mayor.

In the hush that followed, I sensed a shift, a glimmer of hope pushing through the fog of despair. It was in that moment I remembered why I was here. I had spent too long hiding in the shadows, too long allowing fear to dictate my choices. I stepped forward, my voice steady but loud enough to reach the edges of the gathering. "We're not blinded! We're awake! And we're ready to take back our town!"

The crowd erupted, a collective roar that sent shivers down my spine. It was an invocation, a rallying cry that seemed to shake the very ground we stood on. Gavin moved beside me, his presence solid and reassuring. "You've got this," he murmured, nudging me forward.

I locked eyes with Callahan, and in that moment, everything fell away. It was just him and me, the embodiment of power and its reclamation. "You've misused your position. You've taken from us and given nothing in return. It's time for you to step down and let someone who truly cares for this community take your place."

A low murmur swept through the crowd, the momentum building like a wave before it crashed onto the shore. Callahan's face contorted with anger, his bravado crumbling under the weight of our resolve. "You think you can just take my position? You're nothing!"

"Nothing but a community that's had enough of your lies!" I shot back, my heart pounding in my chest. The fog swirled around us, thickening as if it too was eager for the reckoning.

Suddenly, a voice from the back rang out—a young man, barely out of his teens, standing atop a crate to get a better view. "I've seen what you've done, Callahan! We know the truth! You've sold us out for your own gain!"

The crowd erupted again, each voice rising higher, a collective symphony of anger that could no longer be silenced. It was a beautiful chaos, a mixture of frustration and determination that filled the air. In that moment, I felt the shift; this was not just our fight anymore—it was the town's battle cry.

Gavin stepped forward, a fire in his eyes that mirrored my own. "You think you can silence us with threats? You've underestimated our strength. We're done living in fear of your power."

Callahan, cornered by the undeniable force of our unity, staggered back, his bravado slipping away like sand through his fingers. "You'll regret this!" he spat, but the tremor in his voice betrayed him.

"No, we'll celebrate it!" I shouted, my heart swelling with every word. The fog around us thickened, wrapping the square in its ghostly embrace, a shroud of hope rising from the ashes of our despair. We were ready to face whatever darkness lay ahead, together.

The tumult in the square swirled around me like the fog itself, thickening with every shout, every accusation hurled at the beleaguered mayor. His bluster was slipping away, the air crackling with the collective anger of the townsfolk—a palpable force that thrummed beneath our feet. I could feel it in my bones, a burgeoning sense of empowerment rising like the tide. This was our moment to reclaim the heart of Misty Shores.

"Look at him," I murmured to Gavin, my voice barely cutting through the din. "He's like a deer caught in headlights. Who would have thought we'd see the day?"

"Honestly? I pictured it more with fireworks and confetti," he quipped, his lips quirking up in that familiar mischievous grin. "But hey, I'll settle for a good ol' public shaming."

With a nod, I turned back to Callahan, who was scanning the crowd as if searching for an escape route. The desperation etched into his features was almost comical, the once-unshakeable facade crumbling under the weight of his transgressions. "You're making a mistake," he stammered, the bravado fading from his voice. "The people you trust will turn on you. You'll regret this rebellion!"

"Regret?" Mrs. Hargrove's voice rang out, strong and unyielding. "Regret is living under your thumb, Mr. Mayor. Regret is the empty promises you've made while lining your pockets." The crowd erupted once more, echoing her sentiment with fervent approval, the rhythm of our collective heartbeat resonating like a drum in the air.

I stepped forward, emboldened by her words, my heart racing as adrenaline coursed through my veins. "We're tired of being pawns in your game! This town deserves better, and we're ready to fight for it!"

The crowd roared, and for a heartbeat, I felt invincible. But as Callahan recoiled, his eyes darting in panic, I sensed a change in the atmosphere. It was no longer just about him. It was about us facing whatever came next, a battle against a foe who was not only desperate but unpredictable.

Suddenly, from the back of the crowd, a sharp scream sliced through the air, chilling the fervor that had been building. "Look out!" Someone shouted, pointing frantically. The crowd parted like the Red Sea, and a figure rushed forward, cloaked in shadows, moving faster than the eye could follow. My heart leapt into my throat as I squinted against the fog.

"Get back!" Gavin shouted, instinctively moving closer to me as the crowd gasped. The tension in the air shifted dramatically, our united front faltering for a brief moment as fear seeped into the cracks.

"What is happening?" I asked, trying to peer through the gathering mist. There was a flicker of movement, and then the unmistakable outline of a familiar silhouette emerged—a figure I never expected to see tonight. "No... it can't be," I whispered, my breath hitching in my throat.

As the fog receded slightly, revealing the figure, the unmistakable face of Lila, Callahan's right-hand woman, came into view. Her expression was wild, eyes wide with panic, as she pushed her way to the forefront of the crowd, her clothes torn and stained. "You have to listen!" she gasped, her voice hoarse. "They're coming!"

"Who's coming?" I shouted back, confusion clouding my thoughts.

"The people you thought you could trust!" Lila yelled, desperation lacing her tone. "The ones who've been working with Callahan behind the scenes! They're not finished yet!"

The crowd gasped again, a wave of uncertainty rippling through us. The energy that had surged in our favor suddenly felt fragile, like a delicate thread poised to snap at any moment. I could see the shift in the faces around me—concern mingled with confusion. Callahan's panic morphed into a semblance of relief as he caught sight of Lila, an ally suddenly thrust into the spotlight.

"What do you mean, they're coming?" Callahan stammered, his earlier bravado replaced by an edge of fear. "Who?"

"Those who support you, who've been hiding in the shadows. They've always been waiting for the right moment to strike back!" Lila pleaded, her voice rising above the clamor. "You need to leave—now! They'll stop at nothing to protect their interests!"

"I knew we couldn't trust her," Gavin muttered, eyes narrowing as he glanced at me. "What's her game?"

"Right now? Survival," I replied, my pulse quickening as I tried to piece it all together. This revelation added an entirely new layer of danger to our confrontation. The town wasn't just facing the mayor's tyranny; it was facing a network of supporters, hidden threats lurking behind every corner, ready to unleash chaos.

"Enough!" Callahan barked, raising his hand to silence the crowd, though it was clear his authority was slipping. "You think I'm afraid of them? I'm in charge here! We'll deal with them when they arrive!"

But Lila's eyes were wide with fear, and I could see the beads of sweat dotting her forehead. "You don't understand! They're ruthless! If we don't act fast, we'll all be swept away!"

"Why should we believe you?" I challenged, stepping closer, my heart pounding. "You were part of this mess, too!"

"Because," she said, her voice trembling yet fierce, "I don't want to see this town destroyed. We have to stand together if we want to survive!"

"Who are you asking us to trust?" I pressed, feeling the weight of the crowd's uncertainty heavy in the air. "You or Callahan?"

"Both of us," she implored, glancing between us, her expression pleading. "Only together can we stop what's coming."

As the fog rolled back in, I felt the urgency thrumming in the air, a ticking clock echoing in my mind. "This is insane! We can't just trust her!" Gavin shot back, his eyes darting around, assessing the growing unrest.

"Maybe not," I replied, feeling the weight of the decision bear down on me. "But if she's right, and those threats are real... We don't have time to waste. We need to prepare."

Suddenly, a low rumble echoed through the square, vibrating beneath our feet, a sound that sent a collective shiver down our spines. A shadow flickered at the edge of the square, growing larger, ominous, and unmistakably menacing. The crowd collectively gasped, fear creeping back into our hearts as we realized that whatever Lila had warned us about was no longer just a whisper in the fog—it was right at our doorstep.

"Now!" Lila shouted, urging us forward as she grabbed my arm, her grip firm but desperate. "We need to find a way to protect ourselves!"

But just as I turned to follow her, a voice boomed through the thickening mist, reverberating in the air like an ominous bell tolling. "You've stirred the pot, and now you'll face the consequences!"

The crowd froze, eyes wide with fear and uncertainty as the figure stepped into the dim light, cloaked in shadows but unmistakably powerful. My breath hitched in my throat as I recognized the sneering face of a familiar adversary.

"Hello, Misty Shores," the figure sneered, the words dripping with menace. "I hope you're ready for the storm."

And just like that, the fog rolled in thicker, enveloping us in uncertainty and dread, a cloak of shadows hiding the very chaos that threatened to consume us all.

Milton Keynes UK
Ingram Content Group UK Ltd.
UKHW042004281024
450365UK00003B/158